WE CAME TO WELCOME YOU

Also by Vincent Tirado

Burn Down, Rise Up
We Don't Swim Here

WE CAME TO WELCOME YOU

A NOVEL OF SUBURBAN HORROR

VINCENT TIRADO

WILLIAM MORROW

An Imprint of HarperCollinsPublishers

WE CAME TO WELCOME YOU. Copyright © 2024 by Vincent Tirado. All rights reserved. Printed in the United States of America. No part of this book may be used or reproduced in any manner whatsoever without written permission except in the case of brief quotations embodied in critical articles and reviews. For information, address HarperCollins Publishers, 195 Broadway, New York, NY 10007.

HarperCollins books may be purchased for educational, business, or sales promotional use. For information, please email the Special Markets Department at SPsales@harpercollins.com.

FIRST EDITION

Illustration by Buch and Bee/Shutterstock, Inc.

Library of Congress Cataloging-in-Publication Data has been applied for.

ISBN 978-0-06-338318-0

24 25 26 27 28 LBC 5 4 3 2 1

To anyone who has ever regretted joining a Homeowners Association: consider engaging in malicious compliance.

"Love thy neighbor as you love thyself."

—MATTHEW 22:39

WE CAME TO WELCOME YOU

PART I

THE MOVING

When the gates parted and the truck drove into the quiet community, Sol only had one thought: Maneless Grove was exactly like the brochure.

The houses were painted the kind of pastel yellow that didn't attempt to assault the eyes, but also wasn't dim enough to recall the image of an infant's spittle. It was *pleasant*—a word Sol hated. Carefully manicured lawns, which barely stood taller than an inch, welcomed Sol and her wife into their new home—no, their new life.

Even the clouds parted to let down a heavenly ray of sunshine.

It was the kind of place that put the brochure to shame, actually. And that was rare. Sol's eyes jumped from tree to passing tree. Every few feet was another one planted into the sidewalk, medium-size in thickness but nearly as tall as the homes behind it. The white bark caught her attention—she'd never seen trees like this before.

Alice reached out to grip Sol's arm and a surge of energy jolted her.

"I can't believe it," Alice whispered. "We're here."

As Sol followed the moving truck in her own car through the community, she caught brief glimpses of the people who lived in such an impossibly perfect place. A group of middle-aged white women descended upon the sidewalk in a brisk formation, garbed in different styles of athleisure suits from the same name brand. A balding man was checking his mailbox with all the gusto of a divorcé. The truck in front of them stopped short as a self-absorbed teenager crossed the street. While the professional movers yelled from their cab, the pale teen barely noticed, too engrossed in whatever music his headphones were blaring or what was on the screen of his phone.

They moved on, and Sol held back a smug grin. As perfect as Maneless Grove looked, there was no such thing as perfect people. At least she had that to look forward to.

Alice hummed. "So . . . what do you think?"

"It's . . . nice." Before the distracted teen, she was actually thinking it was *too* nice. Like it was all a setup and any moment now, they were going to roll up to one of those prank camera crews that was going to livestream their reaction to the distressing news they didn't *actually* buy a house but rather a landfill or an abandoned penitentiary.

Okay, that's never happened in the history of the world. But Sol's imagination ran on the premise that if anything bad *could* happen, it would happen to *her*. Good things weren't just good things—they were an omen, a warning that the other shoe would drop soon.

From the corner of her eye, Sol watched Alice give a curt nod. The gesture annoyed her, but she bit the inside of her cheek to keep from snapping.

Remember your therapy, she told herself. She imagined sitting across from Dr. Evans again, a man who always wore a tweed three-piece suit like he was trying to conjure up the image of a serious therapist. It was a pity that he could no longer treat her—just one month before Sol's big move, he announced he was going to be working at another private practice in New Jersey and would not be able to telecommute for her sessions. Sol had been with him for such a long time that she was upset at this news—but only because she didn't relish the idea of finding a new therapist, let alone getting to know one.

She could imagine Dr. Evans now. He'd click his pen while giving Sol a polite stare and a polite smile—two things that Sol found patronizing.

He'd start with a question. *You don't like it when Alice nods like that because . . . ?*

Because it was never a simple nod. She was being passive aggressive.

And why do you think she's being passive aggressive?

Because Alice wanted Sol to gush over the neighborhood, to fall so completely in love with it that Sol would never feel anxious or binge drink again, would promise to be nothing but light and love and joy and . . .

You're assuming things about your wife. What did we say about that?

It only created disappointment at best and resentment at worst.

So then why don't you just ask her?

Sol sighed. Catching her wife's gaze, she asked, "What's wrong?"

The words came out like she was chewing gravel. Alice sat silently for so long that Sol hoped she hadn't heard her at all.

Finally, Alice replied, "You don't seem . . . happy."

"It's just a lot for me, okay?" Sol's eyes could've burned through the back of the truck the way she was staring, willing for it to stop sooner rather than later. "Moving is a lot of work. It's stressful. And I'm not good with new places, you know that. I just don't want to jinx things."

Her wife snorted.

"What?"

"For a scientist, you're so weirdly superstitious." Alice patted Sol's leg. Sol froze and Alice clearly immediately realized that was the wrong thing to say. "Hey, it's going to be okay. I promise. You'll be back at work soon, I'm sure of it."

And what if I'm not?

The truck slowed to a stop. They were finally here.

"I'm going to let the movers in," Sol announced. All too eager to get away from the tense situation, she jogged away from the car and up to the front door.

Right off, Sol noticed a difference between this house and all of the others. The paint wasn't just dull, there were light streaks running through it as if it had recently been hit with acid rain. The grass was much taller too, spilling over to the concrete path leading up to the house. Every single home on the block had one of those white-bark trees stationed out front, right at the corner where the lawn and fence met the sidewalk. But theirs had no such tree. Just an overgrown lawn.

Still, it was stunning. Larger than their old apartment and even more importantly, it was owned by them. The details didn't matter. A home is home is a home.

Can't believe we could actually afford this. Though it didn't show on her face, the excitement made Sol's stomach flip. *I'm a homeowner now.*

Sol unlocked the door. "Just . . . put everything in the living room unless we need you to bring it upstairs," she instructed the movers, who were right behind her.

"Will do," replied one of the bulkier men. His name tag said RAN-DAL, and Sol watched as he started with the wooden chairs while his partner brought in boxes.

Sol made her way to the back of the truck to see what she could help bring in. That's when she felt it—eyes, burrowing into her. She turned around quickly.

Movement at a window from across the street confirmed her suspicions.

Someone was watching her.

Don't be so paranoid.

Sol rubbed the back of her neck and took in deep breaths. *While caution is good, not everyone is out to get you,* Dr. Evans would've said. *Instead of expecting every flag to be red, look for flags that are your favorite color.*

What he meant was she should try to look for more positive experiences rather than always expecting negative ones. It was an exercise that still felt odd to her but, again, if she was paying for therapy, she should at least try it.

The street stretched on in such a straight line it eventually met with the sky on the horizon. Aside from the shining sun, there were more of the small trees she'd seen when driving in placed equally distant from each other, going all the way down the end of the street. They were lush—a dark green with hints of a crisp orange trying to push itself through. Nearing fall had that effect, but Sol was surprised to see not a single leaf on the ground anywhere. In fact, she couldn't remember any littering the streets while she drove in.

She sighed. "It's too perfect." Then she laughed at the absurdity of such a statement.

Back at the truck, Sol carefully chose a nightstand to lift over her shoulder and bring into the house. Yes, they'd paid for the movers, but she had to do *something*. Especially if it meant not having to talk with Alice at the moment. She loved her wife, but was there anything more aggravating than having someone dismiss your concerns?

I'm not being superstitious, she thought, walking up to the door. *I'm just . . . cautious. There's nothing wrong with that.* She entered her new home.

The difference between the inside and outside was staggering.

An unbearable heat immediately descended upon her once she stepped over the threshold into darkness. Stifling. The darkness itself was oppressive—as if the sun couldn't bear to let any of its precious light pierce too far into the home. Sol reached for the nearest light switch but flicking it did nothing.

"Ah, shit," she muttered.

Alice suddenly appeared behind Sol. "What's wrong?"

"Jesus!" Sol breathed, clutching her chest. "You scared me!"

She felt Alice move beside her and flick the same switch. Again, it did nothing.

"Might just be the lightbulb," Alice noted. "Or maybe the fuse is out?"

Sol put down the nightstand. She squinted into the darkness and only saw the vague outlines of furniture the movers had dumped in the living room. "I'll check the fuse first. Do you know where it might be?"

"Kitchen maybe?" Her wife shrugged, then laughed. "Or really anywhere."

"Didn't you come here for a house tour a few months ago?"

"You mean the house tour that *you* were supposed to join me on?" Alice's voice traveled from somewhere Sol couldn't see—and then there was light. Alice stood at the living room windows farther into the house. She pulled the curtains farther apart, letting in sun, and wiped her hands on her jeans.

Between all the moments when they bickered, when Sol was so tightly wound she could pop, and Alice was not feeling at all patient— there were moments like this, when Sol watched sunlight drape around her wife and became just a little softer for it. Alice was not much shorter than Sol, with a long torso and hair that was always cut right around her shoulders, just to be pulled back into a rubber band. Despite how Alice complained about her own perceived flaws, her wife was much more careful about her appearance than Sol ever could be. Alice attributed it to her being Korean, needing to keep a stylish wardrobe and being particular about her skincare routine. Either way, there was no doubt she was stunning.

Whereas Sol was the opposite. She wore the same oversize button-down shirts, faded from constant use, and only ever washed her face with soap and water. She liked to think she made up for her deficiencies in other ways, like showing up to a house tour when she said she would. (She didn't.)

Not that she was without cause. The last few months flashed through Sol's mind. A constant circle of anxiety bad enough to ruin her appetite, lack of sleep, and yet another depression that kept her rooted to the bed. During that time, Alice couldn't force Sol to take a sip of water if she tried, let alone go on a house tour.

Dust particles floated in the sunbeams between them. Her wife practically glowed.

"You look beautiful," Sol said. "This place suits you."

Alice looked over to her and smiled. "It suits you, too, jagi."

Her expression softened as she used the Korean pet name. A good sign. She took Sol's hand, squeezing it gently. While Alice wasn't pale by a long shot, her soft bronze skin seemed far lighter contrasted with Sol's deep brown complexion.

"Things might not be perfect, but it *will* get better," said her wife. "We look out for each other—we always have. And now we have this beautiful house. The least we can do is try and make it work."

What Alice called "better" was really just a distraction. A yearlong string of tense work incidents were buried in the back of Sol's mind and she couldn't help remembering there was currently a loaded gun pointed at her entire career. The house was a distraction, something to make her say, *Well, at least I'm a homeowner now. Everything is hunky-dory.*

The problem was that Sol just didn't do silver linings. She was still every bit the twitchy, paranoid person who couldn't sleep without downing a bottle and a half of wine or staying up until four a.m. before passing out on the couch. She wasn't as positive that a change of location would change all that.

"Looking at her hopeful wife, she breathed deeply. "I'll try."

"Good." Alice smiled. Then she pulled Sol toward the staircase on the other side of the living room. "Now, come on. I know I showed you pictures of this place, but they really didn't do it justice."

"Shouldn't we help bring all of our things in first? I think those guys start to charge by the hour after the first two."

"Sol. We can afford it, so don't worry."

It was hard not to—money was always going to be a thing for her. Even holding a PhD and working in molecular research was hardly enough to bring in any significant salary. Her wife, on the other hand, worked a six-figure job in marketing at a fancy tech company—something that went over Sol's head completely. The difference between their paychecks did not make life easier. Sol hated feeling like a mooch.

She trudged after Alice, noticing the way the floor creaked at certain steps and how silent it was at others. Her imagination was running again. What if the house had termites and that's what caused the uneven stability in the floorboards? What if some part of it were weakened enough that it snapped and they fell straight through? Alice assured her there were safety inspections done long before the house could be put on the market, but Sol still cursed her past self for not doing the initial house tour with Alice.

The second story had less actual floor space, in a way that also irritated Sol. The staircase that led up into it shared the same ceiling as the first floor. Had the builders segmented it, Sol and Alice would have had just as much of a spacious upper room that could have been used as an office space. Instead, the staircase connected to the center of a long hallway that functioned like a balcony. Both ends of the hallway led to windows, with a few doors adjacent to them.

Stop being negative, you're a homeowner now, she tried telling herself. *Be happy, be excited. Alice can tell when you're anxious. Don't let her know you're anxious.*

"This is going to be our bedroom!" Alice announced.

Triumphantly, she threw open the last door on the right. But Sol didn't feel any sense of wonder. Rather, the room was once again dark and stuffy, something that made Sol feel claustrophobic.

"I'm going to go find the fuse box," said Sol with an awkward smile. "Maybe this place will look less gloomy if we can actually see."

"It's not that bad!" Alice laughed. The sound lifted the ever-present weight from Sol's shoulders. It wasn't that she just loved and trusted her wife, but that part of the reason she *did* love her wife was because her optimism wasn't unrestrained. If Alice thought something could be done, then that usually meant it could. She was the opposite of Sol in this way. Where Sol saw problems and impossibility, Alice found ways to introduce joy.

Sol paused at the bottom step in the living room, finding a new problem. The living room was becoming cluttered faster than she anticipated. It was probably a bad idea to tell the movers to just throw everything in the living room, but she wanted to be done with the whole business of "moving" as soon as possible. Sol always hated moving. She had done it so many times as a kid—nine times before her eighteenth birthday—that it stopped feeling exciting. In fact, it felt more like a chore.

And the memories it brought up—*God*. Each time Sol and her family moved to a new apartment, a crowd of church ladies would accompany them with rosaries in their hands and a violent prayer on their tongues.

They would move throughout the home slowly, cursing all evil things and demanding they leave before the new family could settle down. It was to keep the family safe, they told her, and very important to do before moving into a new home. But all it did was serve Sol a new flavor of anxiety—the fear that anything could be hiding in the corners of each wall.

Sol took in a deep breath.

This is the last time, she reminded herself as she grabbed a box of old research journals destined for the basement. It would be the last official "move" for . . . well, hopefully, a very long time. Sol knew of those people who always spoke of their "starter homes" or made "flipping houses" their entire career—she didn't know how they could stomach it. What was so good about uprooting yourself every few years?

Sol carefully nudged the growing collection of boxes and furniture apart to make an easier path to the basement. The door needed a few good pushes before it would open.

Sol stood at the top of the stairs and chewed on her bottom lip.

There was darkness that was bearable and then there was this. A hollow abyss where light got lost. It might as well have been a black hole.

Or another omen.

No, it's not. She sniffed, feeling her shoulders tensing already. There was no need to panic. It was just a basement.

Juggling the box on her hip, Sol reached into her pocket for her phone and aimed its flashlight at the floor. As long as she took it one step at a time, she would be at the bottom soon enough. The last thing she needed to worry about was tripping over her feet in the dark.

Knowing me, I'd trip and break my neck. Imagination sprinting, she could already see her funeral. A wailing Alice. A sparse audience watching as her coffin was lowered into the ground. Maybe one or two colleagues would make the time to show up—but she doubted it. Not after how her last few months had been.

Don't think about it, she thought. But it was too late. Her vision became like a fishbowl, and Sol had to stop and breathe for a few seconds before it went back to normal.

You didn't do anything wrong, Sol reminded herself. *You didn't do anything wrong.*

She knelt down on the steps, squeezing her phone in her hand. Sol prayed that Alice wouldn't find her in the dark, unable to breathe and panicking about nothing in particular. At best, Alice would call an ambulance. At worst, Alice would blame herself for pushing Sol to do something new and outside of her comfort zone.

And as much as it brought up unpleasant memories and emotions, this was going to be *good* for her. Owning a home was something she and Alice had always wanted, and now they did! Why couldn't she just be happy about it? What was so wrong with her that she was always looking for an excuse to be miserable? Maybe it was because it was what she was used to. A bad habit, you could say.

After their second anniversary of dating, when they had just graduated from school, Alice revealed how cool Sol always seemed to her—so put together, responsible, down-to-earth, and on top of it all, dedicated to her field. To Alice, Sol was always calm and collected. But even then, on the inside, she was fraying at the ends, juggling familial duties and her own personal secrets.

And Sol wanted to be that cool and down-to-earth version of herself that Alice thought she was. Alice deserved a wife like that. Not . . . not whatever she was right now.

Sol waited until the tension in her stomach lessened and the anxiety attack had passed before continuing down the steps. She carefully put down the box of old journals against the wall and froze for a moment. In the dark, she was certain she heard something rustling, low and indiscernible. Like a fly that was buzzing just within earshot. Or was it white noise? A static-like vibration that was impossible to make out?

For a moment, the noise became clearer—and it sounded like whispering. Was there a radio left behind by the previous owners? Strangely, the farther down the basement stairs she went, the duller the noise became. Until it was nearly gone.

Well, even if it is a bad habit, at least I'm trying to be better for Alice. Sol sniffled again, resolving to put it out of her mind.

Then she went on the hunt for the fuse box.

COMPANY

If the most stressful part about moving was packing, the second most stressful part would be the unpacking. Sol wouldn't get that far though, not now. Not when she had to designate boxes filled with clothes to go to the bedroom and push the couch to the far corner of the living room. The coffee table was the easiest part, of course, and just as useful because Sol could stack *other* boxes on top of it to clear up space.

Things like toiletries obviously went to the bathroom, containers of books lined the wall where their bookshelf would be, and the box wrapped tight with duct tape—not because it was fragile, but because it contained a few of their sex toys they didn't want to spill out if the movers dropped the box—needed to be quickly shoved in a closet until they were ready to place them someplace more appropriate. Or until they got in the mood—whichever came first.

Sol was so fixated on the task of clearing the living room by any means necessary that she almost didn't notice how drenched with sweat she was. The house did its best to keep in the heat, it seemed. She stopped in the kitchen after placing a box of plates down on the island and flapped her shirt a few times to cool herself down. It barely made a difference.

"Thank you again!" Though Alice's voice was muffled by the kitchen wall, Sol could still make out the words.

Through the kitchen window, Sol watched her wife wave off the movers as they drove away. Her hair billowed in the wind, and the grass was pressed flat against the ground as though a force lay on it. And yet behind the open window, Sol felt nothing.

No stir of wind, not even a breeze. Beads of sweat rolled down her neck, and without a second thought, she went to the fridge and stuck her head inside the freezer. It was only beginning to cool since she flipped the fuse switch, but it was much better than the rest of the house.

All this damn hair . . . Sol gathered her curls in a tight fist and pulled them up from her shoulders. Her hair was so thick, heat trapped itself within each coil. Maybe it was time for a trim—or a big cut. Sol always wondered how she'd look with an undercut.

"Sol, where are you?" Alice yelled. Soft footsteps came into the kitchen and stopped immediately, before a bout of laughter came.

"What on earth are you doing?"

Sol glanced at her wife over her shoulder. "Just chilling."

Alice laughed again, then wrapped her arms around Sol's torso and gently pulled her out of the empty fridge.

"It's ridiculously humid," Sol complained, letting her hair fall back down. She twisted herself around to face Alice. "Can't you feel it?"

Alice raised an eyebrow. "Aren't you from the Dominican Republic?"

"First, my parents are from D.R. I was born here. Second, do I look like I'm dressed for the Dominican Republic? No, I'm dressed for *Connecticut.*"

The flickering smile on Alice's face made Sol feel lighter. They still could poke fun at each other, tease each other like they did when they were still dating.

The first time Sol and Alice had met was in undergrad at Yale. They were roommates, in fact. Sol was incredibly introverted, and Alice was a social butterfly, but they were very respectful of each other, never clashing over a dirty room or unwelcome guests. One time, Sol accidentally walked in on Alice changing and though she turned away, face heating up quickly, it was the first time Sol wondered why Alice never *did* bring a guy over, because the girl was seriously beautiful.

Maybe it was out of respect for her, Sol thought, but it was something she thought time and time again, when Alice would come home after a long night of drinking with friends. The way Alice would fall on her bed, with her miniskirt riding up, made Sol want to dunk her head in cold water. Instead, she pulled her blanket over her, left water and painkillers on the nightstand, and turned out the light.

Sol never would have imagined in a million years how Alice could have felt toward her. She never would have thought she could be that lucky.

A loud knock at the door brought Sol back to the here and now.

"Did the movers forget something?" she muttered, moving to the kitchen window. "You tipped them, right?"

"Yes," Alice said, moving away from Sol.

Instead of the two bulky men of few words, Sol saw three people at their front door milling about awkwardly. Great, that must have been the nosiest of their new neighbors.

Alice sped to the door, but Sol decided to stay put and watch from afar.

Of the three, a man stood far off, beyond the shade of the house, and at first glance seemed bored. The black suit with blue shirt and no tie combination made him look casually distinguished, as if he wanted others to know he was a businessman but that he didn't take himself too seriously. His eyes were glued to the roof like he was watching for something that he was sure to catch.

The second member of the welcome brigade was an older woman, and she stood much closer to the house. She appeared short and plump with a head of hair that could only be described as "mushroom-like." Her wrinkles were prominent, and there was something about the way she looked over the length of the house that made Sol even more uncomfortable.

A third woman with sleek black hair stood right at the edge of the door. It was subtle, the way she shifted from foot to foot, dancing on her toes anxiously. It was odd the way the three were clearly together but didn't act like it.

They only came alive when Sol heard Alice open the front door.

"Hello! I'm Teresa," the sleek-haired woman said. She gave a genuine smile, and the others followed suit.

The thing about being Black and butch was that each of those traits already made *certain people* nervous as it was. And their nervousness rubbed off on Sol. It made her overly cautious of the way she stood (not relaxed enough), the way her smile shifted into a neutral line (too aggressive), and even the way she spoke (short, curt, deadpan). She was a deer in headlights in most social situations. So maybe it was better for her to hang back?

If no one ever sees you, they'll assume you're suspicious, her anxiety spoke. *And a suspicious Black person is the worst kind of Black person to them.*

Sol decided to join Alice at the door.

"You must be the new neighbors!" the woman chirped. Gesturing at the others, she added, "This is Hope, and that's Eugene." The pair hurried closer. "We're on the board of the Homeowners Association and just wanted to welcome you to the community."

Sol had been right. This welcome brigade was definitely the nosiest of their new neighbors.

Teresa extended a confident hand, and Alice did her one better— she shook hands with each of them. Even Eugene, who tried to stay away from the shadows, was forced to step in a few feet. Was it Sol's imagination or was that a look of fear in his eyes? Sol glanced at Alice, wondering if she noticed.

"It's so exciting to have a Yale researcher here with us!" Teresa said, still locking eyes with Alice.

Sol's forced smile fell flat. Pushing aside the fact that they assumed it would be the Asian person with a higher education and not the Black person—how the hell did they know what Sol did for a living?

"Oh . . ." Alice's smile wavered. "No, that would be my wife, Sol. I'm in marketing, actually." She gestured to Sol.

Sol gave a wry smile. "Hi." *And fuck you.*

Teresa was taken aback. "Sorry, we shouldn't have assumed . . ."

"It's okay." *It's not.* "Don't worry about it." *Watch your fucking step.*

"So, you're Sol?" Hope, the mushroom-haired woman, tried to ease the tension. "It's nice to meet you. Wow, Sol Song—what a fun name!"

"We actually didn't change either of our names," Alice jumped in, giving Sol a moment to recover.

"Really? Not even going to hyphenate?" Hope frowned, as if the thought had never occurred to her that some married couples actually preferred to keep their last names. For Alice, it was mainly a cultural thing—Korean women kept their maiden names unless they were trying to assimilate. For Sol, it was a matter of pride attached to having a PhD. To be called Dr. Song instead of Dr. Reyes made it feel like it was less *hers*.

"We just preferred not to," Sol said.

"*O*-oh. Hm." Hope's brow furrowed. The awkward silence that followed had a layer of judgment over it. Maybe the older woman couldn't fathom why the younger generation didn't care for the tradition of changing their last names in marriage. Whatever—it wasn't Sol's job to make her understand.

Just pretend you're not offended. Sol tried to maintain a neutral expression, only to further upset herself. Why did she have to be graceful when Hope's low opinion showed itself on her face?

"Of course," Teresa cut in. She seemed to have collected herself, already forgetting about her faux pas. "Sorry to bother you, we know you probably have a ton to unpack and organize, we just wanted to formally welcome you to the neighborhood and give you a little gift."

Teresa stepped aside so that Hope could hand over a small woven basket with two bottles of wine and a set of candles. Sol's eyes widened at the sight of it. Maybe there was forgiveness in Hope's future after all.

Sol glanced to the side, quickly reading Alice's face. Alice maintained a blank expression, polite smile, but her eyes, Sol noticed, were doing a quick calculation, and Sol knew it was about the bottles.

Sol always liked drinking—she joked it was a Dominican trait, something most families did together while watching telenovelas or sports or while sitting in the park, watching clouds go by. And perhaps at one time, Alice would joke that Sol would fit right in with her family, as drinking with Koreans was something of an extreme sport. But what first was a way to calm her nerves became the only way Sol could keep from losing her head in the last few months.

Any time she wasn't at work was spent with a bottle in hand. And Alice didn't like it. Sol wanted to believe she was fine and made noises to her wife in that regard. The two compromised in that they both knew Sol *would* be fine as long as she had a better handle on her bad habit. But it wasn't actually a solution to what Alice thought was a problem and Sol thought was just the natural order of things.

So while the wine bottles were a definite temptation . . . well, it was still a gift. And it would be rude not to accept the gift, right?

"Wow, this is amazing," Alice said, probably thinking the same thing and taking the basket.

"I made the basket and candles," Hope said, beaming. "And our community has a very good relationship with a winery so we often get much more exclusive drinks." Sol felt her face heat up with embarrassment when Hope winked at her.

"Wow, that's . . . nice." She stiffened. How much did they know about her? They couldn't know *that*, right?

"I'm sure you've already heard of our community's motto!" Hope went on.

Ah, right. The motto. *Invest in a neighborly spirit.* Sol had heard it so many times throughout the application phase, she could swear it was tattooed on her psyche. The idea was to always cultivate good habits of checking in on your neighbors and making sure everyone was taken care of. It was, again . . . oddly very nice.

"Yeah, Nadine actually told me about the motto," Alice said. "We couldn't agree more."

Sol stopped herself from gagging. *Nadine.* One of Alice's coworkers who'd been trying very hard to befriend Sol by inviting her and Alice out on a number of double dates. She was so over-the-top it actually worked *against* her favor, and Sol was wary of her as a result.

And yet, here they were, moving into the same neighborhood as Nadine. Last Sol heard, Nadine was on maternity leave. She hoped that motherhood would keep her too busy from gracing their home, but it looked like other people were happy to fill in for her.

Teresa practically beamed, like she had come up with the motto herself. "We're glad to hear that. Not everyone is amenable to our way of living here, but Nadine assured us you would be ideal candidates."

Sol's eyebrow twitched. "Way of living" sounded like they were swingers or part of some extreme religious faction. Maybe even a pyramid scheme.

"Speaking of, inside that basket, you'll find our HOA agreement. You can just sign it whenever you're ready and hand it to any one of us within the next week." Teresa chuckled.

And that was the sound of the other shoe dropping. Sol held back a snort. Asking to sign some legally binding agreement "whenever they're ready" and have it back by the end of the week was nothing short of contradictory. Like they'd already been determined to join something as controlling as a homeowners association.

"Oh, we're still not sure about joining . . ." Alice's voice faltered. She glanced back at Sol, who froze for a split second. Her wife's expression said, *Feel free to jump in anytime!*

Sol cleared her throat, putting all eyes on her. "We were under the impression that it's not required. You know, to join the association," she clarified, after a moment. The stunned look on everyone's face made her feel like she was small again. Did she say something wrong?

"Well, no, it's—it's not a requirement," Hope stammered. "But we would strongly suggest joining as there are a number of benefits to doing so."

"Right, *so* many benefits," Teresa continued, furrowing her brow as she thought up examples. "The fines are . . . much less, if you do join . . . and er—"

"We have special connections with an, um, exterminator who gives us pesticides at a discount!" Eugene jumped in. His cheeks were red with determination. "And if there's ever a natural disaster event that damages the house, we're more than happy to chip in to pay for repairs."

Doesn't homeowner's insurance normally cover that? Sol thought. That was hardly a benefit.

Hope mumbled something about special events, snapping her fingers as she tried to recall volunteer opportunities they engaged in.

Sol watched with morbid fascination as they stumbled over each other, trying to convince her and Alice that it would be in their best interests to sign away their homeowning independence. It wasn't a *great* idea to start with financial penalties, Sol thought, and who cared about getting cheaper pesticides? One of the few upsides of having a backyard was having her own garden, and she would be *damned* if she let them talk her into a lack of biodiversity on her own property.

Hope's and Eugene's voices died down as Teresa spoke up. "If you need extra time to read over the agreement, you absolutely can. Oh! But if you're confused on any of the terms or conditions, we'd be happy to sit down with you and explain anything you need."

It was an interesting first attempt, Sol would give them that, but if they were going to be this pushy about it day after day, she could see a very passionate tirade in their future.

With lots of colorful Spanish curses.

"We'll certainly look it over and think about it," Alice said politely. She passed the basket to Sol and widened the door. "Until then, would you like to come inside? I'm sure we can find a couple of glasses fast and have a small toast!"

Sol groaned internally. She knew what Alice was doing. The more people to share wine with, the less she could have. Alice was staying on her toes.

A ripple of disquiet traveled through their new neighbors. It was very subtle, but Sol couldn't help but take note of it—like watching one of those nylon balloons pop and slowly deflate.

Hope's eyes flashed with an emotion Sol couldn't name. "Oh, we couldn't . . ."

Teresa chimed in, "You probably have a lot to do, and we don't want to take up any more of your time."

Sol couldn't help her relief. She needed at least two to three business weeks to mentally prepare for socializing. They could come back then. Yet despite her relief, something was off. They just about fell over themselves trying to convince Sol and Alice to join the association. Now they were suddenly backing down from a chance to be with them? These were the kind of people who should be inviting themselves in.

"We actually do have a lot to get done." Sol jumped in before her wife could insist it was okay. "So . . . Alice?"

A chorus of goodbyes and *nice to meet you*s followed until Alice closed the door. Her shoulders drooped in the universal sign for *God, I'm more drained than I thought.* Sol wondered if she could get away with a glass or two right now if she could convince Alice to have some. Was it a red flag that she was craving it this much already?

As soon as the door shut, her wife leaned against it and let out a long sigh.

"Well, that was interesting," Sol remarked.

"Sol. Don't." But even Alice couldn't hold back a laugh. "Multiple benefits to joining an association, my ass. And what was that about me working at Yale? God, that was so racist. My parents only wish I had a PhD!"

Sol laughed awkwardly. Unfortunately, she was more than used to being assumed to be the less-educated one in the relationship. Noticing that Alice had already shed her shoes at the door, Sol took the sign to do the same and kicked them aside. She'd set up the shoe rack later.

"Like, was that racist toward you or me?" Alice continued.

"Why not both?" Sol turned the basket around in her hands. She tried not to look like she was checking out the bottles of wine. *Pinot grigio . . . not bad.* When she looked up, Sol noticed that Alice's eyes weren't on her, but rather on the wine. She was doing another mental calculation.

"Something wrong?" Sol asked, putting on her best innocent expression.

Alice mused for a moment. "Just thinking that maybe . . . it wouldn't be a bad idea to have a glass or two? You know, just to christen the house."

Sol tried not to visibly brighten. She only nodded and put the basket atop a large box. "Maybe for dinner?" she suggested. That was reasonable, right? A glass of wine, over dinner?

"Sure, dinner. Let's go unpack."

Alice leaned over and gave Sol a peck on her cheek. Her stomach fluttered, and part of her felt stupid for it because she knew it wasn't the affection itself that made her a bit giddy. It was the fact that she felt like she *earned* it, like it was a good grade on a test.

Good job, Sol, you pulled off the act well.

As promised, they didn't get into the bottles until later on, after they had somewhat rearranged the living room and distributed the boxes and furniture into the appropriate rooms. Dinner was a bowl of mac and cheese, made quickly over the stove, and it was perfect.

"We definitely need to go grocery shopping at some point. I wonder if there's an H Mart near here . . ." Alice typed into her cell phone. Sol glanced over, a little surprised that Alice hadn't bothered to check before applying to buy the house.

H Mart was her immediate go-to supermarket, on account that it sold many of her favorite Korean snacks and ingredients for Korean meals. In short, it was a cultural staple for her in the same way Sol never hesitated to buy plantains or mangos wherever she found them.

Alice groaned. "Ugh, none. But maybe I can still find another Asian market somewhere."

Sol followed her lead, looking into the nearest grocery stores. "There's like three Trader Joe's."

Alice made a face. "I will never shop there. Their tteokbokki are *sweet*. How do you mess that up?"

Sol thought about her mother-in-law's spicy rice cakes and nodded in solidarity.

Alice took a sip of her wine. They'd opened the red with a brand name that was impossible to read due to the overly cursive typeface but still wasn't all too bad. Sol would have to ask for the name later.

"Honestly, as weird as the association were," said her wife, "this wine kind of makes up for it."

"They *were* weird, right?"

Sol always jumped at the chance to talk about strangers behind their backs. It was another Dominican trait in her, passed down matrilineally. It was also a bitch move and she knew it, but she refused to feel bad about it.

"Glad it wasn't just me this time."

A small smile from Alice. "Not this time."

"And how did they even know that one of us works at Yale?" That wasn't information their new neighbors would be privy to. Not unless they had a shady relationship with the bank Sol and Alice applied to for a mortgage.

"Mm." Alice sipped her wine. "Maybe Nadine? She *is* close with them."

It was plausible, sure, but Nadine would have *definitely* mentioned that it was Sol who had the PhD, not Alice.

"Didn't know Nadine was part of the Homeowners Association," said Sol. "Though I can't really say I'm surprised." She paused. "By the way, we're really not joining, right?"

It wasn't that Sol questioned her wife's earlier outright refusal of the association, but rather that Alice had a habit of not wanting to seem "easily won over" in any situation. In the same way that Sol didn't want to be viewed as aggressive (if only for her own safety), Alice didn't want to be thought of as meek or submissive. It was, in short, another careful calculation that had to be done. Better to shut down a conversation now and change her mind later than to be seen as someone who could easily be taken advantage of.

At first, Alice didn't respond. Instead, Sol watched as her eyes caught on something in the basket. She reached in and pulled it out.

"Hey, what's this?" said Alice. She held it up to the light.

It was small, white, and circular. Made from marble.

Sol took it from Alice, flipped it over in her hand. She spotted an interesting carving along the top—a tree with deep sprawling roots. She traced her finger along the grooves, and instantly thought of mosaic art and stained-glass windows.

"Does the neighborhood have a logo?" Sol snorted. "Did we just get branded?" Leave it to an HOA to make a community feel more like a company. "And if so, what is this thing? Are we supposed to use it as a paperweight?" Sol couldn't see any other point to it.

"Maybe it's some sort of coaster?" Alice offered, her nose scrunched in confusion as well.

Sol shook her head. The center curved upward, making it too difficult to balance a cup or glass. "I don't think so."

"Well, it's the thought that counts," Alice said, unbothered.

Sol's eyes snagged on a piece of tape stuck to one side of the marble disc. Glancing back into the basket, she saw an envelope that must have fallen off.

Opening the envelope, she let out a laugh.

"What is it?" Alice leaned over.

It was the contract for joining the Homeowners Association. Sol could count the rules on one hand and yet they were still ridiculous demands.

1. Lawns must be properly maintained, absent of any weeds, with grass no longer than two and a half inches long. The aspen trees found on every property cannot be removed, harmed, or even pruned without prior written approval of the association. Herbicides used must be on the approved list found on page 3 of this contract.
2. Personal gardens are not allowed as they may attract bees and other pests. However, homeowners do have access to the community garden, as well as the proper gear needed if they so wish.

"Pfft." Sol pointed to the second rule. "As if they're going to stop me from having my own garden." It was something she'd always wanted, one of the key reasons she'd been even remotely eager to move here in the first place.

"Just as long as you remember to grow some cucumbers," Alice said. Sol didn't need to ask why. Alice loved to snack on gochujang cucumber salad. It was her go-to comfort food.

Sol smiled. "Of course."

They read on.

3. No political slogans of any kind are allowed on lawns, in windows, or in any places that can be seen by the public.
4. In the event that the homeowners wish to renovate their homes, they must consult the association beforehand with detailed plans, including the hours construction workers can be found on the premises.

5.   If homeowners wish to paint their homes, they must receive prior approval from the association and only utilize neutral colors.

    In return, members of the association have access to the community garden, mini golf, and other amenities* at reduced to no cost.

    *See list of amenities on page 4.

As Sol flipped to the next page, she found a list of penalties that the association would be allowed to enforce—most were dubious, giving no indication of the amount of money they would be forced to pay.

    If a member is found in violation of any of the above agreements, they will be fined.

Fined what? How much money would they have to pay? And would it be proportional to the supposed infraction? For as few as the rules and regulations were, there was no clearly defined way to settle disputes. What would happen if Sol had to go to civil court over something as innocent as waving the lesbian pride flag in her window? Could her entire existence be determined too political for the community?

"There's no way this can be legal."

"Yeah, we're not signing that." Alice took the contract and walked it over to the trash. "Not like they can force us to sign."

Unless they could, Sol thought. There had to be a catch to this somewhere. Every single house they had passed by on the way here was identical. Identical lawns, identically painted houses. There wasn't even so much as an out-of-place pebble. How could they achieve that level of uniformity without micromanaging people's lives?

Teresa had said the fines were lower, but how could they even fine them if they'd never signed? That was suspicious, to say the least.

Sol scanned the page a little more carefully. The same terms applied to other gated communities called Andor's Grove and Horned Medley. She'd never heard of them.

"Hey." Alice's hand found Sol's and she squeezed. "This is going to be good for us, okay? Good for you too. Here, you'll always feel safe, and there's tons of stuff you can enjoy without really having to step outside of the community if you don't want to."

Yeah, sure. Anxiety had a way of making sure Sol didn't step out of the house if she didn't have to, so she wasn't quite sure it was as optional as Alice made it sound. Even when she was younger and went through a number of mental health professionals who struggled to agree on a diagnosis, there was always the common denominator of not wanting to leave her comfort zone. Leaving the comfort zone was for suckers, manic depression be damned.

If it wasn't for the fact Sol's home growing up wasn't safe for her, she might not even have left it for Yale.

So for the HOA to think they could in any way dictate *her* home, *her* sanctuary, they were the ones out of their minds.

"Thanks," Sol said. Her stomach fluttered again but this time she knew it was because she felt understood. Even when Sol thought Alice couldn't have possibly known how she felt, or how bad her mental health issues were, Alice never forced her out of her comfort zone. Maybe to the edge of it but never beyond it. It was in these moments that Sol knew her wife was always thinking of her, and it made Sol soft again.

Sol pulled Alice's hand to her lips and pressed a long kiss into her palm.

Alice blushed. "You're in a good mood, jagi." Then suddenly, as if pressing her luck, she asked, "What do you think about having a dinner party later on this week?"

Sol countered with a Spanish pet name. "Querida, I would rather have a divorce."

"You're so dramatic!" Alice snorted. Sol kissed her palm again and went back to eating until they were both finished. When Sol picked up the wine and walked over to the fridge, Alice spoke up.

"Actually . . ." There was a bit of hesitation in her voice but then she went on. "It's way too hot in here. Why don't we take a bottle to the backyard and drink there?"

Sol raised an eyebrow. "You're sure?" She was almost doubtful and tried to temper her excitement at the thought of drinking *more*. It was probably a red flag at this point. But the taste still coated her tongue and God, did she *love* the way it lingered.

"Yeah, why not?" Alice stood up. "I'll grab a blanket from upstairs. You go on out first."

The moment she stepped outside of the house, a rush of cool air swept over Sol. It was a welcome break from the constant humidity of their home, and she wondered what exactly kept it so hot. She surveyed the yard—a modest size for a modest house. Perfect for a small garden.

There was something lovely about being surrounded by life, gently taking care of it, and keeping it healthy. Children required too much upkeep and pets were a mixed bag of pros and cons. Sol had considered an emotional support dog but the hoops to jump through for certification were exhausting, and ultimately she didn't think the hassle was worth it—either before *or* after.

Lush greenery in the backyard, a place that was squarely within the bounds of her comfort zone yet allowed her to take in fresh air, bask in the sun—how could she not look forward to that? Not to mention that when she eventually went back to work, she would find herself stuck in a lab, surrounded by caustic chemicals and sterile equipment. This could be her little project, something to take her mind off her many daily stresses.

"Alice, what's taking you so . . ."

She stopped. Sol wasn't sure how she missed it, but there was a gnarled tree just at the corner of the house. Large popping roots wrapped around it like veins. Dark brown, unlike the white bark trees she had seen all throughout the neighborhood. It was strange to see it there, so close to the house it almost seemed to merge with it at the base, growing outward like a tumor. Despite only being the very beginning of fall, the tree branches were already bare.

I don't belong here, it seemed to say, and by extension, neither did Sol.

"Yeah, yeah, I'm here," called her wife. Alice walked outside carrying a bundle of fabric in her arms. She followed Sol's line of sight.

"... Huh."

"Did you not see this during the open house?" Sol asked.

"Yeah, but I came to see the open house, not the ugly tree." Alice frowned. "Do you think we can get it removed?"

"According to the HOA, not without approval," Sol said, half joking. The tree was so hard to look at, she wouldn't be surprised if it brought down the property value. Maybe this would be something the HOA would be willing to pay for—if they joined. It was almost tempting considering how expensive tree removal was. "Besides, I don't think we have it in the budget to get it off our property."

"We still have savings."

Sol gave her a pointed look. "And we only have one income."

"But not forever, right?" she asked, as though it wasn't a rhetorical question. Alice wasn't leaving room for any negativity. The pessimist in Sol wanted to argue, to explain to Alice that anything could happen, but the sore subject made her clam up.

"Let's not touch our savings right now." *Just in case.* Just in case the worst happened and Sol had to find a new career.

"If you say so," Alice said, backing down for once.

Sol had a hard time tearing her eyes away from the tree. She stepped toward it. Her eyes climbed the length of the tree, and she tentatively placed a hand on the bark.

"Besides . . . it's dead, so no leaves will block the windows. Hell, none of the branches even touch the windows," she muttered. "And even if there was a storm, the tree is angled away from the house so . . ."

"So . . . ?" Alice mocked her tone.

"So, we can just leave it alone. No point on wasting money on something that's—ow!" Sol jumped away.

"What's wrong?"

"I think I just got a splinter." Sol checked her palm carefully. Weirdly enough, there was a thin layer of ash now covering her hand. But no splinter.

She wiped her hand on her jeans. "Must've fallen off. Anyway, let's open up the blanket and drink." Alice paused to check her phone, suddenly buzzing. Sol raised an eyebrow when she scoffed. "It's just work. I have paid time off until Monday, though, so they can wait."

Part of Sol wanted to ask what if it had been important, but another part of her knew better. With Alice gunning for a promotion, it would have been in her best interest to go above and beyond, answer all calls even if it were in the dead of night. God knows, she had done so in the past—what was so different now?

Sol clenched her teeth as she spread out the blanket and lay down.

"What's wrong?" Alice asked. "You've got that look on your face again. You're anxious."

Underneath the endless blue sky, Sol wanted to feel hopeful. Newly married and owning her first home was not something she ever thought was possible. It was too good to be true. And yet, here she was. A belly full of pasta and wine, cuddling her wife, and a long vacation from work. It should have felt perfect.

"You ever just feel out of place? Like, no matter where you go or what you do, you stick out and everyone can tell you're not supposed to be there?"

"Hm." Alice thought for a moment. "Nah. Couldn't be me, I'm a natural chameleon."

"Ha-ha." Sol rolled her eyes and Alice laughed, teasing her with a nudge.

"I'm joking. You think I haven't felt out of place before? I went from growing up in South Korea to moving to Toronto to moving to *Connecticut*. So many changes like that, you kind of learn how to make yourself fit in."

"Yeah? How did you do it?" Sol turned on her side. She knew that Alice had had some difficulties with the immigration process before but not so much on a social level.

Alice pursed her lips, wheels turning in her head. "Find just one thing you'd be okay with sharing with other people. Maybe an interest or a hobby. If you can bond over that, it works wonders every time."

"Sounds like a lot of work just to not be lonely." Sol sighed, linked her hands over her stomach. Lying flat on the ground, the cool earth felt more welcoming than most people. It never shied or reeled away from her. As long as she wanted to lie upon it, it would oblige. She stared up at the sky. It had never looked bluer, and the clouds hardly moved. She might as well have been looking up at a painting.

"That's when you use it as leverage."

"What?" Sol's eyes flitted back to her.

"Leverage, keep up!" Alice nudged her again. "What's the point of making connections with people if you can't use those connections for whatever you want? Make those people useful to you. That's how you stay ahead in this world."

"That just sounds like manipulation. Were you always an evil genius?"

Alice playfully slapped Sol's shoulder. "It's how most of the world works! Haven't you ever heard of networking?"

Sol frowned. Maybe she was looking at it all the wrong way. What *was* wrong with taking advantage of any connections she had? Wasn't that the point of job references and letters of recommendation? To leverage a connection to achieve further validation? And really, if she went one step further, most communities and ecosystems were made up of smaller interconnected parts and organisms. Relying on one another was how entire species survived.

"What about quinoa? I could be into quinoa," Sol offered. "I feel like the people here are very into quinoa."

Alice snorted. "Stop it! You could *not* get into quinoa. You don't even like oatmeal!"

"Fine." Sol pretended to think meaningfully. "I'm willing to bet at least one of our neighbors is going to be into an all-paleo or keto diet. I could try those."

Alice rolled over in laughter. The sound alone lifted Sol's spirits.

"You are a menace," Alice said, in between catching her breath. "Don't let them hear you say that."

"Even if it might be true?" Sol grinned, surprising her wife with a kiss.

"Mhm." Alice smiled into it.

Loose strands of hair tickled Sol's cheeks and as the kiss deepened, sparking passion between them, there was an audible click that seemed to come from inside the house. They turned and noticed that every light had turned off, every room suddenly darkened. Sol felt Alice stiffen, a concerned look flickering on her face before she shook it off and got up.

"Damn, did we blow a fuse already?" Alice sucked her teeth. "I'll restart the breaker. It's in the basement, right?"

Sol forced herself to focus on the buzz she felt from the wine and not about how that seemed like a bad sign.

Tell me you grew up Catholic without telling me you grew up Catholic . . . Any slight inconvenience was guaranteed to be an omen from God.

Sol leaned into the shifting wind.

Clap!

Sol sat up. Looking over the fences, she couldn't see a single person.

Clap! Clap! Clap!

The clapping continued, joined by others. A slow crescendo that was carried over the wind.

"Alice?" she called out. "What's that clapping sound?"

When Alice returned, she stopped at the doorway, turning her head to listen.

"Oh, that's just the trees," she answered. "It sounds like clapping when it gets windy."

Sol scrunched her face. It was the first time she heard of any tree having a distinct sound like that, but then again, she grew up in a city.

Alice sat down with a second bowl of mac and cheese. They didn't continue the kiss. And that was fine, really. Sol wasn't disappointed, not one bit. She made her wife laugh, a sign that, even if Sol felt completely out of place in a neighborhood where the people could be obnoxiously overbearing, she would still feel at home with the one person who mattered.

Sol kept all this in mind even an hour later, when they folded up the blanket and headed inside. She kept all this in mind as they passed the tree and tried not to think too hard about the fact that it felt like the tree was staring at her.

She kept all this in mind when her dreams were filled with ash.

THE WELCOME PARTY

The nursing home was silent, with the rare sound of an elderly person making their way through the visiting area. Occasionally, a nurse would walk by, pop their head in, and then move on when they only saw Sol and her father sitting at the center round table. All the others were empty, save for the tattered board games that were left on them. A TV sitting on a shelf in the corner perpetually played an old *Jeopardy* episode. Most days, the TV was too loud, but today it was muted.

Sol preferred to visit on Saturday mornings. She liked to have one-on-one time with her dad when no one else was around. It decreased the chances of her making a scene when he started being an asshole.

"How was the move?" Papi asked. Sol kept her eyes down at the dominoes, white ivory pieces clacking as her father's hands pushed them against each other.

"It was fine, Papi."

Actually, she was annoyed, especially since the breaker had to be reset again that morning. She wasn't going to divulge that information, though. Papi would insist on fixing it and the only thing he'd accomplish would be electrocuting himself.

Between paying for a funeral and hiring an electrician, Sol wasn't sure which would be more expensive.

Resetting it was cheapest.

"Y la nena?"

La nena. The girl. It was never "How is Alice?" or "How is your wife?" She was just "la nena." It was the kindest way that Papi ever referred to Alice, but it still annoyed Sol to hear that from him.

"Fine," she repeated, watching him distribute the dominoes. "Any new gossip around here?"

"You are such a chismosa, just like your mother!" Papi laughed. Sol resisted the urge to roll her eyes. The last thing Sol wanted was to be reminded of her mother, much less compared to her. The woman was dead now, so why couldn't Papi just let her memory die too?

Sol pursed her lips tight, willing herself not to retort. Papi would find a way to make it into an argument and the visit would end with security escorting her out of the building.

It wouldn't have been the first time.

Papi put down the first domino.

"Nah, nothing new here. Jackie just had her new baby though, very cute. Would've been cuter if it were my kid but eh, what can you do?"

"Jackie, the nurse?" Sol clarified. "Isn't she younger than me?"

Sol put down the next domino. Papi squinted at the piece, probably trying to do the math in his head. "What does age have to do with anything?"

"Okay." Sol focused on the black-spotted tiles. For a while, Papi hummed to himself as they played. It almost made him seem harmless: a typical Dominican viejo with a wandering eye.

"Do you remember when your mother was alive . . ."

Here he went again.

"Every time we moved to a new place, she always brought those old church women to pray over the house. She would dab the corner of the walls with consecrated oil too."

"Why are you bringing up Mami?" Sol demanded.

This was the second time he'd done so this morning. It was as if her dad had no idea what to talk about with his daughter, so he needed a third party to facilitate the conversation. Just like when she was alive.

"You just moved, didn't you?" He fixed her with a look. "Did you do the same thing?"

"No, Papi. Why would I?" she shot back, although her thoughts returned to the anxiety attack she'd had in her basement. Sol couldn't remember that ever happening when she moved apartments with her parents. While she hated the idea of bringing strangers into the house—especially strangers who would tut at her and her wife's "lifestyle"—maybe it would put her at ease.

Papi *tsk*ed. "You're just letting those demons frolic, aren't you?"

But the only demon here was him. His hands brushed against hers on the table and Sol felt how rough they remained from years of landscaping work. That and a refusal to put on lotion because it was a "female thing to do" left his hands as coarse as tree bark.

"You didn't even like going to church with us," Sol mumbled as she put down another piece. "What are you talking about demons for?"

"Sermons are one thing. Demons are another," he said. "You never know what the last family left behind."

"They left nothing behind but dust, Papi."

Still, maybe she would throw around salt. She heard it had a purifying property.

"You say that now, but you just moved in." He paused. "Did I ever tell you about the Abreus? They were a family that lived down the street from us in D.R., before you were born."

When Sol didn't respond, he went on.

"They didn't always live down the street, mind you. Before then, they lived in a nice part of town. Casa de Campo, really high-end. Mostly full of retirees and viejos."

Sol vaguely remembered Casa de Campo. She had driven past it with her parents on a few occasions and noticed how differently the Ponderosa-style tropical homes shined brightly along the clear beaches. Now that she thought about it, she remembered seeing boats on the water. She wouldn't be surprised if those same retirees and viejos were swimming in cash.

"What about them?" Sol asked dryly.

"They moved into this one fancy house, but after a week, a lot of strange things kept happening. Their youngest, Jose, got sick and the doctors didn't know what to do about it."

He was probably just sick, thought Sol.

"They spent so much money trying to figure out what was wrong, but things only got worse. The mom was pregnant but suddenly lost the baby."

Sounds like bad luck.

"And you're probably thinking it was just bad luck, but you didn't know the mom then. Carolina was a strong, healthy woman. Sexy too, a bunch of us back then would've done anything just for a chance with her."

And, of course, Papi found a way to be gross again. Usually, he only did it once per visit, but this time he managed to sneak another one in. Sol glanced at the clock, wondering if it was too early to leave.

"One day, when they were walking to church, they were approached by a bruja who noticed that Carolina was losing her hair. The bruja took one look at the house and said they had to move or el bacá would steal every bit of life they had."

"I don't know what a bacá is."

"It's a demon. One that's usually summoned in exchange for riches or power. But you have to pay up somehow, and I guess this one liked to take people's health."

Sol blinked. "Let me guess, they decided to move?"

"Of course. Wouldn't you?"

Sol couldn't answer that. Of course it would make sense to get the hell out of a dangerous place, but when it's your home, it's a different story. You'd want to fight for it. Especially when you have to think of the financial logistics of finding a new place to rent *and* paying for the mortgage until the house is sold. Getting a realtor, figuring out equity, tying up all the loose ends with a bank—and wasn't there a study done that showed homes owned by a Black person were valued less than when owned by a white person? It would be impossible getting her money's worth. Forget el bacá, she'd fight every demon from hell before contending with legal fees and homeowning bureaucracy.

Besides, nothing had happened in the house yet. Nothing *would* happen in the house because it wasn't haunted. Instead of demons, the only thing Sol needed to watch out for was her neighbors. The Homeowners Association. It still didn't sit right with her that they knew where she worked—even if they *did* assume it was Alice who worked at Yale. Maybe Alice was right and Nadine simply had a loose tongue. But she didn't like it.

Quiet descended for a moment, and Sol thought that maybe she could finally make an excuse to go. Suddenly, Papi changed the conversation.

"What's the neighborhood called again?"

"Maneless Grove."

"Maneless?" He quirked an eyebrow. "That's a strange name."

"Whatever, Papi." Why was she suddenly feeling defensive about the place?

He watched Sol intently. "Entonces, tell me about the neighborhood."

Sol thought carefully about her next words. "It's nice."

"Casa de Campo nice?"

"Nice enough to have a dozen identical trees planted every couple of feet." And by identical, she meant *identical*. There didn't seem to be a branch out of place. That had to cost a lot of money to maintain.

"What are you talking about?" he asked. "What kind of trees?"

Sol knew she shouldn't have gone there. Papi the Landscaper loved to find any way to seem like the smartest person in the room, and that meant taking every opportunity to talk about his work.

"Tall ones. White ones." She couldn't remember the name. It was probably written on the HOA agreement back home. Sol would have to take a look.

"Birch trees?" He raised an eyebrow, a smirk forming on his lips. Sol threw up her hands in defeat.

"Yeah, sure. Birch trees, I don't know. It's a nice neighborhood with a lot of nice things." She moved the conversation along, carefully thinking about what else she had seen in the brochure. "A mini golf course. A lake. A town hall, I think."

"Sounds like a resort," Papi said.

"It's a gated community."

Which might as well have been a resort. Sol hoped this would be the end of the line of questioning. Mami had also been like this, Sol thought, but specifically about whether or not Sol acted Christian enough for her. Papi was more secular and found a way to be nitpicky about Sol's every accomplishment. Between the two of them, Sol didn't have a shred of confidence growing up. It made conversations like these feel like she was being set up to be the punchline of a joke.

"What about your neighbors? Did you meet them? Are they all white people?" Papi snickered.

"My next-door neighbor is an elderly Black woman," Sol said. "And she's . . . friendly."

"You took too long to say that. What happened?"

Sol bit the inside of her cheek. On her drive out of the community this morning, she'd had the unnerving sensation that she was being watched.

And she was. Just one house over, there was an elderly Black woman standing at her window. She stared directly at Sol, tight-lipped and with a somewhat vacant expression. Sol raised a cautious hand to wave, but the woman didn't reciprocate. She stood there in her floral nightgown and silk bonnet, clearly having just gotten out of bed. Sol shifted from side to side, checking to see if her eyes followed her. They did.

"Nothing." She placed down another domino. "But I haven't met anyone else. Just the representatives from the Homeowners Association."

"The *what* association? What's that?"

Sol thought about how to say it politely.

"It's like . . . a neighborhood organization that collects money to keep the community looking nice."

His face soured. "Sounds like a scam. I don't trust it."

She snorted. "That's not a surprise." When he looked at her again, his smile was gone. The whites of his eyes had grown more pink. Sol steeled herself. When she was younger, making comments under her breath like this would earn her a good smack. Sometimes several, if he was already in a foul mood. Though she was an adult now and wouldn't allow herself to be hit, she always wondered what would be the straw to break the camel's back.

"Why are you always trying to argue with me?" Papi shook his head. "You don't visit me enough and when you do, it's nothing but an attitude."

"You're exaggerating. I visit you every week." Sol put down the last piece and gathered her bag. "I win. I'll see you next week. Bendición, Papi."

Before Sol went home, she made a quick stop at a nearby Home Depot, just to pick up an air conditioner. The humidity in the house was getting to her, and even if Alice wasn't complaining about it as much, she knew this stalemate between her and the house wouldn't last.

The thought made her chuckle—that she was actually fighting with a building—until she drove into Maneless Grove. She stared up at her new house, and it seemed imposing. Foreboding, even. Maybe it was due to her own poverty-stricken upbringing, but having a house like this had always been a pipe dream. Something that she could always look forward to having in the future but not ever expect it to come to her in the present. Hell, it was only thanks to Alice that Papi was living in such style. And now she and Alice were too.

Yet it also felt like it could be taken from them any moment. Throughout the entire process of applying for a mortgage and looking at houses, Sol was consistently convinced things would just fall through. After all, anytime Alice even so much as *looked* at a home, some investor came swooping down like a goddamn vulture and snatched it up, offering much more money than either of them could hope to earn in a lifetime. And yeah, Alice grew up well-off, but she wasn't *rich*.

Sol blamed Zillow and Airbnb fanatics, having read the articles about how both contributed to the difficult housing market. They were either raising the prices of every home in the area just by shady appraisal methods or buying up the homes to rent them out at ridiculous rates.

So when Alice came back to their midsize apartment with news that they would finally be able to close on a house, Sol was skeptical. More than skeptical.

How did they suddenly get so lucky?

Parking in the driveway, Sol took a moment to look up at the house once more. It was lovely, even if it didn't have the same cookie-cutter design as all the other houses. Actually, that was one of its more charming points. If every home was identical, how could anyone even tell which one was theirs? She could drive in circles for hours and not realize she'd passed it. And it's not like any of its flaws couldn't be corrected the way *they* wanted. The dim yellow paint could be painted over with a more vibrant orange. The grass could be trimmed, and she could plant flowers along the walkway to the door. Sol could even replace the muted beige mailbox with one that was forest green.

The longer Sol stared at her home, the less she saw flaws and the more she saw *potential*. It was *their* home. She and Alice could do whatever she liked with it. And as long as they made sure to never join the Homeowners Association, it would remain their own.

Already feeling lighter after the morning's tense visit, Sol turned to get out of her car—and jolted hard enough to hit her head on the roof.

A young white girl stood right beside her car door. She wore a coral dress with a ribbon around her waist and an empty-glass stare. The girl hardly blinked when Sol cracked the door an inch—any more and the door would've smacked into the girl.

"Can I help you?"

The girl didn't answer.

"Where are your parents?" Sol asked. The girl finally turned and raised a pointed finger across the street. There was movement in the window, drapes that fell back against the glass to obscure the inside.

"Do you want to go back? Or just . . . move?" Sol waited for another response but when it didn't come, she closed the door again, trapping herself inside.

It's just a girl, Sol told herself. A little one, probably no more than ten. Her brown hair was brushed to perfection and her cheeks were round. Like a perfect doll.

Unfortunately, Sol did not have much experience with doll-like girls. Or kids in general. Growing up, Sol learned to make herself scarce—not because her parents did not want her around but because she did not want to be around her parents. And that aversion to her parents spread to most adults. It was almost ironic that that aversion was coming back around to small children. Sol placed her hands on the steering wheel and considered going for a drive around the block until the girl went away.

She laughed at the idea.

Running from a child? Seriously? Sol might not have been a people person but to be afraid of an eight-year-old was grounds for a hot topic in therapy.

Sol let go of the steering wheel. She had an air conditioner in the trunk and she was going to deliver it to her wife, creepy-child-blocking-her-escape or not. Maybe she should try a different approach, like introducing herself.

Sol rolled down the window.

"Hi, I'm—" She was cut off by a thick smell of rotting meat. It hit her square in the face like a wave of maggots and decaying flesh. She could taste it in the back of her throat. The revulsion wrung her guts tight and she rolled the window back up to gag in silence.

All the while, the girl stood there quietly. The hand of her shadow twitched, out of sync with her actual body.

Where did that smell come from? It couldn't have come from the American Girl Doll look-alike. She was picture perfect, the poster child of well-adjusted preadolescence.

"Well-adjusted" might be doing a lot of heavy lifting there . . .

Still, she hadn't smelled anything that revolting when she cracked open the door earlier. Maybe something had crawled under the car, promptly died, and was well on its way through the decomposition stage—all in the last five minutes.

I need to get in the house, Sol thought, determination spiking. Or was it desperation? Either way, there were other ways to get out of the car. The girl wasn't going to trap her on all sides now, was she? Or that horrible smell.

Climbing over to the passenger seat, Sol took a moment to crack the door an inch. The lack of a nauseating scent granted her the freedom to fully exit. Once out, she looked over to the young girl.

"Are your parents okay with you being over here?" She glanced at the girl's home. This time there was no movement at the window. How carefree were these people?

Sol waited in awkward silence for the girl to do something. *Anything.* The girl could start wailing in her front yard, prompting community-wide concern, and Sol would sigh in relief.

But the girl, still pretty in coral pink, did nothing. It was enough to make Sol feel rooted to the spot, like she was being held hostage by the girl's silence.

This is ridiculous. It was a child. A small girl, who could do nothing short of crying or even kicking Sol and yes, it would hurt or annoy her, but it's not like this girl was a nuclear bomb. There was nothing short of social conventions that was keeping her outside and away from her wife.

Electing to ignore the kid, Sol grabbed the air conditioner from the trunk of her car and lugged it into the house. Every step away from the girl, while freeing, still felt uncomfortable. Even as she closed the door to the house and kicked off her shoes, she could feel the girl's eyes needling into her through the wood.

"I got an air conditioner!" Sol yelled, pausing by the window to peek out. The girl was now halfway across the street, walking roboti-cally until she got to the front steps of her house. Sol watched the girl simply turn the knob and enter, no knocking or keys necessary. Did no one lock their doors anymore?

"Hey, Alice, have you noticed a weird little girl around here?" she said, dragging the heavy box further into their home. Her knees were buckling already but she was determined to get it as far as the bottom steps.

Alice was sitting on the couch, head lowered as she massaged her temples.

"Alice? Everything okay?" Sol asked, arms straining.

"Huh? Oh, sorry. I'm a little out of it this morning. I have this really annoying headache and painkillers just aren't working." Alice looked over her shoulder—then did a double take and ran over to help. "I thought you were just visiting your dad today?"

"Yeah, but afterward I thought I'd grab this for us."

Sol let out a breath of relief as Alice grabbed the other end. They began to do a crab walk up the stairs, carefully shifting the box's weight as needed.

"Good thinking." Alice didn't speak again until they were at the top and turning down the hallway toward their room. "So . . . how was it?"

"The air conditioner?" Sol furrowed her brow. "I mean, I haven't tried it yet but . . ."

Alice groaned. "Jagi, I *will* drop this."

"I'm kidding!" Sol forced a laugh. They got to the room and gently placed it on the floor by the window. Sol stretched her back. "The visit went as usual. He was being a dick, and gross, and I left as soon as the opportunity presented itself."

"That's still not telling me much." Alice sat on the floor and leaned against the box with her eyes closed. Sol wondered if the light was making her headache worse.

"It's what happened."

"Sol, seriously—when are you going to let me go over and meet your dad?" Alice asked.

"You already met him once, remember?"

It was at Mami's wake. It was cold and dreary out and even though the event was inside a funeral home, the coldness clung to Sol like a ghost. Alice's hand in hers was the only sense of warmth Sol felt the entire time. The other mourners were Mami's friends from church who shared her disdain for the queer couple but at least they had the good sense to avert their judgmental stares. Even with Alice there, Sol barely spoke a word to anyone at the wake. She only had enough energy in her to walk silently toward the coffin, stare at Mami's stern expression for a moment, and then walk to the back of the funeral home.

The crowd parted like the Red Sea. Sol put her head on Alice's shoulder. She didn't hear Papi stomp up to her until it was too late.

"So this is *her*?" He slurred his words. "You had the nerve to show up with the *bitch* you picked over your own family?"

Sol looked up at him. Papi could barely stand on his two feet, he was teetering so much. If someone lightly pushed him, Sol knew he would be on his ass. Still, she stood tall in front of Alice, just in case Papi got a little too rowdy.

"Your mother knew you were so rebellious, but *this* . . ." He gestured to Alice with a look of disgust. "We didn't raise you to be so shameless."

Sol didn't wait any longer. She left, and if her Papi had said anything else, she ignored it. She didn't even go to the funeral. As warm as Alice's hand felt, everything in Sol was dead cold. That day, she blocked her father's number after texting him, *You're dead to me.*

It was years before she spoke to him again. And it would be years—like, a thousand years—before she brought Alice to him again.

"Sol, come on," Alice pleaded. "He was drunk at your mother's wake. And mourning."

"And he was a homophobic asshole. Still is, in case you were wondering."

Sol left the statement hanging and went to find a pair of scissors to open the box around the air conditioner. Hopefully Alice wouldn't press the conversation—it was an old one and it wouldn't seem to go away. Alice let herself believe there *could* be a chance Papi would come around just because her own parents were accepting. On the one hand, it was almost insulting because it implied Alice knew Sol's parents better than she did. On the other hand . . . Sol would be lying if she said she wasn't hoping for the same.

After all, didn't Papi go from calling Alice a "bitch" to "la nena"? That was an upgrade, as far as Sol could see. Not that she would ever admit that to Alice.

When Sol saw her mother lying in that casket, all the coldness she felt just confirmed that there was no coming back from the kind of relationship they had. There was no hope that Mami would ever come around.

It was a misery, but it was also a relief because at least it meant she didn't have to keep hoping.

Now if only Papi would just drop dead.

It took a lot for her to not cross herself in that moment—old Catholic habits died hard. But she fought through that ingrained guilt.

Sol found a pair of scissors behind the mirror in the bathroom. She stared at herself, took in deep breaths. Sol didn't want to talk about Papi. She didn't want to even *think* about him. Alice thought the man was just grieving the first time they met—but Sol knew that look in his eyes. She had grown up with the man. That wasn't just tequila and grief making him aggressive—it was pure *rage*. Tequila just happened to bring it out in him.

And Sol couldn't imagine what she would do if Papi ever laid a hand on Alice.

Gripping the scissors, Sol walked into the bedroom and stopped. Alice was gone.

"Alice?"

"Down here!" Alice yelled from the first floor. Sol frowned. Following her voice down the stairs, she saw Alice standing at the front door with an envelope in her hands.

"What's that?"

Alice opened it and her lips spread into a smile. There was a glint in her eye as she turned in Sol's direction.

"An invitation."

Sol quickly descended the steps, stopping at Alice's side. She snatched the invitation from her wife's grasp to read it for herself. Three balloons were embossed in the center of the page. Below it read:

Dear Song Family,

We at the Maneless Grove Homeowners Association would like to welcome you to the neighborhood with a tour and small welcoming party. We hope to see you today at 3pm. And don't worry—it's a casual event!

Sincerely, the HOA

At the very bottom, an address was stamped.

Sol met Alice's stare and understood the look in her eye. For every no Sol gave to attending a social event, she eventually had to say yes to something else. It wasn't something they ever spoke about, it was just understood between them. Compromise was how marriages survived, after all. If she wasn't going to give in to Alice's half demand to meet her father, then she could at least agree to a social outing.

Even if the last thing Sol wanted to do was *be* social. It was a product of growing up in a very strict church. At mass, at coffee hour, at a baptism or communion or confirmation party—someone was always watching, always judging. If anyone caught her doing so much as glaring at someone, information made its way back to her mother with almost literal lightning speed, and she would then interrogate Sol at home. As such, in these situations, Sol couldn't tell who was an ally and who was just waiting for her to expose some perceived flaw. And even though she had nothing to prove and no one to answer to now, the fear of hyper-surveillance was ever present.

They want to get to know us.

She knew exactly what that meant.

"Wow, we're the Song family, now?" Sol pretended to take issue with how the letter was addressed.

"*Sol.*" Alice pressed.

"I'm joking!" Sol sighed. "Looks like fun."

"I agree." Alice kissed her on the cheek, then paused. "What were you saying earlier, about a little girl?"

Suddenly, it didn't feel as pertinent.

"It's nothing," Sol said. "Let's just get ready for this party."

According to the brochure, Maneless Grove boasted a "small, close-knit community made up of many different kinds of people." Sol didn't buy it. For one thing, Sol had only seen one Black person so far. If they were going to claim any amount of diversity, she was going to have a hard time believing it. And if they were just going to rave about all those supposed "benefits" again, they'd better be willing to actually show it on more than just paper. So far, Sol was unimpressed and suspicious. The more they claimed to be a perfect community, the more she was sure they were either faking it or hiding something. Everyone had skeletons in their closet. The better they were at hiding it, the worse the secret generally was.

Alice hummed as she drove them toward the party. She stopped briefly to curse under her breath as they turned down the same street again. "This place is a maze, I swear." She *tsk*ed, and Sol could only nod. All the pristine streets did look the same.

"We could go home," Sol muttered from the passenger seat. "Didn't you have a headache?"

"It went away." Alice glanced at her out of the corner of her eye. "Fun, remember?"

Eventually they made it. Pulling into a small parking lot, Sol could see a field stretching beyond them. Balloons tied to chairs bobbed in the breeze and an enormous banner read *Welcome Reyes-Songs!* A crowd of people were already gathered and a table of champagne glasses had been prepared.

This wasn't some impromptu event. They'd been planning it for a while. It sent a shiver down Sol's spine.

So now we're the Reyes-Songs? Sol couldn't help but stare at the banner in confusion. It's like they didn't know how to address the couple, so they tried every combination possible.

There was an excitable buzzing—one that didn't seem to come from the people ahead of them. It was similar to that same radio-static noise Sol heard in the basement. Like whispers rising from the grass.

"Looks like we have company," a voice said, and Sol looked at Alice, wondering why she'd said that.

Before she could ask, Hope—the mushroom-haired woman from yesterday—caught sight of Alice and Sol first, excitedly waving them over. The strange buzzing immediately died down.

Sol tried not to visibly recoil. "Why do I feel like we've been ambushed?" she said, looking back at her wife.

"Because we've been ambushed." Alice sighed. "Too late to back out now."

Tentatively, Sol removed her seatbelt. She'd better have a get-out-of-jail-free pass for at least two more social engagements after this.

Hope ran over to them—literally *ran*—as soon as Sol and Alice exited the car. "Hi, we're so glad you could make it on such short notice!" she enthused, almost out of breath from her dash.

Ah, so they were aware it was damn inconvenient. If Sol didn't like them before, they were certainly on her shit list now.

And it only took two days.

Ever the diplomat, Alice said, "It's such a kind gesture, Hope. We're just a little confused. We thought it would be much more low-key—more a tour of the neighborhood."

Hope waved away her concern. "Oh, well, everything that you need to know about can be seen from right here. Follow me!"

Alice's smile grew more strained as they followed Hope out of the parking lot toward the other guests. Sol recognized it as her wife's "marketing consultant" smile. Sol never saw the point in mustering fake smiles. Sol was a scientist. She only cared for the facts, and the facts were that neither of them liked this woman or the association. But she let Alice lead and did her best to keep her distaste to herself.

For now.

In the distance, a man in a camouflage jacket and a five o'clock shadow squared his shoulders. He glared at Sol as the three of them approached, and Sol instantly felt the air go out of her body.

Here we fucking go.

The man was pulled away by another man with red hair. The redhead raised his glass toward Sol, smiling widely. Somehow, that unnerved her even more.

Tossing a laugh over her shoulder, Hope told them, "You see, this is the lawn for informal events. Over there is the lawn for formal events."

Sol gripped Alice's hand more tightly as they stepped onto the lush green grass. Her eyes followed the perfectly rectangular lawn as it stretched into the distance. The formal lawn was taped off from the informal lawn. Who the hell needed two kinds of lawns? And yet somehow even the children who ran circles around the adults managed to obey the limit. Sol immediately noticed the strange girl from across the street among those kids. Seeing her run along with her peers filled Sol with relief.

Finally, normal kid behavior.

Hope continued her chattering. "Right beyond that is mini golf and the building we're next to right now is the town hall."

Sol's gaze skimmed the tall, cylindrical building. It was made from dark wood and the windows looked newly painted white. The town hall stood out in sharp contrast to the rest of the homes in the community, which were painted in muted colors. It made Sol unable to look away.

"Careful!" Alice said to a small boy as he skidded into a sharp turn in front of them. Sol continued to watch, finding something particularly odd about the children. It wasn't until Alice pulled her along that she realized all the kids, despite being utterly unruly, were also stoic and silent in their chase. As if sensing Sol's observation, the young girl stopped in place, then turned to stare back. Sol averted her eyes.

"Alice, do you see that girl over there?" Sol nudged her wife.

"Hold on a second." Alice's attention was on Hope and the crowd they were moving through.

"Teresa, they're here!" Hope called out.

The crowd parted to allow Hope and the couple passage.

Teresa twirled around, hair flowing in the movement and eyes glinting with excitement.

"Welcome! We're so glad you could join us here. We wanted to show you what the HOA is all about." She tilted her head at the assembled guests, her smile smug. "Community spirit!"

"Thank you, Teresa," Alice responded. "Sol and I are just as excited to meet everyone in the neighborhood!" Her hand in Sol's, she squeezed. Only Sol could detect the irritation in her wife's voice at being summoned for this command performance.

Sol seethed silently. She was not someone to have their hand forced—and it was only the warm hand holding hers that kept Sol from lashing out.

Seemingly oblivious, "You two, go on and mingle," said Teresa. "Later, we'll talk business."

And with that, she had just guaranteed Sol would *never* join the HOA. She was pretty certain that was the case from the get-go, but this . . . she had no time for sneaky power plays. There were enough of them in academia.

Hope rejoined the couple, bringing along a group of four middle-aged women Sol was having a hard time differentiating. Each of them wore a different color set of yoga pants and matching top—peach, royal blue, chartreuse, and magenta. No name brand anywhere, but it was all too sleek, so it had to be the more expensive kind that didn't look too ostentatious.

While they didn't go as far as bleaching their hair to the same color, the same middle-parted, curled ends struck Sol as uniquely sorority-like. Eyebrows were even plucked to all hell, colored in with whatever respective shade their hair was. Sol imagined all of them swapping curling irons and eyebrow pencils early in the morning before going on with their day.

"Ooh, I think I've heard of this fashion before!" one woman crowed, one hand waving excitedly, the other holding a glass of wine. She wore the peach set, so Sol internally decided to call her Peach. "Don't tell me. It's very . . . farmer-chic. Am I right?" She gestured to Sol.

She looked down at her bargain-bin men's jeans, open wrinkled button-down shirt, and white cotton tank top that was honestly starting to pill.

"No, uh . . . I think it's just called 'butch'?" Sol met the woman's eyes with a defiant smile. Her wife squeezed her hand again, a signal for her to "be nice." Sol wished there was a signal for "this *is* me being nice."

"Oh!" Peach nodded, bringing the glass of wine to her lips. "Well, *you* wear it very well." She laughed to herself, the others joining in with her. Sol could tell when she was mocked. She squeezed her wife's hand, a signal for "you're hearing this shit, right?" Before Alice could do anything, the woman wearing royal blue wobbled in front of them. Magenta stuck a hand out to steady her.

"Are you all right?" Alice asked.

"She's just started an intermittent fasting regimen," Chartreuse answered for her. Blue's face was vacant of all emotion, striking pity in Sol—until she saw her shadow shake its leg while she stood still. Or maybe it was just a trick of the light where a breeze hit the grass on the lawn.

"She should probably eat something soon." Sol wasn't a nutritionist, but even she knew that when her hands shook in the lab, it was better to grab a snack than trying to handle something as precise as a micro-pipette.

"She's fine," Peach said. "We all take some time to get used to it."

"Right. That and the paleo diet, huh?" She glanced at Alice. Her wife's lips puckered, threatening to break her poker face. Sol decided to make an excuse to go mingle on her behalf.

"It was nice talking to you, though." She waved half-heartedly, pulling her wife along with her.

Alice leaned into her with a giggle. "You're a menace!"

"She started it."

As they moved farther away from the yoga-set women, two men stepped forward to introduce themselves.

"Hi, you must be the Reyes-Songs." A blond man with crow's-feet around his eyes offered up a hand.

What gave it away? Sol wanted to retort. The forced hyphenation of their last names was getting on her nerves. Instead, she turned away, feeling her eyes beginning to water and her nose congest. While she was no stranger to seasonal allergies, they were already well into the summer. And it was not like there was so much as a dandelion on the lawn—where was the supposed pollen coming from?

"I'm Roy," the man continued, "and this is my husband, Finnian. It's great to meet you. Also, don't mind those women—they're always looking for an excuse to bully someone." He whispered that last part, shaking his head disapprovingly.

Sol recognized Finnian as the redhead who pulled that other disgruntled man away. She glanced around, hoping to find him again if only so she knew how to avoid him.

Alice shook their hands but offered no introductions. What would have been the point?

Sol's eyes scanned the event around them. There had to be a napkin she could use to discreetly blow her nose.

The redhead—Finnian—took a moment to swallow his drink. "Sorry I didn't get a chance to meet you yesterday. Usually, the board likes to set aside time to greet newcomers, but I had a prior engagement I couldn't get out of." He stood tall, towering nearly half a foot over everyone else and easily blocking out the sun for his husband, who seemed grateful for the reprieve.

"That's fine." Sol rubbed her eyes, but the irritation was getting the better of her. Even her nose was beginning to run. "Hey, are there any napkins around? I think I'm being affected by the . . . pollen," she said, strained. The lack of any kind of flowers on the field made her claim seem ridiculous. But if Finnian or Roy thought so, they didn't show it.

"Of course. Let me grab you one." Roy sped off.

Alice leaned into Sol with a question. "You're not faking, are you?"

Sol rolled her eyes. "Faking *seasonal allergies* of all things? If I were going to fake an illness, it'd be something like a . . . stomach bug." She frowned. She could do better than that. "Or appendicitis. Maybe even leprosy."

Alice snorted. "Good luck faking that one."

"Here you go!" Roy handed Sol a travel-size pack of Kleenex, still sealed in plastic. Sol didn't waste any time tearing into it. She turned away from the group and half listened in while Alice continued the conversation on her behalf as she blew her nose.

"Sorry, what were you saying before?" Alice asked.

Sol balled up the used tissue and looked around for a trash can. Not only was the lawn completely devoid of blooming flora, but there didn't seem to be a single trash receptacle around. Were people just expected to toss their trash at home? Sol pivoted again and was immediately met with the strange girl staring at her from a few feet away. This time, Sol couldn't look away.

What do you want? Sol wanted to ask. Her mouth flapped open and closed until she settled for a simple wave. The girl slowly waved back. Satisfied with the reaction, Sol rejoined her wife and their new neighbors. The conversation seemed to have found its way back to the Homeowners Association.

"I'm the treasurer." Finnian gave a prideful grin. "And accountant. If either of you needs help with your taxes, you can always get in contact with me, and I'd be happy to look them over."

"That's very generous of you," Alice said. Though her eyes softened, the smile did not. Sol knew she found the offer suspicious. But she was being tactful because someone had to be, and that person definitely wasn't going to be Sol. She was already unnerved by the small child who seemed to take a strange interest in her.

"Stop trying to schmooze your way into having more clients, Fin." Roy rolled his eyes. "I'm so sorry about him. He's always going on about how the benefit of joining the HOA is having . . ."

"Access to pooled resources at every turn," their words came out together, and Finnian laughed. "Well, it's true! I'm sure you've already tried the wine, right? That isn't the *only* perk we have from living in a community like this. We have connections to just about anything we need because here, everyone's got something to offer. What about you two?"

"I'm a senior marketing associate at the N&V Firm," replied Alice. Her shoulders were tightening by the second. "And Sol here is a scientist at Yale."

Sol's stomach clenched. Reactions to learning where she worked were usually over the top. It didn't make her proud. It made her uncomfortable. Total strangers suddenly decided they knew everything they needed to know about her. When the truth was they had no idea what she was capable of. They assumed she must be really smart to work at Yale as if the university didn't hire incredibly ignorant professors all the time. Like the one undergraduate professor she'd had who'd nicknamed her "Punta Cana" after a tourist resort in the Dominican Republic.

Right on cue, Roy said in an exaggerated voice, "Oooh, looks like we're the ones who got lucky!" He laughed. "Two intelligent women and one of them's a doctor."

Sol felt her eye twitch as pressure moved along her temples. Fishbowl vision was going to be coming on quick if she didn't get ahead of it. Stress was always her biggest trigger, and these people were making her hella stressed. And as much as she would've liked to use this as a reason to go home sooner, she somehow knew that making a scene would only cause these people to want to "check in on her" later during the week. And she did *not* want visitors.

Instead, she breathed through the pain.

"Well, not a medical doctor," Sol said. "Just a researcher in the molecular biology department."

"Don't be so modest!" Finnian laughed. "That's still amazing. Okay, so Yale and N&V Firm?" He gestured to each of them before going into deep thought. "That actually sounds familiar. Isn't that . . ."

"The same place that Nadine works?" Alice filled in. "Actually, yes! Nadine's the one who took me under her wing when I started so many years ago. Taught me everything I know."

As she listened to her wife talk about work, it reminded Sol about the other reason she hated people knowing where she worked . . . because she didn't exactly work there at the moment. Her days at the lab were exchanged for days at home where she wallowed in career limbo, and she hated being reminded of it, especially to fake-ass people like the ones at this farce of a get-together. The thought of all that made her mouth feel exceptionally parched—she could *really* use a drink.

"Good for you, taking advantage of any resources you can get!" Finnian raised a glass in a toast and winked at her. "You'll fit right in."

"We're glad to hear that," Alice said. "Do you do a party like this for everyone who moves in?"

"Of course." Finnian laughed. "Have you met Lou? Lou, come meet the Songs!"

Aaand we're back to the Songs. They really did love to flip-flop between the two, didn't they?

Dread filled Sol's stomach when she saw who Finnian was gesturing to. The man in the camouflage jacket stepped up to the group. He had a wry smile, but his eyes were nothing less than malicious toward Sol.

Well, I definitely found him. She decided to let Alice handle this one.

"Lou's a retired veteran. He just moved in last month. Lou, meet Alice and Sol." Finnian quickly introduced them. "Alice works with Nadine—you remember Nadine, right? And Sol works at Yale."

"Yale." Lou repeated, nodding into his drink. "Good to know Affirmative Action's still working in your favor."

Everyone's smile became strained, uncomfortable. Sol wondered how her mugshot would look on the evening news if she got into a fight here and now. The title would probably say something along the lines of "Disgraced Scientist Assaults Veteran."

Nah, they would never use the word "scientist." It would give her too much dignity.

"Just kidding!" Lou smirked. "Don't be so sensitive. We're all friends here. We're a *community*, isn't that right, Finny?"

Finnian gritted his teeth and swirled his own drink in his glass. Roy had the decency to look apologetic.

Fortunately, Alice responded first.

"You're right," she chirped. "It *did* work in my favor."

Lou blinked, suddenly forgetting there were *two* newcomers, not one. "You? No, I mean, you're—"

"Asian?" Alice completed his sentence.

Lou blinked, embarrassment finally showing on his face. "I was just joking. I didn't mean anything by it. Listen, I was stationed in South Korea, so I—"

Sol sucked in air through her teeth, shaking her head.

Sensing that was the wrong thing to say, Lou excused himself. Alice's eyes followed him across the party.

"We are *really* sorry about that," Finnian said. "I mean, we had no idea he was . . . you know."

Sol rolled her eyes. The HOA ran a background check on both Alice and Sol but couldn't tell if Lou was of the KKK variety? She called bullshit.

"Racist," Sol said. "You can just say racist."

"Right." Finnian looked crestfallen. Sol resisted the urge to roll her eyes again. He was not the victim here, she was *not* going to feel bad for him. Instead, she eyed the glass in his hand. How long did Alice say to stay at the party for before using the fake emergency exit strategy? Five minutes? Had it been five minutes yet?

"Here's an idea." Alice broke the silence. "How about we forget about Lou? Just keep him away from us, and we'll consider that apology enough."

Finnian immediately brightened up. "Sounds fair."

As Finnian and Alice chatted a little more about work and taxes, Roy stepped beside Sol while stirring a drink.

"You know, between you and me, I'm *really* happy not to be the only gay couple here."

Sol's forced smile became a little easier. "Oh, really?"

She didn't know what to say or how to feel about that. For so long, she had always been the *only one* of something, whether it was the only Black person in a class, the only Latina in her department, or the only Afro-Latina lesbian on the entire staff. She got used to it the way one got used to sitting on a limb for too long. Eventually the limb would just fall asleep and she had to pretend like acknowledging her tokenism didn't make her uncomfortable.

"I mean, they're a *bit* better about things here," Roy said in between gulps. Sol buried her nails into her palm. Just because others were drinking, didn't mean she had to—she repeated this internally and focused on anything else. The way the air moved over the grass, how Alice laughed at something Finnian said, the kids who were standing a little *too* still . . .

"At least you won't get questions about who the man or woman is in the relationship." Roy laughed then stopped to catch his breath. He did that a lot, she noticed, take a moment to swallow lungsful of air. Suddenly, his breathing became a hacking cough that he muffled with a readily available handkerchief from his back pocket.

"Are you okay?" Sol asked. She wasn't a medical doctor, but the combination of his breathing and coughing reminded her of the first few weeks she visited Papi at the nursing home. There was an elderly man there who had lung disease and was constantly using some kind of respirator.

Roy smiled even as he shook his head. "I'll be fine! Don't worry about me."

That didn't inspire much confidence. Her attention was drawn back to the kids. Every single child was silent, standing still with both hands at their sides and facing a cardinal direction. At some point, Sol noticed that one would suddenly take off running, followed by another who was followed by another. The girl would be last, lingering as long as she could, as if to make Sol even more ill at ease.

It didn't help that they ran in straight lines, giving the appearance of rowdiness but actually seeming more like they were following some sort of unspoken instruction. A very odd version of follow the leader where no one spoke a word. Suddenly, the leading child stopped in place. The next child turned to run elsewhere then stopped there, and on and on until Sol realized they all went back to their previous standing positions.

And again, the girl would be last.

Roy followed her line of sight. "Do you have kids?"

His reaction was nonchalant, as if he wasn't seeing what she was seeing.

Sol shook her head.

"We don't either." Roy went on. "Though we would *love* to adopt one day. What about you? Have you two given any thought to raising a family?"

The invasive question made Sol's skin prickle.

"No, I guess not," she lied.

Adoption was another subject she and Alice danced around, but that wasn't any of his business. Or was it actually a normal thing to ask? Was Roy just making small talk—fuck, was adoption considered small talk? Sol was suddenly all too aware of the location of the drinks on the table, like a magnet pointing north. Her eyes and nose welled up again and she had to pull out another Kleenex for some momentary release.

Unfortunately, discomfort was never far. The longer Sol stood around, trying to act normal, the less she felt in control of her body's temperature. She was both too hot and too cold, breaking out in cold sweat and wanting to shed layers. Oh shit, was this another anxiety attack? Twice in one week? Sol's vision curved and she was back in a fishbowl, now with some asshole tapping the glass.

The only thing that broke her out of the experience was the feeling of foreign fingers brushing up against her scalp.

"By the way, you have such *lovely* hair." Roy murmured, his hand moving up from the nape of her neck into her curls.

Sol froze. The air shifted. Suddenly all eyes were on them.

"Oh no." Finnian quickly retrieved Roy's hand. "Roy, what did we say about personal space?" He turned to Sol. "I'm *so* sorry about him."

It was a small comfort to see that Alice's shocked expression mirrored her own, however, her attention remained on the rest of the party. Every adult in unison went from freezing in place with her, to going back to their conversations. Even the kids turned wordlessly toward each other, as fluidly as they had stopped and stared. The girl remained looking in her direction.

"It's . . . it's fine." Sol stumbled away, toward the drink table. It had just two glasses of wine left and she was going to have *both*, fuck moderation. Clearly being sober wasn't the way to handle these people.

Sol downed the first glass and decided to distract herself with her phone. Bad move. A new email from Dr. Henderson—the head of Yale's biology department—blazed up at her. The subject was titled *Information Regarding Your Hearing: IMPORTANT*.

She raised an eyebrow at the way the university's email set it apart in red lettering. Her thumb hovered over it, deeply curious to know the content. She was already thirsty again.

FROM: ghenderson@yale.edu
TO: mreyes12@yale.edu
SUBJECT: Information Regarding Your Hearing: IMPORTANT

Hello, Dr. Reyes,

I hope this email finds you well. While it is in my best interest to remain neutral due to the sensitive nature of this incident, I must say that the outlook does not look favorable toward you. However, there is still time and so I urge you to disclose any material or information you may have that could shed light on the situation. The committee is pushing for a decision to be made at the end of next week.

    Again, I hope you are well and if you have any questions, you know how to reach me.
    —Dr. George Henderson

Sol blinked. And then she read the email again. And a third time. Each time, her thoughts scattered as she digested the same information. It did not look *favorable* toward her? In all the years she had worked at Yale, spending countless hours in the lab and repeating experiments for the sake of validity, what exactly made them think she was capable of plagiarism? And what the hell was Clarke doing *now* that made her look worse off while she was absent from work?

Sol spun around when someone tapped her shoulder, ready to tear their head off. The sight of the elderly woman from next door made her reconsider.

"Hi, I-I'm Sol," she stammered. What was it about older Black women that made her crave their approval? A deep-rooted issue about her mother, she was sure.

"Corinne." The woman nodded, lips curled. "I'm sorry, have I met you before? You look familiar."

"This morning, maybe? I mean, you were at your window staring right at me." There was her trademark tact again. The accusation would have made anyone else embarrassed. Corinne, however, didn't seem fazed.

As she watched the other woman's expression, it was clear that nothing Sol said rang a bell. "Did I?" said Corinne. "Must've been sleepwalking again. I don't remember that at all."

Did people normally sleepwalk with their eyes open? Sol wasn't sure.

"Right. Excuse me a minute," Sol said, and stepped away. She walked slowly around the edge of the lawn, nursing her second drink and zoning out. The party seemed to continue on around her like an elaborate dance. People turned and moved in a semicircle, pausing to switch into another group. They seemed to intuit Sol's next step and got out of her way promptly. She was grateful for the consideration. Children ran this way and that, back and forth, all without bumping into her. For once, the girl was nowhere in attendance.

But instead of those perfect little eyes boring into her, now it was Corinne who continued to stare at her. Sol felt it. The crowd continued their strange circular movements, an orbit Sol wanted no part of.

She only ventured back to the drinks table when more wine had been poured. All the while Dr. Henderson's words gnawed at her. The fate of her entire career had been taken out of her hands.

I should probably stop after this next one, she told herself. Several drinks later, *I'll definitely stop after this one,* she promised herself.

But she didn't stop until Alice came looking for her.

"Sol!" Alice's voice was shrill. Sol had to be careful when she turned, or the earth itself would fly out from under her. Shit. This wine must be extra strong.

Alice forced Sol to put down the glass in her hand.

"Let's go. Remember that *emergency* we had?" Her wife hissed the word "emergency" like it meant something. Sol's head swam and she couldn't help but giggle.

"Sorry, everyone. I have to get Sol home now. It was great meeting you all, though!"

There was a hum of well wishes as the two shuffled all the way to the car. Alice helped Sol into her seat and fastened the seatbelt quickly.

"I cannot believe you got so drunk in the span of what? An hour? How many glasses did you even have?"

"I dunno . . . this many?" Sol held up a hand and laughed when Alice cursed in Korean.

Once Alice turned the car around, Sol glanced at the rearview mirror. The children had stopped playing. The adults had stopped gossiping.

Everyone had simply come to a complete stop, standing completely still, and watched them drive away.

And when Alice and Sol returned home, the house was just as hot as when they'd left it. The air suffocating and motionless, and Sol too drunk to put the air conditioner in. Sol's head hit the pillow, plunging her into unrelenting heat and darkness.

THE FALL

More buzzing. Fast. Strong. It was torrential, the way it fell over Sol, invading every sense. Her bones rattled. Her teeth chattered. She could taste bland oatmeal rolling around on her tongue. Her feet felt simultaneously too tight in heels and too free in boots. Where was she? Her eyes fluttered so fast, she could never tell. Lights danced beyond her eyelids as voices made themselves clear. Voices that didn't make sense for her to hear.

"Do you think that was a bad idea?"

"Who knew she was going to drink so much?"

"Shh! She might be listening."

More and more voices, some speaking, others arguing, some crying, screaming, *choking*—

"If you don't return that lawnmower, so help me, God—"

"Thiscan'tbehappeningthiscan'tbehappeningthiscan'tbehappening—"

"GET ME OUT OF HERE!"

And then, pressure. Sol felt herself squeezed tight, compact, every atom in her body compressed together by the weight of the universe. The weight got in her ears, tucked itself under her nails, wedged itself into her joints, and squeezed and squeezed and squeezed—until something wrapped itself around her leg, tugging her back to bed.

She jolted up in a cold sweat. The buzzing stopped immediately. Sol glanced around the room, drinking in air in large gulps.

Nightmare. It was just a nightmare. But what a bizarre fucking nightmare that was. That first set of voices sounded like the people at the party. Hope and Finnian and Teresa and other people who she knew by face but not by name. The second set of voices . . . Sol pushed it out of her head. They weren't real, it was just a nightmare.

Then another voice, and for a moment her panic skyrocketed at the sound. *Am I still dreaming?*

No, wait, she knew this one. It was hushed and distant but familiar. And it didn't come with any buzzing.

As Sol slowly got up from the bed, she realized why. The air vent in the lower left corner of the room carried Alice's voice quite well from the kitchen.

Sol listened as Alice opened cupboards, removed plates, and placed them down on the counter. She was cooking breakfast, it seemed—the vent carried the smell of eggs as well as the sound of a sizzling pan. It smelled good, but the humidity surging from the vent was unrelenting. The air conditioner she'd bought was not doing the trick at all . . . and she realized Alice must have put it in the window, and there was just a bit more guilt about last night.

And again, there was the easy flow of Korean. It took Sol a minute to mentally translate.

"Umma, uri gwaenchana." *We're fine, Mom.*

Hearing this made her ball her hands into fists.

She didn't hate her in-laws. Hell, she didn't even dislike them. It was hard to dislike people you rarely interacted with. Any time Sol *did* speak with Alice's parents, it was short and sweet. They always asked if she was eating well and to make sure Alice was too. In fact, Alice talked much more often with her aunt Julie who lived in Canada and helped raise her during high school.

That said, jealousy was a strange thing to feel about somebody else's parents. Especially your wife's. Sol couldn't help but compare the differences in their upbringing and each time she did, Alice won.

On one of their first actual dates, Alice revealed that yes, she was out to her parents, and while their relationship was rocky at first, it slowly got better with Aunt Julie's help.

Sol couldn't even fathom that happening for her, much less that it was possible that other people could still have a relationship with their parents. Most of the gay people she knew in college were in the closet to some degree.

She knew it was irrational, but it felt like a weird form of betrayal to know other people got dealt better hands in life . . . even if she now supposedly shared that hand.

Alice's voice carried again, and Sol's mind went to work translating what she knew.

No, we're not looking into having kids now that we're . . . That last part escaped her. Sol groaned and ran her hands across her face.

Not the kids conversation again. That was something Sol's parents and Alice's had in common—wanting grandchildren. Babies that were perfect for molding into people that parents are traditionally proud of. Like new projects until the projects eventually realize they can have their own opinions and sense of style—then you gotta scrap it. Hope those kids grow up to have their own kids and start over with the new batch.

"*Have you two given any thought to raising a family?*" She remembered Roy asking this at the party. The answer was a clear no, but it seemed like the topic would come up with or without their consent anyway.

Sol and Alice wanted none of it. They didn't hate children—although remembering the silent way the children played at the party yesterday made Sol shudder—it just so happened that neither of them wanted to quit their careers to take care of them. She and Alice saw through the scam of being a stay-at-home-mom and chose to live child free.

Besides, the adoption process was hell and pregnancy was worse. And yet, the two were *still* being hounded to freeze their eggs—if not by parents, then by doctors, by gynecologists—hell, it was part of their *insurance* package if they felt like taking advantage of it. The moment a childless thirty-two-year-old woman walked into a clinic, it was like even the nurses could smell it.

"*You should get it done before you turn thirty-five,*" they'd say. "*It's not too late.*"

As if they were still on the fence about it.

Maybe if Sol introduced Alice's parents to the little girl across the street—or any of the children in the community for that matter—they would back off. Hell, *anyone* might back off if they watched the children's odd behavior at the party. She thought about how they "played"—it was like they were following a set of silent instructions. Maybe it was a new game Sol had never heard of. It's quite possible that she might just be out of touch.

Alice's voice caught her attention again, as the conversation with her parents switched to the topic of the Homeowners Association. Though her mental translation couldn't keep up, it was a relief to hear that Alice's tone shifted to one of annoyance.

Sol was about to stop eavesdropping when something in the vent caught her attention. It was thin and spindly and extended beyond the bars of the vent onto the floor—and it wiggled.

On impulse, Sol stomped on it. When it didn't so much as retract, she reached down and pinched it between her fingers, and she was surprised by what she was touching.

It was a root, still brown with dirt as if it had just pushed itself up from the earth. Sol pulled and pulled but was surprised when it didn't give. She tugged harder—still no dice. Sol peered into the vent—maybe it was just snagged on something?

In the darkness of the vent, something else moved forward just enough for Sol to see a single eye blink.

"Sol?"

"Jesus!" She jolted up and fell back.

Alice came in through the door and tossed her cell phone on the bed. "Whoa, are you okay? What happened?"

Breathing hard, Sol peered back at the vent. The root was gone and so was the eye.

That was a human eye. She swallowed. Yet the vent was small. Only about a foot long. A person couldn't possibly have been in there.

Jesus, was she still drunk?

"I—I think we might have mice," she lied.

Alice's shoulders fell. "No. No, please don't say that. God, I can't stand mice." She went toward the vent. "Was it in here?" Sol stopped her.

"Don't worry, I'll take care of it. But—uh, were you on the phone with your mom? Your voice traveled."

Alice's face scrunched up. "Sorry, did I wake you? I know it's early but with the time difference and the fact I haven't called her for a few days now, she just wanted a quick call to know if we were settling in okay."

The thought of an appropriately worried mother was a punch to the gut. Sol forced her attention away from that.

"A quick call? Is that why I smell fried eggs and . . . bacon?"

"I don't know!" Alice crossed her arms. "Maybe I thought I'd make you a little something to help with that hangover you've probably got."

Sol suddenly felt smaller. "Yeah, thanks." She swallowed. She could taste her own guilt. "I'll come down to the kitchen in a moment. Let me just wash my face."

"I'll make some extra-strong coffee," her wife added, not really smiling, and headed for the stairs.

As Sol stumbled into the bathroom down the hall, she noted the annoyingly high squeak the door made when she opened it. She jiggled it a few times to locate the hinge and frowned at it, promising to herself that she would get it replaced somehow. Maybe Alice would appreciate that. Maybe it would be Sol's own fun little project that would get Alice off her ass about the drinking. Honestly, though, could Alice really blame her? She was already dealing with *a lot* without the added stress of having to socialize on such short notice.

Sol's career was hanging by a thread because of that plagiarism accusation, and she couldn't do a single thing about it. Her dad was a homophobic asshole who found a way to piss her off *weekly* and then the moment she thought she could catch her breath, she was whisked away to some party to have her personal space violated by complete strangers. And yet, she was expected to deal with *all of that* while sober?

Absolutely not. While Alice could be upset about Sol getting a little too carried away with the booze, she couldn't pretend like it wasn't a disaster waiting to happen.

Sol turned on the bathroom sink. Holding her hands out in front of her, she paused for a moment. It was faint, but there was still a trace of dirt on her index finger. So she hadn't imagined it, right? Sol plunged her hand under the running water and scrubbed it clean. Then she splashed her face a few times.

And if she hadn't imagined it, just what *was* that in the vent?

No. "I imagined it," she muttered to herself. "I only imagined it." Hangovers were a bitch.

After all, how could a person fit into such a small vent? And maybe the root was not a root but the tail end of a mouse. That could explain why the rest of it didn't come through when she pulled. Not to mention, Sol was barely awake yet.

Maybe her brain hadn't fully booted all the way up, and parts of it were still playing catch-up. She didn't know. She was a molecular biologist, not a neurologist. No, she had simply imagined it the way she imagined those whispers in the basement.

You're looking for faults when there aren't any. This is all new—or, in terms of the microaggressions, not new at all—and it's throwing you.

When Sol managed to get herself down to the kitchen, still breathing deeply to clear her mind, she was stunned by the sight of a plate stacked with her favorite comfort food.

"Yaniqueque?" Sol sank onto the kitchen stool. "You made yaniqueque? What's the occasion?"

It was a very simple Dominican snack, truth be told. Simply fried dough, but it went well with breakfast, and Sol bit into it heartily. The salt made her mouth water and she relished how chewy it was.

Considering how snippy Alice was earlier, Sol didn't think it was meant to be an apology of sorts. And now that she thought about it, if all of this was for a hangover, it was a lot of work. An instant ramen cup and some painkillers would've done the trick.

"No special occasion," Alice said, dipping a piece into egg yolk. "Just thought it wouldn't be a bad idea to have some."

She was lying. Sol could see it in the way Alice avoided her stare. And actually, she had avoided looking Sol in the eye upstairs too.

"Mhm. You're lying, querida," Sol pointed out, softening the accusation at the end.

Alice sighed. "Well, I didn't want to bring it up *now* since you just woke up, but . . . what the hell was that yesterday, Sol? You got completely carried away. I thought you said you were going to try harder."

"I *am* trying harder." She sat up and poked her yaniqueque toward Alice. "And if you haven't noticed, we *just* got here, okay? Give me a minute to settle in before you decide whether or not I'm fucking up."

"You got drunk at the welcoming party."

"I don't do parties!" Sol shouted. "You knew that. It's why you came up with the idea of us leaving after five minutes, do you remember that? Christ, Alice, what more do you want me to do?"

Alice rubbed her temples. Ironic, because Sol was the one getting a headache from all this bickering.

"Look, I didn't want to start a fight over this. I'm just . . . I'm just worried," Alice said. "Can you give me that much? Am I allowed to be worried?"

Sol deflated, slowly. As much as she wanted to blame someone, Alice was not her enemy. She didn't cause Sol's descent into paranoia and madness, nor was she the reason Sol was required to take a leave of absence while the academic hearing went on.

That rat bastard Clarke was.

Sol slowly pulled out her phone and opened the email before showing it to Alice. She watched her wife's face as she read quickly. Alice's expression went from a look of mild confusion to wide-eyed shock.

"I saw this email during the welcoming party," Sol explained. "So sorry that I went a little overboard, but . . ." She didn't want to say she needed it, nobody *needed* to get day drunk faster than bad news traveled. Except she *did*. Regardless, Sol let the sentence hang in the air and Alice nodded, understanding that this was an explanation for her behavior, not an excuse.

"This is why I worry about you being home alone all the time while I'm at work," Alice admitted. She tore at the dough. "I'm worried about you having nothing to do and feeling bad about it because then you get into this spiraling mood, where all you do is day drink, pretend to watch TV, and pick up a new DIY hobby that you drop within a week. Remember when you tried soldering?"

She didn't remember it, and that was part of the problem. Being blackout drunk while using a dangerously heated metal implement was probably not the best way to spend a Saturday night.

The bathroom hinge quickly ranked low on her priority list. Sol put down the yaniqueque and cleared her throat.

"What else is there to do?" Her voice was low, even. Because from Sol's standpoint, she was already doing *a lot*. Therapy, processing the academic probation, recovering from months' worth of exhaustion—all while remaining as close to sober possible—was *very fucking difficult*. What else could she possibly do to put Alice's mind at ease?

"I mean, would it be such a terrible thing if you went for walks every now and then?"

"Why? So someone can call the cops on me for being suspicious?"

Alice's mouth dropped. "They are not that racist."

Sol raised an eyebrow. "That guy touched my hair without asking at the party!"

"Okay fine, that was out of order." Alice gave in. "But you haven't met *everyone* yet."

That much was true, but if those few were any indication of what the rest would be like, Sol would rather eat glass.

Sol shook her head, chomped on another piece of yaniqueque. "Must be *really* easy for you to give them the benefit of the doubt . . ." She trailed off as she chewed, but she was rapidly losing her appetite.

Alice sat up straighter. "What do you mean by *that*?"

Oh joy, now Alice was catching an attitude.

"Nothing."

"No. I want to know, Sol." Alice drew in a breath through her nostrils. "I want to know what you mean."

It was moments like these when Sol realized just how stark the difference was between how she and Alice regarded their white neighbors. Sol was always on guard around white people. She had to be out of self-preservation, and it was like every time she interacted with them, they only proved her right. But Alice was . . . well . . .

"I'm just saying, Lou had two *very different reactions* to the both of us."

Alice let out a derisive laugh. "I knew you were going to go there."

"It's true, though," Sol said, back stiffening. "Remember the time a cop pulled us over and had me get out of the car?"

"We are *not* splitting hairs over who has it worse." Alice turned away from her.

"He made up something about me matching the description of a suspect from a nearby robbery and asked me what I was doing in the area. Then he made me do a sobriety test."

"You were drunk!" Alice argued. "You were practically sweating sangria!"

"Alice, you were the one driving."

Their eyes locked, and her wife released a small exhalation. Sol felt her anger rising as the silence stretched between them. Alice wasn't going to concede, that much was obvious.

"Right." Sol stood up and collected a few more yaniqueque in her hand.

"What are you doing?"

"What does it look like I'm doing? I'm going for a walk. Like you said."

Alice pinched the bridge of her nose. "Oh my God. You don't have to be a bitch about it. A simple no would have sufficed."

"I'm going to grab a jacket. It looks a bit chilly outside."

Sol hadn't taken even thirty steps out of the house when her nose began to run.

For fuck's sake, how is there so much pollen? She stopped momentarily to sniffle and rub her eyes. Once her nose was fucked, the eyes were always next to suffer. She wanted to turn back but didn't want to prove Alice's point. Fuck it, she would have to deal with it for the next half hour.

Sol was halfway across Corinne's lawn when the woman called out to her.

"Mind if I join you?" Corinne asked, already leaving her home. She wore a long blue dress and a sun hat that matched a cane. It was almost startling to see her like this—coherent and chatty. "I'm an old woman, you know, I need to keep some sort of daily exercise routine. Walks are easy now, but they don't get any easier with age."

Sol slowed her pace to let the older woman join her—it didn't seem she had much of a choice. "How's the moving in, dear?" Corinne asked.

It took her a while to answer with a mouth full of yaniqueque. Finally she said, "Uh, yeah, it's actually going pretty well. Alice—my wife—is very good at unpacking smaller things and I like to take care of the heavier stuff." Like rearranging furniture and building the new bookcase Alice needed and pointing out the blatant racism in their new neighborhood.

I don't really want to talk about Alice, though.

Sol's eyes traveled across the street, almost expecting the little girl to make an appearance. For once, she was absent. Sol sniffled, stopping snot from dripping down to her upper lip. It wasn't so much the grossness that put her off, but the discomfort of the sensation.

"Good to hear. I'm happy for you," Corinne said. "Is something wrong?"

"Nothing. Just allergies. Do you know who lives in that house over there?" Sol had to turn to point in its direction, but Corinne hardly spared a glance.

"That would be the Kennedys."

"Huh." Sol couldn't help but stare at the house. It was identical to both houses on the left and right, but unlike the other two, the curtains were always down.

And yet, in this moment, Sol felt like she was being watched by that secretive home more than any other home in the community. No one else had curtains closed to the outside world.

No one except the Kennedys and me. And Sol had nothing to hide, she just enjoyed her privacy. So maybe the Kennedys were the same way? Sol rubbed her eyes again. Irritation was wearing her down.

Realizing something, Sol asked, "Were they at the party? I remember seeing their little girl. What's her name?"

"Veronica," Corinne answered again, keeping her gaze focused ahead. Sol's fixation on the house had slowed her down considerably—now *she* had to catch up to *Corinne.*

"Do they always let Veronica run around unsupervised?"

She was truly obsessed. She shook her head. Sol hoped she didn't sound nosy, bitchy, or both.

Corinne's eyes looked at her from the side and she quirked up her lips.

"It's a safe neighborhood," Corinne remarked. "The kids can go just about anywhere they like. But they're never really unsupervised. Someone's always watching."

Sol felt the sting of judgment. Clearly someone was always watching. Her parents only lived across the street, of course they would be keeping an eye on Veronica from the windows. Just because Sol had a rough childhood doesn't mean she should expect the same for Veronica.

And now I feel bad for not talking to everyone at the party. Veronica's parents probably *were* there and she missed her chance to be a well-adjusted adult welcomed into a community because she was too busy getting drunk and paranoid. Typical.

Alice definitely deserved an apology for that behavior.

Between the shame and the awkwardness and the snot, Sol became immediately uncomfortable with the silence. The yaniqueque she was eating would only last so long. She racked her brain to come up with a new topic for small talk.

"Hey, we've been having issues with the wiring," Sol said. "Every now and then, we have to reset the breaker and we're not sure why. Do you know what might be causing it?"

"Well, there was a fire previously," mused Corinne. "Maybe it's damaged the wiring."

"Really?" Sol furrowed her brow. "Doesn't look like it. I mean, it does look a little different from the other houses." Muted. Dull. Even a few inches shorter if Sol stared at it long enough. But no sign of fire anywhere.

"Oh, it's a . . . very special house, I'm sure."

What does that *mean?* Sol almost opened her mouth to ask, but Corinne cut her off quickly.

"Do you need a tissue?" The woman was already rummaging into her bag. "I know the pollen must be killing you. It did for me when I first moved in. But it does eventually subside when you get used to it."

Thankful, Sol buried her nose into the soft Kleenex and blew as hard as she could. It didn't fully un-fuck her nose, but it did help. At least now she could do a facsimile of taking a breath.

"How long have you lived in Maneless Grove?" Sol asked, balling up the used tissue and banishing it to her pocket. The last thing she wanted to do was litter in front of this old woman. She looked around at some of the houses and could *feel* the windows on her.

Yes, littering here seemed imprudent.

"Ha! All my life, it feels like. My husband, Winston, and I moved in early in the eighties, though we'd been trying to move into a place this nice since the seventies."

"You're married?"

"Widowed now." Corinne sighed. "Winston died just last year. You just missed him."

"I'm sorry to hear that." Sol frowned. Maybe the awkward silence was better. She tore into more of the fried bread. "How are you doing otherwise?"

Corinne laughed. "Wonderful, actually! I mean, I miss my Winston but, in this community, you really feel the love and support from others that make you feel like everything's going to be okay."

Now Sol was wondering if the two were living in two different neighborhoods. So far the "love and support" she felt from others seemed a little bit conditional. As in they would *love* it and *support* them if they joined the Homeowners Association.

Gritting her teeth, Sol could only manage a "That's . . . great."

Maybe Corinne's experience of living in the community was just different from Sol's. She *did* move in before Sol was even born. Maybe Corinne and Winston were brought in from an older agreement before these newer and pushier residents came in. Corinne didn't seem like the kind of person who was interested in bylaws and regulations. She probably signed away as long as it meant she could have a home.

Sol could only imagine what would happen if she *did* join the HOA. Sure, it would get their passive-aggressive tactics off her back, but that wasn't the same as being completely left alone. She and Alice were already ambushed with a forced social event. What was next? Being showered in bland pasta casseroles? Hosting uninvited guests for dinner? If Alice and Sol didn't put down their foot down and establish boundaries, these people would never learn.

And if Sol were being honest, their insistence on uniformity felt a little too close to the way she had grown up. Mami and her church friends were very particular about everything, and that included Sol. Growing up in a very religious household meant long skirts, no makeup or jewelry, being modest in all manner of speech, keeping herself "pure" (which really just meant never even thinking about boys—which, in hindsight, probably would have been more than welcome), and so on.

Then there were the comments. From an outsider's perspective, they were harmless, one-off observations, but Sol knew they were much more than that. They were judgments, an underhanded way of letting the other know they did not approve and they expected you to get in line sooner rather than later. These women—past and present—made Sol very wary of any kind of "close-knit" community she came across, Maneless Grove included.

No, she much preferred to keep her space. Wasn't that the point of a house? To finally have something all your own? A castle, in some of white America's parlance? That's what she hoped this move would be. And in the unlikely event that Alice died an early and untimely death, Sol would become an alcoholic shut-in who might or might not try her hand at writing a memoir. Maybe she would adopt a cat.

But the drawbridge would be *up*.

Already halfway there with the alcoholic shut-in part of your plan, according to Alice...

Corinne had a sly smile on her face when she glanced over to Sol.

"You're not really into it, are you?"

"Into what?" Sol pretended not to understand. Her focus was back to her congesting nose. Her eyes were welling up again.

"You're very closed off. A bit reserved, kind of like a hermit."

That was definitely the more polite way to describe her.

"I'm just an introvert." Sol sniffled.

"Mhm."

It was the trait Sol hated most about herself. She never felt comfortable around others. It took work, an inside knowledge of how socializing worked. Was she smiling enough? Making enough eye contact? When she said goodbye, was she expected to give a handshake or a hug? The stress of these questions tore at her stomach, deepened her social anxiety, and filled her with a sense of self-hatred she was sure no one else was victim to.

And when it felt like every house and tree and bird was staring at you, and your head was stuffed to the gills, it only made this all the harder.

The two only just then rounded the first corner of the street. God, this was going to take forever. Sol wondered if she could make up another emergency that required her to turn back and run straight home. Or would two emergencies in one week be pushing her luck?

Do I even have *any luck?* she thought. Also, *I need to invest in a shitload of Benadryl.*

"I guess what they say about opposites are true," Corinne mused. When Sol gave her a confused look, the older woman explained, "You know, because at the welcoming party, your wife seemed to really enjoy socializing."

"Ha, don't remind me." Sol couldn't be more upset about that—and upset at herself. Given the chance, she still wouldn't change anything about Alice. But God, she wished someone had warned her about the trials of being an introvert married to a social butterfly. It was like slowly jogging through a marathon and being sporadically told you needed to sprint for at least the next half mile.

"How *did* you two meet?" Corinne asked.

Somehow the question managed to catch her off guard. It wasn't an exciting story, nothing dramatic about it.

"We were roommates in college."

"That must've been nice."

Sol shrugged. For a while, it wasn't anything. It just *was*. They weren't friends, just people who lived together in the same room. Most of the time, they hardly spoke a word to each other. Alice was always off somewhere hanging out with her crowd of friends and Sol was practically chained to her desk, studying. If it wasn't for the fact their names were printed on the door of their room, they probably wouldn't have even known each other's name.

Things between them didn't start to change until Alice came back to their room drunk one night and accidentally crawled into Sol's bed, cuddling her like it was a normal everyday occurrence. At first Sol froze. She was shocked, then angry, then embarrassed. More than anything, Sol wanted to move her into her bed, but Alice was heavy and out cold.

Sol went to Alice's bed instead, leaving the drunk girl in hers, and noticing for the first time ever that Alice's pillow smelled like pomegranate. It was a soothing smell that somehow made her heart pound so loudly that she hardly got any sleep that night.

The next morning, Alice apologized profusely only to be surprised by Sol getting her a bacon, egg, and cheese sandwich on a bagel, together with a bottle of water and some Tylenol.

"Greasy food and water usually help with hangovers," Sol had said.

Just like Alice had done for her this morning. Ugh. How had she not seen the connection?

Because I'm a selfish, drunken—

Corinne interrupted Sol's self-loathing with another question.

"When did you two start dating?"

Sol was grateful for the fact that question started with "when" and not "how." The "how" was a story Sol never got used to telling, particularly because it wasn't a good one.

"Sometime around junior year?"

Sol and Alice had been in freshman year when that bed incident happened, and normally they would have been given different roommates the following year and that would have been the end of that. But for some reason, they decided to stick together. Maybe it was because Sol never ratted Alice out for underage drinking or that Alice had the common decency to not bring the parties back to their room. Whatever the cause, they just clicked.

"That's so sweet. You two were practically kids."

Sol laughed. She never thought of it that way. At the LGBTQ+ club on campus, there were more than enough jokes about them being U-Haul lesbians. Living together before they even started dating made it seem like they jumped the gun, even if the dorm's lottery system introduced them first.

And how many years had they stuck by each other, dating or not? It had to have been over ten years now. From age eighteen to now, that was fourteen years of just knowing each other.

Corinne and Sol rounded the corner. Just two more to go. The safety of her pollen-free home was so close, she could almost breathe.

"So, are you working, Sol?"

Sol felt all the air get sucked out of her.

"I'm . . . on a sabbatical." That was definitely one word for it. "Probation" was another. She tried not to sound too sad. "It's like a long vacation."

Corinne reached over and patted Sol's arm.

"Good. No sense in working yourself sick."

Sol winced. Images of what initially caused the "sabbatical" flashed through her mind. While she was never close with her colleagues, it was the arrival of a new one—Clarke—that pitted them against her. Her late nights made him look bad, while her impeccable writing made it easier for her papers to get published. Sol was always in her own world, a seemingly more efficient one, and her success was an impediment to his.

When the freezer in her lab suddenly went off, she didn't even think to check if it was only unplugged. Instead, she rushed the frozen specimen home, cleared out her own freezer, and sat it in there until she got a report of what caused the sudden power failure. Except . . . there simply wasn't one.

Not long after, some of her reports went missing, making Sol question her sanity because she absolutely did write them and she knew she always placed them in the upper drawer of her filing cabinet . . .

Finally, there was the accusation of plagiarism that was looking like it was going to end everything she'd worked so hard for.

Sol shook her head. A lump was rising in her throat—she pushed it down. Everything would be fine. Sol knew she didn't plagiarize. Her name would be cleared.

Her mental health, however . . .

Corinne snaked her arm around Sol, pulling Sol to her side for extra support. Her heart jumped in response and she immediately worried whether she was sturdy enough for Corinne. Was she walking too fast or too slow for her?

Sol found herself slouching and carefully walking in step. For a moment, her shoulders ached—then she felt her entire body relax into a sigh.

All at once Sol knew that Corinne's husband, Winston, was diabetic, that the two had been married for over forty years, and that, until recently, Corinne worked in HR at a small oil company. Sol knew all of this so quickly that she didn't have time to even question how she knew it. There were no words, but the information still flowed between the women effortlessly.

Best of all, she didn't even feel congested.

This is weird, thought Sol.

Another thought quickly went, *No, it isn't.*

And even if it was, it didn't matter. This was *pleasant*. This was *easy*.

It bewildered her, and yet she also realized how much she wanted it. The easy. Socializing *never* came easy with Sol. Why not drink it in while she could? These feelings steamrolled her before she could process it. After all, it wasn't Corinne's fault she walked in her sleep and maybe Sol's drunken state cast their interaction at the party in a worse light.

Just enjoy it. The thought slithered in. *Enjoy being part of a whole.*

A vibration in Sol's pocket broke the silence, and it felt like something was tearing inside of her. She nearly tripped as she fished her phone out of her pocket, ruining the harmony of their steps so fast that Corinne let go of her arm.

"Hello?" Sol scrunched her forehead, mind in a fog. Congestion returned like a bad ex.

"Sol? Listen, I'm sorry. Okay? I didn't—I didn't mean to push you.

I know you're already trying your best," Alice said, quietly. "Can you come home? Unless you don't want to. Your choice."

Well, now Sol felt like an ass for storming out.

"Uh, sure. I was just walking with Corinne, our next-door neighbor. You remember her, right? From the party?"

"Oh!" Alice's voice shot up in surprise. "Wow. I don't think I had the chance to talk with her. We still have some yaniqueque left. Bring her over, I'd love to finally meet!"

"Okay, be there soon." Sol hung up and turned to Corinne. "Sorry about that. Alice was just saying that she'd love to meet you. Are you free now?"

Corinne didn't move or blink. Her smile never faltered and her posture barely budged. Yet Sol was absolutely sure she felt a wave of hostility rise from the elderly woman.

"Corinne?" she repeated.

"Why, of course!" the older woman finally responded, any animosity gone. "Come on, let's go!"

Though Corinne and Sol linked arms again for the rest of their walk, it was no longer effortless or calming.

The moment Sol opened the door, she was greeted with a wave of sweet peppermint.

"Alice, we're here." She took one step forward and stopped. Corinne hadn't moved an inch since they got to the front door. Her eyes were pointed upward, staring at something on the roof. Sol looked to find nothing wrong with it.

"Corinne? Aren't you going to come inside?"

A few seconds later, Sol started to repeat herself and was cut off by the sound of crashing plates.

"I'm okay!" Alice yelled. Sol decided that was a lie and sped to the kitchen, where she found Alice attempting to shove an enormous number of cups and bowls in a small cabinet. Her back was to Sol, and she was surrounded by the smallest bowls, which had inevitably spilled out.

"What are you doing?"

"I thought she might like some tea, so I put a kettle on the stove and tried to get some mugs but uh . . . I forgot I didn't exactly get them all to fit the first time." One mug was already threatening to fall back out from the corner. Sol quickly went to grab it.

"Can you at least come and say hi to Corinne really fast?" Sol said, helping Alice relieve the overfilled cabinet by placing many of the bowls on the counter. "She seems freaked out by the house already." Sol tore a handful of paper towels off the rack and tried clearing her nose again. The roughness was a stark contrast to the soft Kleenex everyone in the neighborhood handed her, but it still did its job.

Alice frowned. "Huh? Why?"

"I don't know. Just say hi to her so she can get on with her day, okay?"

"Okay, okay. You don't have to tell me twice."

Sol started her way back and paused at the unusual sight of Corinne already halfway up the stairs, eyes glued to some fixed point. Sol didn't care what she was looking at—what she wanted to know was, what was Corinne doing there?

Sol raised her voice. "Um, excuse me?"

Corinne's facial expression shifted, and she turned to look at Sol. Looking down at Sol and the steps, she seemed confused. And that made Sol pissed.

"I-I'm so sorry, I don't know what I was thinking—" Corinne's hand went out to the banister, missing it by just a centimeter before taking a step backward. Her foot grazed the next stair beneath her, confirming it was there.

And then it wasn't.

The next second felt like an eternity. Sol stared at the disappearing step in shock. It was there. It had to be there—but it wasn't.

Before Sol could shout or run to Corinne, she fell.

There was an audible snap. A shriek of pain. Alice darted out from behind Sol and ran straight to Corinne's side. Assessing the damage, all she could do was yell, "Sol! Call an ambulance!"

Sol was frozen. Corinne hadn't slipped on the step. The step had simply vanished.

Sol stood there, entranced by the impossibility of it all.

For half a second, she thought the step that Corinne stood on was just twice as high as the others—except that was an impossibility as well. She would have noticed if that were the case. *Alice* would have noticed. They would have marked the area and looked into getting a carpenter to fix this mistake. It would have consumed their thoughts for much longer.

It didn't. There was only one possibility. The step had disappeared.

"Sol? Sol!"

Sol snapped back to the present. Alice cursed under her breath and lunged for the nearest house phone. She was so upset that she was still yelling when speaking to the operator.

"Yes, hello, there's an elderly woman here who fell and broke a bone, I think."

Alice's voice faded to the background. Sol walked hesitantly toward Corinne, who openly sobbed in pain.

"H-help me, please!" she begged.

Sol looked back to the step Corinne had missed.

It had reappeared.

THE INCIDENT

S ol was an expert in psychiatry office decor. Hardly a surprise given the number she'd been in and out of during her childhood. At some point, it stopped being a point of shame for her and instead became something of a game. She liked to categorize the types of therapists based on their office. Some therapists liked to hang movie posters and place popular show memorabilia along the desk as a way to show they were "relatable" or "just regular people."

Some kept their offices devoid of all personality, preferring to keep cream-colored walls blank and use generic Ikea furniture to emit a strange "nonthreatening" atmosphere.

Then there was this one. This office, belonging to one Dr. Nieman, was pretty much standard issue.

Sitting on the mandatory couch, Sol's eyes scoured the walls, which were lined with books like the *DSM-V* and *Chicken Soup for the Soul*. Dr. Nieman's desk was large and mahogany, and the carpet matched. Sunlight brightened the light-blue walls. It almost felt *too* bright in here, like the woman was trying to subconsciously tell Sol to lighten up. Directly behind the leather chair that Dr. Nieman occupied, two doctorate degrees hung on the wall—one in psychiatry and one in psychotherapy.

And then there was the therapist herself—Dr. Nieman. She looked . . . *fine*, all things considered. An older woman, with smile lines etched into her face even when she wasn't smiling. Blond hair that was only blond from the bleach. Her roots were already exposing her to be a natural brunette. She was one of those white people who Sol wanted to say didn't look *entirely* white. Some non-white ancestry showed up on her face somewhere, Sol just couldn't pinpoint where.

Dr. Nieman was the first on a list of therapists that Sol was "interviewing," so to speak, before deciding which one she would stick with for the remainder of her treatment. Though, Sol hoped the woman was good enough that she wouldn't need to see anyone else. Having to go through the same intake session over and over with different people was guaranteed to stress her out nearly as much as the welcoming party.

Click-clack. Click-clack. Click-clack.

The silver balls of a Newton's cradle drew back Sol's attention. She wondered if the line of balls that graced her desk kept swinging long after she was gone.

Click-clack. Click-clack. Click-clack.

The rhythm kept her attention, ironed out her anxieties. It was strangely calming to watch. Maybe this was a good sign.

"If I remember correctly, you wanted to meet after you finished moving. Are you all settled in now?" began Dr. Nieman.

She remembered. Sol perked up. That was a *very* good sign.

"Yes." She cleared her throat. "I'm all settled in."

"That's good to hear." Dr. Nieman smiled. It was a professional smile. She was a professional, trying to keep Sol at ease throughout this initial appointment.

That was suspicious.

No, it isn't. Sol kicked herself for her immediate apprehension. There was no reason to believe Dr. Nieman had ulterior motives. She was just doing her job.

It didn't help that all Sol could think about were those damn stairs.

"So why don't you tell me about what your goals are for treatment, and we'll start from there?"

"Yeah, that sounds good," Sol said, trying to feign nonchalance, but she couldn't stop her nails from picking at the seat cushion. "I think my main concern is my anxiety. Whenever I feel like something is wrong, I get fixated on it, trying to prove that it's actually wrong."

Like with the stairs. She tried to shake it from her mind.

"I see. And is there anything making you anxious now that you'd like to work on first?" Dr. Nieman rested a hand on her cheek. She had a look in her eye like she was welcoming Sol to admit that seeing *her* was making her nervous. It was, but not any more than her new home situation.

"My neighbors," Sol offered. "They're kind of . . . odd."

"How so?"

"They're like . . ." Sol paused to sigh, not knowing where to start. "There's a motto for the neighborhood—which is weird enough already, right? Like since when has there ever been a motto for a neighborhood?"

"Mm, I can think of a few. 'East Coast, Beast Coast,' for one." Dr. Nieman smirked. Sol felt herself deflate.

Please don't be one of those. The woman didn't look like she knew fun little colloquialisms like that one. It was a little young for her age range. And who was she showing off for?

She probably sees younger clients all the time. Sol tried to give her the benefit of the doubt and relax. It was hard to relax, though, especially with a new therapist. Sol didn't want to make herself seem like a handful within the first few sessions, but she also wanted to make sure she could trust whoever was across the room from her. It was almost funny. Most people didn't like to sleep with others on the first date; Sol didn't want to look crazy during the first real session.

"Sure, I—I guess." She tried to mirror her therapist's expression. "But that one doesn't count. That's for an entire part of a country. I'm talking smaller, a little neighborhood."

"What's the motto?"

Sol made air quotes as she told her, "Invest in a neighborly spirit."

Her therapist gave a small laugh. "That doesn't seem so terrible."

"It's . . . that's not the point." She waved her off. "It's weird, isn't it?"

"Hm, a little odd but ultimately harmless, don't you think?"

Sol bit back her words. She wanted to argue but, really, Dr. Nieman was right. It was a harmless thing to have, a neighborhood motto. Yet it bothered her so much.

"I guess it's . . . fine," Sol grumbled, not fully convinced. Dr. Nieman tapped her pen against the desk a few times, nodding sagely.

"Have you ever tried dialectical behavioral therapy?" she asked.

Sol stiffened. "Isn't that for people with personality disorders?"

That was a red flag. Going from talking about anxiety to a personality disorder was such a huge leap in a short time, Sol's discomfort was growing by miles. Forget the stairs, did she really want to continue treatment with someone who was so eager to diagnose her?

Dr. Nieman's smile seemed to widen. "It sounds like you're familiar enough with it—but it's not *solely* for those with personality disorders. In fact, it's been used to help treat people with similar struggles as you."

Now it sounded like Dr. Nieman was just trying to sell her on it. Or was she still on high alert from earlier? Shit, was she shooting herself in the foot already with this therapist?

"We don't have to get into that for now. It's just a possibility for the future," the therapist said, skillfully smoothing over the discussion. "Is there anything else you'd like to work on if you pursue treatment with me?"

"I guess I could work on my social skills," Sol mused.

"How does your support network look?"

Sol frowned. "I have Alice. My wife." She knew how pathetic that sounded the moment it left her mouth. A network was more than one person, it was a group of people. And sure, maybe she didn't *relish* the idea of juggling more than one relationship at a time, but it was a healthy thing to have a community to rely on.

Not that she would ever admit that to Alice.

As if reading her thoughts, Dr. Nieman chuckled. Sol sunk into her chair.

"Okay, don't worry, we can work on that as well. What about your parents?"

"God, no." Sol rubbed her eyes. Confusion flitted across the therapist's face and Sol knew she had to explain. Was there a way for Sol to give her the SparkNotes version of the situation with her father? Thirty-two years' worth of a fraught relationship seemed like too much ground to cover in one forty-five-minute session.

"He's a homophobe and I'm a married lesbian."

Dr. Nieman slowly nodded. Though her face was unreadable, the line seemed to have sufficed.

"That's quite a lot. Why didn't you lead with that?"

Sol shrugged. It wasn't that she didn't *want* to talk about it. It was that there was nothing to talk about. It wasn't interesting to her. Why should it have been interesting to Dr. Nieman?

You're paying the woman to listen to you bitch about your life, the least you can do is tell her everything.

She still wasn't going to tell her about the stairs, though.

"Too much to unpack." Sol left it at that. "I visit him once a week at the nursing home and that's still one time too many."

"I'm sorry, you still visit him?" Dr. Nieman's confusion returned. Sol's mouth flapped open. Was that so difficult to believe? "How does your wife feel about that?"

"Not happy, but not because I visit at all—it's because I don't let her come with me."

"And why is that?" Dr. Nieman's expression was . . . not unkind, but not entirely neutral. Her brow was deeply furrowed, mouth parted slightly like she was trying to figure out a complex math problem. It unsettled Sol, to feel so entirely alien to someone who was supposed to treat her.

Is that how I look when I'm studying parasites? The tiny creatures were the crux of so much of Sol's research, but she never thought she would ever be looked at in the same way.

"Sol?" Dr. Nieman pressed.

"Because . . . sometimes he can get violent?" She thought that would be a given. Did straight people not know how dangerous homophobes could be? "He doesn't even refer to her by her name. He just calls her 'la nena.'"

"Sorry, is that Spanish?" Dr. Nieman furrowed her brow.

"Yeah. I'm, uh, Dominican."

"Oh, I didn't know you were Dominican. I thought you were just . . ."

Black. Sol completed her sentence.

Referral or not, she was immediately crossing Dr. Nieman's name off the list. This therapist was clearly not for her.

Dr. Nieman cleared her voice.

"So you're worried he'll hurt her," Dr. Nieman said, face returning to a neutral expression. It wasn't a question.

"Well, yeah," she said. "You can't trust homophobes to keep their hands to themselves." She hoped that was obvious now.

"Has he ever hit you?"

Sol almost laughed. "I grew up Catholic. Of course he's hit me. 'Spare the rod, spoil the child' and all that." It was when she was very young and very small. Whenever she threw a tantrum, or broke a plate by accident, or hell, even spilled milk, she'd earn a few smacks until she learned not to do it again.

"I don't mean if he hit you under the guise of discipline," her therapist clarified. "I mean if he's ever hit you due to your sexuality."

Sol pursed her lips together and looked down.

"Once. And it wasn't even because I came out." She took in a deep breath, cautiously going down that memory lane. "He was drunk, like he always was. And yelling across the house about how all gay people were disgusting all because he accidentally sat next to a gay guy on the bus."

"How did he know the guy was gay?"

Maybe it was because Sol knew that she would never see this woman again that she wasn't bothered by the prodding into such a traumatic memory. God knows she would never tell Alice this. The way her wife tiptoed around her *more pressing* work issue drove her insane as it was. Then again, she didn't like how hard Alice came down on Sol for her drinking either.

Maybe I just don't like confrontation.

Sol shrugged. "He probably didn't. I think he said something about how shameful it was for a man to cross his legs and just made the assumption. Anything slightly less than full-blown machismo is a sign of gayness, I guess," Sol continued. "Earlier that week, I met a girl who had two moms. I don't remember the girl's name anymore, but

I remembered her mom seemed really nice, so when Papi started up about gay people being disgusting, I said that couldn't be true."

In that memory, there was a silence that followed, the kind that tightened around her throat. Sol remembered being so small that Papi towered over her, blocking out the light of the living room. She stood firmly in his shadow as he asked her if she thought she knew better than him. She said no, but—

"He slammed my head into the wall." Sol pushed the words out if only to end the memory. "And told me not to speak back to him again that way."

For a moment Dr. Nieman was silent, and that made Sol nervous. When therapists went silent, it was because they were going to throw her a curveball.

"You know, Sol . . ."

Here it was.

"From the little that I know about you, you're pretty successful. You work at Yale, you have a beautiful wife and now a beautiful house. And it doesn't seem like he has anything hanging over you so I have to ask—what keeps you going back to your father?"

All the air left the room. Sol slowly sat up.

"Well . . . he's my *dad*," she said, shame hot beneath her skin. It always felt like a piss-poor excuse to routinely visit someone who was downright despicable as a person, with zero redeeming qualities. And yet, he was the only person other than Alice who knew everything about her. He'd been there since the literal day she was born. Sure, she didn't exactly open up to him, but he knew her nervous tics, could read her easily, and had an astonishing way of finding and pressing her buttons all at once. There was a saying, familiarity breeds contempt—and it made her wonder if that was why her father was so callous with her. He knew too much about her and he didn't like it. If it wasn't for the fact that Alice was such a loving force in her life, Sol would readily believe that maybe she really *was* just unlikeable.

But even with all that said (or unsaid) . . . *dad*.

"I understand," said Dr. Nieman, doing the sage-nod thing again.

"But there are many queer adults who have cut off contact with abusive parents. They almost always go on to live better lives without them. Why is it that you don't do the same?"

Sol wanted to scoff. If she didn't visit her dad weekly, he would probably hunt her down to the detriment of his own health. Would he get far? Probably not. But the fact of the matter was, he would still *try*, and that left a nasty taste in the back of Sol's throat.

"I just . . . have to, okay? It's a Dominican thing." Another piss-poor excuse. She said it rarely as a trump card, to get non-Dominicans to drop something. But no one could dissect someone else's culture without seeming like an asshole, and she was pretty sure Dr. Nieman wasn't an asshole.

"I see." She leaned into her chair. The session didn't go on for much longer after that.

During the drive home, Sol's mind went back to the *real* reason why she visited Papi. It was the thing that brought her and Alice together, coincidentally, but it still was a terrible memory.

Sophomore year was the year that Sol became more involved on campus—but not just with any club—with the LGBTQ+ club aimed at providing a safe space for queer students. It was called REFUGE, and it was the one place she felt she could breathe. She started going, proclaiming to just be an "ally" but, before long, she admitted to being something more—something that she couldn't wear on her sleeve as proudly as the other students did.

She was something that needed to be kept a secret from her parents. Except that wasn't possible forever.

It happened during winter vacation of sophomore year. Sol was home and studying physics at the kitchen table. A textbook was opened up in front of her with a notebook she was scribbling in next to it. Mami was cooking, frying up chicken for dinner. Papi stumbled home, somewhere between buzzed and drunk.

Mami pretended not to notice. She always pretended not to notice when Papi wasn't quite sober, something that Sol hated with every fiber of her being. She knew it was because he was a man, he was given liberties that she could only dream of. What Sol didn't know was that at that moment, Mami had a bigger issue to deal with.

"Marisol, how is school?"

"Fine," she'd said, reflexively.

"Joined any clubs lately?"

Sol stiffened but tried to keep her cool.

"I don't have time for clubs, Mami." It was partially the truth. She really couldn't afford to waste time anywhere else than at her desk.

Mami fell silent and then went to the fridge. She brought out a large head of lettuce, and Sol knew that the food must have nearly been done since salad was the last thing to prepare.

"I was on Facebook earlier, you know . . ." Mami said, grabbing a large knife. She chopped a little slower than Sol was used to seeing, as if she was only partly preoccupied with the vegetable. "Just scrolling . . . but then I saw a picture of you at some event."

Sol instantly knew what she was talking about. REFUGE had a yearly fall event, a potluck that was supposed to entice new students into giving them a try. Most students brought store-bought items, including Sol, but it was a very laid-back event where people got comfortable and could unwind after a long day of studying.

"You seemed very comfortable at REFUGE," Mami continued.

Sol was always careful not to upload any pictures of herself online with REFUGE. Hell, she was careful not to take *any* pictures with them at all. But someone must have snuck one and then tagged her on Facebook.

I should have just deactivated that fucking account.

Except that would have made Mami even more suspicious.

"A friend of mine invited me." The lie rolled off her tongue and she'd hoped it was convincing. Listening closely, Sol realized Mami had stopped chopping.

Papi shuffled into the kitchen, burping something fierce. Sol smelled Corona on his breath but she knew Mami wasn't paying attention to that.

"Is the food ready yet?" he asked, eyeing the stove.

"Did your friend also give you this?" Mami reached into the pocket of her gown and pulled out a small rainbow flag pin.

Sol's blood drained from her face. She thought she had kept it squarely hidden away.

"I found it while cleaning your room." At this moment, Sol noticed that Mami hadn't bothered to drop the knife. Instead, she was gripping it, so tight that her knuckles were strained.

Papi looked over and furrowed his brow. "¿Qué es eso?"

Mami came closer and Sol jumped up to her feet, not liking how the knife was pointed at her.

"Mami, it's not a big deal . . ."

"Not a big deal?" she yelled, and threw the pin against the wall. She waved the knife at her as she screamed, "Do you know you're going to hell for this?"

Sol backed away, hands up and eyes glued to the knife. "I don't know what you're talking about . . ." Her back hit Papi and she was immediately afraid that he was going to keep her there, facing the knife, facing possible death.

The look on Mami's face was nothing short of homicidal.

"Hey, hey, calm down . . ." Papi said, putting Sol behind him. She was so surprised by the action that she didn't think to run. She was still frozen by the certainty that this was how she was going to die.

"Calm down? Our daughter is disrespecting us *and* God with what she's doing. I knew I shouldn't have let her go to college!"

The knife was lower now, but Mami still didn't put it down. Sol's heart was jackhammering so hard she thought she might have a stroke. Part of her was watching the scene from the corner of the ceiling.

"I'm not doing anything . . ." Sol murmured, not quite believing what was happening. That despite doing everything she could to keep up her scholarship at Yale, despite having *excellent* grades throughout the hardest courses, she was still a disappointment to her mother. The idea cut into her, making all her efforts seem useless. Sol's eyes watered and she looked to her books, still on the table.

"I'm going to study in my room," she announced weakly, and maneuvered around Papi to stack her books. She hugged them to her chest, makeshift armor against a glinting knife. Sol sniffled and for some reason it enraged her mother.

"Good. You should be *ashamed*," Mami declared.

Sol's face contorted into one of anger—a mistake, in hindsight.

"I'm not *ashamed*," Sol spat. "I'm *angry*. I'm working hard at school and you're more upset about if I'm gay or not."

"*Are* you gay?" Mami's face was hardened. She stared into her daughter's eyes, but it was in the silence that she found her answer. "You're going to *hell*."

Even with a tear rolling down her cheek, Sol scoffed as she turned her back to her mother, "Well, then I guess I'll see you there."

It happened faster than she could blink. Sol was pushed—not just pushed, *attacked*. She was facing Papi when it happened, shocked when his arms came out to grab her. She thought he was going to hit her so she flinched, but then Mami came in barreling from behind.

Suddenly, Sol was on the floor. Her books were covered in blood and when she looked at herself, she realized it was coming from her arm. For a moment, she was numb. Then a sharp pain settled in. The world around her was muted and loud all at the same time.

"You are going to hell!" Mami screamed. "You are going to *hell*!"

Papi held Mami back. The knife was still in her hand, blade dirtied with blood.

"Go to your room," Papi had urged her.

Still in a state of shock, Sol did just that. She wrapped her arm in an old T-shirt, only beginning to panic when the blood soaked through the fabric and showed little sign of slowing down.

Did Mami nick an artery? Was Sol dying? She felt lightheaded but part of her was sure that if an artery *was* hit, she'd have been dead before she got halfway down the hallway. Still, the amount of blood flowing was worrying, and the pain was truly unbearable.

When Mami calmed down—or when the screaming abated somewhat—Papi entered Sol's room. The bleeding finally slowed.

"Come on, I'll take you to the hospital."

It went without saying that Sol would not say a word about being attacked by her mother. She'd long forgotten what story they told the doctors—probably something that involved a bad fall—but Sol did not forget the events that transpired. She couldn't forget because even when the stitches were finally gone and she was healed, there was still a scar in its place.

A reminder that her mother tried to *kill* her.

Papi on the other hand, for all his gross machismo and sexist double standards, made *some* attempt to shield her. Tried to pull her out of the way, even took her to the hospital. Sol never knew why. He was unpredictable at best.

That didn't completely absolve him from letting Mami disown her, news that she was given at the start of spring semester that year. If it wasn't for Alice, Sol might have dropped out entirely.

No, he was definitely on Mami's side about Sol's sexuality. When she thought about that ride to the hospital, there were no apologies, no fussing over Sol or how she was feeling. Papi didn't take her to the hospital out of love but out of obligation. That was something she didn't understand at the time. Now she understood.

He saved her, whether he meant to or not.

The least she could do was visit him.

THE ARGUMENT

It had only been two days since Corinne fell and broke her hip, but Sol still no longer trusted the stairs.

"Sol, gimme a break," Alice groaned upon getting home late in the evening. "Are you really still doing this?"

Sol was propped up on the couch, which she had spun around to face the staircase, an old video camera in hand and a bowl of popcorn beside her. There was a pillow and blanket folded neatly at the end, and Alice probably thought that Sol was never going to attempt to climb the stairs again. On the coffee table in front of her was a mess of papers, handwriting that went from neat to rushed back to neat again, and a short stack of their rerouted mail. One letter was already torn open, from the HOA, reminding everyone that the association board member elections would be happening in just two months. Sol considered sending back a letter reminding them that the elections were none of their business.

"I ordered pizza," Sol responded, writing in a journal.

Alice rolled her eyes as she went to the stairs. She had theories for what happened, none of which came close enough to actually being useful or even possible. While Alice was at work, Sol took to staring at it from every angle, measuring the length and width of each step and comparing it to all others.

Corinne slipped on the fifth step from the bottom. Five was an odd number but it wasn't cursed, not like the Biblical six or the superstitious thirteen. That particular step was only half a centimeter taller than the others, which should have made it easier for it to connect with the heel of Corinne's foot.

No matter how Sol thought about it, the old woman shouldn't have slipped. Not unless the stair really *did* disappear.

Maybe she just lost feeling in her leg halfway up the stairs? It was a better possibility.

"How was work?" Sol asked half-heartedly.

"Constant meetings and mostly unhappy clients." Alice shrugged. "What else is there?"

Sol frowned. Truth be told, she had very little idea what it was like to do Alice's job. Marketing seemed to be full of connecting with *people* and figuring out what made them tick so you could convince them to buy a product. It essentially boiled down to feelings—things Sol couldn't be bothered with most of the time. And even when Alice tried to explain to her how there was actually quite a lot of math and analytics involved when it came to evoking an emotional response in someone, Sol was in over her head. To this day, she couldn't tell you what made Alice fall for her, so she definitely wasn't going to understand how to get other people to fall for whatever product might be for sale.

Alice kicked off her Mary Janes at the door with such force that Sol thought she was trying to use them as projectiles. She shuffled into a pair of house slippers with a huff and paused to rub her eyes.

"Something wrong?" Sol asked.

"I might have to work more late nights this week." As she headed to the stairs, Sol noticed Alice's eyes were not on the steps but on the mess of papers on the table. Sol sheepishly gathered them into a stack.

"You've been working late nights often."

Alice stopped at the first step. She leaned against the banister, a deep frown expressing acute distaste. "It's this company we're trying to partner with. They've practically been harassing me, making sure to add all the little specifications needed for their AI, completely ignoring the fact that I do not work in the tech department." She took one step up. "And now I look like I'm micromanaging the tech side and stepping on people's toes, and it all adds up to me playing peacekeeper to two sides and still trying to do my own work." Alice took a deep breath as if just the thought of her day-to-day exhausted her.

Sol didn't know what to say so she instead focused on Alice's feet, continuing up the steps at a leisurely pace. The closer her wife came to the fifth step, the more intensely she stared. What were the odds that it would happen again? That the step would simply become undone under the weight of another person? Ignoring the fact that for the last two days, Sol watched Alice ascend and descend the stairs without issue, she was eager to find a cause for what made Corinne fall.

"And then I come home and see that you're getting obsessed again," Alice grumbled.

"I am *not* getting obsessed." Sol jumped up. Alice gestured to the table, the collection of papers sitting like a piece of damning evidence.

It was easy for Alice to dismiss what had happened as Sol's eyes playing tricks on her. Sol couldn't fault her for that. After all, Sol did have trouble sitting still. At the university, whenever there was any downtime, she found ways to fill it with work. While the PCR machine ran, Sol reviewed her notes. If Sol was getting ready to begin gel electrophoresis, she made sure to bring a book or academic articles to read during the process.

"Okay, fine, I might have *too* much time on my hands," Sol said. "But in my defense, I know what I saw." And what she saw was the step disappearing and then reappearing.

If that were possible, what else could the house do? Could the banister shift away from a hand? Could the walls give off warmth as if the house were a living creature?

Could a blinking eye spawn in the vents?

Though Alice remained silent, Sol could hear the gears in her head turning. Wondering if there was any point to arguing with Sol. Wondering if she had any energy to deal with this. The look on her face was nothing short of exhaustion. Her wife seemed to have had one hell of a day. Sol's shoulders fell, concern for Alice trumping her curiosity.

"Why don't you go take a shower?" Sol offered. "I'll be up soon."

Alice's mouth twitched. It was quick—a small smile forming before she pressed it back into a line. Sol had seen that look before. Her concession definitely made Alice feel better, but she pretended to be stubborn and think about it anyway.

Alice let out a long-suffering sigh. "Okay. But only if you're sure." She crossed her arms.

Sol held in a laugh as she met her at the steps and pulled her into a kiss. "I'm sure," she murmured.

Alice hummed as she kissed her back, hands lazily wrapping around Sol's waist. They stood there for a moment, relishing the comfort they found in each other's arms. There was something about feeling Alice's weight on her that filled Sol with deep satisfaction. It felt *right*. And the more she pressed herself against Alice, the more fulfilling it was.

Alice did the same. They fell into each other, kissing and pressing until it was obvious they weren't just going to stop there. When Alice's fingers grazed Sol's skin under her shirt, Sol quickly peeled it off.

Breathless, Alice pulled away just long enough to ask, "Where'd you put—"

"The strap? It should be in the closet upstairs." Sol tossed her shirt aside with the same motion that she grabbed Alice's ass. With how frantically they were pulling at each other, Sol couldn't tell which of the two started the ascent. She just noticed how tentative their steps were—how careful they were being as they went. It was for good reason, of course—how embarrassing would it have been to fall because they were too busy getting it on to pause for the few seconds it would take to just walk up normally? And if either of them happened to hurt themselves, Sol was *not* going to be the one to explain the situation to the paramedics.

Still, the slow progression made Sol all too aware of the stairs again. She peeked down, eyeing the fifth step with curious intention.

What if something happens when we're both on it?

"Never mind," Alice scoffed, quickly letting go. "Clearly you're not into this."

Sol was stunned. Confused, she stood there as Alice stomped the rest of the way up.

"What? No, that's not it," Sol argued, short of breath. She didn't realize how quickly she became winded.

"I can literally feel you thinking about it!" Alice raised her voice. "You're not subtle."

Sol narrowed her eyes.

"First of all, I don't know who you're yelling at like that but it better not be me," she said. She had all the love in the world for her wife, but she drew the line at being yelled at like a child.

"*Sorry*," Alice spat, then shifted from one foot to another. She ran a hand through her hair and sighed. "Look, it's been a long day, okay? I'm not in a great mood."

Yeah, that much was obvious. Sol frowned and awkwardly picked up her shirt. She could understand having a bad day—she had an awful string of days not too long ago and it nearly resulted in alcohol poisoning.

What she didn't understand was Alice's overreaction.

"Whatever. It's fine," Sol mumbled, putting on her shirt and returning to the couch. Sex was definitely off the table. She might as well finish looking over her notes. Though she wouldn't admit it, Sol had to admit it felt a little silly to be . . . *preoccupied* with the stairs. The more she looked at the measurements and her theories, the more she wondered if Alice was right. Maybe she was getting obsessed.

She stopped when she realized Alice hadn't left. She looked up to see her wife still standing in the middle of the stairs, arms crossed and deep in thought, like she wasn't sure if she should say something else or not.

An actual apology would be nice, Sol thought. But she wouldn't press it. Alice had had a rough day. The least Sol could do was to give her space to process it.

She decided to smooth things over with a question.

"Hey, have you been . . . seeing anything weird lately?" Sol couldn't believe she hadn't thought to ask this before. They lived in the same house together, they literally shared the same bed. Why would Sol be the only one who noticed something odd?

Alice stiffened. "Weird like how?"

Tension returned. Sol could practically feel the cracking of eggshells as she approached the subject.

"I don't know, like you see something in the house that shouldn't be here? Like—"

Alice immediately held up a hand. "Stop. Please don't bring that stuff in here."

"What?" Sol blinked. "What stuff?"

"Creepy stuff. Don't talk about it. It'll be attracted to our house."

Sol let out a careful laugh. This was a joke, right? Alice's face made it clear it very much wasn't a joke. "You're serious? What, are you suddenly afraid of ghosts?"

"Shh!" Alice hushed her. "I said don't talk about that stuff!"

Sol's eyes widened in amusement. And here she thought she knew Alice inside and out. Turns out her wife could still surprise her after all these years.

"Don't laugh." Alice scowled as she ascended the rest of the steps. Sol chased after her, a mischievous desire to tease her wife more.

"No, don't go!" Sol said, giggling. "Let's talk about this. Or not talk about this. Does it still count as talking about it if we're talking around it?" Sol put a hand on Alice's shoulder. She slapped it away.

"If you're not going to take me seriously, then don't follow me!" Alice quickened her pace to the bathroom and shut the door behind her. The next sound that came through was the rush of the shower, telling Sol that the conversation was over.

Sol chuckled under her breath. It wasn't that she wasn't taking Alice's concerns seriously. It was just that it was . . . well, *cute* that Alice held some superstitious beliefs. And when it came to teasing Alice, Sol couldn't help herself. It was just too fun.

But if Alice preferred to be left out of her experimentations, Sol would oblige. Besides, she never *said* that she believed something supernatural was going on in the house. She just wanted to be able to rule out the possibility of a gas leak. That was a much more reasonable theory than ghosts.

Sol slowly descended the stairs—pausing for a moment on the fifth step. It didn't move, didn't shift, didn't do anything that warranted further study. Sol felt both relieved and frustrated. She wasn't sure what she hoping for, truth be told. A repeat of Corinne's fall? An explanation for what she saw in the vent? Couldn't she just chalk it up to her eyes playing tricks on her?

For some reason, she couldn't. The memory of both events nagged at her, begging her to pay attention.

Pay attention to what? Sol wasn't sure. And because she couldn't justify this compulsion, she kept it to herself. Sol returned to the coffee table and picked up her notes. Pages upon pages scribbled with detailed information about the dimensions and material of the stairs. It said everything and it said nothing.

Pay attention, pay attention, pay attention, something told her.

Sol sighed. "I really do have too much time on my hands."

And then she crumpled the pages into a ball.

That night, when the house was filled with silence and Sol couldn't sleep, she went into the bathroom and lifted up her arm. A line that was a shade lighter than the rest of the arm crept from the back of her elbow up to her shoulder.

She traced the scar with her other hand, taking in deep breaths as she recalled what happened after it initially healed. She was back at college for spring semester and rooming with Alice once again. The two were more than just roommates—they were friends by then. But sometimes Sol would feel Alice's eyes on her when she was studying, or her hand would linger on her shoulder just a beat too long when she was passing by.

Before winter break, she thought it was a sign that Alice might have been interested in her—she at least knew that Alice liked girls. They'd had that conversation at the start of sophomore year. But after winter break? There was a dull pain in her arm that would soon become a scar and the memory of Mami looking at her with pure revulsion in her eyes.

Sol avoided looking anyone else in the eye after that. She was too afraid of seeing her reflection in them and finding what Mami saw. Something that needed to be *erased*.

"Sol, you're really cool," Alice had said. Sol jolted up from her desk at the sound of Alice's voice. Heat was spreading from ear to ear and she turned to look at Alice, not in her eyes but at her nose. Sol gave her a curious look.

"What makes you say that?" she said, voice hoarse.

Across the room, Alice was sitting in bed, her knees holding up a notebook as she wrote. Earbuds in her ears, and Sol thought she heard the faintest sound of Thirty Seconds to Mars.

"You're really serious about your studies," Alice said in earnest. "And responsible. I bet your parents are really proud."

The heat in Sol's face gave way to a sudden chill as all blood drained away. The last thing she wanted to talk about was what her parents thought of her. She looked down at her arm and felt the bandages underneath her long sleeves. Even when Alice had accidentally seen it and asked about it, Sol made up a half-baked excuse about a nasty fall.

"I wouldn't say they were proud," Sol murmured. And at that moment, as if Satan knew exactly when to strike, Sol got a text from Papi. And Papi never texted.

Sol read the text. Reread it. Put down her phone and took a deep breath. The world was swinging out from under her. Even when she knew it was coming, she still wasn't ready for the freefall. It wasn't until Alice was crouched next to her that Sol knew she was crying.

"What's wrong?" Alice asked, urgent. "Is it your arm—do you need me to get someone?"

With shaking hands, Sol slowly passed her phone to Alice and let her read it. It was just four words but the weight of them crushed Sol.

You can't come home.

"What does this mean? Sol?" Alice looked to her but Sol couldn't answer through her racking sobs. Instead, Alice pulled Sol into a tight hug. She cooed Korean into her ear, things Sol didn't understand, but the softness made her cry harder, body tensing with the need to expel every awful thing that had taken up residence in her. When she was done drenching Alice's shirt with tears and snot, Sol felt something akin to absolute emptiness. Her life was over. She couldn't keep a heavy course load *and* work enough to rent a place for just a few months out of the year.

The first thing Sol said after all that crying was, "I'm going to have to drop out."

And the first thing Sol heard Alice say was, "No, you're not."

Sol's mouth fell open. The certainty in Alice's voice was enough to make her question reality.

"Listen, every year, my parents offer to get me a short-term rental so I don't have to fly back to Korea whenever school is out," Alice explained. "I usually say no because I stay with Imo in Canada anyway, but if I take their offer, you can just stay with me until classes start up again. Sound good?"

Sol didn't know what to say to that. Why was Alice going this far for her? Sure, the two might have gone from just roommates to friends in the last few weeks, but suddenly offering to keep her housed while she focused on studying felt . . . suspicious.

"Why?" Sol asked. She didn't know much about Alice's family structure, much less why she preferred to fly to stay with her aunt in Canada instead of seeing her parents, but there had to be a catch. Nothing good came for free.

Alice looked thoughtful for a moment. Then, as if giving up, she shrugged.

"Why not?"

Guilt rising, Sol shook her head. "No, I can't let you do that. First of all, are you sure your parents can actually afford—"

And that's when it hit Sol why Alice was always out late and partying. She was one of *those* rich kids.

"Don't worry about my parents," Alice huffed. "I'll deal with them. Just . . . be my roommate. You're already really good at that."

The joke caught Sol off guard and she laughed. Still, Sol was hesitant. The last thing she wanted was to become a burden on someone else.

"Hey . . ." Alice stopped her with a smile and a knowing look. "I know it's weird, that I'm suddenly offering you this. But I promise I don't have any ulterior motives. You deserve good things, you know. Besides, we have more in common than you think so . . . maybe it's a good idea that we stick together?"

Sol met Alice's eyes and saw her reflection—but instead of an object of revulsion, she saw something else. She saw love. And maybe not love like in a romantic way—Sol couldn't imagine that someone like Alice would ever like *her*—but love in the way that sea otters held hands so they didn't drift away from each other. Love in being seen and *understood*. Love in knowing that she wasn't completely alone.

Sol didn't get why Alice was so comfortable taking her parents' money and not seeing them for years, but that was okay. She had all the time in the world to learn more about the strangely charismatic Korean girl she met at Yale.

And that night, when the lights were out and the two settled into bed, Sol somehow found the nerve to ask something ridiculous.

"Hey, Alice?"

"Yeah?" Her voice sounded so far away.

"Do you mind if . . . just for tonight . . . we sleep in the same bed?"

The answer came in the form of rustling bedsheets across the room, and then movement beside Sol.

"This kind of pillowcase feels nice." Alice yawned without a care.

"Thanks. It's satin." Sol paused, then went on to explain, "It's . . . supposed to be better for Black hair. Bonnets tend to give me headaches."

"I see."

The rest of sophomore year went on with tender moments like this. Small smiles, lingering touches. Sol tried to keep herself from expecting anything more from Alice—it was already too much that she was gracious enough to share her apartment, but it was impossible to keep the flutters in her stomach from growing into strong buzzes.

The day that Sol moved into Alice's apartment, with nothing but a box under each arm, she found a small present at the foot of the bed.

Satin pillowcases.

Alice was always looking out for Sol, like she said she would.

Now the two were older, married, and living in the same house. For Sol, this was the epitome of hitting the jackpot. She won. If she didn't think about her job situation at all, she might even say she was *content* with her life.

Sol splashed water on her face. The nagging feeling that something was amiss refused to relent, even hours later.

Pay attention, pay attention, pay attention.

She tried to erase the feeling from her mind, but it was persistent. Her hands massaged her scalp, a calming sensation that helped her stay grounded, until her finger brushed up against something thin and hard. In the mirror, she watched herself pull out a twig.

This couldn't be right. Sol hadn't left the house all day—when would a twig have found its way into her hair? It couldn't have been sitting in it for days either; Sol definitely detangled her Afro just yesterday.

Sol twirled the twig slowly while she thought about every possible explanation.

And then the twig *twitched*.

Immediately, Sol dropped it into the sink. It fell quietly against the porcelain and all Sol could hear was her own heart, jackhammering away from shock.

"Sol? Are you okay?" Alice's voice floated in the house. Did Sol yell? She didn't realize it. Opening the door slightly, she answered, "I'm fine! I just . . . stubbed my toe." When Alice didn't respond, Sol assumed she was satisfied with the answer and looked back into the sink.

The twig was gone.

THE INTRUSION

S omething was trying to get into the house.

That was the first thought Sol had when she woke up and heard a suspicious tapping at her back door. Not a "who" but a "what," and it jolted her upright, heart speeding up with every tap. Strong sunlight was already filtering in through the windows, suggesting that she had slept most of the morning away—which also meant she was alone. Alice was likely already at work, and now Sol was here to deal with the intruder.

Maybe it was just an animal. Sol wanted to believe that. A bear or maybe even a deer had managed to make its way into a gated community, find its way to her home specifically, and somehow overcame the fences and gates that closed off her own backyard. And now it was trying to find a way out by going through the only other naturally occurring exit found in nature—a door.

Yeah, of course Sol couldn't believe that. But it was a hair better than thinking something nonhuman lurked beyond the back door. She looked around and quickly picked up her laptop to use as a shield and weapon. It was a shit idea, really, and she made a mental note to convince Alice to have a gun somewhere in the house. Just in case.

The tapping wouldn't cease, only pause. At some point, the intruder gripped the handle and pulled but was barred by a lock. Sol cautiously peeked through the blind—and yelled.

"What the hell are you doing?" she yelled through the glass.

"What?" Hope scrunched her brow. "I can't hear you."

Sol cracked open the door. "I said, what the hell are you doing in my backyard!"

"You weren't answering your front door." Hope blinked, innocently. "And I saw that your car was still in the driveway, so I figured you might've been home, just in your backyard."

Sol stared at her, incredulous. Just to make sure she got all that right, she repeated it back to her.

"You came to the front door and rang the doorbell. Didn't get an answer, so you decided to go into my backyard, confirm that I wasn't there either, then tried to come in through the back door?"

If Hope spotted the absurdity of her actions, she didn't show it. Instead, she pouted like a worried aunt and tilted her head to get a better view inside the house.

"Well, I thought you might have been in trouble or something!" she said. "After all, you haven't gone to work in days, you haven't signed the HOA agreement or given us a spare key to your home."

Sol would've pulled the door closed another inch if that didn't mean closing it altogether.

"I'm sorry—what do you *mean* give you a spare key?" The longer she stood here, doing this insane dance with Hope, the more she felt like she was tumbling through the Twilight Zone. Everything Hope did was normal while Sol could not be more clearly the odd one out.

"It's part of the agreement. Once you join, the HOA gets a spare key to your house. You know, in case of emergencies." And then Hope perked up with a *smile*. She smiled like this made perfect sense, to allow a board of strangers that much entry into Sol's life, into her *home*, and that if Sol could just get with the program, this would all be over.

And now Sol's nose was clogging up. Damn pollen.

"Okay." Sol sniffled. "Okay, fine, I'll pretend like that's a completely sane thing to do. *What* is it that you came all this way for, Hope?"

"I was just coming over to pick up your HOA agreement."

And that's when Sol shut the door.

"Hello, Sol?" Hope's muffled voice was accompanied by more tapping. "It's okay, I can come back tomorrow!"

"Do not come back tomorrow!" Sol shouted. "We are *not* joining the HOA!"

She stomped halfway to the living room and stopped. There was nothing after that, no more yelling on Hope's end. She was suddenly quiet, which puzzled Sol. After lacking the foresight to *not* trespass on the property, could Hope really be so easily discouraged?

Tucking her laptop under her arm, Sol returned to the back door and peeked through the blinds. Hope was already gone. Sol huffed. Good riddance. Hopefully, no one would ever bother them again about joining the HOA. So many of their rules were overreaching and their penalties were vague at best, but the idea she'd give strangers a key to her house? That they could just invade her space whenever?

Who would ever want to live like that?

The maniacs of Maneless Grove, apparently.

I should shred the agreement. Realizing she could do exactly that, she stomped over to the kitchen and plucked it out of the basket. Tearing it in half, she dropped it in the trash can and just for extra measure, flipped it off.

Go to hell, you stupid fucking association.

"We'll see you there."

Sol froze. It didn't sound like Hope, but who else was around to respond to something she said?

Thought. Sol was thinking that, she didn't say it out loud. No one could have responded. There was nothing to respond *to*. She was just . . . tired? Stressed?

Sol made her way back to the couch.

Once is happenstance. Twice is a coincidence. Three times is a pattern. The vent, the step, and the twig. And now the voice? That was four times. If three times is a pattern, what was four?

Sol's thoughts cycled between these incidents. Each time, she *thought* her eyes were playing tricks on her. She *thought* it was just a sign that she was stressed, a symptom that all her internal worries about her job were starting to manifest in strange visual hallucinations. But Sol was hardly even *thinking* about her job when she pulled that twig out of her hair and she *still* saw it move.

Pay attention. Pay attention. The compulsion worsened.

It was bad enough that Sol couldn't go to work to get her mind off this. But now she was convinced that something was wrong with the house—and she badly needed a drink.

I can't talk to Alice about this. For all her teasing just the night before, Sol found out that Alice really *did* believe that talking about ghosts or spirits attracted them. Her wife downplayed it as being a "Korean thing," the same way that Sol downplayed her loyalty to her abusive father as a "Dominican thing." It meant "don't ask, because I don't want to talk about it."

Fine, Sol wouldn't force the topic on her. But she *did* need to talk to someone about this.

Maybe she shouldn't hesitate about talking to a therapist about the house. Maybe Sol *was* losing it. She *was* considerably stressed out about her job, the pollen kept her inside while the lack of cool air seemed to want to push her outside—as if the community and house were working together to drive her nuts—and now these overstepping neighbors were getting on her nerves. Stress-induced hallucinations happened, right? Even if she had no history of hallucinations before, there was a first time for everything.

Sol fell onto the couch and spotted something new on the coffee table—a Vicks nasal spray with a note beside it.

For your allergies. —Alice

The thoughtfulness of the gift warmed Sol's heart. Even after a terrible day at work, Alice was still looking out for her. Sol pocketed the spray, vowing to make good use of it before taking a cursory look around the rest of her home. They had already completely unpacked, and aside from the broken-down moving boxes sitting in the corner, waiting to be taken out for recycling, the house was spotless. She would have to figure out what to do with the rest of her day.

Sol's stomach grumbled.

Looks like I'll have to make myself breakfast first.

There was what could be called a "quiet neighborhood," and then there was a ghost town.

Sol felt like she was driving through the latter. It wasn't even how it *looked*. The houses all looked picture perfect, brochure-worthy, the definition of the white-picket-fence American Dream that everyone's always raving about. The lawns were immaculate, the streets were well-paved with not a single piece of gravel out of place. Small trees were planted equidistant apart, adding some greenery to the landscape.

As Sol drove, she noticed that every single window had its curtains open, inviting in sunlight and the eyes of nosy onlookers.

And Sol was feeling particularly nosy. She parked her car on the empty street and walked the length of a few homes. She tried to look like she was busy and obviously going somewhere she was invited, but her eyes kept wandering to the windows. Peach curtains pulled apart. The back of a white love seat faced outward. Sol could imagine the homeowner sitting down and reading a book there as they basked in the sunlight.

Sol went over to the next house. It was . . . identical. Peach curtains, white love seat. A *Live Laugh Love* sign posted on the adjacent wall. Sol didn't remember seeing that in the previous house, but she wasn't going to circle back to check now. She sped up to the next house.

Again. The same indoor arrangement.

"What the fuck . . . ?" Sol bent down, pretending to tie her shoes. She glanced over again. From her new viewpoint, she noticed a hanging light coming down from the ceiling. One of those hanging lights on a chain. The vintage copper cover gave the house a bit more personality than the last. But how could she be sure all the previous homes didn't have that?

Sol sniffled, congestion sneaking up on her. She quickly cleared her nose with the spray and mentally thanked Alice for her consideration. Sol stood back up and walked at a more leisurely pace. Maybe not *every* home had the same setup. She and Alice definitely didn't have any hanging lights or a white love seat in the window. Maybe the only reason these houses did were because they made a bulk order from a catalog. Finnian and Roy *did* mention that everyone liked to take advantage of whatever discounts the HOA afforded them. So maybe this all made sense. No need to be alarmed over bland decor.

Not that Alice would care. Just because Hope was trespassing onto her property that same morning didn't make it okay for Sol to snoop outside of people's homes and cast a wide net of judgment over them.

But where *were* the people? Sol twisted herself around. Not only was her car the only one on the street, it was the only car *at all*. No one's vehicles were parked in their driveway. There were no signs of life anywhere.

Then it hit her, and it was a gut punch. *They're at their jobs, Sol.* It was the middle of the day, of course. A wealthy neighborhood like this meant people had to be working high-paying jobs. Again, that made sense. There was once again no need to be alarmed. She had too much time on her hands if she was going to be finding reasons to be suspicious of others. If anything, she was the suspicious one. The one Hope had noticed *didn't* seem to be going to her job.

Because I might not even have that job. Because I've been too afraid to even look at my emails the last few days.

Sol sighed. Turning back to her car, she froze at the sight of Veronica just standing in the middle of the street. The little girl stared at Sol with the same unreadable expression she always had, wearing a pink summer dress. It took a moment for Sol to find her voice.

"Veronica? You should get out of the street. It's not safe." The advice felt a little dumb, considering there seemed to be no one else around for miles. "Actually, shouldn't you be in school? Do your parents know you're out here?" Sol had driven a considerable distance away from her home. Her parents surely couldn't be watching from across the street *here*.

Veronica didn't move. Her eyes flickered to something behind Sol, but when she turned to check, there was nothing but one of the large trees. When Sol turned back, Veronica was already walking away, a straight beeline in the direction of her home.

"Wait!" Sol jogged to catch up. The air around her changed. It was subtle at first—the smell of fresh cut grass gave way to a compost-like stench. And then it became putrid and wet.

Sol gagged, tasting what could only be described as mold and pus in the back of her throat. It was enough to bring her to her knees, but Sol steadied herself with a hand on the hood of her car. Veronica stopped just a few feet away. Was it the angle, or did the little girl's shadow stretch longer than Sol's did?

There is something very wrong with this girl. Or maybe there's something wrong with me. If Sol could get a lungful of clean air, she might have even cooked up some theories, but the ability to think clearly was stanched. Complex thought was reduced. All she knew was she needed to get home and this little girl needed to get home, and between the two of them, Sol was the one with a car.

"Do you . . . need a ride?" Sol spoke in short, quick sentences. The more she opened her mouth, the more she could taste rot. Yet if she tried to breathe through just her nose, the pollen practically delighted in choking her with snot. It felt like she was drowning in the middle of an open street, surrounded by air she couldn't breathe and trees that weren't able to save her. They needed to leave, *now*.

Veronica nodded. Sol quickly unlocked the doors and rolled all the windows down, praying she could get away from whatever was causing this smell.

On the drive back, Sol glanced at Veronica through the rearview mirror. The child opted to sit in the back rather than beside Sol, a decision that made Sol feel equally grateful and guilty. Just like before, Veronica looked like the picture of health. Her dress was ironed out, her pigtails were brushed, her skin was clear of any dirt that would've been normal to see on a rowdy and adventurous child.

Except Veronica didn't *seem* like a rowdy or adventurous child. She seemed like a little robot, if anything.

And what the hell is that smell? Because it didn't seem to dissipate as they drove away.

"Is everything okay at home?" Sol asked, cautiously. What she really wanted to know was if everything was okay here and now. Because something about the girl's look made Sol feel haunted, like the two of them weren't the only ones in the car.

Veronica just nodded again, staring into thin air and not at Sol.

Soon enough, Sol turned into her driveway. Veronica got out of the car without any help or prodding and went straight to her home. This time, Sol followed, if only to be able to meet the girl's parents face-to-face for once. It was only right, it felt, to meet them after giving their latchkey kid a ride back to safety. If Sol had a daughter who ran about without supervision, even she would want to put a name to the face of the adult who kept their kid safe.

Just like last time, Veronica crossed the street without looking both ways. She went ahead of Sol, getting to the front door first and disappearing into the house before Sol even put one foot on the sidewalk.

Determined to meet Veronica's parents, however, Sol came to the front door and knocked politely. After a few seconds, no one answered, so she knocked again. Then she rang the doorbell. She heard the chime echo through the house and die in silence.

What gives? Sol could clearly see the parents' car sitting in the driveway. A thin layer of dust coated it, like it hadn't seen a wash in a month. Which was odd in and of itself, but so was the fact there was a car there at all—again, she hadn't seen a single other car besides her own on her drive and walk. Throw in a little girl who wasn't at school . . . clearly one of them *had* to be home.

"Hello? Veronica, are your parents home?"

If they were, no one answered. Sol's stomach roiled and she gritted her teeth. What, so she was good enough to spy on from across the street but not good enough to meet face-to-face? Or were they so hands-off with their own daughter that they didn't care if she stumbled into trouble?

Sol surprised herself by jiggling the doorknob. She didn't remember reaching for it. It was just suddenly there, pressed into her palm.

Sol stepped away from the door, disgusted with herself. She'd almost become Hope, and it bothered her how easily the action came to her. She looked to the window again. There was movement behind the curtain, for sure. Someone was home with Veronica. It was both a relief and a point of anger. They were just pretending she didn't exist? Sol may be an introvert, but the idea that she was *nothing* to others was brutal, and not at all akin to wanting to be left alone. She dealt with this shit at Yale, she didn't need it across the street from her home . . .

Slow down, Sol. You need to calm down.

You need to breathe . . .

Easier said than done.

Before peeling herself away from the house, Sol yelled, "Mr. or Mrs. Kennedy, if you're home, you should consider keeping a closer eye on Veronica. I found her a little farther from home than I'm sure you're comfortable with."

Sol waited a minute for a response. No movement, no yelling. All silence, all secretive.

Fine, if that's how they wanted to raise their kid, who was she to interfere? Then next time she found Veronica half a mile from home, she would leave the little girl to her own devices. It wasn't her problem.

Sol huffed as she crossed the street back to her own home.

Someone's always watching, my ass. There wasn't a soul around. No one except a strange-ass little girl and her standoffish parents who didn't seem to care that she wasn't in school. Or was she home-schooled? Considering how odd the girl seemed to be and how much of a shut-in her parents were, Sol didn't put it past them to homeschool Veronica. But she had to have friends, right? Sol did see her playing with the other neighborhood kids during the party. All of them were probably at school and Veronica was the odd one out. Poor kid.

But not my problem.

Sol went inside and plopped back on the couch. With a clear nose and that horrible stench gone, she could breathe in deeply. There was no doubt in her mind now that it came from Veronica, but Sol couldn't figure out how. She definitely didn't smell like that during the party. Sol would've noticed. Or would she? Sol was suffering from allergies even then, and then quickly got drunk. The most she remembered from that party was that awful email and Roy and Finnian pissing her off.

She frowned to herself and picked up the camera. Would it be weird of her to point it across the street? She just wanted to see Veronica's parents at least once. She needed to put a face to the girl's parents. After all, they knew what Sol looked like. Hell, they even knew her name, assuming they were at the welcoming party. All Sol knew about them was that their last name was Kennedy and they had a little girl who never spoke and smelled like she'd lived all her life in an open grave.

Sol didn't want to spy on them, but she wasn't, not really. Once she caught proof of their existence, she would watch the recording once and delete it. Nothing suspicious or weird about that. In fact, she was really just being cautious. She might have been pissed that they allowed Veronica to roam the streets like a wild animal, but a child was still a child, no matter how bad they smelled.

Sol grabbed the camera's charger and brought it to the plug closest to the window. Deleting her previous recording of the stairs, she pointed it out toward Veronica's house. In a day or two, she would check it and confirm that at least one of the girl's parents were home. As long as they moved the curtain just enough for her to be able to zoom in on their face, Sol would be satisfied with that.

And then Sol could move on with her life.

THE HOSPITAL VISIT

Sol picked things apart like it was a job—she was doing it now. The passing neighborhoods were pretty if not quaint; the greenery was beautiful but not as lush as inside Maneless Grove. She hated to admit it, but the world beyond Maneless Grove seemed much more dull and boring.

She looked down at the Tupperware of chocolate-chip cookies she baked in the middle of the night. They were for Corinne now, but when she was baking them, they were for no one in particular. She just needed something to do with her hands, and insomnia often made her productive in ways she never considered being.

Alice never had much of a sweet tooth so when she woke up that morning and asked who they were for, Sol said the first name she could think of other than the Kennedys. She was desperately trying not to think of them, or their strange daughter who was out and about across the street already. Having checked the camera, Sol only found disappointment. Nothing stirred within the house. No one ever came out to get the mail or check the windows. It was just Veronica opening and shutting the door behind her before going on her way.

Sol thought about bringing this up to Alice but had a feeling that admitting to spying on her neighbors across the street would not go over well. So, Corinne it was. It made Sol appear thoughtful, which she realized was something she felt she desperately needed to prove to her wife.

What she didn't expect was Alice's insistence on joining Sol.

"Are you sure you're okay with going?" Sol asked.

It was a Tuesday—Alice should've been at work. But one look at the cookies and she immediately called the office to say she'd be getting in at noon, after a quick visit to the hospital. Maybe it was because Alice was never the sort to call out of work for *anything* that they wished her well. Maybe they assumed that Alice was the one injured.

"It's fine." Alice waved her off. And then they fell silent for the rest of the ride.

To say that Sol's feathers were ruffled was an understatement. Why wouldn't Alice look at her? Hell, she hadn't even noticed the camera at the window, something that Sol spent time and energy making up a believable lie for. She was *going* to say that it was a matter of security. After Hope tried to intrude in their house, Sol wanted video proof in case they had to go to the police over it.

But Alice said nothing about the camera. She just preferred to go straight to bed after work, complaining of a headache and a need to be unconscious for a few hours. It felt a little bit unfair to Sol. Buying a house was supposed to bring them closer together—or at least provide a distraction to Sol's current work mess—but instead it seemed like there were new problems cropping up all around them. As Alice drove, Sol kept her eyes ahead until they turned into the hospital parking lot.

Should I ask Corinne about the stairs?

The thought surprised her, as she felt like she had given up on that issue days ago. But if she had *really* given up on it, why would she have dug up the crumpled notes from the trash?

All right, fine, maybe she wasn't *completely* over it. She was momentarily distracted with the Kennedys but who could blame her? The likelihood of someone leaving their home was statistically higher than seeing a structural part of the house exhibit a spatial anomaly. And yet, it was still 0 for 1 on that account.

So maybe this would be it. Sol would be able to get to the crux of the issue once and for all by asking Corinne if what she saw was really real.

And if Alice was right, and Sol only *thought* she saw the step disappearing, then she would apologize to Alice, clear the living room of her notes and video camera, and head back to their room for much-needed sleep.

But if Corinne confirmed what Sol had seen, then . . .

Alice wouldn't believe either of them anyway.

That was what was so frustrating about Alice coming. Yes, she liked Alice being near. But now, when she needed to get to the truth of things, it just felt like her wife would be in the way. Corinne was old, possibly with faulty vision and bodily function. What if Corinne didn't even remember? The fall down the stairs was fast and painful. She probably didn't even realize she fell until her bones fractured, a flood of neurons firing pain signals to the spine and up to the brain. She probably didn't want to remember it.

Sol was feeling less and less sure of her plan by the time she and Alice made their way to the third floor, where they got further directions from a nurse.

"Mrs. Monro? You have some visitors." The nurse let them in through the door after confirming it was okay.

Corinne looked like she was being consumed by blankets. The sea of white cloth swaddled her as she swallowed spoonfuls of applesauce.

"Hi, Corinne," Alice said meekly. "Do you remember me? I'm Alice, Sol's wife."

Corinne shrieked with happiness and put down her spoon. "Well, come on over!"

Sol watched Alice be pulled into a genuine hug. For a moment, she recalled her irrational anger at the nosy woman and felt bad. It was apparent that even if Corinne was snooping around, her bony frame could do nothing to really harm them.

She's at least friendlier than Abuelita, Sol thought begrudgingly. Memories of Sol's grandmother were bleak. Always yelling. Always scolding her about the length of her skirt. Always something about hell, brimstone, and fire. There was never a moment where Sol wasn't being disciplined for some innocuous slight.

Still, she remained beyond the reach of Corinne's hug and simply raised the cookies in view.

"Oh, you shouldn't have," said the old woman, placing the cookies onto the tray in front of her. The plate of food she neglected consisted of a half-eaten bagel, scrambled eggs, and sausages. The only thing Corinne had completely polished off was the fruit cup that came with it.

Would cookies be too difficult for her to eat? Shit.

Ever more socially capable, Alice broke the awkward silence. "We just wanted to apologize for what happened at our home," she started. "Sol probably surprised you and it caused you to take a bit of a tumble. Are you okay?"

Sol couldn't help but notice how Alice skirted over the fact Corinne was somewhere she shouldn't have been in the first place. Sol watched Corinne's reaction closely. She expected her to freeze up or laugh awkwardly but the woman only shrugged.

"Fractured my hip, if you can believe it. But I guess things like that happen when you're old."

"I'm sorry to hear that," said Alice, the corners of her mouth pulling downward, probably hoping the home insurance covered accidents. "Do the doctors know when you'll be able to make it back home?"

"It really depends on whether they can get me an aide." Corinne sighed, dejected. "They don't quite feel comfortable enough letting me go home knowing that the same thing can happen or worse with no one around."

"That's a good thing, though, isn't it?" Sol's voice came out a panicked squeak. Alice and Corinne both stared at her, waiting for her to continue. Sol's heart felt ready to leap out of her chest from the pressure. "I mean, you know . . . it's better to be safe than sorry?"

The cliché seemed to work.

"True." Corinne nodded. "And, really, I am fortunate to live in such a connected community. I'm sure before long, others will notice my absence and come to help me figure out the next steps."

Invest in a neighborly spirit.

"Mind if I use the bathroom?" Alice pointed to the door behind her. When Corinne waved her off, she slipped inside quickly.

"So . . ." Sol shifted her weight from foot to foot. Without a social buffer, Sol felt the question bubbling up inside of her and rising to the surface. "I'm sorry, I know it was probably traumatic for you, but I can't get it out of my mind."

"What do you mean?" Corinne asked.

"The fall—to me, I guess, it looked like the floor fell out from under you. Well, not fell but just disappeared. Like it was there one second and gone the next and when I came closer, it was there again. Alice didn't see what I saw because she was behind me, and I know it's impossible but—can you tell me? *Did* that actually happen?"

Sometime during her rambling, Sol noticed a subtle change in Corinne's expression. It was mostly in her eyes, the flicker of emotion that went from puzzled to a strange mix of confused and fearful.

"I-I don't understand what you're talking about. I—where was this?"

Sol stood dumbfounded. There was panic in Corinne's voice now as the old woman's rambling continued. "I didn't do anything—it wasn't me!" she protested. "She made me! She . . ."

"Corinne, who is 'she'?"

Corinne looked to have gained a moment of clarity. And then her eyes darkened.

"You have to get out of there," she whispered. "Get out of the house. Get out of there." Corinne grabbed at Sol's arm, gripping her with ferocious strength. "It's not safe. Don't trust it—don't trust the neighbor. Please, you have to go!"

A rush of water flowing through pipes made Sol jump backward. Alice would be coming out shortly. Sol could already hear the sink running.

"What are you talking about? Which neighbor?" Sol swallowed. She didn't realize her throat was dry.

The bathroom door opened. Corinne's fingernails left tiny crescent moons in Sol's forearm.

Alice's gaze swept over the two of them as she reentered the room. "Corinne? Are you okay?"

The old woman had a single tear streaking down her face.

"Oh, yes, I'm—I'm fine. I think. Yes." She sucked in a deep breath and wiped away the tear. "Strange. I can't remember . . ." Her voice trailed off.

"Knew we shouldn't have left her alone too long."

"We can't risk them getting too suspicious."

The sudden voices came with a high-pitched buzzing. Loud and painful enough to knock Sol to her feet. She pressed her palms against her ears just as Alice came to her side.

"What the hell is that buzzing?" Sol shouted. It was piercing her eardrums and shooting across her skull. Vertigo took her hostage, as she had the sensation of falling endlessly, unable to find her bearings.

And then she smelled vanilla. Her wife wrapped her tight in her arms and cooed softly, grounding her instantly. Slowly, the buzzing receded.

"Are you okay?" Alice looked her over, eyes wide with concern.

A knock at the door stole their attention.

"Corinne?" An older man with a bouquet of flowers and a pregnant woman with a protruding stomach stepped into the room. "Alice, I didn't know you were going to be visiting today! Oh, sorry. Were we interrupting something?" She looked between Sol and her wife.

Nadine.

Alice helped Sol to a nearby chair. "No, you're fine. Sol, what happened?"

"I . . ." She didn't know how to explain. Swallowing unease, Sol shook her head. "I just had a sudden sharp pain. I'm fine now."

"Are you sure?" Alice frowned. Sol was never a good liar but she hated it when her wife saw her in a bad way. Sol hoped it wouldn't happen again, at least not while Alice was around.

Sol nodded. Before Alice could respond, Nadine pulled her into a hug.

"I'm so glad to see you again!"

Shocked but polite as ever, Alice returned the hug—and the enthusiasm. "You too!"

"How are you settling in?"

The sight of Nadine made Sol roll her eyes. And here she thought she was on an extended break from the overly friendly and patronizing woman.

"Great! We're doing great," Alice said brightly. Too brightly for Sol's taste. "Thanks again for your help in getting us into the neighborhood!"

Sol wanted to blend into the background. It was only a matter of time before Nadine tried to hug *her* too.

The pregnant woman waved her off. "Oh God, don't worry about it! The wait list has been a mile long for years. When I heard that you and your wife were looking to buy a house, I couldn't think of a better addition to our community. Besides, what good is it being the president of the Homeowners Association if I can't swing my weight around for a friend?"

"God, the office just isn't the same without you." Alice glanced to Sol. "Nadine, you remember my wife, Sol."

With her blood running cold, Sol could only manage a shallow "Hi."

Nadine's eyes lit up, excitement so potent that Sol felt compelled to stand up, at least for a moment. The woman pulled Sol into a side embrace, careful not to add pressure to her stomach. "Of course! I'm so happy to see you're doing well again, Sol."

As opposed to what? Sol thought, annoyed. Did Alice tell Nadine about her nervous breakdown? She shot a look at her, but Alice didn't blink.

"And you two remember Terry, my husband."

"Nice to see you again." Terry meekly waved and kept his distance. Sol was grateful for that. From the corner of her eye, she watched Corinne's expression turn blank. Her eyes followed the new visitors, but they were completely void of any emotion.

"Terry was the one who made your little good luck charm." Nadine grinned. Sol and Alice traded a confused look.

"I'm sorry, what charm?"

"Oh, my mistake. It was the little round marble carving with our community symbol." Nadine nudged Terry's side. "I told you, you needed to add a little explanation for what it is. It's basically our neighborhood's totem, if you will. Whenever you want something to go your way, you either break it with a hammer or you bury it somewhere on your property. It's a little superstitious, but hey, can't argue with the results! I've seen so many amazing things happen with others. Winning contests, getting a new job . . . promotions."

She winked at Alice. "Really think you should give it a shot. Think of it as feng shui that gives a surge of good luck."

That's definitely not how feng shui works, Sol wanted to say, but she waited to see Alice's reaction first. As if the mildly racist statement went in one ear and out of the other, Alice gave back a beaming smile.

"Well, I'm not really one for superstitions . . ."

Sol snorted, earning a hard nudge in her side.

"But maybe I will. Anyway, we've gotta go. I'm due in the office soon, but thanks again, Nadine, you're the best."

"Anytime!"

"Ready to go, Sol?" her wife asked.

"Uh, sure. Feel better, Corinne." Sol squeezed her hand. Corinne refused to let go. "Corinne?"

It was slight, almost a tremor, but Corinne shook her head and tightened her grip. She mouthed something over and over and a chill went up Sol's spine.

"You okay there, Cor?"

Nadine came up and placed a hand on Corinne's shoulder. All at once, Corinne melted. Her jaw went slack and she blinked rapidly as her hand fell away from Sol's.

"Yes, much better." The words sounded mechanical. Corinne didn't even look up at Sol or Nadine. She just had a far-off stare and sank into the bed.

"Poor thing," Nadine cooed. "She must be exhausted. I came by to bring her some of my relaxing chamomile tea and another one of Terry's charms. Hopefully, it will make her feel at home." She reached into her bag to bring out a thermos and another white stone piece. She carefully put both on the table in front of Corrine and locked eyes with Sol. "I'm glad you at least got to see her awake before heading out. You know, you two really do fit right in."

Nadine's smile was perfect and her eyes matched it. Yet there was a coldness radiating off her that made Sol shrink away.

"What makes you say that?" Sol asked, panic growing in the back of her mind.

She looked surprised at the question but handled it with aplomb. "Well, you came all this way to visit Corinne and you even brought cookies. That's such a neighborly thing to do." Nadine patted Sol's arm.

"We were already on our way over here for a different reason so we thought we'd visit. Two birds, one stone and all."

"You were?" Sol was suspicious. What reason could she possibly have to be at the hospital?

Nadine's answer came with a look to her stomach.

"Oh!" Sol felt stupid. "Sorry, I didn't realize . . ."

"That I was pregnant?" Nadine laughed loudly and looked back to her chuckling husband. "Sol is too nice. I'm just joking but there have been concerns about the baby."

"Oh no, is it serious?" Alice was back at Sol's side, clearly more invested in this than she was.

"We're still not sure," Nadine said. "But don't worry! I'm sure it'll all be fine. If all else fails, we still have our good luck charms."

Oh joy, she's one of those women. The kind that bought into the whole healing crystals thing. For the sake of the baby, Sol hoped Nadine wasn't anti-vax.

"If you need anything at all, you know you can rely on me," Alice offered.

"I know I can." Nadine smiled warmly at her. Maybe it was just Sol's paranoia, but she thought the look in Nadine's eyes was too conspiratorial. "It was great to see you two again."

"You too!" Alice looped her arm into Sol's. "Come on, Sol."

Sol waited until they were out in the parking lot before speaking again.

"What was that?" she demanded.

"What was what?" her wife repeated.

"That!" Sol gestured vaguely toward the hospital. "You saw Corinne. She looked genuinely afraid. And then she got weird around Nadine."

Alice opened her mouth and shut it. "Yeah, that was . . . really odd. But I'm sure it's nothing nefarious. I mean, Nadine and Terry have clearly been around her longer. Maybe she's got early-onset dementia or Alzheimer's and got confused for a second, I don't know."

The explanation was so . . . rational that Sol wanted to believe it. Besides, that's what she was trying to get at with the stairs, at least.

Finding a simple, undisputed reason for why things are happening the way they are. Occam's Razor and all that. Yet there was a creeping sensation that there was more at work here. Something just beyond her understanding of the world.

Am I going crazy?

For once, Sol hoped the answer was yes.

"Staying up late again?" Alice was hesitant, like she knew what Sol was *really* doing. Pretending that she was going to crawl into bed after Alice was fast asleep, only to "accidentally" pass out on the couch.

Sol's guilt became heavier when she answered, "Yeah."

Because yes, that was *exactly* her plan. And it made her feel worse that Alice saw through her so easily.

The lack of answers she received at the hospital coupled with even more suspicion made Sol not trust anything or anyone around her, save for her wife. She didn't want to go up those stairs or look into the vent or find something squirming in her hair again. And at least two of those things could be avoided if Sol stayed in the living room.

Hell, if it were up to her, she'd be sleeping in her car. But if she woke up to Veronica staring at her through the windshield, she might have a heart attack. The couch was a better compromise.

Sol let Alice head to bed first while she boiled herself a mug of tea. It was a healthier substitute for when she wanted to drink herself into unconsciousness, though she hadn't done so in quite a while. Which Alice didn't even seem to notice, which bugged her just a little bit. *If I'm going to be sober, don't I at least deserve the credit? Right.*

After the day she'd had, Sol had a feeling she'd need it—the drink or the flowers.

Half an hour later, Sol was curled into the couch. She was surprised to feel like she didn't need to fight the cushions for a comfortable position.

With the lights out and half a mug of chamomile tea, sleep came for Sol immediately.

Unfortunately, it didn't last long.

Sshht.

Shhhttt.

The sound that awoke her was hushed. Slow. It sounded like some-one dragging their feet through sand. Sol's eyes cracked just a bit, but she could not move. Sleep paralysis. Of course, she would have sleep paralysis now of all times. She'd been wired lately, unable to reconcile reality with her expectations. She was always waiting for the other shoe to drop, and it showed in the way she couldn't accept the good that did happen.

Her eyes adjusted to the dark. She could see what was making that sound now, a shuffling humanoid figure across the living room. Sol's heart beat loudly and rapidly. This wasn't real. It wasn't real. It was just sleep paralysis and during these moments, her brain was throwing hellish nightmares against the wall just to see what would stick.

The figure came to the edge of the table and reached for the mug Sol left on the table. It poured the contents onto where the mouth would've been and the tea evaporated on contact.

"*Hhhhh.*" The figure put the mug back down and passed by Sol with-out acknowledging her. It was smoking. The irritation to her nose and throat became too much of a struggle to keep quiet; Sol coughed.

The figure stopped.

It turned in Sol's direction and began shuffling toward her.

It's not real, it's not real, it's not real.

Because if it was real, then the disappearing step was the last thing to worry about.

The chanting in her head eventually turned into *Wake up, wake up, wake up!*

The closer it came, the more Sol realized the shuffling sound wasn't the figure dragging its feet. It was from its body crackling with every move. The figure was burnt through and through, and its skin contin-ued to flake off, only for it to dissipate.

Sol was whimpering now. The figure stepped in front of her and crouched to her level. Soot fell off, stroking Sol's face. If it wasn't for the terror of it all, she'd have thought it was snow.

Even with the figure close, she couldn't make sense of its features. There was a deep wheezing sound, but Sol couldn't see a mouth or a nose.

"*Leave,*" the figure said.

I would if I could!

It couldn't hear her thoughts, though. That part of her brain didn't communicate to the nightmare and instead she watched in horror as it stood back up and turned to the staircase. The creature climbed the steps one by one and Sol screamed internally for it to stop. As if knowing the layout of the house, it continued from the top of the stairs to the right, where Alice was sure to be.

The moment the creature slipped beyond the hall, Sol suddenly found herself able to move. She jumped up, her foot colliding with the mug on the table—it smashed against the floor. Sol ignored it, lunging up the stairs two at a time and running to the bedroom. The door was thrown open and Sol crashed into Alice.

"Oof! Sol, what the hell?"

The light flicked on. Sol checked the closet and under the bed. There was no one in the room besides them.

"I thought I saw . . ."

Alice gasped. "You're bleeding!"

There was a stinging in her feet that Sol neglected while running— she assumed it was from stomping on the ground. It wasn't until she looked down that she realized she was actually injured; cut from the broken mug she stepped on in her pursuit of the creature.

Mierda.

"Sit down, I'll get some bandages."

Even after having her feet cleaned up and bandaged, Sol couldn't calm down. She went from door to door, peeking around every corner just to make sure they were alone.

"You need to stay off your feet, jagi," Alice said, coming with her.

"I only have a few cuts, I don't have a broken foot."

"Are you sure you saw someone in the house? It sounds like it was just a bad sleep paralysis dream."

It *did* sound like that.

Yet it had been years since Sol dealt with sleep paralysis. The panic and fear that overwhelmed her during the event always melted off in seconds upon waking up. But this? This was different. She couldn't shake the feeling that whatever had been shuffling through the house was still there. It felt like it was all around them, in the room next door, in the walls. Sol couldn't go back downstairs to the couch. She needed to be with her wife.

"Sorry for the mess downstairs," Sol mumbled, holding Alice close in bed.

"It's fine," Alice yawned, already half asleep. "Wasn't my favorite mug, anyway."

"Was it a pain to mop up the tea? Or did the floor soak it up?" She hoped it wasn't the case. Warped wooden flooring was expensive to fix.

"What do you mean? There wasn't anything to mop up."

THE LUNCH DATE

Toxoplasma gondii. A persistent if not particular parasite, one that made a habit of traveling through all sort of vehicles. Contaminated utensils, undercooked meat, even drinking water. By far, outdoor cats must be its favorite method of transport. It started with just one contaminated bird or rodent. The cat would ingest some part of an animal that hosted *T. gondii* and its life cycle would be kickstarted. Sexual reproduction in the cat's intestines gave way to cysts shed through feces. And the unsuspecting human that came along to clean out a litterbox? That would be its next host.

Sol sat in the basement, cross-legged in front of a box containing her journals from earlier experiments. It was mostly numbers and figures, including the strength of herbicide used to inhibit the growth of *T. gondii*, but she needed to ground herself in something familiar. Something that distracted her from the concerns she had about the house. Sol had committed to memory so many facts about the parasite, but it was different when she opened her journals. It was like she could be transported back to the lab, if only in memory. The smell of a sterile environment. The feel of latex gloves. The indentation her goggles made on her face.

God, she would do anything to be taken back to that. Pushing aside a binder, Sol froze at the sight of something even more familiar than her lab notes.

A flask. An eight-ounce container filled with Everclear that made her mouth water. She hid the damn thing from Alice when they were packing, hoping she would never have to use it. In her defense, it wasn't like Alice made her agree to *quit* drinking. She just had to tone it down, be a little bit more mindful of time and place.

And the basement in the middle of the day was not the time *or* place to get shit-faced. Besides, she had to go for a drive in just a few minutes.

Sol shoved the flask to the bottom of the box. Out of sight, out of mind. Instead, she opened up another journal, one with crude doodles of *T. gondii* along the edges. She wasn't sure what about *T. gondii* fascinated her. They were worse than bugs. They were tiny and could wreak so much havoc on a host—the same entity that it so badly needed to survive. It was like "mutually assured destruction" was written somewhere in the parasite's molecular code.

It could also survive for a long time within the bodies of warm-blooded animals, perhaps even a lifetime. And most people—provided they had a healthy immune system—would be none the wiser. Sure, there were flu-like symptoms. Muscle aches and swollen lymph nodes that people would shrug off with a 200 mg dose of Tylenol and a hot cup of TheraFlu. But it would always be there, festering and living out an entire life where it didn't belong.

Like me.

Sol's phone alarm finally sounded. She turned it off and stood up, taking in a deep breath.

Alice was out, working. The house had cooled considerably as if the building itself finally decided to breathe. It was suspicious. And yet, Sol found herself able to rest easier, exhaustion from sleep deprivation chipping away at her consciousness. Maybe that was why it took her an unreasonably long time to find her way out of the neighborhood. The identical houses and roads made Sol lose track of where she had been and there were more than a few times where she was certain she had gone around in a circle.

What the hell is the layout of this place? She pressed onward, determined to get away from Maneless and from the suffocating pollen. But the neighborhood tricked her time and time again. Sol imagined she was going against an unseen force—but maybe it was just her own tiredness. Eventually, she found the gates and exited.

Alice had been beyond delighted that Sol would be leaving the house today to meet a colleague from Yale. Well, "colleague" may have been the wrong word for someone who worked in an entirely different department. Friend, maybe? Dr. Amir Kazan had sent her an email asking if she was free for lunch. They often had lunch together—or had, when she'd been a fixture on campus—and he was the only person at work outside of her department who knew about the incident that was on the verge of destroying her career.

Amir was late. That wasn't unusual. He was always late, but it was never by more than a few minutes. Sol sat at a round table by the door of Eli's Eatery. A tall order of some incredibly sugary and highly caffeinated drink was in front of her as she quickly checked new emails. Anything to keep from thinking about last night's mishaps.

Putting down her phone, Sol noticed white flakes on her sleeve. They were tiny, fine specs. If Sol wasn't wearing a dark-blue flannel shirt, she might not have even noticed it, though she wondered what it might have been. Just the look of it made her want to sniffle.

Damn pollen. She brushed it off.

"Sorry I'm late," Amir said. Sol jumped at his sudden appearance. He was already sitting across from her and held his hands up defensively. "You just seemed really focused, I didn't want to interrupt." Amir smiled sheepishly. The light scent of coffee clung to him and she felt herself calm down immediately.

Amir was known at the university as kind of a heartthrob celebrity figure. Not that he did anything to deserve celebrity status, but word of his good looks spread fast throughout the campus. The Indian man had deep-brown skin and a thick mop of hair that he always had to brush out of his face.

His only flaw was being a history professor.

That and the caffeine addiction.

"Hey, Amir. How are your students?" Sol asked, trying to kill any thought of her postdoc research. It was strange. While Sol did experiments and generally stayed away from the idea of teaching, Amir was the opposite.

"Only fifteen students dropped my class within the first week, so, you know. That's an improvement."

Sol couldn't help but crack a smile. "I keep telling you, you're a regular heartbreaker."

"Please." He waved her off. "I've got a wife and three kids and a growing beer gut. At some point, it has to kick in that I'm off the market forever."

"Maybe after you start balding, it'll sink in," she teased. "Speaking of family, how are they?"

There were very few people Sol cared enough to ask about, and Amir's family just happened to make the list through association. There was Meera, his wife, a lovely Punjabi woman who Amir swore had a singing voice that belonged at Carnegie Hall. He had three girls, the oldest a precocious teen named Jazmine and a twelve-year-old named Preeti, and the youngest had just been born in the past year. Sol wanted to say the name was Nana but she couldn't remember.

"Ahh," Amir groaned. "Jazmine's gotten herself obsessed with something called 'true crime TikToks.' I can't understand it but every other week, she wastes hours watching videos about some missing-persons case. If you want to know about a true crime, it's these videos killing her grades."

"Ugh—dad jokes?"

"I'm a dad! I get to make them!"

"Have you considered taking her phone away?" Sol knew the suggestion would place her on Jazmine's shit list for years to come, but she made it anyway. "At least while she has to study or do homework."

"Meera tried, but Jazmine said she needed the internet to *do* homework so, you know. Back to square one." He shook his head in exasperation, then turned his attention to Sol. "What about you? How is the move going? Is everything going well?"

The question was loaded. The look in his eyes made her feel uncomfortable, like he was pitying her.

It's just sympathy, she knew. Amir was a very sympathetic person. The two commiserated over their personal work struggles—Sol in recalibrating equipment and Amir in failing students. And then when Sol stopped going to their lunches during the beginning of her troubles, Amir sought her out. What he found was not good. The cracks in her armor were visible. Even when he offered to help her keep watch over the lab and equipment to make sure no one tampered with it, she acted as if she had no idea what he was talking about. Was she too proud to accept help? *Cuando viene la soberbia, viene también la deshonra*, Mami would quote Proverbs 11:2. *When pride comes, then comes shame.* Ironically, Sol couldn't stop feeling like it was shameful to admit she needed any help at all. Ever.

All that mattered was that Amir had witnessed Sol's fall from grace.

And even worse, she cared about what he thought of her.

Sol hesitated. Then she decided to lie.

"It's . . . fine." It would be more fine with a bottle of pinot, but that was something else she hid from Amir.

"Hm." Amir took a sip of his coffee. "You know, it's a good thing you never took up a career in acting because you're not very good at it."

Now Sol couldn't help but chuckle.

"It's fine, Amir," she repeated, but her voice cracked.

"Yeah, that was actually worse than before." Amir leaned into the table. "What's going on?"

"I . . . I got this email from Dr. Henderson." She opened it up on her phone and turned it to Amir. She'd been looking at it off and on for days. It felt emblazoned on her forehead like a Scarlet A.

"Oh!" His eyes scanned it. "Oh." Then his furrowed brow deepened. "Mhm." Finally, "That doesn't sound good."

Sol scoffed. That was an understatement.

"But it sounds like Dr. Henderson is on your side. Silver lining, right?"

That much was true. Though Sol would hesitate to call Dr. Henderson a friend, and he was whiter than Hellmann's, he had always been a supportive colleague. And he'd remained objective and evenhanded, not jumping to conclusions about the allegations.

Except his objectivity seemed to be pointing to Sol actually being guilty of what she was accused of, at least according to the email.

So *was* he on her side? Time was now coloring Sol's memory, tainting every interaction she'd had with that man. Like the many times they would bump into each other so early in the morning even the mice in the building were still sleeping. Once or twice, they'd have coffee together. Not that they'd ever had a meeting of the minds, more like they happened to be having coffee in the same place at the same time. Was Dr. Henderson really a kind man with an appreciation for Sol's early-bird nature or was he only ever tolerating her?

Like a parasite.

"Hey!" Amir said loudly, interrupting her thoughts.

"Sorry." She shook her head. "I didn't get much sleep last night."

No thanks to the creepy creature in my house.

He grimaced. "Well, tell me about the new home!"

That was the last thing Sol wanted to talk about.

"It's uh . . ." She cleared her throat. "The neighbors are nice?"

It was the lie of all lies. She'd never met the Kennedys, Corinne's hospital outburst kept her on her toes, and Hope trespassing into her yard made her want to buy a gun. And that didn't even broach the topic of the last-minute welcoming party full of bigots and microagressors, the creepy behavior of the children, or the fact most of the neighborhood seemed like a ghost town with identical homes inside and out.

Honestly, the more she thought about it, the more problems Maneless Grove seemed to have.

And there was absolutely no way she was going to bring up the disappearing staircase, the dancing twig, *or* the strange voice she heard when she was *absolutely* home alone. She could only imagine how it would look to Amir. Local scientist, nearly blackballed from research, starts hallucinating in real time. Even *she* didn't really want to believe what she experienced.

Amir raised an eyebrow. "That's all you have to say? That the neighbors are *nice*?"

"What do you want me to say?" She sank in her seat and toyed with the straw in her drink.

"Tell me about what it's like to actually *own* a house. Are you and Alice considering renovating? Redecorating?"

Shocked, Sol's face fell. "We *just* moved in!"

"People have renovated homes before moving." He shrugged. "I've seen it on those home improvement channels. Just remember not to do an open floor plan, those always knock out the load-bearing wall."

"I'll be sure to keep that in mind," Sol said, deadpan.

"Okay . . . so no house talk. How's Alice?"

Sol rubbed her eyes. "Uh, fine."

Amir gave her a long look. "You know, every time you say something's 'fine,' you never say it in a way that's actually believable. What's going on? Trouble at home?"

"You could say that." She sighed. For a moment, she was silent, trying to find a way to skirt around the crux of the issue. Alice was definitely acting weird. A little more spacey, always going straight to bed after work. She hadn't been as quippy with Sol as normal. Sol would make a sarcastic observation about the neighborhood or their neighbors and Alice would just stare into the middle distance, like she didn't hear her.

But at least a quieter spouse was easier to deal with than the growing number of odd occurrences in their new home.

"I'm just not . . . settling in as fast as she is." That was as close as Sol could get to *Listen, I watched part of my house fucking disappear and almost kill an old woman. I think my house has been trying to suffocate me and if not, attack me with twigs and roots. And a charred body came to visit last night . . .*

Amir leaned back and crossed his arms. "What if you didn't stay inside all the time?"

Sol eyed him. "How do you know I'm inside all the time?"

He laughed. "Knowing you? It's hardly a leap."

"Shut up." She scowled. She didn't realize how much of her was an open book until she was around Amir or Alice. Though the more she thought about it, the more she realized how similar the two were. Alice was quite popular on campus when they were in college, and so was Amir. Both seemed to really enjoy Sol's company despite Sol being a hermit. Their personalities were similar as well—Amir and Alice were very good at being tactful without pulling their punches.

This was as close to an Alice stand-in as she could get, and she didn't realize until now how much she needed that . . . especially because Alice was adamant that Sol not talk about "creepy things."

"Hey, Amir." Sol was hesitant. "What would you do if your wife started seeing things around the house?"

"Like what?" He furrowed his brow.

"Like . . ." She racked her brain for something similar to her situation. "Let's say she said she watched a spoon just fling itself across the room." Sol stared at Amir, willing her poker face to do its job. Amir's eyes searched hers and while she was sure she read his expression as confusion, part of her wondered if he was already on the verge of questioning her sanity.

After a long quiet moment, he answered, "I guess I'd like to see proof?"

Right. Sol was already using her video camera, though, and from what she could see, the incident wasn't replicating.

"What if she couldn't get proof?" she asked.

Amir scratched the back of his head. "I guess we could just get rid of it?"

She blinked. "Just like that?"

"It's just a spoon. We could get another one."

Sol could *not* just get another staircase. Even if she could, though, that wasn't an answer she was looking for.

"Hold on." She shifted in her seat. "You're telling me that if your wife told you she saw an inanimate object move on its own but couldn't give you proof, you would . . . accept that and get rid of the spoon?"

"I don't know if I'd say I would accept it." Amir was defensive. Sol could see that in the way his shoulders squared up and he leaned farther into his chair. "This is kind of a weird hypothetical, Sol."

"I know but just . . . humor me."

"Okay . . . I guess I'd wonder where the spoon came from?"

Sol furrowed her brow. "Like the origins?"

"Or who we got the spoon from."

She hadn't considered that. Not that finding the origins of an entire house was possible, but she could reasonably find the previous owners and ask them for their experiences living in the house.

Though that begged the question—why would the previous owners decide to leave such a nice neighborhood?

Sol looked at Amir and caught him pursing his lips together in deep thought.

"What is it?"

"Huh? Nothing." He shook his head and then, as if to keep words from spilling out, he grabbed his drink and brought it to his lips.

"You were thinking hard about something. Spit it out."

"*I'm* the one that's hiding something?"

"Amir . . ."

"Okay, fine but . . . I'm pretty sure I'm wrong, okay?"

Sol furrowed her brow as he continued.

"I've been hearing something about a new position opening up in the biology department."

Sol's stomach became so tight, she thought everything was about to come up.

"What? Who did you hear this from?" God help her, Sol hoped it wasn't from a reliable source. "And is it my position?"

"I don't know! I was just talking to Clarissa in HR and she mentioned she had to start making room in her schedule to review applications for a new biology position. She didn't say what kind of job or when this position had opened up."

Amir scratched his arm nervously. "Honestly, I thought you had quit suddenly. That's why I invited you to lunch—but then you showed me that email and I knew you didn't and—hey, I said I could be wrong!" he repeated defensively.

"Right. You could be." Sol nodded as she put her head in her hands. "Fuck."

Sol didn't know anyone from HR personally, much less someone named Clarissa. But the budget for the biology department was always tight, which was why Sol had gotten *very* good at grant writing in the years she worked there. If a position opened up, it was because there was suddenly room in the budget.

Was Sol already fired?

What would she tell Alice? What would she tell Papi? No, Sol wouldn't accept this. She wouldn't let it happen. No matter what.

Is that really up to you?

She was sure Amir said other things during the lunch. She was sure they had an awkward hug goodbye, and she must have gotten to her car, although she couldn't remember the walk. It was all she could do to not completely disintegrate even as she felt her world crumbling around her.

This wasn't a hallucination. This wasn't a disappearing step or a bad smell. This was real, this was her life . . .

And she was pretty sure it was over.

THE SCREAMING

Sol was well above the speed limit, but she didn't care. Her thoughts ran much faster than the car. She had to think fast—what could she show Dr. Henderson to prove that she didn't plagiarize her work? What could she show anyone? The answers had to be in her basement somewhere. That was where she kept boxes of her research papers. Granted, she'd pored through them for hours at a time when the initial accusation occurred, but maybe she missed something. She *had* to have missed something.

If not, Sol could kiss her entire career goodbye.

She pressed harder on the gas pedal the moment she entered Maneless Grove. There was no one in the streets, so who would care about her speeding? The only person she ever seemed to keep running into was—

Veronica, who quite suddenly appeared in the middle of the street again.

Sol hit the brakes. The car skidded for what felt like miles, her chest pressed against the steering wheel from the sheer force. The honking blared in her ears but not quite as loud as her own heart pounded.

Sol just hoped Veronica had enough sense to get the hell out of the way in time.

Eventually, the car did stop. Sol peeled herself away from the wheel and put the car in park. She jumped out onto the street. Veronica was still standing in the middle of it.

"Are you crazy?" Sol yelled at the little girl. "Why the hell are you standing in the middle of the street? I could have killed you!" Adrenaline-induced fear made Sol break out into a cold sweat, enough that a slight breeze made her shiver. Despite the cooling weather, Veronica still wore a blue summer dress and sandals.

And she only stared with both hands clasped behind her back.

Sol's sharp anger intensified. Where the fuck were this girl's parents? How did they not teach her not to stand around in the middle of the street? She stomped over to the girl, pushing forward even when that rancid smell invaded her nose again. It was ironic in the worst way possible—the only time Sol could breathe in this neighborhood, and it was when she didn't want to take a single breath. Something was seriously wrong with this girl and Sol was starting to lose it when it came to her.

"Come on, get in the car. I'm taking you to your parents."

For a second, it almost looked like Veronica's eyes widened a hair. She shook her head slowly, stepping away from Sol.

Sol huffed. She didn't have time for this.

"No, I need to have a long conversation with your parents—" Sol grabbed Veronica's arm and the girl immediately let out a long, piercing scream. Sol stumbled backward, anger turning to shock. Veronica ran off, gripping something that glinted in the sunlight.

Okay . . . what was that all about?

Stranger danger, maybe? I guess I shouldn't just be touching other people's kids, but what the hell am I supposed to do? Let this little girl run wild and get herself killed?

Stunned, Sol only managed to watch the girl run out of sight. Her eyesight wasn't good enough to confirm from a distance . . . but was Veronica holding a knife?

"Veronica?" Sol yelled, somewhat concerned. A kid her size should *not* be running around with a knife. To be fair, she shouldn't be running around at all, at least not without adult supervision. Should Sol go after her? Or was it bad enough that she essentially tried to force the unwilling child into her vehicle? Sol twisted herself around, looking at every home. No cars in the driveways and no curtains shutting out the outside world. No one was home, again. No one saw her grabbing Veronica. Or speeding. Or almost running the little girl over . . .

Guilt overshadowed Sol's concern. Maybe it would just be enough to go to her parents' door again. She'd knock and knock and would make it clear that she wouldn't leave without speaking to *someone* face-to-face. Veronica's behavior needed to be addressed. Getting back into her car, Sol's bones shook as she drove carefully down the road. She wasn't too far from her home. Within minutes, she parked right outside of the Kennedys'.

I did nothing wrong. Sol took deep breaths, gripping her steering wheel. She was just a little concerned. And angry. Anyone would be angry if they nearly committed vehicular manslaughter. Should Sol have been going too fast? Probably not. But there would have been no danger at all if Veronica knew enough not to stand in the middle of the street.

That was right. Sol was not entirely at fault. And again, she was just concerned for Veronica's behavior. That was what she would tell the Kennedys. They would have to understand. Self-assured, Sol went to their door and knocked. After a few silent minutes, she rang the doorbell. Someone was home. They had to be. Their car was still in their driveway. And if they wanted to make it seem like they *weren't* home, they'd have parked in their garage like Alice did in hers.

Sol knocked again.

"Hello? I'm your neighbor from across the street—my name is Sol. I'm here to talk about your daughter's concerning behavior." Sol hoped her yelling was loud enough through the door. "I'm not going away until you open the door." She shouted—then sniffled.

Ah hell. Not the allergies again. Sol patted her pockets down for that Vicks nasal spray. She had left it in the house. Sol knew she could just as easily run across the street and return but she wanted to wait just a little longer, just in case. She pressed her ear against the door, hoping to hear any signs of life. There was only a deafening silence.

And a disgusting, rotting smell. Sol fought the urge to hurl. It was even worse than how Veronica smelled. And how was that possible?

Sol could think of one way. She rushed over to the window, hoping she was very, very wrong. She hoped it was silly of her to worry like this. But now that she thought about it, why else would the HOA want an emergency key to everyone's home? That didn't sound normal unless there was a past incident that made it necessary to become a rule.

Please don't let me see what I think I'm going to see. Not to sound callous, but she didn't have time for this. Her own job was on the line and she didn't want to worry about people she'd never met. Except . . .

What if she was right?

The curtains were getting in the way again. Sol searched for a gap somewhere. If she could just find an inch where she could peek in, maybe even curve her hands around her eyes to block out the glare of the sun, she just might—

Sol jumped away from the window. Her blood became ice and her heart was halfway to skipping town.

She didn't see that. She refused to believe it. But when she took another breath, the awful smell made sense. Sol ran to the car and grabbed her phone and dialed 911.

A crowd of people gathered on the sidewalk in front of the Kennedys' home. With an ambulance parked right out front, it was hard to blame them—but where the hell did they come from? Wasn't the neighborhood completely empty just an hour ago? They stared from a safe distance, far beyond where the stench could reach. Their eyes moved in unison, Sol noticed. And every direction one person leaned, the rest would follow, like they were part of some weird flash mob. Every so often, the sound of clapping hands erupted but when Sol turned to look, it was clear it wasn't coming from them.

Right, it's the trees. Because *that* made it less creepy.

"This house belongs to the Kennedys." She hugged herself tight, tearing her eyes away from the crowd. "I never got to meet them, not properly. I only ever saw their daughter go in and out. She's a little girl, maybe about eight years old."

"And where is their daughter?"

Sol shook her head. "Ran off. She was playing in the street and got spooked when I was coming home." She decided to leave out the part where she accosted the girl for her dangerous behavior. That wasn't important. What *was* important was what Sol saw just beyond their window.

The paramedic sighed to themself and looked back to their partner. The two of them donned gloves and face masks in preparation for what they were going to stumble upon. Their partner, a short, stocky woman, rolled a stretcher with a large black body bag onto the sidewalk. The neighbors parted easily to give them access.

"You said there were two of them, right?" the woman asked.

Sol nodded. "Right, two." She watched the taller one walk over to the door and turn the doorknob. It barely budged.

"It's normally left unlocked," Sol offered weakly. The paramedic glanced at her with a tired expression.

"Do you know anyone who might have a spare key?"

"Excuse me!" a familiar voice shouted. A disturbance among the crowd pried itself through and Nadine walked briskly to Sol and the paramedic. "Sorry, what's going on here?"

"This woman said that she saw two dead bodies in the living room of this home," they answered. "Do you by any chance have the key to let us in?"

"Of course, I do but—Sol, I wish you had called me beforehand. The Kennedys are just a nice, quiet family, I'm sure this is just a big misunderstanding." Nadine chuckled.

"Sorry, are you *laughing*?" Sol's face fell.

Nadine's voice quickly died down.

Sol pressed on. "I came over here because Veronica has been behaving really oddly. I just wanted to talk to her parents about it, but when I looked through the window, I saw . . ."

Sol's mouth went dry. The image was too startling to repeat but she could see it again, clear as day for someone who only had an inch to peer through.

Swinging feet. Two bodies elongated from gravity, close to snapping from decomposition. A thin line of rope or cord—Sol didn't get a good look at it—stretching from the ceiling to each body. The first time Sol could put a face to the name "the Kennedys" and they were both blue and purple and *swollen*. A mass of bugs chewed greedily on their flesh. Sol's own skin itched with that knowledge.

And Nadine's first instinct was to *laugh*? To call this a misunderstanding? No, Sol *knew* what she saw. The stairs be damned, this was not something that could be brushed away so easily.

Sol's eyes welled up again. She sniffled.

Fucking allergies.

"I'm sorry, Sol." Nadine reached out, but Sol pulled away. "I didn't mean to make you upset. I'm just . . . concerned because I just had breakfast with the Kennedys this morning."

"Yeah? Well, they're dead now," Sol spat. It didn't take long for a body to start decomposing—just because they were alive and well a few hours ago didn't mean Sol didn't just see them hanging from their necks recently.

The paramedic interrupted. "Ma'am, sorry to interrupt, but if you have the keys to their home, could you please unlock the door? We need to get inside."

"Yes, right, sorry." Nadine pouted, stepping up to the door. She pulled out a ring of identical keys and undid the lock. The moment the door was pushed open, Sol steeled herself for the overwhelming smell.

But none of that came.

The paramedics gave each other a puzzled look before entering with the stretcher. Sol leaned far enough to get a quick look inside. A column got in the way of the view of the living room, where Sol knew the dead bodies hung.

Still, it was silent. After another minute, the paramedics exited the home, looking equal parts relieved but also annoyed.

"Ma'am," the shorter of the two addressed Sol. "Are you aware that reporting a fake emergency is a crime? We could have you arrested for this."

"Oh, I'm sure that's not necessary . . ." Nadine interjected, but Sol hardly heard her.

"I'm sorry, a fake emergency?" She blinked. "Are you joking? The bodies are right there."

"There is nothing inside the house," the taller paramedic said. Their tone was serious. Sol studied their expression for a moment and then their partner's. Neither of them was lying to her.

Sol's own legs felt like jelly.

"No, you have to be . . ." She pushed her way past Nadine and the other paramedic and into the home of the Kennedys. She turned the corner on the column and looked into the living room. There she saw exactly the same setup as every other home. The white love seat in the window. The peach curtains, which were closed to keep out prying eyes. The *Live Laugh Love* sign on the wall.

And the only thing that was hanging from the ceiling was that same vintage light fixture, turned off as if to conserve energy. The whole house was darkened and covered with a layer of dust. There was an abandoned Barbie Dreamhouse in the corner, evidence that a little girl did live here, at least.

But the place was empty. And there was no stench. Nothing that made sense of Veronica's odor, and nothing indoors that matched what Sol saw.

She was frozen to the spot. The impossibility of it all was enough to make her crack.

What the fu—?

She balled up her fists and located the inch of window gap that she had peered through. A thin sliver of sunlight trailed far enough inside that Sol knew exactly where the bodies were supposed to be.

She stood in it. Looked up to the light fixture directly above her. Everything else was what a regular, cookie-cutter, Stepford Wives house should look like. And yet, an hour ago, she saw two bodies hanging where there were none.

Sol's chest tightened. Her mind ran in a loop; the certainty that she was literally standing in the spot where bodies hung, where insects congregated, made her skin crawl. Except they weren't there—not the bodies, and not a single bug. That was a good thing, right?

She should feel relieved. Veronica's parents weren't dead. She only thought she saw something horrifying.

Sol followed the line of sunlight back to the window. Outside, Nadine was chatting casually with the paramedics. She had one hand on her baby bump, and the other gesticulating, with a wide smile like she was just at another barbecue.

To their credit, the paramedics did not seem amused. Sol trudged out of the home, a mix of white-hot shame and nausea firmly embedded into her core.

"I . . . I saw it. I know I did. They were there," Sol muttered, bottom lip trembling.

"Oh, look who it is!" Nadine chirped. Sol looked up to see the crowd parting again, allowing Veronica to pass through. "This is the Kennedys' daughter, Veronica."

The girl stepped forward tentatively with wide eyes.

"Don't worry, sweetie, you're not in any trouble," Nadine comforted her. But the look on the girl's face only reminded Sol of Corinne. Veronica pursed her lips together and fidgeted with the hem of her dress. Wherever that knife was, the girl must have known to get rid of it before coming back.

"Hey there." The shorter paramedic crouched down to Veronica's level. "Do you know where your parents are?"

"W . . . work . . ." Veronica's voice was barely a whisper. It was the first time Sol ever heard the girl speak and it was a little raw, like she hadn't had a drop of water in days.

She probably hasn't if her parents were dead. Sol's eyes wandered to the car that was still parked in the driveway. If her parents *were* at work, where the hell did they work? Clearly not at home. And if they didn't work from home, what was Veronica doing here?

"Sol?" Nadine gestured to her. Veronica had stepped in front of her and raised her arms.

"You . . . you want a hug?" Sol asked, incredulous. Feeling the pressure of expectation from the paramedics and the crowd, Sol bent down. Veronica wrapped both arms around her neck. Sol stiffened. She hadn't noticed it before when she grabbed Veronica, but the girl's body was cold to the touch.

"*They're in the roots,*" Veronica whispered. And almost like she flipped a switch, a powerfully decaying stink permeated Sol's nose. It took every bit of strength in her not to start retching in front of everyone. Sol looked around, confirming that no one was reacting to the smell. But how were they ignoring this? Was this like that disease where people lost their sense of smell, only she was smelling things that didn't exist? And hearing things? What the hell was that about the roots?

Was she having a stroke?

"Aww," Nadine cooed. "She's such a sweet girl. And don't worry, Sol. Honestly, I'm glad you cared enough to want to do a wellness check on your neighbors. It really shows that . . ."

Sol hardly heard anything else after that. Once Veronica let go of her, Sol jumped up and made a beeline for her own home.

"Ma'am!" one of the paramedics shouted.

"Let her go," Sol heard Nadine say, a hint of steel in her voice. And for some reason, even though she was either in distress, a liar, or both, the group of onlookers parted in unison and let her go.

"Feel better."

THE ROOTS

t took a little bit of digging—and a nap to sleep off the two glasses of wine she'd gulped down immediately upon getting home—but Sol finally found it: the papers containing the history of the house. The previous family were called the Watersons. It took a bit of googling and sleuthing, but she was able to find Laura Waterson's Facebook page. So much of the woman's life was public—Sol didn't even have to friend request her to see everything she posted.

She scrolled back, far beyond her own move-in date. Far before she and Alice had even heard of Maneless Grove. Sol hoped to find some evidence that it really wasn't just *her* having a hard time adjusting to the house or the neighborhood. Maybe some typo would reveal deep-seated insecurity about reality or an ill-placed photo would hint at the slow unraveling of the woman's mind. Was it a little messed up that she hoped Laura suffered some manic-depressive attack? Perhaps. But Sol badly needed evidence that it wasn't just her. Unfortunately, the photos on Laura's Facebook didn't quite suggest a profoundly unsettling truth.

Instead, what Sol found was this: The Watersons were a family of four—a man, his wife, their daughter, and a son, and they were the kind of people who flipped houses for a living. They moved into a place for a short while, fixed it up, then put it back on the market at an increased value. Mr. Waterson was an architect, which was presumably where his passion for house flipping came from.

Laura Waterson looked like your average white mom with beach curls that only just brushed the top of her shoulders. She was covered in freckles that made her seem lightly sunburned—or maybe she really *was* lightly sunburned, at least in one of the pictures. A quick journey through her photo album showed that no, she actually did just look like that. The more Sol compared her situation with what Laura's profile suggested, the more alienated she felt. After all, Laura fit the status quo. She was a loving wife and devoted mother. Sol couldn't imagine wanting kids. Laura was delightfully feminine. Sol could practically hear Mami scolding her for looking like a *man*, as if a woman's worth was determined by how accurately strangers could guess her gender. And what was so wrong with being a butch lesbian? Would she have an easier time if she dressed more femme, like her wife? If she fulfilled the requirement of womanhood by becoming pregnant—or adopting?

Sol continued scrolling. Laura's smile looked easy—but even when she wasn't smiling, the woman looked pleasant enough. Approachable. No one would ever accuse her of having a resting bitch face. There were also photos of Laura cutting her hair, dyeing it a shade lighter, and overall just having fun with her appearance. Sol wondered what it was like to have the freedom to do so without everyone pointing out how inherently *different* it made you.

Laura had several posts in a row detailing just how grateful she was for her family, her job, or well-adjusted attitude. Sol barely lived in the same zip code as "grateful." Laura was Hashtag Blessed. Sol was a pound sign away from being admitted to a mental facility. Her skin itched, feeling less and less human, and more like . . . well, a *parasite*.

Laura looked like she *belonged* in a place like Maneless. So what was it about this house that chased her away?

It was a long hour filled with gut-wrenching anxiety before Sol decided to send a message. Then she turned her phone screen down to keep herself from staring in anticipation. The couch was still turned toward the stairs, the camera once again positioned in the same direction. After the situation with Veronica and the Kennedys, Sol decided she was better off deciphering the mystery of the stairs. At least then, she wouldn't be inconveniencing emergency services or calling concern to her own mental health.

I know what I saw. Sol gritted her teeth and leaned forward with her elbows on her knees. One way or the other, she was going to get answers.

Though her back was turned, Sol's mind was on Veronica and even Corinne. The old woman said not to trust the "neighbor." The little girl said "they" were in the roots. And both seemed to be somewhat afraid of Nadine, a pregnant woman in an annoying position of power in the Homeowners Association. Was she the neighbor that Corinne was referencing? Sol had no other clues to suggest otherwise. She could only seethe quietly in the silence of her home. But, as spacious as it was, Sol still felt like something was closing in around her.

She imagined it was a noose.

Sol didn't realize she had fallen asleep until she was jolted awake by Alice's shout the moment she got home.

"I'm home!"

Sol quickly rubbed her eyes just as there was a clatter of keys on the coffee table. By the time she looked up, Alice was already at her side with both hands pulling her up and planting a long kiss on her cheek. She was beaming with a smile Sol hadn't seen in days.

She had started up the stairs when Sol found her voice. "You're in a good mood."

Alice replied with a twirl and looked back with a wide grin. "Is it obvious?"

Sol's lips quirked up in a small smile. Her chest felt lighter. Maybe the issue was that Sol always isolated herself. It was hard to feel human when there was no one around to remind her that she was—and spending time with Amir or Alice always seemed to do the trick. If she could somehow keep those two around 24/7, Sol could imagine being hopeful for once. But hope dampened when Sol realized something just as important—that Alice would be *pissed* when she found out what Sol did today.

Her lips became a straight line again. "Y-yeah, I'd say it's pretty obvious." She gulped. "Did something good happen?"

Alice leaned against the banister, kicking her shoes off before picking them up. "You remember that promotion I've been gunning for at work?"

Sol floundered. This seemed like the first time she'd heard about it. Did Alice actually tell her about it before and she forgot, or did Alice misremember who she spoke about it with?

I have to tell her about the Kennedys. Normally, the admission that she saw *hanging dead people* would be kept a secret, but considering she dragged the paramedics and even *Nadine* into the situation, she knew the information would get around to Alice sooner or later.

And it was better if it came from Sol.

"Uh, s-sure?" Sol stammered, picking at her nails. "What . . . was this promotion for again?"

"To lead my own marketing team!" Alice gave Sol a questioning look. "I'm pretty sure I've mentioned this to you before."

Trying to keep her mind off the corpses she saw, Sol said, "You might have—I'm sorry. Tell me again."

Alice rolled her eyes but still couldn't contain her excitement. "There's a new lead position open ever since Andrea left. You remember Andrea, right?"

No, I don't remember Andrea. Sol was starting to feel worse. Was she always this disconnected with her wife's work life? Was she always just so obsessed with her own?

I have to tell her about the Kennedys, the thought repeated. Sol pushed it back with the sound of her wife's voice.

"Anyway, Andrea's gone, and her old team is wrapping up their last campaign before a new one starts. And I might be the one to lead it!"

"Wow, that's—that's huge!" Sol wasn't exactly sure what it meant— was this a promotion or wasn't it? But Alice was ecstatic and that was enough to celebrate. It'd been a while since she'd seen her wife beam with pride and now that she saw it again, Sol wondered if it was because she had been such an energy vampire.

"Thanks!" Alice said, glowing with pride.

Suddenly, she knew she couldn't tell her. She couldn't be the one to suck the air out of the room (which was saying something in that stuffy house). Sol couldn't do that to her, especially when Alice was working so hard. She deserved to be happy, even if just for a moment.

No—I'll tell her later.

Alice turned up the stairs but stopped at the top. "By the way, how was Amir? You had lunch with him today, right?"

Sol nodded, a crushing sense of disappointment over her. Here Alice was about to achieve one of her longtime goals and all Sol could say for herself was *I managed to leave the house for more than five minutes—and by the way, I caused a major incident (and possible felony) in our neighborhood, and I might lose my job.* Her stomach twisted with anxiety, and she was already thinking of the next drink she could sneak to soothe it.

"Amir's doing well," was all Sol could manage in response to her wife's question.

"Okay." Alice paused, furrowing her brow as if she wasn't sure what to do with that answer. "Well, I'm going to shower. Think you can handle cooking up some kimchi fried rice for us?"

Sol scoffed. "Pretty hard to fuck that up." Though it wasn't exactly cooking together, at the very least it wasn't another night of subpar takeout. She watched Alice disappear up the stairs to the bathroom. The loud squeak of the hinges was enough to change her mood from stressed to annoyed and she swore to herself that she would get that fixed if it was the last thing she did.

It was another night of silently watching Alice's favorite variety shows together during dinner—until Alice went completely silent, and excitement from her earlier news clearly abated. When Sol looked over, she noticed Alice was rubbing her forehead and wincing.

"Something wrong?"

"Just a headache."

Sol offered to grab ibuprofen from the bathroom, but Alice waved her off.

"It hasn't really been working for me lately. Maybe I'm just tired." Eventually, Alice decided to head to bed early.

With nothing else to do, Sol opened her laptop and looked up Google Maps directions for how to leave the neighborhood. There were so many dead ends and streets that curved around to the same road that it was driving her mad whenever she or Alice needed to head out and they always took the same route just so they wouldn't get lost. But it wasn't the most efficient way to the highway—at least, it didn't seem to be, and it made her wonder who was even in charge of the development of the community. It should not have been complicated to find an exit.

Sol accidentally clicked on Google Earth and sucked her teeth, but ultimately let it load. From above, the entire community looked lush and beautiful. There was the lake she never got to see, sectioned off by what appeared to be a second set of gates. Sol knew from the torn-up agreement that only Homeowners Association members had access to it, which was fine since she never cared for swimming anyway.

She recognized the large informal and formal event lawns on both sides of what was likely the town hall. Christ, even from above it was very much circular. Sol squinted and zoomed into the image. The roof had an odd design—thick straight lines going down with small hatches at the bottom. She could have sworn she'd seen something like that before somewhere. Sol found herself walking toward the kitchen and felt she was in the right direction. Looking around for a second, she noticed the welcome basket was long gone but the odd stone carving was still sitting on the far corner of the cabinet. Sol grabbed it, lifting it up for closer examination. She couldn't be entirely sure, but the image on Google Earth seemed like a geometric version of that same marble tree carving.

"Talk about keeping on brand." Sol snorted, drawing a finger across a line. It was very well crafted, she had to give the HOA that. Sol set it down and went back to the computer.

They're in the roots. Veronica's voice echoed in her head. Sol was ready to dismiss it as child nonsense—she still wasn't even sure she'd heard Veronica say that. Because even if Sol *did* see the girl's parents swinging from the ceiling, what the hell was she supposed to do with "they're in the roots"? The phrase meant nothing to Sol.

Unless Veronica meant it literally. She could have meant that her parents were buried under a tree, perhaps. That would *almost* make sense . . . if Sol hadn't already seen them inside the house. Dead and decaying, but they were there.

Except . . . they weren't, were they?

The corners of Sol's eyes stung with tears. The image of her neighbors silently judging her, of Nadine being so *patronizing*, the annoyed expression of the paramedics . . . all of it made her feel so small and stupid. It reminded her of the first incident at work. The unplugged freezer nearly ruined her *T. gondii* samples. And it was such a simple fix that when Sol put in a request for a new freezer, it was met with amusement. How was she supposed to know the freezer was unplugged? It shouldn't have been. Who would have unplugged it? Why would *she* have unplugged it? But for weeks afterward, every time Sol went to check on her samples, a snickering coworker would remind her to check the plugs as if it was the most common occurrence in the world.

Were they laughing at her now? Grabbing coffee together during office hours (because no students ever came this early in the semester) and making fun of their exiled colleague? Were her neighbors laughing behind their peach curtains at the hysterical Black lady that just moved in? She didn't know. She was never good with interpersonal relationships. She only knew how to not get in people's way. That's how she was raised. Children were the most convenient when they were seen, not heard. Now she was an adult and had trouble fitting into most social spaces. When she did seem to gain the attention of others, it was always bad . . . just like with her own family.

Sol rubbed the tears out of her eyes.

Whatever. Her neighbors could get bent if they thought they were going to gaslight her. She knew what she saw, but fine, she could mind her own business from now on if it pleased them; she just hoped they'd do the same to her. Because no one was going to make her feel like she didn't belong.

As Sol moved the cursor away from the top view of the town hall, she came across a smaller area, surrounded with black picket fences and rows of bare dirt with the occasional vegetation here and there. She reoriented the camera and saw that it was the community garden they spoke so highly of. What she thought were just decorative shrubs were actually part of the garden—tall bushes of blackberries lining the inside of the fences. With how bare the rest of it looked, she could only imagine they had either already harvested a lot of food or were just beginning to grow them in the photo.

Sol leaned forward, zooming in on the image. There were tall thick trees farther into the garden. The branches reached far and the leaves were so dense that they cast a dark shadow over much of the grass. Sol could only imagine how any undergrowth was able to get sunlight. Any bare scrap of land in the garden maintained a rich brown complexion.

Sol wasn't an ecologist—but her father being a landscaper came with the privilege of certain knowledge. She recalled him coming home one night, grumbling about rabbits tearing up a client's garden.

"And that's supposed to be *my* fault somehow? If you don't want rabbits, put up a fence!" He cursed under his breath. "Now I have to waste more time throwing blood meal everywhere."

Sol's imagination ran wild as a child—she imagined her father literally spraying blood from a hose over a row of hydrangeas. Of course, she eventually learned that that wasn't what blood meal was. The compact powder was a slaughterhouse byproduct, and useful for many things . . . including promoting plant growth and composting. Even learning that didn't shake the creepiness of plants needing blood.

They're in the roots.

She looked back at the screen once more. The beautiful garden suddenly seemed suspicious. Sol shook her head and scrolled away from the trees, yet again wondering why she was so obsessed with all this but not navigating away at all. She came across a hulking figure with red hair.

Is that Finnian? It sure as hell could have been him. The red hair was bright as ever and an easy match. Maybe he had just lost weight over the last couple of years. Or it might not actually be Finnian. White people often looked very similar, after all.

Regardless, Finnian waved at the camera, seeming as welcoming as the first time they met.

Though he was frozen, stuck in mid-pose and face blurred by Google, Sol had the odd feeling that he could see her anyway. With a start, she closed the laptop and got ready for bed.

Sol settled in on the couch and stared at the ceiling in the dark. Though the sleep paralysis incident was still fresh in her mind, the mystery of the stairs took priority if only because she was awake when it occurred. Now she wanted to sleep, but the nap she accidentally took earlier left her feeling more refreshed than ever.

That and the stinging in her feet didn't do her any favors. Sol flexed one of them as she turned, convinced that her wound was going through the unpleasant transition from open to scabbing.

Then the stinging turned to twitching.

Sol shifted to a seated position, carefully moving out toward the light switch. Once the living room was bright again, she sat down on the floor to inspect the bottom of her feet.

Something bulged out from under the bandages. Sol's breath caught in her throat. The pain of it made her shake but even so, she slowly unwrapped the gauze. Whatever was under there pushed against it and Sol fought the urge to vomit as an overwhelming stench flooded her nose. Stifling her breathing, she pulled the gauze off.

A putrid brown liquid leaked from her wounds.

Again, Sol gagged from the sight but even more disturbing were the strands of hair that seemingly grew from them.

No, not hair.

Sucking in a sharp breath, Sol pinched the end of a strand and pulled. It *hurt*, and yet the idea of these things in her feet hurt more, and so she kept pulling. More strands came with it. It was scraggly and wooden—roots. They were fucking *roots*. Never mind that there shouldn't be roots inside her at all, Sol just knew she had to get them *out out out out out*

Yet, the more she pulled at them, the more it felt like she was unraveling tissues and tendons in the meat of her foot. Like they were somehow *her* roots. Her leg jerked and she had to hold it down at the ankle as she breathed.

The threads, the strands—the *roots*—all became bloody, and beads of sweat rolled over her forehead. A droplet fell into her eye and blurred half her vision. She ignored it. She had to—there was no other choice. This was inside her, and if she could get it out, she'd be better. She'd have proof. She'd know that everything she'd been dealing with the past few days could be excised. She tore at her foot with hands that were so slicked with blood, it became harder to pull the roots. But she didn't need to.

The roots *moved*.

Not just moved, but shot into the floorboards with speed and force, pulling her feet flat against the ground.

Sol could feel some of them moving farther, piercing through the living room floor and the basement until they met back with the earth, still connected inside her. Other tendrils went in the other direction, snaking up her leg and wrapping around her so tight she couldn't move. They pierced Sol's skin, drinking up her blood as though she were the only source of water for miles.

Sol blinked and suddenly saw the Kennedys again—dangling from her own ceiling. It wasn't electrical cords or wire or strong twine . . . roots had strangled their necks. Worse, now that she knew that, she could once again hear a mix of their voices thrashing the inside of her skull.

"They're in the roots! They're in the roots!"

Their bulbous eyes held her in their tortured gaze. Figures moved in the corner of her vision. She looked—more rooted victims, people she didn't recognize. An elderly Black man with a tree branch growing out of his ear. A young redhead with a heart replaced by compost; worms wiggled in her chest cavity as she groaned.

Everywhere Sol looked, dead people stared back. Roots penetrated their bodies. Their thoughts were filled with pain and even then, they whispered, *"They're in the roots . . ."*

In the dark, Sol spotted a young person with one arm amputated grinding a fine white powder in a bowl. He stepped forward, eyelids rotted away to accentuate wide, malicious eyes.

"Stay part of the whole so we can live."

And then he blew the powder into her face.

Sol couldn't stop screaming. The sensation was burning. The agony of the roots shot straight through her spine. She felt her muscles harden, joints fusing together and trapping her in a stillness she couldn't break from.

And then she was pushed to the ground.

"Sol!" Strong arms wrapped around her center and held her tight. "You're okay, Sol. Everything is okay."

"What happened? Where am I?" she asked, feeling a soft but cold ground underneath her. Wet grass pressed against her hands and feet, and she was covered in a layer of cold sweat. Sol shivered as she looked to Alice. She wore a tired expression, eyes wide with concern. "You were sleepwalking and digging. I found you out here because you started screaming."

It took a moment for Sol's eyes to suddenly adjust to the daylight all around. She looked down at her arms. They were covered with dirt and so much of the grass beside the tree was pulled out. Suddenly, a different image came to her—one of pale hands at that same tree, burying something important. Sol blinked and found herself home again.

"Everything okay over there?" The voice came from around the corner of the house, just on the other side of the fence that separated the front lawn and the backyard.

"We're okay!" Alice stood up first and poked her hear around the corner of the house. "Sorry about that, Terry. My wife just had a night terror!"

Sol carefully came to her feet. The bandages were gone and standing with her wounds against rough earth made the pain worse.

Terry didn't move on.

"You gave us quite a scare, there." He laughed awkwardly. "Thought I was about to stumble upon a dead body like in one of those crime shows!"

"Oh, were you out jogging?"

Aside from the chatter, the neighborhood was quiet. Sol eyed Terry suspiciously—where did he come from? He certainly didn't live nearby.

How do I know that? Sol shook the thought from her head. Thoroughly embarrassed and shaken by the nightmare, she gestured to the house to let Alice know that she was heading in and would wait for her inside.

First, it was a few seconds. Then it was minutes, five, and then ten. Sol busied herself with washing the dirt and blood off her hands and feet, gingerly wrapping them again in clean bandages and going into the kitchen to make coffee—even if she really wanted vodka. Still, Alice didn't make an appearance.

In the kitchen, Sol found the odd marble carving that the association gifted them. The one they said to break or bury for "a surge of good luck." Sol sure as hell didn't believe in luck but if it got Alice inside the house quicker, she'd consider grabbing a hammer and breaking it open.

Where is she?

Sol hugged herself, relieved to feel soft skin and not jagged roots digging into her flesh. The only prickles of pain came from her own still-healing feet. When Sol sat down, she checked them again, tracing the thin scabs that were now coming apart. Her fingers came away with a few drops of blood, but that was it. She hadn't torn them open, she didn't pull out roots, and those roots didn't connect her to a sea of dead people she didn't know.

Except for the Kennedys. Did seeing them through a window really mess her up like that?

Which brought up the more pressing question: *Did I actually see them?*

Nadine claimed to have had breakfast with them early that day. Veronica said they were at work. Granted, Nadine could've been lying, and Veronica was a very strange little girl . . . but the paramedics didn't find any bodies anyway.

Sol had nightmares before—but none so vivid as that. And Sol had never had hallucinations or visions or anything like that. She knew what schizophrenia looked like too—she had classmates and colleagues who were schizophrenic and aside from minor personality quirks, they were very normal people.

Whatever Sol was dealing with was not normal.

Once more she wondered, *Should I tell Alice?* If Alice didn't believe her about the stairs, she sure as fuck was not going to believe her about the roots. Sol's stomach tightened. The longer she and Alice lived in this community, the more estranged she felt from her own wife. Wasn't buying a home supposed to be a huge milestone for them? Shouldn't it have brought them closer together?

She'd never felt more apart from her.

She shook her head. What was it Dr. Evans said? To paraphrase, assuming things about how her wife felt or thought was bad. She needed to be open and honest with Alice . . .

. . . but probably not about the Kennedys or the roots. She'd have to find a new therapist to talk to about those things.

Eventually.

Nursing her second cup of coffee, Sol peeked through the curtain of the window to get a good look at the man who had captured her wife's attention. Terry's head was cut off but from what she could see, he was dressed in a tracksuit and was making good use out of it. Sweat glistened on the back of his neck. She watched him hold out a hand and pass something to Alice. It looked like a pill bottle.

"What the fuck?" Sol whispered.

Without warning, Terry turned, and she was caught. She jumped away from the window, spilling coffee onto the counter. "Fuck!" By the time she finished wiping it up, Alice had come in through the front door. Her arms wrapped around Sol's middle from behind and squeezed tight.

"Do you need me to stay home today?"

Guilt rattled Sol. She wanted to say, *Yes, please stay home and make me feel a little less insane* and even, *Of course, let's watch some variety shows together, I promise I won't alienate you with my latest mental illness issue of the week.*

Except she couldn't do that. Alice had work, she had a promotion she was working hard for, she didn't have time to babysit Sol through her madness.

"It was just sleepwalking, querida."

Alice *tsk*ed. "You know I hate it when you do that."

"Do what?" Sol asked.

"Act like your problems are just your problems."

"Aren't they?" Sol muttered, and instantly regretted it. Though Alice still hugged her, the silence that followed only deepened the rift between them.

Shit, I really am a problem. Sol wished she could take back those last ten seconds. Instead, she changed the conversation. "What was that thing that Terry gave you?"

Alice froze and pulled away. "Well, I was complaining to Nadine about how I was getting odd headaches and nothing was working, so she gave me something that she says helps her with the usual pregnancy pain. Terry was bringing them over when he heard us."

She held up a little blue pill bottle and shook it. It sounded full.

"Are pregnant people allowed to take ... *anything* while they're pregnant?" Sol scrunched her brow as she looked at it closer. There was no label, which made her feel a bit nervous. And as she turned it over, she noticed the same symbol of the community on the bottom.

"Where did she get these?"

"I'm not sure. But she vetted it with her doctor, and she said the OB signed off on it so ... if it's safe enough for her, it should be safe enough for me. Honestly, I would do *anything* to get rid of these headaches. It's really hard to focus at work. But that's not what we should be talking about," Alice said as she snatched the bottle from Sol and shoved it in her pocket. "*You* haven't been sleeping well in general."

"I'm fine," Sol mumbled.

"And now sleepwalking and a night terror all in one? When's your next appointment with ... what's her name? Dr. Newman?"

"Dr. Nieman. And we didn't hit it off so well," she admitted. "But don't worry! I've already got an appointment lined up with someone else."

And it was the next Monday, but Sol knew that if she answered with that, Alice would ask if she could see them sooner. Sol preferred not to act like she was experiencing crisis after crisis after crisis when meeting a new therapist. The last thing she needed was being 5150'd.

"*I'm fine,*" she repeated. "I promise."

Yes, Sol was still shaken by her bizarre experiences in this house. Yes, it was relief that *this* was an experience she felt she could speak openly about with her therapist. Maybe she'd never dealt with sleepwalking or night terrors before, but those were much more normal than, say, seeing a burnt figure shuffle through her house while she was asleep.

And it was *leagues* more believable than if she told the therapist about the staircase incident.

Alice pursed her lips together. "I don't feel good about leaving you by yourself. You're just going to keep isolating yourself and that's going to make things worse." Somehow Sol could hear the addendum *And drink.* "How about this—I was speaking to Terry, and he said Nadine would love some company while he's working. You should go over there and spend the day with her."

Sol thought for a moment.

"If you won't go, I'll work from home today."

"Don't do that." Sol groaned. "Won't it look bad if you're looking to get a promotion?"

"You're more important, jagi," Alice insisted. The words, while kind and warm, made Sol feel undeserving of them.

"Fine." Sol swallowed. "I'll stay with Nadine. But only for today!"

And maybe I'll even find out what the hell is going on with the Kennedys. It had to be a lie that she had breakfast with them, right?

Alice gave Sol a long look and then a tight hug. It was enough for Sol to know how reassured Alice felt about her safety.

"I'll go get ready for work. Why don't you get ready and I'll drive you over, okay?"

As they kissed, Sol felt another prick of pain from the bottom of her foot.

Nadine's house was large. Or maybe it just felt that way? All things considered, it was identical to every other house in the neighborhood—the only difference was the open floor plan. Nadine had knocked down the wall that separated the kitchen from the living room.

Hope that wasn't the load-bearing wall Amir was talking about.

Still, since the moment Sol stepped into the cavernous space, she felt the vastness press against her skin. Taking a sweeping glance of the room, Sol's gaze stopped on four specific things: the white love seat by the window, the peach curtains, the hanging vintage light fixture, and the *Live Laugh Love* sign on the wall.

Sol sat with her legs pressed together, palms down on her thighs, and knew she was fully exposed to Nadine from across the room.

"Are you sure you don't need any help?" Sol nervously shifted in her seat. It wasn't possible, but Nadine's stomach looked like it was going to burst from the pressure.

"Oh, please. You're the guest. You just stay right there," Nadine said. Her voice carried easily. The little kid inside Sol felt like she was being yelled at.

And if things couldn't be worse, Sol's feet were still prickling. She planted them firmly onto the floor, hoping it would be enough to stop the itching.

"So, how far along are you?" Sol asked, tossing the question over her shoulder.

"Eight months!" Nadine chimed.

And you're still able to move around this much?

The woman waddled when she walked, but it wasn't pronounced and, if anything, she swayed with a grace that Sol found herself envious of. More, there was no complaint of nausea or pain or swollen ankles, nothing that most pregnant women complained of. It was like she didn't notice she was pregnant at all.

Maybe their visit to the hospital really paid off.

Sol steeled herself, watching Nadine return to the couch. It felt a little silly to feel threatened by her. What could this woman do to Sol when most of her energy was spent housing a new life? Why were Corinne and Veronica so afraid of her? There was something, though—something off. Alice loved her, talked about her all the time, about how much of a mentor and positive force she was. And yet . . . at the Kennedys' . . .

Sure, she'd helped. But she'd also brought a crowd. Took over. Dismissed Sol and her claims.

Made her invisible. Irrelevant.

"I'm really glad you decided to come by, Sol," Nadine said as she placed a tray of store-bought sugar cookies on the table and two mugs of what smelled like peppermint tea. "I've always wanted to get to know you better."

"There's . . . really not much to know." Sol shrugged, feeling a little put on the spot. "I'm married to Alice and I'm a scientist." *Was* a scientist, she didn't say. Nor did she mention she was currently experiencing what someone could generously call "employment issues."

"Nonsense! I'm sure there's more to you than you're letting on." Nadine chuckled. "But I can understand feeling shy. The truth is . . . we really do need to talk. About what happened at the Kennedys.'"

And there it was. Of course this wouldn't just be a social moment. Sol's stomach flipped. Needing to do something with her hands, she picked up her mug and sipped the tea. It was bland.

How did white people make *peppermint* bland?

"Yeah . . ." she murmured into it. "I'm really sorry about any trouble I caused."

"No, no, don't worry about it." Nadine waved her off. "Honestly, I'm glad you were so concerned about your neighbors. It's a good thing. I was just wondering . . . did you tell Alice yet?"

When Sol didn't answer, Nadine sighed.

"I thought so. It's okay if you'd rather keep this between us. But you should know that it did put us in a little bit of a tight spot. After all, we had to convince the paramedics not to report you."

The news jolted Sol into spilling her tea onto her shirt. It shouldn't have startled her—she knew this was a possibility. But to have it spelled out so blatantly still shook her.

"You stay there, I'll get a napkin." Nadine excused herself, leaving Sol to hyperventilate on the couch. If they pressed charges and this ended up on her record, it would be the nail in her career's coffin. They wouldn't even *need* proof that she had plagiarized her report. This would be enough to judge her as a person with poor character.

"Hey, hey, it's okay," Nadine cooed upon returning. She patted Sol's chest with a napkin. "You're okay." As soothing as it should've been, Sol's anxiety ramped up again. She snatched the napkin from Nadine's hand and cleaned herself up.

"Listen, Sol, I didn't want us to do this. But if something like this happens again, you would be fully on your own. The association can only protect its own members."

"Excuse me?" Sol blinked, realization setting in. Here came the blackmail.

"We have legal counsel in case of emergencies," Nadine explained, hands raised in defense. Great, now the woman looked like *she* was afraid of *Sol*. Sol didn't even so much as raise her voice.

Nadine continued, "All I'm saying is that if you ever needed help, it would be advantageous for you and Alice to join first rather than keeping us as an afterthought. And of course, all of this stays between us. I'm sure Alice would be very upset if she knew what happened."

Sol studied her face, too shocked to respond. She could read between the lines easily though. Nadine wouldn't tell Alice, but only if the two just signed on the dotted line. Of course, if Sol had an outburst here and now, she would just look like a perpetrator. She glanced down at the woman's stomach. Nadine could get away with just about anything in this state.

"And . . . it would *really* help me out," she admitted, chewing on her bottom lip. "You got the letter about the new elections coming up, right? With this baby on the way, people are talking about pushing me out of the presidency. I haven't been able to take part in events in a while, so I can understand why, but I just—I can't let it go."

"You'd want me and Alice to vote for you?" Sol scrunched her face. "No offense, but even if we *did* sign the agreement, I don't think we'd care enough about the elections to vote. It's just so . . ."

"Silly?"

Voting on the chief party planner? Yeah, something like that.

"It's not our thing." Sol settled for a more diplomatic answer.

Nadine shook her head, a bubbly laughter rising through her chest. "You just don't understand yet. But you will."

What's not to understand? Your invasive policies? Your ability to fine us for growing flowers? No, I understand all too well that you're deranged. Sol bit her tongue. The last thing she needed was to give Nadine a reason to tattle to Alice.

Another reason.

"Now, I wasn't lying when I said I wanted to know more about you," Nadine said, a charming smile finding its way onto her lips again. Like she hadn't just made a thinly veiled threat. "Where do you go shopping? You have such an interesting sense of fashion!"

The backhanded compliment stunned her. Sol looked down at her comfortable men's jeans and oversize blue flannel button-down. She left the shirt opened to a gray tank top. In contrast, Nadine wore a floral-pattern maternity dress. A gold hoop bracelet dangled from her wrist. It reminded her again of Laura, of the status quo.

Of how Sol did not belong.

Parasite.

"I just . . . buy whatever's on clearance, I guess," she said, trying hard not to scowl.

"Oooh, how economical!" Nadine cheered. Sol wanted to stick her face in a pillow and scream. No, she wanted to stick *Nadine's* face in a pillow and . . .

Outside, she could hear the trees rustle loudly, shaking her from her thoughts. Nadine looked out the window at the sound and then smiled at Sol.

"And where are you from again? I know your last name is Reyes so I imagine you have a little Spanish in you."

Sol narrowed her eyes at that statement. While it was a surprise to know Alice hadn't told Nadine much about her, that meant Nadine—and just about everyone else in the neighborhood—would be making their assumptions about her.

Again—*more* assumptions. She wasn't so naïve to think they didn't have preconceived notions about the Black lesbian in their midst.

Like when they assumed Alice was the one with the doctorate.

You're about to get some Spanish in your face if you don't stop with this microaggression shit—

Once more, a sound from outside seemed to react to her violent thoughts.

Let's rein it in for today, she told herself. *For Alice.*

She put down her mug, determined not to let Nadine win. "Right.

Uh. Well, I was born in New York, but my family's from the Dominican Republic."

"Ooh! Fun!" Nadine carefully leaned over to grab her mug. It was preemptively painted *World's Best Mom* and filled to the brim. As Nadine blew across it and took a sip, she said, "You know, I've actually been to the Dominican Republic before."

"Really?" She didn't want to know where this was about to go . . .

"Yup! Went over as a part of Habitat for Humanity and built homes for so many families there."

Sol tried not to show her discomfort. "Oh. H-how was it?" Now she really didn't want to know, but the tidbit of information had hit her like a truck, and she couldn't think of any way out of the conversation short of cursing out a pregnant woman that her family's home country wasn't a white-savior fantasy camp.

"It was so beautiful! And the culture! Ugh!" Nadine's hand went across her heart. "Your people are truly resilient."

The more Nadine spoke, the more Sol wanted to crawl deep into the recesses of the earth and scream. To drag this woman down with her and let the dirt pile up on her after Sol climbed back out. She reached over the table and grabbed a sugar cookie. Maybe if she signaled to the woman that she was done talking, the conversation would be over immediately.

"I even got to learn a little Spanish while I was there!" *Nope.* "Let's see . . . what do I remember . . ."

Sol hoped she had a case of amnesia.

"Oh! ¿Quieres una galleta?"

The mispronounced words caused Sol to cringe for more than one reason. A flash of her mother looking down at her disapprovingly went through her head. The phrase had a double meaning, at least in D.R. The more innocent one meant "Do you want a cookie?" Whereas the slang meant "Do you want to get hit?"

But Nadine couldn't *possibly* know that.

Nadine gave Sol a sympathetic smile as if she saw the memory herself. She reached for a cookie and Sol flinched, then cursed herself for it.

Another small smile—was it satisfied?—touched Nadine's lips. "Yeah, I was never great at rolling my *rs*." She laughed. "I think I might actually have some photos somewhere, let me see if I can find them." Nadine shifted to the edge of the couch, getting ready to stand up.

"Oh, you don't have to do that," Sol said. She really did not want to see photographic evidence of Nadine parading around her parents' home country *fixing* it. Because while her parents were assholes, she had to have *some* pride over where they came from.

Instead, Sol found herself asking, "Why don't you tell me about yourself, Nadine? Like . . . when did you move here?"

Nadine furrowed her brow as she grabbed another cookie.

"Huh. I guess it's been five years, now that I think about it! Time really flies."

"Really? Five years? You really seem like you've been here for much longer."

"Do I?" Nadine smiled. "Gosh, I hope so. You know, I do really love this community. It's just wonderful the way everyone invests in a neighborly spirit, don't you agree?"

Not at all. In fact, Sol couldn't help but notice how often they said it, like they were afraid they would forget if it wasn't mentioned at least once a day. Nearly everyone she'd spoken to brought it up at every opportunity.

Instead, she said, "It sure is something. So, five years here, you wouldn't say that you're, I don't know, on bad terms with anyone, right?"

Nadine seemed genuinely surprised by the question. "I can't say I am."

"Not even Corinne?"

Nadine's response was something like a shrill giggle. "That woman can be so silly."

Sol pressed her back against her chair. "In what way?"

"You'll find out soon enough." She continued to giggle, so high and piercing that Sol thought she was going to choke on her cookies. "Sol, don't let me be the one to eat all of these! Go on, take a few more. I promise you, they're delicious."

Sol hadn't even finished eating her first one. She opened her mouth to respond but then at the last second grabbed another cookie. Hunger dug into her, and she quelled it with a mouthful of carbs. She looked down at the bite mark and noticed flecks of white.

Ugh, is that flour? Are these even cooked fully? And yet for some reason she took another bite. It didn't taste like anything but an actually decent sugar cookie, so she kept eating.

"Do you remember when we met at the hospital?" Sol blurted as soon as she swallowed. "Corinne looked at you like she was afraid of you."

"Me?" Nadine's giggle started up again and she rubbed her stomach. "Do you really think she has any reason to be afraid of me?"

Something lurched inside Sol. Surprised by the sensation, she didn't notice at what point Nadine had put one of her cookies back on the tray.

"I don't know. But I can ask her." Sugar melted on Sol's tongue, its sweet taste morphing into the feel of heartburn in her ribcage. She rubbed her chest uncomfortably. "I'm sure she'll tell me."

Nadine put another cookie down. "Let's hope you get the chance to do that."

Sol froze, heartburn melting into nausea. "Why wouldn't I get the chance?"

There was another lurch. So strong that it kicked Sol into the fetal position, dropping crumbs everywhere.

"Are you okay, Sol? You don't look so good."

"I'm fine," she lied, forcing herself to sit up. She took another bite even as her stomach rejected it. "Just haven't had much to eat today."

"You're holding your stomach," Nadine pointed out. "Are you feeling sympathy pain? I've been told I have that effect on others, but I thought my husband was just saying that to butter me up."

It wasn't pain as much as it was a discomfort. Sure, Sol's stomach felt like it was ballooning, but she could just as easily look down and see that she wasn't. Sympathy pain, right. That's all it was.

"Maybe if I get up for a second . . ."

"Of course!"

Sol stood up, deciding that maybe walking would lessen the tension in her body. She passed around the couch and went to a shelf lining the wall with frames. She was surprised that most of the photos were of people Sol had met once or twice. Like Hope and Finnian, sharing the grill at a barbecue. Fireworks were going off in the background; Sol assumed it must have been the Fourth of July.

Then there was Nadine in a wedding dress beside her husband. The man had a clean-shaven face that clearly had not seen the sun in some time. The top half of his face was half a shade darker than the bottom half. It made him look odd. A few more photos of them revealed that the man definitely used to have a beard—but more than that, there was a boy in some of the pictures. He had Nadine's brown hair and was almost as tall as her husband.

"I didn't know you have a son." Sol held up the photo to Nadine. "How come I haven't seen . . ." Sol stopped. Nadine was no longer smiling.

"Yes, I did." Nadine wobbled as she stood up and came around the coffee table. Her hand grazed the edge of the frame before taking it in her palm. "He was sixteen in this picture, I believe . . ."

Sol watched Nadine's expression. It was the first time she had ever seen the woman not cheerful. The lines on her forehead were more prominent and Sol noted the way Nadine studied the photo. She almost looked confused, as though she wasn't sure what emotion she should have been feeling at the sight of the photograph.

Okay, so her child was likely dead. *Shit.* Sol was now feeling bad for her ill intentions, her mouth as full as if her foot had been one of those cookies. It was more than her faux pas too—her not-so-subtle accusations about Corinne were leaving a bad taste as well. Nadine probably just had some typical bad housewife history with the older woman. Or maybe Sol just misread Corinne's expression.

It wouldn't be the first time I read into things incorrectly, she thought wryly.

The silence grew uncomfortable, and that was saying something considering how the morning had gone.

"What was his name?" Sol wasn't sure what made her ask other than a need to not be standing there saying nothing at all.

"Sean."

Sol floundered for something else to say. "He . . . looks happy."

"He was." Nadine placed the frame face down and stepped away.

A cold, gnawing sensation ate at Sol. She followed Nadine back to the couch and rested her hand on her shoulder.

"It must have been hard for you." *To lose him.* Sol didn't need to speak the words out loud. Nadine slowly nodded with a blank stare.

"Everything happens for a reason, I suppose," she said. Her voice cracked at the edge of that sentence and Sol felt a sharp pain dig into her palm. She pulled back to massage it but kept her attention on Nadine.

"I'm sorry."

Nadine didn't speak at first. She turned to Sol, but her stare was pointed toward the shelf.

"Are you religious, Sol?"

"Not really." Sol rubbed the back of her neck. Her answer felt awkward, like a half truth. She quickly amended it. "My parents were, though, so I kind of grew up in a religious home."

"I don't think I ever believed in a higher power. Only what I can see, a more tangible way of living." Nadine breathed. "But moving here, to Maneless Grove, it's taught me a little bit about how the two can be closer together than we ever thought possible."

"Uh-huh?" Sol's hand burned. She shook it at her side and flexed her fingers.

"When you live in a community like this, you come to realize that everyone can be part of something greater. A greater good, a greater state of being. Even the dead stay a part of us long after they pass. We all take care of each other, you know?"

Sol stammered, "Sure, right." She wasn't sure where this line of questioning was going.

"You and your wife, you applied to live here, not just because you wanted the house but because you also wanted that, right? To be part of a community?"

Sol tensed up. This was getting into territory she didn't like. Truthfully, had Sol known what they were signing up for, she might not have agreed to buy the house, despite the deal they got and the scarcity of inventory anywhere close to Yale or Alice's job.

"Yeah, I thought so." Nadine sighed. It reminded her of when Corinne called her hesitancy for what it was. Was she that easy to read? Guilt settled into Sol's stomach.

"It's not the community . . ." Sol said haltingly. "I'm just kind of a loner."

Nadine muttered something and then quickly stood up.

"I'm going to get a refill on my tea," she said.

Before Sol could respond, Nadine went back into the kitchen. It wasn't until much later on, when Sol went back to her home, that she realized what Nadine muttered was a vague threat. Even worse was the fact that she'd been staring in the direction of her son's photo, a cold gaze in her eyes.

Nadine said, "Loners don't typically do well in our community."

THE LONER

S ol could not get out of Nadine's house fast enough.

"Are you sure you have to go so soon?" Nadine asked when she came back with her tea, her mouth curving downward in that same fake look of concern. Sol could swear the woman had about three expressions she cycled through for any given moment. Nadine stood in the way of the door, like she instinctively knew Sol was trying to escape before she came up with the idea.

"Yeah, I just remembered . . ." Sol searched for a good lie. "We have an electrician coming by! Corinne mentioned there was a fire and we think it messed with the wiring somehow." It wasn't *entirely* unbelievable, and actually something they *did* need to look into—she just hadn't actually initiated it yet. If Corinne knew of a fire, then Nadine definitely knew about it.

"Oh, I see. Hm." Nadine furrowed her brow for a moment. One of her three expressions, for sure. "Well, okay. Just remember what we talked about."

Sol pretended she didn't know what she meant.

"About not causing trouble again," she reminded Sol. "There's only so much we can do to cover you without you being a member."

"Right, of course." Sol nodded. "It won't happen again."

Just please open the damn door.

Nadine smiled again, taking a beat as if listening to something before obliging. Sol took long strides to the sidewalk. From the corner of her eye, she saw Nadine standing at her wide-open door. Smiling a Cheshire-like grin and watching Sol leave.

"Get home safe, Sol!" She waved.

Sol returned the wave with barely a turn back in Nadine's direction. What a weird thing to say, *Get home safe*. Sol intended to. What did she think was going to happen to her here?

What she was more worried about was her wife. When Alice dropped her off at Nadine's house, it was with the added (but unsaid) expectation that she would stay there until Alice returned. She didn't realize it until she looked up her address on her phone and saw how far away Nadine lived, despite being in the same neighborhood. Without a car, it would be a long walk home. If it wasn't for her feet, she might have welcomed it. She thought about the last hour she'd spent with Nadine and told her feet they'd just have to deal with it.

The graying skies made the outside air chillier than Sol liked, but she wouldn't turn back now. It was a relief to be out of that large house. What did Nadine need all that space for, anyway? It was mostly empty. And yet, the stuffiness could not be overstated. Sol felt like she had been squeezing herself into an invisible box. Maybe she was, in other ways.

You're out now. It's over.

As if to confirm that, Sol looked behind her, startled to see that Nadine was now standing on her lawn. Still watching Sol. Waving at her. Sol waved back again with a nervous smile of her own.

Let's get home faster—sorry, feet. She doubled her pace and turned the corner. At least now, Nadine couldn't see her.

Still, she could practically feel the woman's eyes tracking her, even now.

It wasn't quite a jog, but it was almost Olympic-level walking at this point.

After a few blocks were between them, disappointment slowed Sol's thoughts and pace. She didn't figure out what was up between Nadine and Corinne. She hadn't even broached the topic of Veronica or the Kennedys. Instead, Nadine got the jump on her, making it known that she would be holding it over her head until Sol and Alice considered joining the Homeowners Association. Did they really have to convince the paramedics not to press charges? Or was that another lie that suited Nadine? It hadn't seemed like they were really going to follow through when the one paramedic had brought it up . . . right? The more time she spent with that woman, the more Sol knew Nadine was caught up in her own self-importance. Which meant Sol was also right not to like her. She had such a slimy personality.

What the hell did Alice see in her?

Sol looked up and stopped in her tracks.

Rows upon rows of identical houses stretched on for what looked like miles into the horizon. Manicured lawns taunted her, and the tall trees surrounded her like she was the enemy—and she was outnumbered. Sol didn't know how far she walked but it couldn't have been that far. Maybe if she turned back, she would find Nadine standing outside her house again. Sol ran back.

Nadine was gone. Or maybe just back in her house. Was there anything outside that could point as a landmark to where she was? There had to at least be a street sign.

Her skin itched. Her nose twitched. Sol's eyes watered. And once again, Sol had left the nasal vapor spray at home. How many times was this going to happen before she learned to keep it on her? Sol pulled out her cell phone. GPS would have to be her savior.

She quickly entered her address. Except this time her screen glitched, and she impatiently tapped it again, scrolling down and hoping it would refresh and fix itself. Then it loaded the map. Just the map. No directions. Not even the little blue dot that would tell her where she was in this maze of a neighborhood. Sol zoomed out.

More houses. More streets. Squares and lines identical to the ones before them. Sol refreshed her phone. The screen came back to that map. She restarted it and tried again. Still, the same odd map.

It had worked before. She had bars. How was she suddenly in a dead zone?

"This cannot be happening to me," she breathed, half seething, half hyperventilating. She needed to get home. In fact, she *wanted* to get home, even if she was tormented with visions of rooted people and phantom steps. She would rather be in a house that was somewhat familiar to her than on the street where the indistinguishable homes were deeply disorienting.

Where *she* was the anomaly.

What if she walked up to a home and knocked? Just waited for someone to answer the door and help give her directions? There weren't any cars on the street to indicate anyone else was home, but considering the crowd that formed outside the Kennedys', she had to believe all the cars were tucked squarely away into their garages.

What if she just asked for help? What's the worst that could happen?

The worst that could happen is I get shot, she grimly thought. Or someone calls the cops . . . and *then* she gets shot. Just look at her: a sleep-deprived Black Latina wearing men's jeans and an oversize blue flannel. She didn't look like she belonged there, much less *lived* there. She realized, too, that she hadn't gotten a new driver's license, so she couldn't even prove her address. On top of all that, she remembered that asshole Lou from the welcoming party. What if she made the mistake of knocking on *his* door? If anyone looked trigger-happy, it was him.

Imagining that scenario stressed her to the point of blurring her vision again. The fishbowl came down around her and she had to sit on the sidewalk and breathe deeply. Great, now she looked like a strange person suffering a mental breakdown. This couldn't have waited until she got home?

Except she couldn't get home, and her vision got blurrier.

Sol took a deep breath. There was another solution to this problem. She could just keep walking. If Sol continued in the same direction, she had to eventually reach an end to the neighborhood, or reach a decent enough landmark that could point to her location. Hell, maybe if she moved, her GPS would recalibrate itself without any fuss.

"Are you lost?"

Sol jumped up. She blinked rapidly, hoping to clear her vision. The figure in front of her came into focus—a pale teen. The same one that absentmindedly crossed the street in front of her when she first moved in. Veronica's actions now seemed less a personal flaw and more a symptom of something larger. The boy pulled his headphones down and rested them around his neck.

"Yeah, sorry. I went out for a walk and my—my GPS isn't working," she stammered, straightening her back. "I'm Sol, I just moved in about a week ago. You might have seen me at the welcoming party?"

The teen stared at her, unblinking. His gray eyes made the boredom etched into his face more pronounced.

"Uh, right. Do you think you could help give me directions?" Sol thought quickly. She didn't want to give this kid her address—that seemed a little uncouth. She needed some other landmark to help guide her home.

"The town hall. Do you know how I can get to it?" If she remembered her time using Google Maps correctly, the town hall was a straight line and a few simple turns from her house.

Without another word, the teen turned and started walking. Sol followed at a distance.

"How did you get lost?" he asked.

"I'm not sure." Her face grew hot with embarrassment. "I guess it's kind of hard to find your way when everything looks the same."

The only sound from the teen came from his trudging feet. It was like watching a zombie shuffle forward.

"Do you still have no connection?" he asked. Sol quickly checked her phone. The connection wasn't the issue—it was that her GPS wouldn't cooperate.

Suddenly, a sense of vertigo hit Sol like a truck. She fell to the ground on her hands and knees and froze as the neighborhood shifted around her. Trees rustled softly, though she didn't feel the slightest breeze.

It was bad enough this was happening in public—but in front of a kid? Embarrassment wasn't a strong enough word for what she was feeling.

But luckily, it stopped. The vertigo melted away, and Sol finally felt safe enough to stand on her own feet.

"Sorry, I don't know what—" Her voice died. Not only was she not surrounded by the rows of irritatingly identical homes, but Sol was immediately *very* close to the town hall.

Close, as in it was just across the street from her. The imposing white tree forest stood behind it, tall and seemingly staring directly at her.

It reminded her of the same scene at the Kennedys'.

Forget the Kennedys. Just moments ago, she saw nothing on the horizon but more empty houses. How did they get here so fast?

"We walked," the boy answered. Sol didn't realize she said anything out loud. But now that she found the town hall, she could use it as the true north landmark it was and book it back home.

"Thanks." Sol swallowed. She took a step back from the teen, and then another step. The teen only tossed a look over his shoulder and went on. Toward the town hall.

Wait, no, he wasn't going toward it, he was going past it. The teen appeared to be going straight into the woods.

Sol blinked. If there was any time to run in the other direction, now would be the time. Whatever this kid was doing in the woods, it wasn't any of her business.

Curiosity killed the cat.

Sol was too Black to be entering her version of a horror movie. But then she glanced back to the rows of houses that stretched on forever. The endless cookie-cutter homes were another hell she didn't want to experience again. It was like something was playing with her. The neighborhood was equal parts mocking her and refusing to let her go.

The forest ahead of her was still. Uncaring. There was a dead silence that was only interrupted by a distant clap of leaves. She listened intently—no birds. No crickets. Nothing was ruffling its feathers or zipping through shrubbery.

Just an eerie dead silence.

Shit, maybe I'm already in a horror movie. The question now was, how would she, the singular Black person, die? Would it be after following a suspicious kid into the woods and possibly getting mauled by a bear? Or would she rather meet her end at the hands of the Waspy elite, in a neighborhood that seemed to gaslight her to madness?

She followed the distant figure of the boy, through the trees and away from the neighborhood. The temperature quickly dropped in the shade. A chill ran up her arms, wrapping around her body. She shivered under cold sweat.

Sniffling, Sol continued forward, ignoring how many times she wiped the running snot onto a sleeve. The trek would be more tolerable if she could breathe through her nose. Or had on an extra layer.

Sol looked to the sky. Sunlight trickled down through tree branches and yet any warmth was stripped down by the time it reached her. It was like the sun was just a cosmetic. There so she could see where she was going, not so that she could enjoy it.

In the distance, sudden movement caught Sol's attention. She squinted, almost certain she saw a figure. But the light only revealed soft haze. Her eyes were playing tricks on her—again.

Sol slowed her pace and stared into that middle distance. Her nerves became sensitive to the idea that something just might be staring back. She didn't get the chance to push down against that thought—as the boy immediately broke into a sprint.

Sol followed—not fast enough to spook him further, just enough to keep up. Creeping vines whipped her shins and slowed her down, but soon enough, she spotted him again.

But he wasn't alone.

Sol stopped behind a tree. The boy met with a group of other kids, who seemingly waited for his return. From where Sol stood, they were all of varying ages. Older teens and preteens and the smallest child looked about six. She even spotted Veronica in the mix, the only girl in a summer dress (wasn't she freezing?) among older kids who wore all-black clothing or torn jeans with graphic tees.

And they were all incredibly pale and completely silent. Standing with blank faces, or milling about aimlessly, not a single one uttered a word even when the newest arrival came.

Every head turned to him, simultaneously. Then they moved to him in quiet unison. When he presented a butterfly knife to them, everyone gave a synchronized nod, as if they were all of one mind.

A chill went down Sol's spine. This was a mistake. She shouldn't be here. Whatever was going on, Sol absolutely did not want to become witness to it.

She peeled away from the tree and took a step back—only to notice something odd about it. Large strips of the bark were carved off the tree. The white gave way to an ashy black. Her eyes flicked back up to the kids. For a moment, she was relieved to see they didn't see her there. Instead, their attention was on another tree. They stood around it in equal distance while the boy stepped forward with the knife.

He began carving into it. Slowly and methodically, until a large piece of bark fell away. Sol watched as he tore it into pieces, then passed each one out to the group. When the last piece was given away, the entire group turned toward Sol. She froze in place, but ready to run if anyone so much as took a step forward. Was she fast enough to outrun a group of kids? She didn't think so. They had a knife. The only thing she had on her side was her size.

Still, Sol would fight kids if it were a life-and-death situation.

For now, she waited. The kids all watched her with blank expressions—it was hard to get a read on what they were about to do.

Until they moved. Sol flinched before she realized they were only lifting their arms. With the bark pinched between their fingers, they quickly popped it into their mouths and swallowed it whole. Sol's face fell.

"Are you sure you should be—ow!" She hissed, feeling an immediate cutting sensation on the inside of her own cheek. Sol tasted blood.

She pressed a finger inside her mouth and withdrew it—nothing. Just saliva. But she tasted rust and copper all the same. Ahead of her, the kids dispersed. All walking in different directions, it was the first time she'd seen any of them move independently of the others.

I should . . . I should go, she thought, turning back.

She found the neighborhood quickly, as though it had always been there, just a few steps away. Sol's head swam with confusion and anger.

"Hey there, Sol!" a man chirped from around the corner. Sol

jumped. She didn't see the redhead at all until she stepped onto the sidewalk in front of his lawn. How did he know her name?

"It's me," he said, waving. "Finnian."

Oh fuck off, you're not Finnian is what Sol wanted to say. This man was easily a couple of inches shorter than the one she saw at the welcoming party. Hell, he was almost her height. A person can gain or lose weight easily, but no one *loses* their height that quickly.

But that smile . . . it was uncanny. Doubt crept in the edges of Sol's mind. Was he really Finnian? The red hair wasn't quite as vibrant. Maybe he wasn't a natural redhead like she thought. It could've just been a dye job fading.

But the height . . .

Finnian held a rake in his hands and stood over a pile of leaves. He widened his eyes, concerned, but kept a relaxed smile on his face. "Are you okay?"

Sol opened and closed her mouth, floundering for a response. "I'm fine." She settled and rubbed her arms. The taste of blood had oddly faded. "Hey, all of the kids are supposed to be in school, right?" She needed to know, just to make sure. They couldn't *all* be homeschooled. That was odd.

"Of course. Where else would they be? I saw the school bus just pick up the last of them this morning. Why?"

Sol had never once seen a school bus enter or exit Maneless Grove.

"Well, why hasn't Veronica been in school?"

Finnian hummed for a moment, eyes glazing over. Sol gritted her teeth, impatient.

"That's the Kennedys' kid, am I right? I believe she's homeschooled." As if to avoid looking at her, Finnian returned to raking. Why did it seem like he was lying to her? More, why did she care about the stupid kids in this stupid neighborhood? Sol moved on before Finnian called back out to her.

"Before you go, I wanted to ask—are you planning on joining the HOA anytime soon? Nadine told me you might be, so I need to know, for tax purposes."

Not this shit again. Sol kept her back to him and rolled her eyes.

"Uh . . . I'll have to get back to you on that. Need to talk it over with the wife first." She tossed a look over her shoulder. "You understand."

Finnian's response came in the form of a nod and a tightened grip on the rake.

"Right, of course," he said. His eyes darkened, but the smile remained as neighborly as ever. "You have a good day, Sol."

"Too late," she muttered.

THE CHISMOSO

Saturday morning Sol was back at the nursing home. The recreation room was empty as usual, and the television was off this time. The nurses stepped around occasionally to check in on them. If they were worried that Sol and her father would end up in another screaming match, they didn't show it. In fact, Sol prepared for this by bringing a container of plátanos maduros. The fried plantains were her father's favorite, and she knew he wouldn't turn them down.

If only he knew not to talk with his mouth full.

"So, what's new with your neighbors?" He smacked his lips and licked his fingers before reaching for another piece.

"Now who's being chismoso?" Sol mumbled.

"Hey, if something happens to my only hija, I need to know who might be involved."

Sol fought the urge to roll her eyes. "Papi, even if something did happen to me, what would you do about it?" He sure as hell wasn't all that helpful when Mami stabbed her. Whatever the kids were doing in the woods, or however her neighbors treated her—that was *her* problem. Not his.

"Hey, I might be left to gather dust in this nursing home, but I still have a lot of strength and life in me." Which he underlined with a coughing fit, sending bits of plantains flying over the table. He wiped his hands over them, but it only succeeded in creating small oil streaks across the table. Sol regretted not bringing napkins.

"Went down the wrong pipe."

"Mhm." Sol slowly went over to the water dispenser and brought back a full cup. Papi eagerly drank it down.

"So nothing going on at home?" He raised an eyebrow.

Sol thought about how she'd answer that—and how the conversation would go. She wouldn't even know where to begin, so she'd probably start with the most recent thing and talk about the kids in the woods, and her neighbor lying to her about all of them going to school. But if she did, he'd ask why she doesn't report them and then she'd have to talk about the situation with the Kennedys, and how *she* nearly got reported for making a 911 call about a false emergency.

Then she'd have to explain how she was now practically being strong-armed into joining the Homeowners Association even though she didn't want to join.

Up until this point, Sol had seen, smelled, heard, and even *felt* odd things that didn't make logical sense. And to make matters worse, she had no way of proving these sensations were real to anyone else. Any therapist she'd see would probably have her institutionalized, her wife would consider her insane, and her job would be gone before she had a chance to prove her innocence.

What could she actually tell Papi that didn't revolve around her fucking things up?

I could talk about Nadine. Sol almost snorted.

If she told him about Nadine and what she'd said about her own child, he'd for sure think that the kid killed himself. Papi would even imply that poor parenting might have been a root cause. The man wouldn't know what mental illness looked like if it was heavily prevalent in his own daughter.

Which, of course, it was.

Not like I'm the poster child for having a great relationship with my mom. She instinctively rubbed her scar. At least seventy percent of her trauma was absolutely due to poor parenting, just not in the way Papi would think.

"Nope," she finally answered.

Papi sucked his teeth. "What about work? Is that going okay?"

Sol clenched her fists. The last thing she wanted was to talk about work. Luckily, he didn't know her work situation or the ongoing investigation. It wouldn't do him any good to know that someone was actively trying to sabotage her career in a major way.

Besides, if he knew she wasn't technically working, he'd wonder why she still only visited on Saturdays instead of every day of the week. She couldn't have that. One day with him was enough.

"Yup. It's all good. Work is . . . fine." Sol thought back to Amir calling out her bluffs. She really needed to learn how to lie better.

Papi stared at her long and hard and she stared back. Sol grabbed the last plantain and chewed it slowly. Her mouth watered as she tasted salt mixed with a comforting sweetness.

With the plate of maduros finished, Sol came to her feet.

"Whoa whoa whoa. Where are you going so soon?"

"I'm visiting someone in the hospital."

"Who? La nena?"

"No, Papi."

"But clearly someone more important than your own father, huh."

A prickling pain started in Sol's palm. She rubbed her hand and grabbed her bag.

"I don't have time for this." Sol slung her bag over her shoulder. "I'll see you next week, Papi. Bendición." She gave him a quick peck on the cheek and power walked to the door. Alice had already been waiting in the car for over thirty minutes.

"Everything okay?" Alice perked up, unlocking the passenger door.

"Peachy. Can we go now?"

Alice took in a deep breath and drove.

"You know, I was thinking . . . why don't I go in with you next time?"

"Hard pass." Sol leaned into the window of the passenger seat.

"You don't think he'd like to actually meet me one day? You know, when he's not blind drunk and in mourning?" Alice asked, referring to the one very brief meeting at the wake.

"We've been over this. I'm pretty sure he doesn't."

"You met my parents!" Alice argued.

"We had the wedding in Korea—it would've been weird if I didn't." Besides, the worst thing her parents were willing to do to her was imply that Sol was too dark. Which . . . well, it wasn't great but it also wasn't a stab wound. Sol kept these thoughts hidden—she didn't need to unpack any of it. Some things were better left in the dark.

At a red light, Alice tapped her fingers against the steering wheel and took a slow breath. "Are you . . . ashamed of me?"

"What?" Sol jumped up. "Where's this coming from?"

"You've never formally introduced me to your parents. Your mom died without ever meeting me."

"And with any luck, my dad will die without ever formally meeting you again too." Sol knew it sounded harsh. Still, she had her reasons—reasons that Alice didn't need to experience firsthand. It was lucky that Mami died before the two got married a few years ago—no unexpected guilt over not inviting her own mother to the wedding.

Alice continued, "I'm starting to wonder if your dad even knows I exist at all."

"Querida, he literally saw you during Mami's wake. Trust me—he knows you exist." Sol gritted her teeth, thinking about how her father still didn't refer to her by name.

"We didn't exchange two words, Sol!" Alice protested. "I could've been anybody to him. How do I know you're not still in the closet with them? We've put your father up in a nice nursing home . . ."

"Something he is *still* complaining about, by the way," Sol interrupted. "Alice, I know how it looks. But believe me, you don't know what they were like. What he's like now. My childhood was not like yours."

Alice scowled. "You think I had it easy? I was practically exiled. My parents found out I was gay, and almost *immediately* sent me out of the country to live with Imo. Had to wait years before they could *deign* to speak to me again."

"That's not—" Sol scoffed. *That's not the same thing,* she wanted to say but bit back the words. It didn't seem like they were going to see eye to eye on this. She turned away from Alice. "Forget it."

"No, go on."

Sol focused on the road ahead. "My point is, I don't want to put you in a position where you'll get hate crimed by my dad. That's the only reason I don't want you to meet him."

Alice was quiet for so long, Sol thought the conversation was over.

"Why do you assume I'll get hate crimed?"

"Because I'm his daughter and it happened to me." Granted, Papi wasn't the one holding the knife but he didn't exactly take her side either. Weeks later, he even kicked her out while she was still healing from the stab wound.

They fell silent. The long drive to the hospital felt even longer. She longed for the time skipping that a glass of wine would bring. Sol leaned into the window and watched as they grew closer to Maneless Grove on the way. From the outside, it looked so innocuous. Just another gated community that had better funding than most public schools. The prickling in her hand intensified and she shook it, hissing in pain.

"What's wrong?" Alice glanced over to her.

"Just having a weird pain in my hand. It's been happening a lot lately."

"A lot?"

Sol sighed, already regretting her words. "It's fine. Probably nothing."

Alice raised an eyebrow, letting Sol know she did not think it was nothing. "Well, it's a good thing we're already on our way to the hospital, huh?"

Sol groaned loudly. "I don't need to see a doctor! I'm fine!" Her only objective was to check in on Corinne. She didn't want to be the one to get checked.

"You say that literally every time something is wrong—last time, you even passed out at your desk."

"That was months ago," Sol pointed out. "And I was resting my eyes."

"With your face planted on the keyboard long enough to type out three straight pages of key smashes?"

Sol didn't respond to that. The morning had been bad enough, the last thing she wanted to do was rehash old arguments with Alice. Sol noticed how Alice gripped the wheel tight and put a little more pressure on the gas.

Christ, if it's not one argument, it's another.

Sol massaged her eyes. "Alice? You wanna take it easy there?"

"Why? It's fine." She emphasized the word with a bite.

"You're going to get us killed."

After a moment of silence, Alice relaxed her foot. She lowered her voice. "I don't get it. Why are you always like this? It's like you don't trust that I want you to be healthy and happy."

Sol deflated. "Querida, you're just about the only person I actually trust." *And I'm always happy when I'm with you.*

Well, maybe not now. Sol was exhausted, and it was barely noon. But that was normal after she visited her father. Seeing a doctor would not fix that. Getting her job back would probably fix that. Or proving to Alice that there was something off about the neighborhood and its people. Sol was losing confidence fast. And when she wasn't confident, she didn't feel good about herself, and when she didn't feel good about herself, it was like the universe was setting out to prove she was right not to.

"I still don't feel like that's healthy. I can't be the only person you trust. You need to make friends, jagi."

"Amir."

"You work with him."

"Name one friend that *you* have that isn't a colleague," Sol said. "And people from college you only talk to on social media don't count." Alice floundered.

"Okay, point taken. We're both busy adults who don't have much of a social life outside of work. But I want that to change, Sol. I want us to make more of an attempt to—to be real people and have a better safety net."

A thought occurred to Sol. "Wait, a safety net? Is this—did your parents say something to you?"

"N-no," Alice answered a little too slowly.

"Oh my God."

Alice turned the car into the hospital parking lot.

"Okay, fine, they did, but they had a point. One day we're going to be very, very old and will need just a little extra help getting around. And it's not like we've had a talk about, you know, having kids or anyone to take care of us."

"Are you saying that moving into Maneless Grove was a retirement plan?"

Alice fell quiet but that was still an answer in itself.

"We are in *our thirties!*" Sol felt the need to point out. "We are not that old to need a *retirement plan.*" It felt ludicrous to even have this be a point of concern for them. Yes, Sol wanted to lay down her roots somewhere, but she didn't mean for them to think about where they would *die.*

And she definitely didn't want to imagine being surrounded by the likes of Nadine and the HOA in their old age.

Sol leaned into her seat, staring out the window toward the hospital. As soon as they found parking, she clicked off her seatbelt and jumped out of the car.

"Sol! Where are you going?"

"I'll meet you inside," she said. She suddenly needed space. A lot of it.

The security guard at the entrance barely spared her a glance as she filled out the visitor's log. He only pointed in the direction of the elevators when she announced where she was planning to go.

"Can you please wait up?" Alice's voice shrieked, earning her more than a few stares from those in the waiting room. Sol turned to look and slowed in her tracks. Alice nearly collided with a man, and he held her arm to keep her from falling.

"Terry! Oh my gosh, what are you doing here?" Alice asked breathlessly.

Great, Terry. Nadine couldn't be far behind. Sol was in no mood for small talk.

From afar, Sol could only read Alice's expression. Her eyes widened and mouth dropped open.

Christ, something serious must have happened. Now Sol was the asshole.

Alice caught Sol's eyes and mouthed a name that made her stomach turn.

Nadine's here.

Ah, shit. Sol's shoulders fell.

The next minute, Alice was at her side, taking her arm and pressing her close. It always felt good to have Alice close. Sol felt an unfamiliar calm descend, rinsing her mind of stress.

Looking around, Sol could see they were now in a completely different part of the hospital. She barely blinked, how did they manage to get all the way here?

"Wha . . . where are we?"

"I told you already, we're going to quickly visit Nadine before Corinne. Weren't you listening?" Alice pouted. She said it so sincerely, Sol worried about the possibility of her blacking out. She shook her head like she had water in her ears.

"Can't we go see Corinne first?" Sol asked. Where had the last few minutes gone? She was always stressed and keeping busy—she knew what it was to lose time being preoccupied by something. This was not the same thing.

The door in front of them was slightly ajar. They were in the emergency department wing, which clicked in with the idea that something happened to Nadine. Sol wasn't sure how she knew that, though.

Alice approached first and knocked.

"Come in!" Nadine chimed. She looked pleasantly surprised, and she rubbed her stomach. "Alice, Sol—what are you two doing here?"

"We heard about what happened and wanted to check in since we were already here for a visit."

"We?" Sol whispered. Alice had *not* filled her in on what happened with Nadine. Or did Sol actually black out while Alice was talking? Maybe she was right—maybe Sol did need to get a checkup. Behind them, Terry sidestepped and came forward with a bottle of water.

"Oh, Terry, you told them about the fall?" Nadine's mouth fell open. She looked mildly inconvenienced, but Sol wasn't buying it. "It was nothing, really. Just tripped over my feet and smacked into the kitchen counter. I yelled so loud, Terry jumped up immediately and called an ambulance."

The four fell quiet and while Terry and Nadine looked at each other, cooing softly toward each other, Alice's eyes were burning a hole in Sol's temple.

Say something, her eyes said. Sol swallowed before she did.

"You're okay now, right?"

"One hundred percent!" Nadine beamed. "Just had to get an X-ray for my head and a sonogram to make sure this little one was okay. She's fine."

Again, Sol and Alice were genuinely speechless and had nothing else to ask.

A knock came from behind them and a nurse awkwardly shuffled in. His eyes jumped from Sol to Alice to Nadine and he held up a stack of papers.

"Your discharge papers," he explained before handing it to Nadine.

"Looks like I'm already on my way out. Come on, why don't we all get some lunch? I'm starving!"

Sol had a thought.

"Actually, I came to see Corinne. Alice is hungry, though, so why don't you two head to the cafeteria and grab a bite?" She didn't want to leave her wife alone with the weird pregnant woman, but Alice and Nadine were friends, no matter what Sol thought of the other woman, and she didn't think there was much to fear . . .

Other than Nadine telling Alice about the Kennedys.

That was a risk she was willing to take if she could get a chance to finally talk to Corinne. The old woman was her only witness to the strange happenings in her home. All she needed was for someone to confirm her suspicions, then she would . . . well, she hadn't thought that far. But validation was needed so Sol didn't feel like she was really going insane.

Alice blinked in surprise. She hadn't said a word about being hungry, but even if it was true, it would be odd for Sol to offer up her company so easily. Sol met her eyes and tried hard to communicate that what she needed was Alice to keep Nadine busy and away from Corinne. If she was as easy to read as Alice claimed her to be, the message would be clear.

"Are you sure?" Alice asked, brow furrowing in confusion. Sol nodded and glanced at Nadine. The woman maintained a perfectly polite smile. Sol didn't trust that.

She turned back to her wife and said, "Of course. I won't be long, I promise."

Before either could say another word, Sol stalked to the nearest elevator, eager to find out why Corinne was so afraid of Nadine.

Except when she got there, Corinne's bed was empty. Her name had even been taken off the door. Sol hunted down the nearest nurse to ask, "Excuse me, where is the elderly woman in room 211?"

The nurse took one look at her and then toward the door. "That patient? I believe she was discharged a few hours ago. Why? Are you her daughter?"

Sol didn't answer that. Corinne said that the doctors didn't feel comfortable discharging her until they could get her an aide—did they find one for her that quickly? Or did someone from the community pick her up like Corinne said they would?

She seemed really afraid of Nadine, though . . . And coincidentally, Nadine was here again, when Sol wanted to see Corinne. As mildly suspicious as this felt to her, it could also (very easily) be a coincidence. Sol took deep breaths. Corinne was now probably back home. That was fine, Sol lived right next door. She would just pop over and resume their conversation.

Sol shuffled back to the elevators and down to the ground floor. Finding the hospital cafeteria took just a few minutes (and a request to security personnel), but once she was there, she scanned the room quickly. There were a few doctors chatting, carrying trays of lo mein while workers set out hot plates of food on the "Grab 'N' Go" counter. A small family of three aimlessly trying to get a fussy child to eat a spoonful of rice.

But no Alice. And definitely no Nadine.

Sol immediately pulled out her phone and called Alice.

"Hi, you've reached the number of Alice Song . . ." Voicemail. She called again just to get the same result. That was odd. Sol quickly walked to the parking lot and was met with an empty space where their car should have been.

Did she just fucking ditch me? Sol stared in shock. No, that couldn't be it. Alice would *never* leave her stranded. She would never leave without telling Sol first. It was basic decency as a spouse.

Except there was the empty parking space to prove it. And as Sol's eyes quickly swept the parking lot, she couldn't find their car at all.

The anger turned to panic.

What if Nadine told her about what happened at the Kennedys'? Just because she said she would keep it between them didn't mean she meant it. In fact, she pretty much implied that she would only do so if Sol and Alice joined the Homeowners Association, and that had yet to happen.

Sol's stomach twisted. How long did she think she could get away with Alice not knowing? Nadine was Alice's best friend, after all. It would have to come up at some point.

And if Alice didn't already know now, Sol would have to be the one to break it to her ASAP, if only to kill the guilt and panic that built up every time Alice and Nadine got together. Hell, Sol would tell Alice *now*, if she would only pick up her damn phone.

Sol forced herself to take in deep breaths.

It wasn't *ideal* that she couldn't reach her wife, but as Sol gripped her cell phone tight and stared at the pavement, she knew there was only one thing she could do—go home and wait.

She pulled up a rideshare app and ordered a car.

It was difficult for Sol to sit still. For two hours, she paced across the living room, peeked out the windows for signs of Alice, and even stood outside the door, as if that would summon her home. Twice, Sol went over to Corinne's house and knocked. No one opened.

Strange. Where could an old lady with a broken hip possibly go?

Sol retreated to her kitchen and stared at the marble gift. Like the tree in the yard, she could feel it staring back.

Don't be stupid. Sol turned away from it. *Breaking that thing isn't going to bring Alice home sooner.*

Sol went back in the living room, but the image of the gift remained with her.

What is it about that thing?

She had no answer, but she could practically hear *something* telling her to break it and find out.

It was all she could do to not down a bottle of vodka.

I still have that Everclear. It was just one trip down to the basement. Sol was tempted to take a few calming sips but if, on the off chance, Alice was already upset after finding out what happened with the Kennedys . . .

Sol didn't want to think about what a nightmare scenario it would be if Alice came home to find her drunk. So she waited.

When Alice finally returned, she looked worn down. Shuffling into the house with her shoulders curled inward, Alice barely got through a yawn before being attacked by a question.

"Alice, what happened? Where did you go? I kept calling you, but your phone went straight to voicemail."

"I'm sorry, Sol. I didn't mean to worry you." Alice leaned into her for a hug. Her arms were weak as they wrapped around her, and her foot fell heavily on Sol's. Alice forgot to take her shoes off at the door. "My phone just died as soon as we left the hospital, and I swear I didn't remember your number. We were just at Nadine's place, since her husband made dinner."

Relief hit Sol immediately. If Alice knew anything about the Kennedys, she wouldn't have spoken to her, much less hugged her. She'd yell at her, maybe curse her out a few times, but she wouldn't be as calm as she was now.

Her phone died. Sure, that was possible—except Alice was never known for ignoring the charge on her cell phone. She always made sure it was at least at seventy percent and on just in case there was an issue at work. It wasn't like her to let the charge get so low.

Her relief flipped back to anger.

"But why did you leave?" She needed to know. "I said I was going to be right back and you just . . . left?" What possible reason was there for *that*?

"What are you talking about? I waited at least twenty minutes. I assumed you were going to be longer so I texted saying we were heading out. You said it was fine."

Sol pulled back. It also wasn't like Alice to just blatantly lie like this. "You just said your phone died. So did you text or did it die?"

"*Obviously* it died after I texted." Alice hiccuped, scowling at Sol. "What's with this interrogation?"

"I barely took five minutes." Sol pulled out her phone and went into her texts, turning it around to show Alice. "I came straight down to the cafeteria and didn't see you anywhere. So *obviously*, you never waited *or* texted. See? No text from you."

Alice stared at the phone with distaste. "You probably just deleted it by accident." She rubbed her face sluggishly and Sol noticed she spoke with a slur.

"Are you drunk?"

"Maybe a little."

Sol watched Alice stumble across the room. It was like watching a puppet made of spaghetti attempt to mimic a person. It wasn't just odd, it was completely out of character for Alice to drink so much. Worried that her wife would trip and hurt herself, Sol put aside her anger and helped Alice walk straight. They would have to talk about this in the morning, when Alice sobered up.

"How did you get home like this? Didn't you drive? Or did Terry bring you?"

"Left the car at Nadine's. Terry and I were too drunk. Gonna pick it up in the morning." She yawned. So Alice walked the entire way from Nadine's house? How did she manage it in this state? Sol was completely sober when she tried to make the trek and ended up in the woods with a bunch of kids eating tree bark.

Sol's nose tickled. Alice must've been covered in pollen.

"You hardly ever drink like this," Sol muttered, still trying to keep her anger in check. *Because if this were me, I'd be in the doghouse for days.* But the drinking rules must've been different for the both of them.

Alice rolled her eyes. "Just because you like to drink when you're upset doesn't mean the rest of us do."

"*Wow!* Okay!" Sol let go of Alice just as they got to the stairs. "So this is what we're doing now? We'll just lie and be dickheads to each other tonight, is that it?"

Her wife could use the banister for support and crawl the rest of the way to the bedroom, for all she cared.

"Don't be so dramatic," Alice said, then grumbled something under her breath as she climbed. It almost sounded like *Nadine said you'd be like this.* Sol's eyes snapped wide open, irritation practically being stoked into rage.

Before Sol could ask Alice to repeat herself, she watched her wife stop in her tracks at the top. Alice stood up straight, eyes widening at something down the hall with mild confusion.

"Sol, did you open the window?"

Sol took a moment to stare down at the steps as if to say, *I dare you to disappear on me,* before quickly ascending them. Right where the hall ended, a window that was always closed, always locked, was completely open. Sol's mouth hung open as she thought back to the last time she had opened *any* window in the house. The only two she ever bothered with were the kitchen window above the sink and the window in their bedroom, where they'd installed the air conditioner.

That one was always shut—until now.

"Well, whatever, just remember to close it before you go to bed," Alice said, shuffling to the bedroom. "Don't wanna let any bugs get in the house."

Sol slowly went to the window and hesitated to shut it. In any other circumstance, she would assume there was an intruder. Yet when it came to all that she had experienced, it was more like the house had a mind of its own—and an attitude. At any moment, Sol would find another thing to be wary of, another impossible circumstance. It wasn't enough that she couldn't understand Nadine and Corinne's relationship, there was this underlying fear that Sol could not trust her home.

She went back to the coffee table and picked up her water bottle. Sol drank down about half of it when her cell phone buzzed.

It was Laura.

Hey Sol! Glad to hear you're loving the house. My husband did his best to restore it after the fire. You're welcome to come over on Monday to chat more about it!

Then Laura sent her address. Sol blinked, having many more questions than she wanted answers to. When Corinne briefly mentioned a fire, that had been the first time Sol had heard about it. Granted, she wasn't too invested in even looking at the house, much less knowing its history, but Sol wondered if Alice had known about a previous fire.

What if she didn't? Would Sol tell her? She rubbed her eyes, the indignation at being lied to—and lied to *badly*—still simmering in her mind. Why would Alice lie to her about waiting *and* texting? And worse yet, why would Alice accuse her of deleting the text?

Whatever the reason, Sol would find out. Unlike with Corinne, Sol had the advantage of living in the same home as Alice. She would wake up early and demand truthful answers out of her wife.

And she knew exactly how she'd do it.

THE EVIL PLACE

*P*assing out on the couch is starting to be a bad habit of mine, Sol thought at the sound of her phone alarm. She groggily rolled over and felt around for her phone on the table several times before she found and silenced it. She lay there for a moment longer. Thinking about it now, it was a good thing she *did* pass out on the couch, considering how loud the phone was. Alice would be annoyed by the jarring sound—especially hungover.

Alice.

Sol sat up, memories of last night coming back to her. It was rare for Alice to get drunk. And completely out of character for her to lie about not ditching her at the hospital. The one thing Alice never did was lie—at least not to Sol. She could lie to her coworkers, to her parents, even to her aunt Julie—but never to Sol.

It was like Alice was suddenly a different person.

Sol rubbed her face. Alice was probably still deep in drunken sleep upstairs. She thought about going up to check on her—then thought of something even better.

When they were in college, Sol would leave her painkillers and water because it was all they had near them, but now with a well-stocked kitchen, she could go a step further and make Alice haejangguk—hangover soup. It helped to ease the usual nausea and headaches that hangovers brought. Having made it so many times, Sol even had the recipe memorized.

Would self-righteousness make it taste better? She knew how guilty she felt after Alice made her a full Dominican breakfast, but if Sol was going to make a lot of it, she might as well have some too.

She tiptoed into the kitchen and did her best to get all the ingredients in order on the counter without making too much noise. Though the recipe made for a savory meal, the end result was still a very hydrating soup that would help Alice feel better the moment she ate it.

Garlic, doenjang, Korean red pepper flakes, mirin, fish sauce, sesame oil—all these were going to be mixed together into a sauce. The main soup was made of napa cabbage leaves, green onions, shiitake mushrooms, and soybean sprouts. There was the option of including ox bones, but that added another four hours of work and Sol did not get up *that* early, so premade ox bone soup concentrate would have to suffice as a substitute.

For a side dish—because Alice would jokingly complain about not having banchan for someone who could survive *solely* on banchan—she opted to make gochujang cucumber salad. Sol noticed that Alice hadn't gotten around to doing it since they moved in. That was fine, Sol could take care of that for her. It would be another way to show Alice how *thoughtful* she was being, despite Alice acting completely out of pocket the night before.

Unfortunately, there were only two cucumbers in the fridge. Not a lot, but Alice could make it last a day or two—long enough for Sol to go grocery shopping. She put back the large container she was planning on using and instead put a much smaller Tupperware on the kitchen counter.

As she finished preparing the banchan and storing it in the fridge to marinate a little longer, she suddenly heard the front door slamming shut. She ran to the front door to see Alice walking in with two Trader Joe's bags.

"I'm home!" she yelled.

Sol's mouth hung open as she eyed the bags.

"I . . . I didn't know you left." She crossed her arms, a little miffed and kicking herself. Had she slept upstairs with her wife, she would have noticed the empty house before she put in all that work for hangover soup.

"You went to Trader Joe's?" Sol made a face at the bags. "What happened to 'I will never shop there'?"

"Got up really early to get the car—you were passed out on the couch and I didn't want to wake you. Then when I got to Nadine's, I realized we needed to go grocery shopping anyway so I went to Trader Joe's because it was close by," Alice explained. "The Asian market is too far and I didn't feel like making the trip. Now shut up and help me, these bags are heavy."

She handed one off to Sol. There was an assortment of jars clacking around in it and Sol peeked in to see a number of spices with quirky branding as she followed Alice back to the kitchen. Alice stared at the mess on the counter and glanced back at Sol.

"What's all this?"

"I thought you were hungover so I made you haejangguk and that cucumber salad you like." Sol frowned. "By the way, did you get more cucumbers?"

Alice cursed. "Shit, I knew I forgot something. How many do we have left?"

"None now. And we're out of gochujang."

"Not anymore, we're not!" Alice grinned, pulling out the small Trader Joe's brand. "But thanks anyway. I'll probably have some after we put this away."

Sol watched Alice move about enthusiastically for someone who could barely walk straight after last night.

"Are you sure you're okay? I thought you drank a lot."

"I did—but remember those pills Nadine gave me? Those worked a wonder. I barely feel anything at all—it's like I'm nineteen again."

As Sol handed Alice small jars, she thought carefully on how to broach the subject.

"Hey, we need to talk."

Alice paused to look at her, a wry smile on her lips. "About what?"

"About last night?" Sol raised an eyebrow. She was not getting out of this that easily. "When you lied about leaving me at the hospital and sending a text?"

Her wife frowned. "That wasn't a lie. I really did send you a text."

Ah, so she was going to double down on it. Fine. Sol crossed her arms, defiantly.

"Then show me the text on your phone."

Alice straightened her back. The frown had quickly morphed into a scowl, and she dug into her pocket for her phone. After a few seconds of tapping the screen, Sol could see it—not the text. But the doubt in Alice's eyes. She furrowed her brow and her mouth dropped open.

"It should be here. I remember sending it," she muttered, now scrolling and tapping more violently.

"Is it possible you just *accidentally* deleted it?" Sol threw the accusation in her face. But the more Alice searched her phone, concern and confusion deepening on her face, the more it was clear she was not lying. Or at least, she didn't *think* she was.

Is it happening to her now? Strangely enough, hope ballooned in Sol's chest. Finally, she wasn't the only person being affected by something odd.

It isn't a disappearing stair, but fuck it, I'll take it.

"Ugh, whatever!" Alice slammed the phone down on the counter. "Fine, I'm sorry I left you at the hospital without making sure you were fine with it. Are you happy now?"

Not yet. Sol picked up Alice's phone and gestured to it.

"Has stuff like this been happening to you lately?" she asked, ignoring her wife's apology. "Like you thought you saw something but it's not there anymore? Or you heard someone say something while you were completely alone?"

"What?" Alice's eyes widened. Then she pressed her hands against Sol's mouth. "Stop talking about that! I don't want to hear about things like that, you'll just attract it."

Sol pushed her hands away. "Whatever's happening is already attracted to us! Don't you want to know why this is happening? Figure out how to get it to stop?"

"There's nothing to figure out!" Alice shouted. "I sent a text, but my phone glitched and deleted it. That's it, end of story." She went back to unloading the bags, ignoring Sol's stare.

"Fine." Sol threw her hands up. "If ignoring things is your way of dealing with them, then whatever. Do what you want."

But that didn't mean Sol was going to follow her lead. Instead, she turned around and started cleaning up the mess she made trying to make haejangguk.

What a waste, she thought as she poured the food into a Tupperware container. Sol was planning on having some herself for breakfast, but her appetite was now ruined.

"Good." Alice stopped for a moment. "Huh. I don't remember getting this." She pulled out a container of quinoa.

Sol tossed a look over her shoulder. Pettiness told her to ignore Alice the way her own concerns were being ignored. But she was *married*. Civility was owed even during times of strife.

Sighing, Sol asked, "Did you pay for it?"

"Give me a second," Alice murmured, fishing for the receipt and taking a careful look. She sucked her teeth in disapproval. "Goddammit. I think someone accidentally put their stuff in my basket."

"What a tragedy." Sol rolled her eyes. Civility turned to pettiness really fast.

If Alice noticed, she didn't make it known. She turned the container over in her hand. "How does anyone even eat quinoa? Are you supposed to just swallow it by the spoonful or cook it first . . . ?"

Sol shrugged. "I don't know, I'm not white."

"I'm pretty sure white people aren't the only ones who eat quinoa," Alice said. Sol finished loading the dishwasher before facing Alice.

"Probably not. But I bet if you asked any of the white people here how to eat quinoa, they would know. I'd put money on it."

Alice snorted. "Would you, now? How much?"

"Mm." Sol pretended to think for a moment. "Ten bucks."

Alice gave Sol a long look. "Make it twenty." She brought out her cell phone.

"Who are you calling?" Curiosity piqued, Sol leaned over her wife's shoulder.

"Who else?" Alice asked. "Nadine."

"Of course." Sol nodded. "The woman you ditched me for."

"I did not ditch you!" Alice argued. "It's just—oh, it's ringing. Hold on."

If there was any justice in the world, Nadine would not pick up. Sol prayed fervently that the passive-aggressive pregnant woman would do literally anything else other than pick up her cell phone.

Hey, God, I know we haven't spoken since literally Catholic school but if you could just do me a favor this one time—

Unfortunately, after a few short rings, Sol heard Nadine's voice pick up.

"Hey, Nadine, really sorry to bother you but I was wondering if you had any good recipes for quinoa." Alice took in a sharp breath. Sol winced. Nadine's voice was too muffled for her to understand but she could only imagine what the busybody was telling Alice right now. *Hey, just wanted to know if you were going to join the HOA. Sol said she would talk to you about it, you know, after she nearly caused a problem at the Kennedys'. Oh, you didn't hear about that? Let me tell you in excruciating detail.*

Sol felt her blood draining from her face. Alice slowly reached into her back pocket. She fished out her wallet and removed two ten-dollar bills and mouthed the words *fuck you* to Sol. Relieved, Sol sighed and pocketed the money.

"That . . . sounds great. Thanks." Alice stopped herself from hanging up. "Oh? Yeah. I'll ask." She muffled the phone with one hand and turned to Sol. "Nadine's got reservations for a group spa day. Apparently she won them in a contest? Do you want to go? It would be you, me, Nadine, and Bethany."

Sol's stomach turned inside out. Her first instinct was to blurt out, *Who the hell is Bethany?* but she bit back the response.

After a moment of contemplation, Sol nodded curtly.

Alice's mouth dropped open and she stared at Sol as if to ask, *Are you sure?*

Just about every time she tried to get answers or investigate, she would turn around and there was Nadine, getting in the way. It happened with Corinne, and she wasn't sure how but Sol was certain it happened with the Kennedys. She wanted to turn down this invite— maybe if she did, she would have more breathing room to figure things out . . .

. . . except Alice still didn't know what happened at the Kennedys'. So obviously she couldn't leave her alone with Nadine.

"Yes," Sol repeated out loud. She didn't like it, but it was necessary.

"We're in!" Alice said into the phone, excitedly. Her smile widened, brightening the room. The look of it made Sol feel . . . okay about her decision. After all, even if she didn't care for the spa, at the very least, it made her wife happy to see her socializing for a little while. That was always a plus.

"This Saturday? Okay, sure! See you then." Alice hung up. "We'll meet in front of her place at ten a.m. this weekend. Is that okay?"

Sol's face dropped. "Ten in the morning? That's usually when I go see my dad." And she had already missed one Saturday with him. There was no telling how he would react if she missed two.

Alice pouted. "Can't you just go see him on Sunday? Or literally any other day?"

"I mean, sure, but then he'll keep expecting me and that's . . ." It sounded like a bad excuse. It *was* a bad excuse. There was no reason why Sol couldn't just visit any other day. Sol opened her mouth to agree when Alice stepped on a verbal mine.

"Besides, it's not like you have anything else going on."

"What does that mean?"

Alice gave her a funny look. "It means what it means, Sol. You're literally home all the time. You're not working. You go to therapy and that's about it. You can make time for your dad whenever."

Sol balled up her fists. Alice wasn't wrong, though, and Sol knew it. She really wasn't doing anything else. Just planning to talk to the previous homeowners. Eventually build her garden. Her schedule was pretty open.

But she didn't have to say it like that.

It's like a switch just flips, she thought. One minute Alice was her usual, charismatic self. The next, she said shit that stung and pretended like Sol was being overly sensitive.

"Right. Okay." Sol shuffled out of the kitchen, feeling off about the interaction. Alice was usually more sensitive about her break from work, calling it a time of recovery. She never implied it was just Sol "doing nothing," even if Sol felt like it was.

Which is why it hurts so much now.

When Sol finally drove up to Laura's home, she was surprised. Having been surrounded by homes that were all identical for the last two weeks, she had forgotten that houses outside of her community were allowed to be a little eccentric. In the windows of the top floor were Christmas decorations that screamed, "We just never got around to taking these down." The front lawn boasted a vegetable garden that stretched around the right side and continued to the back. Radish leaves grew straight up, ready for harvesting, and a range of herbs looked to be just starting out.

Sol slowly got out of her car and walked to the front door in a fascinated daze. Laura had given her a range of time to visit, and Sol was firmly within that range. Not too late, not too early. She knocked a few times, waited until she thought she heard the shout of a woman coming to the door.

"Hello?" Laura furrowed her brow. Sol froze, quickly realizing just how disheveled she looked compared to this stay-at-home mom. Sol's Facebook profile photo was several years old at this point, with her hair in crochet braids from a summer vacation in the Dominican Republic. She wouldn't blame Laura if she didn't recognize her right away or even slammed the door in her face.

"Sol?"

Sol breathed. "Yes, actually."

"Oh my goodness, well, come on in!" Laura said giddily. "I was always wondering how that place was doing."

Sol followed Laura to the living room and sat on the edge of the couch. A small child collided with her as she went and she yelped in surprise.

"Randy, what are you doing up, honey?" Laura crouched down to the boy and glanced between him and Sol, a strange look on her face that Sol couldn't understand.

"I had a nightmare." The boy stared at Sol through his curls, snot running down his face.

"Mommy has a guest now, okay? Come on, I'll tuck you back in." She picked him up and quickly took a few steps back from Sol. The forced friendly smile on her face only made the action more alarming.

She's nervous.

"I'll be right back."

"Take your time," Sol answered.

With his head leaning on his mother's shoulders, Randy maintained eye contact with Sol until they climbed the staircase. While they were gone, Sol took a moment to take a lap around the living room. It was certainly much more lived in than Sol's home was currently. There was a stack of pristine coloring books scattered around the television stand, an unplugged iron right beside it. The coffee table had a glass center and was decorated with fake flowers in a small pot.

The walls were painted a light green, a fun contrast to the yellow frames that hung on the walls displaying a number of family vacation photos. One of them was on a ski lift and Sol wondered what it was about white people that they liked to show off where they've vacationed. A photo album was one thing, but the walls of the house seemed more of a brag.

"Sorry about that."

Sol quickly turned, mildly startled. Laura didn't seem to notice.

"That's my son Randy, he suddenly got sick this morning so he's staying in. Would you like some water? I'll get you some water." Laura exited to the kitchen and came back with two glasses. She forced another smile, and Sol kept the glass between her hands. She refused to drink anything from a woman who was acting this weird.

"Is everything okay?" she asked tentatively. "You seem a little skittish."

Maybe it was her own smile that was making Laura nervous. Sol's resting bitch face had a side effect of making smiles look sarcastic. She tried to tone it down without looking too serious.

"Me? No, everything's fine." Laura took a short sip. As if the cool water helped calm her some, Laura finally settled into a nonchalance that Sol was envious of. "So how's the house? My husband did his very best to match its design to the others in the neighborhood as requested. Though, if I were to be honest, he didn't do very much."

Sol decided not to press her on her current state. No, she came to talk about the house so that was what she was going to do.

"What do you mean?"

"Well, the house you live in had experienced a bit of a fire. It was mostly the upstairs that was damaged, but we were told that it had spread to some parts downstairs and might need to be looked at."

Sol's friendly smile was cracking. "I didn't notice anything off."

"That's just the thing! You know, we saw pictures of the wreckage and the community there asked if we were sure about taking on the work. But by the time we got there, it didn't seem anywhere near as bad." Laura pursed her lips. "It was so weird—like the house just started healing on its own." A nervous laugh. "Sounds crazy, doesn't it?"

Sol wished it did. At least Laura seemed to be loosening up. Sol was glad—it would make things easier if only one of them was anxious, and Sol had staked her claim on that long before she drove over.

"That sounds like a good thing," Sol offered, trying to sound casual. "Less work, and at least you didn't have to worry about Randy getting into the electrical wiring or something."

Laura's demeanor changed. Her grip on her glass tightened and she broke eye contact with Sol to stare at her glass. "Mhm."

Okay, now Sol was getting tired of being treated like a threat.

"Is . . . is this a bad time?"

Laura looked at Sol again—*really* looked at her, like she was searching her eyes for something. Whatever she found made her drop her shoulders. Sol hadn't even noticed how tense they were.

"Sorry, I thought you might have . . . but there's no way you would have, because you only moved in after us." She let out an embarrassed chuckle.

"What are you talking about?" Sol was fully confused. Laura leaned onto the edge of the seat and looked at Sol.

"I'm not a superstitious person. I'm not a religious person, and neither is my husband. So when we heard about the suicide, you know..."

Laura stopped. "Oh. You didn't ... know about that?"

The idea of something like that happening in Sol's home made her jaw go slack.

"I'm sorry, a *suicide*? I thought it was a fire. You said it was a fire."

"Right but the fire was caused by ..." Laura trailed off again.

Sol's eyes widened. "Wow," she whispered to herself. "No one has told me about this. So the previous homeowner killed themself?"

Laura's face twitched as if deciding how much to tell Sol. "Not a previous homeowner. Another resident. A teen, maybe a young man, I think? I don't remember the details except that ... someone else from the neighborhood broke in and just set flame to the whole thing."

Sol blinked. She couldn't wrap her mind around it. Normally, when people decided to ... take their own lives, it was in the comfort of their own home. To break into another place to do it was beyond odd.

Maybe they didn't want their body to be found? If so, then a fire was the worst way to *not* draw attention to themselves.

"That's ..." Sol had trouble finding an appropriate word "... tragic." She settled on that.

Laura's face bloomed with sympathy, as if Sol was the one who knew the resident personally. "I'm so sorry. This must be a shock to you."

"Right. A shock." She cleared her throat and reached for her water. She was definitely feeling parched now. "I'm sorry, you said it was a teen?" She thought of the odd kids in the woods, eating tree bark like it was a snack. Veronica wasn't a teen but her parents were ... not around. And now there was this past suicide in her own house? Something was very, very strange in Maneless Grove and it seemed like only the kids were showing symptoms.

"I think so, a little on the older side," Laura answered.

How many people knew about this? Corinne knew there was a fire, but she didn't mention a *suicide* on top of that. As omniscient as Nadine seemed to be, she had to have known too. Did no one think to run this information by her?

Does Alice know?

No, she couldn't have known. There was no way Alice would just hold that information from Sol. She could lie to her about the hospital business and the text, but she wouldn't stoop *this* low.

A fire is one thing. A suicide is another.

The burned creature from Sol's night terror flashed in the back of her mind. She swallowed the bile rushing up her throat.

Laura interrupted Sol's thoughts. "Are you okay? You look a little sick."

"Yeah, I'm fine." She wasn't fine but Sol would have to process this later. As if trying to fill the awkward silence, Laura continued.

"I'm sure you noticed how quiet my Randy is. The truth is, he wasn't always like that. He used to be very loud and creative. You couldn't stop him from drawing on the walls . . . but now I can't even get him to use his coloring books."

Sol glanced to the books she saw before and noticed again they were in perfect condition.

"I don't know what happened, honestly. At first, my kids just stayed at my parents' house and visited during the weekend to see how progress was with the new house. But when we realized there wasn't much damage to the structure, we brought the kids to stay with us. And that's when the trouble started."

"Trouble?" Sol perked up.

"Yeah, Jules—that's my daughter—started having nightmares and Randy wouldn't stop digging around in the backyard."

Sol curled her hands. She could feel dirt underneath her fingernails.

"He just insisted that there was something he had to dig up." Laura paused to take another sip of water. "And I think that just made the community angry because I mean, here we were just trying to fix up the house and my son's over there tearing up the yard! Wait, I think I have a photo on my phone, I'll show you."

It took a few seconds of scrolling through but when Laura turned her phone to Sol, she hardly recognized the boy in the photo. He was paler, with soulless eyes that swallowed everything. Just like the other kids in the community.

The boy she had met, though still creepy, was less watered down—as if he were recovering from an illness but wasn't fully back to health.

In the photo, Randy was crouching with dirt up to his elbows beside a tree.

"I couldn't make heads or tails of it and my husband thought I was going crazy saying that there was something wrong with our son."

"Is that why you left?"

"No, not at first. We left because—well, you've seen my house here. You think I could get away with any of this back at that community?" She gave a self-deprecating laugh. "Some of the HOA members were so upset at Randy's obsession with dirt, I knew they would never dare let me have a garden!"

"But it was the backyard? How did they even see it? Why would they care?"

"You know, I'm not quite sure. But one day, a couple of them had come over and noted the agreement and its rules on gardens and whatnot and that was that."

That was that. As if a child should be subject to an HOA agreement.

"Lovely people, otherwise, though," Laura went on. "Very neighborly."

Sol cringed and, needing a break, she asked, "Could I use your bathroom?"

"Of course! It's upstairs, second door on the right."

Sol couldn't escape fast enough. The brief recess let her catch her breath and rethink what the family experienced. Laura didn't know much—that was obvious. And while Randy might have been a better source of information, he was sick and needed rest more than she needed answers. Squashing any disappointment she had, she ran cool water over her face and dried her hands.

Sol jumped when she pulled the bathroom door open. Randy stood there, still and silent as a statue.

"Sorry, did you need to use the bathroom?" she asked.

Randy didn't answer at first. He just stared at her with large, emotionless eyes.

"You're in that house?" he said in a whisper. "Did you find the thing in the backyard?"

"What thing?"

He looked down. "There's something stuck under the tree. It's in the roots."

They're in the roots.

Sol's blood ran cold. She didn't want to know what "it" was. She'd rather leave it dead and buried. And yet, this might be her only chance. Still, Sol hesitated to ask what she needed.

"Randy, have you . . . ever seen something move or—or disappear on its own at that house?"

Randy gave a thoughtful look before nodding, and Sol's stomach became a pit.

"Hey!" Laura shouted, running up the stairs. "What did I say about you being out of bed?"

She slipped in between Randy and Sol, eyes seized by fear again. Sol took a few precautionary steps back, which seemed to help Laura relax.

"Go back to bed, okay?" She kissed his temple and watched him go back to his room.

Then she stood up. "Sorry, I promise it's not you. It's just . . . I've seen how the other kids acted in that community and it only struck me as odd when Randy became the same way. I thought you might've known something about that."

"I wish," Sol muttered. She was still doing her own half-baked investigation, and nosy neighbors were still getting in the way.

"Is there anything else I can help you with?" Laura asked, still dancing on her feet. Sol's nerves rattled. If one more white woman treated her like *she* was the threat . . .

"No, but thank you," she said. "I need to head home."

"Sure. It was nice to meet you."

Sol didn't believe it was.

As soon as she got to the door, she quickened her pace to the car and pulled out to the road.

The first thing she thought was, *I don't want to look for it.* Whatever had driven Randy to the dirt of the backyard, whatever she was digging up in the sleepwalking episode she had a few days ago—she did *not* want to unearth it. Just the thought of it felt a little like opening Pandora's box, knowing that there was possibly something deeply disturbing hidden away in a place that was so easily accessible. In her backyard, of all places.

There might not even be *anything,* Sol reasoned. Randy could have lied. Or could be confused. It could have been a startling coincidence at worst, a prank at best.

But she didn't quite believe that. And so, just in case, Sol stopped at the nearest Home Depot. She quickly walked to the gardening aisle and picked out the first trowel and gardening gloves she saw.

After parking the car in the driveway, she went straight to the backyard and right up to the tree. The longer she stared, the more the veiny exterior unnerved Sol. She never saw any other tree like this in the neighborhood. It was a completely different species, practically a scar to the uniformity of the trees that lined the streets.

You could say the same thing about me and Alice, she thought. Then, *Papi would probably know what this is.*

She started experiencing terrifying visions right after she touched the damn thing. Randy was probably the same way. Sol took out her phone and quickly took a picture. If she couldn't figure it out, she'd show him during her next visit. Hopefully, he would just be her last resort.

Sol knelt down and examined the disturbed dirt as she donned the gloves. It was dark black, almost wet, from where she had dug the last time. And yet, it also seemed as if the hole was already patching itself up, like a wound closing.

Forcing the pointed end of the trowel into the ground, she dug underneath a raised root. When nothing fantastical happened, it was both a relief and disappointment. She didn't quite *think* she'd hear a scream, but it wasn't out of the realm of possibility either. Sol kept digging.

It felt like a year passed before the trowel scraped against something solid.

Sol had to get on her stomach and shine her cell phone light to get a good look. Something moved in the dirt. A long, fleshy appendage broke into the light and Sol jolted up and backward, expecting a hand to come rushing through. She gripped the trowel with both hands, ready to strike at a moment's notice.

When a hand didn't emerge, Sol cautiously crouched down again. No, it wasn't a hand or even a finger—it was just a worm. *Get a grip, city girl*, she mocked herself, then used the trowel to push it aside. It wiggled fervently in protest but once it was completely out of the way, she plunged both of her hands into the soil, feeling around the solid structure that stopped her trowel. It was cold and unnerving, definitely not a rock or a root or something that might naturally belong there, but she continued until she finally pulled out a small and sleek wooden box.

The box was dark brown and glossy. There were no markings on it, nothing to point to a previous owner.

Sol's heart was loud in her ears. *It's just a box. A box I was compelled to dig for. A box little Randy was obsessed with. Just a box that is in no way evil or demonic or buried under this tree to hide something sinister . . .*

She thought all this even as she undid the rusted latch and slowly opened it.

Confusion replaced her fear in seconds. Sol wasn't sure what she thought she'd find. She *hoped* it would be nothing at all, but there was definitely something in there. It took her a moment to discern what, but she eventually concluded it looked like a stack of diary entries. Yellowed pages with dirt-stained edges stared back at her and as she reached inside to pull out the first one, she squinted at the blurred words.

That's when time stopped—the moment they became clear:

If you're reading this, LEAVE—this is an EVIL place.

PART II

MARCH 20

I thought I was going insane. The sharing, the forgetting, the need to be part of something—I knew it wasn't normal but I needed it to work. I needed to be normal. But it doesn't stop where you think it will. Eventually, it takes everything from you, chooses what you can keep and what you have to forget.

I don't know how it does it. I don't know how it works. I've been trying to type up my observations but every time I do, it gets deleted. Only handwritten stuff stays so I can only write what I see.

And what I see is that something about this place changes people. I don't know why it hasn't worked on me yet—or maybe it already has. Maybe I've already forgotten. I don't know what to do. I don't know where to go. We all moved here because it was supposed to be good for us. It was supposed to be a great place to raise a family—at least that's what they told us.

I didn't know that this is what they would do once we moved in.

If I had known, I wouldn't have come.

THE VOICEMAIL

Sol jumped at the sound of the front door opening. She had been staring at the pages for so long that her eyes felt strained, and she quickly rubbed them before hiding the pages underneath her laptop. The box they came in was already hidden away in the basement. Sol had a feeling she was going to get sucked into these pages—she just didn't know for how long.

Apparently a few hours, she thought.

"I'm home," Alice sang. Sol turned around on the couch.

"H-how was work?" Sol's throat felt dry. How long had she been sitting there, reading just those pages? It hadn't felt very long, and yet the sun outside was halfway toward setting.

"Better than most days." Alice yawned and winced, bringing a hand up to her head. She muttered a curse in Korean and patted her pockets down, looking for something. "What did you do today?"

"Reading." Sol swallowed. She decided not to mention the creepy little boy and his helicopter mother. Her wife wouldn't understand why Sol had searched them out. And for some reason she also didn't tell her about digging in the yard or *what* she was reading. She kept thinking back to that first page, and how it ended.

If I had known, I wouldn't have come.

Alice raised an eyebrow. "You seem tense. Is something wrong?"

There were so many things wrong Sol wasn't sure where to begin. As much as she wanted to believe this was all a weird prank, the writing was much too advanced to be done by a child. More, what would Randy have gained from it? No, it didn't quite add up, and was therefore a nonstarter with Alice.

"I just . . . woke up from a bad nap," Sol lied, and checked her phone. There were two missed calls and an email. One of the calls was from a Dr. Moore. She didn't know a Dr. Moore and stared at the caller ID in confusion until it hit her—it was supposed to be the next therapist to interview on the list. Meaning she was supposed to have therapy today.

Fuck.

The other was an unknown number. It had left a voicemail.

Alice rubbed her forehead. "I'm going to shower and take another one of those magic pills from Nadine—I think I left them upstairs. Do you want to get started on dinner?" she suggested as she ascended the stairs.

Sol nodded and shuffled into the kitchen, clicking on the voicemail. The voice that she heard boiled her blood.

"Hey, just calling because I heard your academic hearing is this Wednesday. Fingers crossed it all goes well. The labs haven't been the same without you. How are you doing otherwise? If you think about it, this could really be a nice vacation for you. Academia isn't for everyone, you know. You may want to rethink if it's for you. Hope to hear from you soon!"

The voicemail ended. Sol put down her phone.

The last person she needed to hear from was the man who started her slow descent into paranoia. Clarke had already done everything from tampering with her experiments to "forgetting" to invite her to biweekly staff meetings. After the third time he "accidentally" left her out of an email chain about one of the sterile hoods being sent for maintenance, she knew he had it out for her. Unfortunately, by then, her reputation among the other scientists was on thin ice because she was now being seen as someone who hoarded time and resources for her own benefit and ignored departmental procedure.

And yet it was only when she caught Clarke leaving her office on the day the findings of her experiment were due that she truly knew something had to be up. She couldn't prove it without it being a he said–she said situation, but it was so clear he was the reason she was being accused of plagiarism. Clear to her, that is.

All of which was to say that whoever gave Clarke her number was going to be on her shit list forever.

But it wasn't just that she was going to lose her job that really got to her. It was the fact that even after many years of keeping her head down, doing her work, she could still be so easily pushed out of academia at the whims of some white guy who only got there less than a year ago. She was already aware of all the ways she didn't quite fit in with the other scientists.

What could she have done to prevent this? Be more charismatic? Appear less gay? Sol had thought if she kept to herself and didn't cause any trouble, she was safe. And yet, whether it was in this house or at work, trouble still found her.

She didn't belong in a lab, she didn't belong in this neighborhood, she didn't belong anywhere, it seemed. Her PhD was the only thing that even gave her any credibility when it came to Alice's parents. They didn't like that their daughter was gay, and they didn't like how dark Sol was—but at least she was a doctor, right? Without her degree, she wasn't even good enough to be married to Alice.

White-hot anger flowed through Sol and her vision blurred. *Will my worth always be predicated on how others perceive me? Will that perception always be clouded by my skin color? My gender? My sexuality?* She almost snorted.

Of course it fucking will.

She gripped the kitchen counter, her knuckles straining and her breath shallow. It was all she could do to not scream or throw things or just break down and start sobbing. It was then that her eyes caught on something white on the counter, a muddled bit of brightness through the sheen of her almost-tears.

The marble totem from the housing association.

A burst of good luck, huh?

She didn't believe it would do anything for her situation, but at the very least it was good for smashing. She gripped the flat side and brought it down against the kitchen counter over and over again until she heard a sharp crack. It split perfectly in half.

Sol stared at each broken piece through tears. She would give anything for that bastard Clarke to get what he deserved. Anything for her name to be cleared.

By the time Alice came down for dinner, Sol had already tossed the gift into the trash. It barely served its purpose of making Sol feel better, and she hated the reminder that her childish reaction—Sol smash!—wasn't going to have any actual effect on her life.

This is it, she thought. *I'm going to lose my job.*

She ate her stir-fry in silence, only half mumbling answers to whatever questions Alice was asking. They finished up dinner and Alice seemed surprised when Sol decided to go to bed early.

At night, she had trouble sleeping. Her mind kept replaying everything—every incident that occurred at work, every incident that occurred at their new home. They clawed at her like needy animals, but none was so tremendously upsetting as the idea that she was going to have to choose a new career to go into. What could she *do* outside of the sciences, really? Perhaps the only consolation was that, without her salary, they might not be able to afford this house and might need to move out . . .

She swallowed that back down, guilty at how easily she was willing to give up on Alice's dream because her own was crumbling around her.

Sol brought her cell phone back to her face, seemingly clinging to the device as a way to not run downstairs for a drink. The email she neglected was from Dr. Henderson and said that her hearing was on Wednesday at nine a.m. sharp. She looked at the timestamp and then went back to her voicemail folder.

Ha. Of *course* Clarke was the first to break the news, his call coming almost a full hour before Dr. Henderson's email. The dick probably had friends in high places who let him know. But even if she showed this voicemail to everyone at the hearing, it wouldn't be enough to absolve her of plagiarism. They probably wouldn't see anything untoward about it at all.

She was fucked.

Later that night, Sol still couldn't sleep, but now it was because her mind kept going back to the pages buried under a dead tree.

They're in the roots, Veronica had said. Randy basically said the same thing, referring to the journal. It was aggravating, because having read those pages for hours, nothing in particular jumped out at her. The journal spoke of nothing in specific, just made vague, ominous warnings about a potential threat. Sol couldn't even be sure if the author was talking about the home or the community.

It was a waste of time. She *should* have been more concerned about herself. About her job, and her future.

Pay attention. That nagging feeling seemed to grow bigger. There was just something about those pages . . .

Sol tossed and turned, her only solace that Alice was a deep sleeper. The urge to wake her up, to get her take on all this, was both selfish and necessary, but ultimately Sol decided to let her get some sleep. Alice was having a stressful time at work, and it wasn't fair to add Sol's stress—especially when half of it was about a mysterious book—to hers.

Her headaches are getting worse, Sol thought, and gently rubbed Alice's back. The small sound of appreciation was almost enough to break through the craze clouding Sol's mind. But knowing her wife had a touch of comfort wasn't enough for her to fall asleep. Sol was losing her job in just a matter of hours at this point. So she turned around and lay in bed with her back square against Alice's and just stared at the wall. Surprisingly, her thoughts finally did drift to something other than her job or the journal.

She thought about Corinne, whose house was just on the other side.

The old woman still hadn't made an appearance at all since she was discharged from the hospital, something Sol found mildly concerning. This was in itself strange, as Sol had never been one to care for her neighbors and had only met Corinne a handful of times at best. She wasn't sure, then, why she was so concerned . . . but she was. If—*when*—Sol's termination was made official, Sol would have to force herself over there if only to keep from going stir-crazy in this house.

Sol squeezed her eyes shut, willing them to stay dry. She took a few breaths, in and out. The tears were dissipating—but they were replaced by something worse. Sol's vision stretched on all sides. While Sol attempted to blink the fishbowl effect away, other sensations snuck in. Her back was sore and her hips had a radiating pain that felt bone deep. Her eyesight worsened and she was suddenly parched. Looking up, Sol realized the ceiling was painted a different color and her body weighed on the bed heavier.

And there was whispering. Low, buzzing, similar to what she heard in her basement. At first Sol thought it must've been Alice—maybe she had gotten up in the middle of the night to call her parents again for some reason. That must've been why the bed felt emptier.

Sol turned to see if Alice's side was empty, only to find her own breathing grow shallow, almost pained until it became nothing more than short gasps. She couldn't breathe. She could hardly move.

Not another sleep paralysis! With that realization, Sol would've expected the sight of the demon if it wasn't for the fact the lack of air in her lungs kept her attention. She was panicking and her eyes were pricking with tears, but she could make no sounds. With as much momentum in her body as she could muster, Sol tried to rock the bed— maybe Alice would come rushing back and wake her if she noticed something was wrong. But the bed hardly moved even when her head slumped to the side. Right as her last moments of consciousness were being taken from her, Sol looked into an unfamiliar mirror from across the room and tried to scream.

It wasn't her room.

It wasn't even *her.*

As bad as her eyesight suddenly was, the person in bed was an entirely different shape—wearing a long-sleeve floral nightgown. She had seen that nightgown once before.

It was Corinne.

Sol jumped up in bed with a gasp. She looked down at her hands, patted herself all over. She was back in her body—of course she was. It was just a *really* shit dream. Sol pressed her hand over her chest and repeated that to herself. Her heart still wouldn't calm down.

"Jagi?" Alice murmured, still half-asleep. She turned over to Sol. "Are you okay?"

Sol took a moment to catch her breath.

"Just a bad dream, querida."

"Another one?"

"Yes, it's okay, though. Go back to sleep." She rolled out of bed, hoping that a glass of water would help her parched throat.

Alice said nothing after. She was out in seconds.

Downstairs, Sol chugged water like she'd gone weeks without it. She curled her hands into fists to keep from shaking.

Just a dream.

She stepped out into the living room and paused. Whether spending the night on the couch or in bed, the nightmares were intent on finding her, it seemed. Sol rubbed her eyes. She was wired again. She needed sleep. But sleep wouldn't come.

Fuck.

Sol sat on the couch and tugged the pages out from under her laptop. Maybe if she tired herself out from reading, she could have a dreamless night. Or at least a restful one.

It was just a dream, she repeated.

She just wished she could believe herself.

MARCH 27

It starts small.

Little buzzing noises here. A little gift exchange there. You think everyone is being so friendly, so neighborly, but the truth is they're picking you apart. Figuring out what part of you fits and what doesn't.

They'll know too much about you and they'll let it slip from time to time. They can't remember everything, can't remember what you've told them and what you haven't. But they know it all anyway, and they'll use it to get to you.

I never told Teresa that I was thinking about buying my own car. I never told anyone about it—so why would she bring up the fact her husband owns a dealership? Why did she wink like that? Everyone says I'm being too sensitive. They said I'm being ungrateful. But I hear the buzzing, I hear the voices, and I know that there's more to them than they're letting on.

THE SACRIFICE

Morning came with the whining sound of an ambulance siren. Groggy, Sol sat up. Her neck ached like she slept on it wrong, and she found a page of the journal stuck to her cheek. The siren continued as she took in her surroundings.

Right, she'd been reading on the couch. When did she fall asleep? Behind her, Alice peered through the windows with a cup of coffee in hand. The smell of caffeine woke Sol even better than the alarms had.

Sol rubbed her eyes. "What's going on?"

Alice didn't look away. "I think . . . I think Corinne just died."

"Corinne . . . *what*?"

Sol wasn't sure if she heard that correctly. She joined her wife at the window, squinting in the glare of the sunlight. A stretcher carrying a large black body bag was wheeled into the back of the ambulance. Aside from the paramedics, two women stood outside of Corinne's house, arms wrapped around each other in loving embrace.

Sol threw the front door open just as the ambulance pulled away from the curb. The silence of the vehicle stunned her even as she walked barefoot onto the street. The back of the ambulance soon disappeared on the next turn and she looked to the women, recognizing them as pregnant Nadine and Teresa. Tears streaked their faces, a sight that made Sol feel embarrassed.

"Oh my gosh, Sol!" Nadine wailed, racing to her. Sol couldn't pull away even if she wanted to, the pregnant woman's grip was as strong as iron. "This is so sad . . . !"

Teresa came beside Sol, joining in on the forced hug. The effect was strangely dizzying.

"You must've been close with Corinne," Teresa mumbled.

"Why do you say that?"

"Because you're crying."

Sol's hand touched her face and came away wet. Her vision blurred but she shook her head.

"No, I-I barely talked with her," she said. Yet the tears continued to fall.

"It's okay, Sol," Teresa pressed, rubbing her back. "No one's judging you here."

The overly familiar gesture made Sol nauseated. She didn't want to be touched or patronized. She wasn't a *child*. Pushing the women away, she marched back into her home and slammed the door. Right there, Sol collapsed. She couldn't bring herself to go to bed. She couldn't even stand. With her back pressed against the door, she wiped her eyes over and over, willing them to stop leaking. Her chest continued to constrict, as if squeezing every drop of emotion out of her.

A pruning is always felt by the tree.

She looked around, wondering if she'd just heard that. But there was only Alice, and it wasn't her voice. *Why did I think that, then?* She'd attribute it to something Papi said once or twice but that man was hardly ever poetic.

"Sol?" Alice stood a few feet away. Sol's sight blurred too much to make out her expression but it didn't matter. Alice dropped to her knees and cradled Sol as she cried.

What the hell was going on with her? As she'd told Nadine and Teresa, she'd only known Corinne for, what, a week and a half? Two weeks at most. To be so utterly affected by the old woman's death? It didn't make sense. She didn't even remember when she started crying. But the wave of emotion was so overwhelming, so persistent, that Sol screamed into Alice's shoulder. Alice's only response came in a tighter embrace. Sol closed her eyes, hoping that a few minutes of darkness would help calm her.

When she opened her eyes, Alice was gone. Sol was on the couch and alone. She sat up on the couch and checked her phone. There were two notifications. One was a text from Alice.

Had to go to work. I'll call you later to check in and I'll pick up some food on the way home for dinner. -A

The other was an email from Dr. Henderson.

FROM: ghenderson@yale.edu
TO: mreyes12@yale.edu
SUBJECT: RE: Information Regarding Your Hearing

Dear Dr. Reyes,

Dr. Clarke has come forward about tampering with not only the paper you submitted, but also a number of your experiments. This comes as a shock to many of us and while we take a moment to reevaluate the situation, please know we are deeply apologetic for the undue stress this has placed on you. I will email you again regarding the status of your position and how we intend to move forward.

Best regards,
Dr. H

Sol stared at her phone in utter bewilderment. She read and reread the email with increased disbelief. If she had been shocked by Corinne's death and her reaction to it, that was nothing compared to this.

He admitted to it?

Why?

What could possibly be Clarke's motive? Considering his voice-mail from just the day before, there was nothing to indicate he felt any remorse. No, it seemed like he'd been gloating, letting her know that his Caucasian maleness was so bulletproof, he could risk rubbing it in even as he usurped her spot. Sol quickly went into her contacts but stopped herself. Even if she did reach out to him, she was not going to get any satisfying answers. This had to be another ploy.

Regardless, relief flooded the room. It was like the world made sense again. Everything was going to go back to normal. She would get her job back and Clarke would be fired and blackballed.

Gripping her cell phone, Sol dialed.

"Hello, Dr. Moore? Sorry about yesterday—do you think you can squeeze me in today?"

Dr. Moore was, thankfully, a Black man. It was a small relief to see that. Maybe Sol would have an easier time with someone like him, rather than with Dr. Nieman.

His office was colorful, to say the least. He had interesting paintings reminiscent of the Harlem Renaissance. In one, there were Black people dressed in silk dresses and suits against a midnight blue sky. Streetlights poured down on them, highlighting their joyful expressions as they enjoyed a nightlife filled with dancing and music. In another, a small Black boy slept in bed while dreaming of playing the trumpet, drums, and guitar. An abstract painting used sharp blocks of secondary colors to illustrate an everyday scene of Black people waiting at the bus stop.

Based on this, Sol couldn't tell what kind of therapist he would be, and that was probably a good thing. She couldn't waste time psychoanalyzing the person who was supposed to psychoanalyze her. She already had her hands full at the moment.

After the initial shock of Clarke's decision wore off, she was suspicious and antsy once more. Sitting down built up so much energy, she jiggled her leg to work it off. Not to mention, the idea of having to go through the intake process *again* annoyed her, but it couldn't be helped. She didn't like Dr. Nieman and doubted she could tell her anything without the woman making it sound like it was all in Sol's head.

And she refused to believe *that*.

"You seem energetic," Dr. Moore began, pointing to her leg. Sol laughed. "Energetic" was a nice way of putting it. Sol forced her leg still and thought about what to say next. She decided to start with an apology.

"Sorry about yesterday."

Dr. Moore shrugged it off coolly. "It happens. Besides, you were the only one I had to see anyway so, really, you gave me a day off." He chuckled at his own joke and sniffled. "Did something happen that made you forget?"

Oh good, small talk. Sol's favorite.

"It wasn't anything big." Sol chewed on her thumbnail. "I just lost track of time with a . . . project." She settled on that word. It might as well be one now, considering what just happened.

Dr. Moore opened a drawer on his side of the desk and produced a box of tissues. "Sorry, you don't mind, do you? My allergies must be acting up."

"No, go ahead," Sol responded, eyes sweeping her clothes for pollen. She was probably carrying some on her—there always seemed to be some on her now.

"You said you were working on a project?" He blew into a tissue strongly, making Sol even more grateful for her own nasal spray. Congestion must've hit him hard. "Sounds like fun."

"It's definitely something," Sol mumbled after blowing into a tissue too. How much could she trust her new therapist with? She couldn't get proof about the stairs for her wife or show the paramedics where the dead bodies were, how was she going to convince this man that something was indeed wrong with the neighborhood?

She couldn't. But one thing was for sure, if she didn't start talking about it—and do it fast—Dr. Moore would just start the actual intake process.

"So why don't you tell me what's brought you to my office?" he asked.

There it is. The start of intake. Luckily for Sol, it was an open-ended question. She could spin this.

"There is something really strange about Maneless Grove—the place where I live."

Dr. Moore's face grew concerned.

"Strange how?"

Sol took a moment to read his expression. He seemed genuinely curious, not at all jumping to a conclusion before hearing the whole story. That was a good sign.

"Well, lately, I've been noticing a lot of odd things. People who repeat the exact same information. Kids that silently follow some kind of unspoken instruction—they move like they're a unit." Sol felt like she was mentally shifting puzzles pieces around. Things had to click together one way or another. "Two kids I've spoken to said something was in the roots—and do you know what I found under a dead tree in my backyard? A box full of journal entries."

"Okay." Dr. Moore slowly nodded his head. It was clear Sol already lost him. "Let's back up here. First, it sounds like you're concerned about people's behavior."

"It's more than just that, it's . . ." Sol chewed on her lip. How was she going to explain this? The knowledge that something was deeply *wrong*, and if she didn't figure it out sooner or later, it was going to sucker punch her before she could brace for it.

Pay attention. The persistent feeling cropped up every time something odd happened, like something whispering to her, trying to serve her a clue.

"You ever just feel like a place is built just as much to keep people in as it is to keep them out?" Sol remembered all the times she was driving around Maneless Grove, how easily she got lost. When she went on foot, the community stretched on endlessly around her until a teenager broke her out of the loop. All the trees, save for the one in the backyard, utterly identical.

And the constant *insistence* that this was a community, for people to *invest in a neighborly spirit*. To sign the damn HOA agreement and be locked into their idea of what a home should be. The physical gates were the least of Sol's problems.

Dr. Moore leaned forward. "Are you saying you're feeling trapped?" His voice was careful, soft. Like he was tending to a wounded animal. The look in his eyes told her he was trying to make sense of what she was saying. Her shoulders dropped. She was putting it all out there, clear as day. How much more literal could she be?

Sol sighed. "I . . . sure. I'm feeling trapped."

He leaned back into his seat, exhaling with a sense of relief.

Maybe she was going about this the wrong way. Dr. Moore hadn't experienced Maneless Grove for himself. He couldn't know or even begin to understand what she was talking about.

"What is it about this place that makes you feel that way? Maneless Grove, that's what you said it's called, right?" he asked.

"For one thing, it's a gated community—"

"Ah!" he interrupted. "That makes sense. It's a gated community. Let me guess, a lot of white people?"

Sol gave a short nod.

"Right. For people like us," he said and gestured between them, "it's easy to feel out of place in an environment like that. It's just not made for us, you know?"

Sol stilled. The validation should've felt good, but somehow it made her feel worse. Like he was saying she *should* feel alienated in Maneless Grove.

"It was the only place my wife and I could afford." She shrugged. At the mention of "wife," Dr. Moore's eyes widened and he attempted to cover the reaction with a long nod. Sol internally groaned. It looked like he just assumed a Black patient wouldn't be queer.

"And is your wife . . . ?" His voice trailed off, and Sol couldn't be sure what he was asking.

"Is my wife . . . what?" She pursed her lips together.

"Is she, you know, lacking in pigmentation?"

Sol stared at him for a moment longer before it clicked in.

Oh my God, not this again. He was asking if she was white. Because every time a Black person was in a queer relationship, it was expected to be with a white person. Sol blamed the movies for that. They were always incredibly lacking in diverse interracial relationships.

"She's Korean," Sol finally answered.

"Really?" The tone of disbelief in his voice nearly made Sol drop her jaw. To think she felt relieved by seeing a Black therapist. If she didn't have to justify her being Black to a white one, she would certainly have to justify being queer to a Black one.

Everywhere I go, I'm the odd one out.

"That's a surprise," he continued. "I didn't know they were particularly accepting."

They weren't, not at first, but Sol didn't like how he was now turning the focus on that part of her life.

"Yeah, that's not what I wanted to talk about today."

"Of course. How are your neighbors?" He changed the subject quickly.

"Well, one of them just died," she said, deadpan.

"My condolences. Were you close?"

The question reminded her of Teresa's words. *You must've been close.*

Sol shook her head. "We hadn't known each other long. But . . . I liked her more than the others," she admitted. Maybe that was part of the reason Sol was hit so hard. Corinne was actually nice and not in the same passive-aggressive way the others were. She never overstepped (except the first time in their house), and she genuinely seemed like someone Sol could get along with.

And she was the only person in the neighborhood who was trying to warn me about something. Sol just didn't know what.

And now she never would.

"Would you be interested in grief counseling, Sol?" Dr. Moore asked. "It would be in a group setting but—"

"No." Sol quickly cut him off. "I don't, uh, do well in group settings."

"Oh." His eyebrows shot up, as if he learned something unexpected from Sol. "Well, that's understandable. It's not for everyone."

The long pause afterward made Sol consider leaving right then and there. No matter what, Dr. Moore just didn't seem like the therapist for her, either.

"Are there any other issues you would like to work on? Any goals you might have?"

By the time the session came to a close, Sol didn't feel any better about, well, anything. Maneless Grove was still a dense, impenetrable mystery that she was pretty sure her therapist didn't believe her at all about. And the job situation still didn't make sense, because Clarke was not someone with a working conscience. There was no reason he would suddenly throw away his career even if he *could* feel guilt. The idea made her foot heavy on the pedal and she didn't think to slow down until she was hitting the dead ends and curves that she was trying to avoid on her way home. Because everything looked the fuck-ing same.

Would it kill anyone to exercise at least a little *creativity?* The houses still did not provide enough indication of who lived in them—or if they were occupied at all. The people seemed to move around her any-way, slowly, in the corner of her vision, sliding about as if following her, but always just out of sight. The neighborhood, for all its insistence on being a picture of static perfection, no cracks in the concrete or grass taller than an inch, felt like it had the attitude of a bored cat. Tracking her quietly, setting up dead ends to piss her off like it was a game.

Ready to pounce.

I fucking live here, she thought loudly. Sol had signed all the papers with her wife. Okay, not *all* the papers, but all the ones she was legally obligated to. She was not going to be made to feel like *she* was the one who was out of place. Like *she* was lost.

"Mierda, you have to be kidding me . . ."

Sol's grip tightened on the steering wheel. While she didn't hit an-other dead end, she had somehow driven to the town hall instead of her driveway. There was a sneaking feeling that this strange building was laughing at her, finding her attempts amusing.

What is it with everyone thinking I'm either dangerous or a goddamn comedian?

And what is it with me thinking this building is judging me?

The last time she was lost, she had looked for the town hall, know-ing she could find her way home from there. But now, Sol looked down one street, trying to recognize any landmarks that would have given her a hint about the way home. But every house, from the mailbox to the curtains on the windows, was identical, making Sol even more furious . . . and just a touch desperate.

She sucked in a deep but slow breath—in through her nose and then out through her mouth. It would do her no good to lose her shit now of all times. She turned the car to the right and continued away from the town hall. One way or another, she'd find her way home.

And she did—but not right away. No fewer than six houses away from the town hall did she find the only other landmark in the neighborhood that would have mattered to someone like her. She remembered the look of it from the Google Earth image—the dark wooden fences lined on the inside with tall, luscious shrubs. The garden caught her eye like a hook caught a fish, and she slowed to a stop before she realized she was reaching for her seatbelt to unclick it.

"Hey, Sol!"

The shout was muffled by the glass of her car but it still made her jump, as if it was also directly in her ear. Hesitantly, she got out of her car and looked for the source of the voice. Farther in the garden, Finnian was the carbon copy of his own Google Earth image, with the same wave that was suspended in time. Sol's skin prickled with unease.

"You know, for an accountant, you seem to have a lot of free time on your hands," Sol shouted.

Finnian blinked, not expecting a sudden accusation. "I could say the same to you, Miss Scientist."

Sol narrowed her eyes. It was like playing "spot the difference." The redhead was similar enough to his photo, but not quite the same as the one she met at the party or on his lawn. He seemed thinner than he had recently, and if she looked closely enough, she could swear there was a mole on his right ear that she didn't see before.

"That's Dr. Scientist to you. What are you up to?" She leaned over to get a better view. The pictures really didn't do it justice. Long rows of raised garden beds with sprawling leaves, stems shooting upward, and swollen berries splashed this section of Maneless Grove with more color than just green. And that was just what she could see from this side of the fence.

Sol leaned in farther. A boot stuck in the ground gave her pause until she saw it was worn by someone crouching in the shrubbery. Sol froze, almost expecting it to be a dead body, until he stood up.

"Sol, it's nice to see you again," the man said, delighted.

"Do I know you?" And then it struck her. "Lou?" Sol gawked. He barely looked like the same person who accosted her at the welcoming party. Lou smiled, a clean-shaven face brightened even more by eyes as blue as the sky. Sol was unsure how to react.

"Lou just recently joined the Homeowners Association so I'm showing him around some of the facilities," Finnian cut in.

"Would you like to join, Sol?" Lou asked.

Sol raised an eyebrow. "You're kidding, right?"

Lou couldn't even imagine that Sol earned her place at Yale—now he was inviting her on a garden tour? And what happened to the deal Finnian made with Alice during the party? Keep Lou away from them and Alice would let bygones be bygones.

Sol sent a look to Finnian but he remained unbothered by this. The redhead must've had a short memory.

"Of course! The more the merrier." He turned to Finnian. "You don't mind, do you?"

Finnian chewed his bottom lip. "Normally, it's only open for members but . . ."

Sol rolled her eyes.

Finnian winked at Sol with a sly smile. "But if Lou doesn't mind, I'm sure it's fine."

"Are you sure?" It sounded less like a genuine question and more like a rhetorical one. Anger often made her sarcastic. She cleared her throat. "I wouldn't want to get you in trouble. The fines looked pretty hefty." There was the sarcasm again. The HOA agreement didn't mention a specific monetary amount. Just "perpetrators will be fined."

Sol waited for Finnian to catch this but he ignored it.

"Don't even worry about it. Fines only come after the first warning and I haven't broken a rule since moving here." He walked to a part of the fence that wasn't obstructed by shrubbery—that should've been Sol's first clue that it was the gate. He undid the latch on his side and swung it out, waiting for Sol to enter.

She glanced between Lou and Finnian, hesitant.

"Oh, just so you know, we *were* planning on having a couple of glasses of whiskey in the garden center."

Be strong, Sol. "I have to drive."

"I can drive you home," Finnian offered. "And don't worry, it would stay between us."

More secrets between her and Alice. Was this going to be held over her head too? Sol looked to Lou.

"What made you decide to join the association?" She couldn't imagine the guy could be sweet-talked into doing anything if it involved Black people. "You didn't seem like the type."

Lou took a moment to respond. "You know, when I joined the military . . ."

Sol gritted her teeth. When she asked, she wasn't expecting his life story.

"I had a lot of anger," he kept on. "I was violent in school. Kicked out by my parents. I thought, what the hell, maybe I could be part of something bigger than me." Lou chuckled, reliving a memory that Sol didn't want to sit through. He was angry and had nothing better to do than go into the military. That was the life story of nearly everyone who ever went into the military who wasn't a poor kid who had to choose either the army or crime.

Yet he continued as if this was all so fascinating, while her mouth was already wondering what kind of whiskey Finnian had tucked away. "Now, no one ever tells you this, but the military has its own set of problems that just exacerbated a lot of my own mental hang-ups. I got worse."

The military *made you racist?* Sol didn't know Lou when he was younger, but she was pretty sure he brought that kind of baggage with him to basic training.

"But I think that's because it was the wrong place for me; the wrong people."

You mean Black and Brown people?

"What I was really looking for was in *this* community." He ended the story—which wasn't really a story in the first place—with a smile that *almost* convinced Sol there was such a thing as inner peace. As if coming to one of the whitest places on earth somehow cured him of his prejudice.

This man has to be on crack, she thought. Or recently experienced head trauma. Because something was deeply wrong with him—this was *not* the same man she met at the picnic. What did they do, water-board him?

Note to self: Do not *sign the HOA.*

As if she needed any further reason.

"Not to interrupt . . ." Finnian gestured to the gate. "But are you coming, Sol?"

Sol took a deep breath and entered. She wasn't going to be swayed to sign because she had a drink. And, if she joined in with these two, she might find some more clues on what was *really* going on in the association. And if she didn't find clues, there was still whiskey at the end. Win-win, either way.

She looked around, her eyes wide. The garden was large enough that it could have been its own housing development.

"I didn't realize it was this big." Sol blinked. Sure, she was told it was a community garden, but she didn't expect it to be massive. It was practically a farm. Had it looked this big online? She couldn't remember, but didn't think so—it was like there was no way this amount of space could have fit inside the fence. And yet, here she was, following the two men. Finnian pulled off a pair of gardening gloves and tucked them under his arm as he walked. He pointed over to the far end of the garden, where a small cluster of trees grew.

"Those are our apple trees—they don't fully ripen until just about the beginning of fall, but when they're ready, members are free to take as much as they'd like for whatever they'd like. Though mostly, we like to make them into apple pies."

"Gosh, I haven't had a freshly baked apple pie in years," Lou remarked.

"You're in luck!" Finnian patted his shoulder. "We'll probably have a baker's dozen for our fall festival."

Sol quirked an eyebrow. "You guys do your own fall festival?" She hadn't heard anything about that. Was it a mandatory event or exclusive to Homeowners Association members?

Finnian laughed, as though he heard Sol tell a joke.

"We like to have small events throughout the year, to sort of mark our time together. There's the Winter Wonderland where we ice-skate over the frozen lake and drink hot chocolate, the Spring Social—which you just missed, but we're also coming up to our end-of-summer bonfire. I hope you can make that at least. It's the most important in our annual calendar."

"That's . . . a lot of events."

"It's one of the ways we maintain community."

Sol stopped in front of a garden bed. There was a plaque installed at the base, nearly golden. She crouched down to it.

It read, *Corinne's bed.*

Sol felt her hair stand on end. The image of Corinne slowly suffocating flashed through Sol's mind and her chest began to constrict. A firm hand met her shoulder.

"This was Corinne's favorite garden bed," Finnian said in a low voice. "She used to come here all the time when she was missing her husband. She said she loved to see the marigolds that he helped plant."

"I thought he died," Sol muttered, watching him from the corner of her eyes. His face twitched and he suddenly pulled back.

"Right." Finnian cleared his voice. "He did. Though here, we like to believe that the dead are always with us."

Lou shouted something from the other end of the garden, grabbing Finnian's attention. Sol stood up, but stayed put, preferring to watch the two men from afar. She just couldn't understand it. How did Lou go from every racist veteran stereotype to a zen creature that caressed flowers carefully, like he wanted to make sure he didn't startle them.

Sol's nose began to run again. She sniffled hard, then went into her pockets for the nasal spray. She was not going to be caught dead without it—not anymore. After a few sprays, Sol could breathe again.

Several rows over, Sol spotted the exact kind of trees planted all over the neighborhood and in the woods. Tall, mostly thin and white. Making sure Lou and Finnian were preoccupied, Sol came closer for a better look. For a moment, she thought there were carvings, short etchings that repeated up and down the bark.

This is just what it looks like. She took a quick photo of the trees.

"I see you're interested in our aspen trees." Finnian's voice startled her. She nearly dropped her phone. How did he sneak up on her like that?

"Is that what they are?" Sol asked. "Hey, do you know if these trees are edible in any way? The bark, I mean."

If Finnian thought the question was strange, he didn't act like it. "Hmm, I suppose it can be made into a kind of tea. But I wouldn't know beyond that."

Sol continued through the grove, then tripped over something hard. Another plaque.

"Why was this here?" She crouched down to inspect it. It had no name—instead, there was just a phrase.

For all the Nameless.

Finnian suddenly gripped her arm. "Well, I *did* say we like to honor our dead community members." He forced her to her feet with a sweet tone that didn't match his actions. "But if we kept doing it for *everyone* in a community as big as this we'd be up to our necks in plaques!"

Sol twisted away from him and looked around for Lou. Wherever that man went, he sure chose to be conveniently far away.

"Looking for someone?" Finnian smiled. *No*, bared his teeth. His jaw was squared and a spark of malice shot through his eyes. She pulled back and he blinked several times, softening his expression. His shoulders loosened and he shook his head.

Sol swallowed. "I should . . . get home. Thanks for the tour."

As if understanding why, Finnian nodded. "That's what good neighbors are for." His expression grew serious. "You know we're all in this together."

"Sure, yeah." Sol stumbled away from him and out of the garden. She thought she might have heard Finnian and Lou yell a goodbye but focused on settling in her car for a few minutes, pressing her palms into her eyes to shake off the dread she felt from being around Finnian.

For a moment there, Finnian acted *exactly* like Lou had. Or at least the version of him from the welcoming party. If anything, he seemed even *more* feral.

He could still be in shock over Corinne's death.

Except people didn't act like that when they were in shock. She rubbed her arm, still feeling the pinch from how Finnian grabbed her. She hoped it wouldn't bruise.

Sol put the car into drive, hoping to get as much distance as possible between her and the garden.

For all the Nameless.

Finnian could dress it up all pretty in whatever faux-kind language he wanted, but calling people "nameless" was not a way to honor them. It was just another way to say they were unimportant. Just one of many. No need to distinguish one from another.

"The Nameless Grove," Sol said to no one in particular. Maybe that's what the community was originally called. A collection of people, like trees, all connected through a root system, helping one another survive, or thrive depending on how one looked at it. Who knew where one began and another ended. If everyone's the same, if everyone moves and becomes part of a whole, to be one organism, it was much more powerful than being by yourself.

No one would want to move into a place called Nameless Grove. But switch the *n* and the *m* and suddenly, it sounded more luxurious, didn't it?

I need to get those journal entries.

This time it seemed as if Sol had no problem navigating back to the house. Shaking her head, she parked in the driveway and only spared a glance at the Kennedys' home through the rearview mirror. Veronica hadn't made an appearance in a while and as concerned as Sol should be, she thanked whoever was listening for her absence.

Sol practically jogged inside, making a beeline for the coffee table. She pushed aside her laptop and found just one entry. She looked around, even checked between the couch cushions, but nothing. The stack of entries was missing. As she sat down, she noticed something new sitting on the edge of the coffee table.

A thin, wiry twig.

"You're back," Sol whispered, as if greeting someone. She knit her brow together and leaned forward, studying it. Last time, the twig lay starkly on the porcelain sink. This time it blended into the dark brown coffee table, a fact she finally noticed because as far as she had seen, there were no dark brown trees anywhere in the neighborhood. All of them were a pale white, with black scars exposing the inside.

The only tree that matched this little twig was the one in her back-yard.

She didn't want to, but there was no way she could just leave it there. Maybe it wasn't a twig, but a figment, but at least by reaching for it she'd know if she had truly snapped. She wasn't even sure what she wanted: for it to be real or it to be fake. So she let her finger waver just above it, shaking and refusing to come down.

The twig poked up.

Sol jumped back, a loud crash echoing through the house.

"Shit!" her wife yelled. Sol blinked—Alice was home a lot earlier than usual. Loud clanging metal told Sol she was in the kitchen, and she rushed in, concerned that her wife was reorganizing the overfilled cupboards again. Instead, she found Alice standing just fine in front of the stove.

"Hey, you," Alice said in the kind of tone of voice that said she wasn't in a good mood.

"Querida? You're home early. Is something wrong?" Sol looked around for the source of the crash. A large rogue pot rolled its way to the fridge. Sol stopped it and brought it back to her, glancing over at the busy kitchen counter. An array of banchan—small vegetables and meat side dishes—were huddled together as Alice put pots and pans into the dishwasher. Sol spotted gamja jorim next to jangjorim and in-stantly knew it was going to be a very hearty meal.

"Wasn't feeling well." Alice avoided meeting her eyes. "Thought I'd take a half day."

"So you decided to come home early and make dinner?"

Alice replied like she hadn't realized it. "Oh. Yeah." Sol took her elbow and gently pulled her around so they were face-to-face.

"Querida, what's wrong?" Sol was not a particularly emotional per-son. She had a rough time articulating what she was feeling herself, but when it came to Alice, she was a little more tuned in. Alice only re-treated into herself when she was disheartened. Sol took her face into her hands and searched her eyes for answers. If she had answers, she could help. What good was she to her wife if she couldn't?

"I . . . didn't get the promotion."

Sol thought she didn't hear her correctly. But then Alice sighed again and cast her eyes down. Sol recognized this expression easily—because she wore it often herself. Shaken confidence, doubt in her own abilities, a resigned acceptance like this was what she deserved.

It gutted Sol to see her like this.

"What? Why?"

Alice shook her head and pulled away. "Same old reason. There was only one open spot and someone else was more qualified."

In Sol's eyes, there was no one more qualified or dedicated than Alice. Beyond her subjective gaze, though, Sol couldn't imagine there was someone doing better work than Alice. She got home so late most days—it seemed impossible all her efforts would go unnoticed. Impossible, that is, if it weren't for the fact that they were two people of color. Or two lesbians. Or two women.

It just made it all the more frustrating, knowing how much of their lives they'd spent pursuing their careers, only to find so much depended on others' perceptions of them. If it wasn't for the fact that Sol was also a workaholic in her own right, she might have even complained once or twice, but their ambition worked just fine for them. At least, until a moment like this, when it didn't.

Would it be a dick move to say I got my job back? She wasn't sure. It would've been good news, but with Alice looking as down as she was, Sol felt like it might've sounded like she was bragging. She was, after all, known for her tactlessness.

Just another secret, she thought. Pursing her lips together, Sol moved to help Alice clean up the counter.

"By any chance, did you see a stack of old papers on the coffee table?" If her track record was any indication, Sol wouldn't be surprised if Alice didn't know what she was talking about. Like everything else in the house, its disappearance would be just one more mystery.

"Yeah. I threw them out."

"Okay. Wait—what?" Sol stopped in her tracks.

"Do you think I can't read? I told you not to bring that shit into our house," Alice said, throwing a ladle down in the dishwasher with more force than needed. The sharp metal clang brought a tension with it that Sol didn't know how to react to.

She chose her next words carefully. "You said I couldn't talk about it. Am I suddenly not allowed to have my own hobbies?"

Alice laughed bitterly. "You call that a hobby? Where did you even find those things?"

"What does it matter?" Sol scowled, refusing to give her any information. "They were mine. You don't see me tossing any of your belongings whenever I'm in a bad mood."

"No, you just get blackout drunk," Alice retorted, stirring the pot on the stove.

Sol scoffed. "Wow! You are *on one* today, aren't you?"

Alice didn't respond. So now she was giving Sol the silent treatment? Fine. Sol had some reading to do anyway. It was lucky that Alice missed one of the pages when she cleared house.

I'll have to find a better hiding spot after I read it. One that wasn't just *under* her laptop.

Sol nearly walked past the counter when she caught sight of a white envelope addressed to them.

"What's this?" Sol opened it and recognized the HOA letterhead immediately.

Terms and conditions for joining the association—

Sol gasped and dropped it. She'd *shredded* this not too long ago. Shredded and tossed it in the trash. What was it doing back in her home, on her kitchen counter?

As if answering the question, Alice said, "I found that in our mailbox. Teresa thought we might need an extra copy for some reason."

For *some* reason? Like digging through their trash? Did Hope find a way to break into their house? Sol knew the association was pushy, she didn't think they were *that* pushy. And yet the evidence was in her hand.

Sol turned just as Alice picked up a dirty knife. The sensation was brief, and superficial, but still brought back memories from long ago.

Memories of her mom looking at her angrily when she was blindsided by the thought of her daughter being gay.

Sol's breath caught in her throat and the room spun. Alice grabbed her before she fell.

"Shoot, Sol. Hold on." Alice tore paper towels off a rack and wiped Sol's arm down. The red line across her skin turned out to be a sauce. Nothing to panic about.

Sol pushed Alice away, getting to her feet faster than she could fill her lungs with air.

"Wait—" Alice pulled her back. "I would never hurt you. You know that, right?"

The first time Sol told her the truth about the stab wound, Alice was livid. She couldn't believe a mother would ever harm her own child, even in a fit of anger. It was probably the only time Alice was grateful the woman died before they could meet—because Alice would've fought Sol's mom herself. And as interesting a sight as that would've been for Sol, it was enough for her to know that at least her mother couldn't do *Alice* any harm.

It took Sol a moment to find her voice. Though she was upset that Alice would throw away something that wasn't hers, she had to know that it wasn't because she didn't respect Sol.

She was just afraid.

But so am I. And yet she wasn't even allowed to talk about it.

"Yeah," Sol answered, still refusing to meet her wife's eyes. "I know that."

There was a pause. Alice slowly let go of Sol's arm.

"By the way . . ." Alice breathed. "I heard that the viewing is this Friday. I got the details from Nadine—she thought you'd want to know."

Sol frowned. What viewing? Then she remembered and confusion warred with guilt. Her feelings about Corinne were more complicated than she realized. The old woman was just that—old. But her death left a bad taste in Sol's mouth and with everything else going on, she was having a difficult time processing any bit of news around her.

"Do you know how she died?" She felt strange for asking, but also felt like she had to know.

Alice shrugged. "Nadine didn't say."

"Wouldn't say or didn't know?"

"I didn't really ask, but it seemed like she knew, but didn't say."

That's suspicious. Sol briefly felt guilty for that thought as she nodded. Now definitely wasn't the time to tell Alice what she suspected about why Nadine wanted them to buy this house. But she couldn't put it off forever.

Sol gave Alice's hand a squeeze. "Yeah, I think I'll go."

APRIL 3

I met a woman today. Another resident. I was out walking, trying to get my bearings in this neighborhood. It can get so confusing, so fast. I think I looped around certain houses a few times. It's not easy knowing where you're going when everything looks the same. When every tree is identical to the next, down to the branch.

I know this because I've noticed. I think if I took the time to count the leaves, it would be the exact number on each tree too.

That's how I met her. I was standing in front of her house when she came out. She invited me in for hot cocoa. I don't know why I decided to go inside. I think the chilly weather was getting to me. Besides, she was pretty thin and looked harmless. I doubted she could do anything to me.

I regretted it the moment I stepped inside. The way she looked at me . . . it was like she could see through me. And even though it started off like a normal conversation—asking me how I was adjusting and if I liked living here—it took a weird turn superfast. I remembered thinking I wish I were literally anywhere else and she suddenly asked me, if I could go anywhere else, where would I go. Then I thought somewhere it didn't feel like I was being interrogated and she laughed like she heard me.

Right before I left, she said that Maneless is a very open

and honest neighborhood. Everyone knows everyone . . . and everything. But if I wanted a bit more privacy, there was at least one other place I could go—assuming I could find it.

I don't know what that meant. And I know I can't talk to Mom or Dad about how weird the conversation was. I'm sure they would just say I was overthinking it and I should've thanked the woman for the cocoa. I'm pretty sure they wouldn't even bother to ask me who the woman was.

Which is a good thing because . . . even though she told me her name, for some reason, I just can't remember it.

THE MANELESS MISSING

In the days before Corinne's viewing, Sol took her time reading the remaining journal entry. Though it was only one page, it still wasn't easy, with how smudged the writing appeared and how delicate the page was—she had to handle it very carefully or else risk tearing it in two. In the middle of reading, she developed another fishbowl migraine and had to lie down for a few hours, effectively keeping her from getting very far.

It was . . . interesting. The author went from barely giving any indication of having a grasp on reality, to naming Teresa outright. And she knew it was the same Teresa because she remembered her husband, Noah, definitely owned a car dealership. Though, how Sol learned that, she couldn't remember, because she'd certainly never met the man . . .

Regardless, she felt a little closer to the author. They were something like comrades now, weren't they? She compared her struggles to theirs. Believing they were going insane, hearing buzzing noises, everyone being weirdly *friendly* but in a way that didn't feel kind. Sometimes people did mention things that they couldn't know, not without watching her closely. Like when Hope came by and mentioned how Sol hadn't left her house in days.

What worried Sol the most was the mention of "forgetting." It was in the first entry. They mentioned being forced to forget things and change in order to be part of the whole. She didn't think she forgot anything . . . but that was kind of the whole point, wasn't it?

If it wasn't for the fact Sol already met the Watersons, she would have thought the entries belonged to one of them.

It could be someone who lived there before them. Before the house was burned down.

Whoever it was, she hoped they would be easy to find.

Sol sat in the parking lot for a very long time. Long enough that she had to turn the car back on for air-conditioning and closed her eyes as she felt the cool air brush her cheeks.

I'm just meeting Amir, she told herself. *I have every right to be here.*

She did—she actually did. Her job was safe after all and even if it wasn't, that didn't mean she'd get in trouble if she *was* found here by anyone who knew her situation.

Besides, she was nowhere near her department. All of Yale's science departments were in a cluster, including the chemistry department, the physics department—hell, even the interdisciplinary bioethics department was clear across New Haven, on the complete opposite side of the scattered university buildings where she was. Chances were very low of anyone from her department seeing her here.

Which was of incredible importance to her, because what would she even say to them?

Hey, how's it going? Great to know I'm not a plagiarist, right, ha-ha. Thanks for having my back.

No, she wasn't ready to face anyone, much less those who probably actually liked Clarke and had only tolerated her.

Sol stepped out of the car and instantly regretted it.

"Dr. Reyes?"

Slowly turning around, Sol locked eyes with Dr. Henderson, the department head. Somehow, even going through the statistical improbability of her home twisting and turning around her, moving objects, and a strange, burning figure in her home, nothing made Sol feel as small as being in front of this man. Dr. Henderson was a short, balding white man with a consistently confused expression on his face, almost like he was not entirely sure what he was seeing or what he was doing. Which all belied the brilliant mind that made him head of one of the most prestigious science departments in the world.

And it wasn't just his scientific acumen (the number of papers with his name on them that were actually *written* by Dr. Henderson awed

Sol) or even his administrative competency—he was just one of those pure polymaths that seemed good at all things. There wasn't a day Sol didn't see him finishing a new sudoku or crossword puzzle at breakneck speed, for instance.

And on top of all that, he was a decent man. When rumors began to fly about her mentally unraveling, he checked in on her more and more. There was a wisdom and kindness in him that routinely shocked her, and there were times she had to recheck her bias against straight white men when confronted with her boss.

Then there were times she was reminded of people like Clarke and Lou, and she was back to where she started. But those two weren't here—it was just Dr. Henderson, a generous mentor who she might have even liked to have as a friend.

If, you know, I had any.

"It *is* you," Dr. Henderson said dryly, because that was also the kind of man he was. Seemingly devoid of emotion even while he acted with it. In one hand he held a Starbucks coffee and in the other a leather briefcase.

"Hi, Dr. Henderson." Sol fidgeted with the car keys in her hand. "How are you?"

"I'm well." He nodded, though upon closer inspection, it might have just been his tremor. Dr. Henderson was always hard to read. "I should be sending an email sometime in the next week about when you can resume working . . . that is, if you're interested in coming back."

The question stunned Sol. There was never any question about her wanting to come back if or when she was cleared. Maybe others would have done differently—they could have sued or thought of an exit strategy, very quick to cut and run if the situation called for it. Sol was the opposite. Or rather, she was a deer in headlights, too slow to make a quick decision, too rooted in place to move.

"You don't have to answer right away. Do take your time," Dr. Henderson replied. He turned for a moment and then stopped. "Dr. Reyes—regardless, I'm glad you seem to be doing better."

And then he went on. Sol tried not to read into that too much as she followed in his direction.

"Dr. Henderson . . . what are you doing all the way over here?" Sol asked out of curiosity.

"Hm? Oh, my daughter has a concert in the music hall."

Sol didn't even realize he had a daughter. Maybe she should've paid more attention to the man who was going out of his way to help her through a difficult time.

As Dr. Henderson stood on the corner of College Street, waiting for the signal to change, Sol swallowed her pride for a moment.

"Dr. Henderson! I wanted to say . . . thank you."

For once, his expression changed. He knit his brow together in genuine confusion and stared at her.

"Dr. Reyes, you are a brilliant and dedicated scientist. I looked at all the evidence and made a decision that the data bore out, so there's no need to thank me. The confession did help, though. I'm just glad he admitted to it, especially since I don't necessarily understand what it was that caused Dr. Clarke to take such shameful actions against you in the first place."

I could think of a few reasons why. She was Black, Latina, gay, a woman—literally any one of those could have been targeted.

"Well . . . thank you, anyway. And speaking of Dr. Clarke . . . do you know what made him decide to confess?" She figured it was well within her rights to ask now that Dr. Henderson brought him up first.

He frowned at first, tilting his head up as he thought. "You know, I'm not sure. At first, some of us thought his email might have been hacked. But then he called later to confirm that he not only regularly intervened in your experiments but he had also gained access to your computer and rewrote part of the results. Just yesterday, while we were meeting to discuss his further employment with us, he turned in his resignation."

Sol let out a slow breath. She expected relief to fill her lungs once again. It was a rare feeling but it did come between moments of paranoia and obsession. This time, however, she didn't feel relieved. Just cheated out of a real answer. She loved the result, but it made absolutely no sense.

Dr. Henderson shook his head. "I can't fathom why he did what he did—either the sabotage or the confession. Sure, I could ascribe some sort of prejudicial motive, but it wouldn't have benefited him unless he is only guided by pure hate. You two were on different tracks in terms of your studies, and even tenure wasn't something you were competing for. But if it was pure bigotry, then why confess? What caused the change of heart? I'm curious, to say the least. But, more, I'm just glad the truth came out. As I said, you're a diligent researcher and what happened to you was wrong." Another sigh. "So please just know that if I can help to right that wrong even a little bit, I would be happy to."

The light changed. He pointed to the other sidewalk and gestured at Sol.

"I'm actually heading the other way," she said.

"You have a good day, then, Dr. Reyes."

Sol watched him cross the street, feeling lighter than she thought was possible. Aside from his mental capabilities, Dr. Henderson always seemed indecipherable to Sol. She had never been sure where she stood with him as colleagues, just that he was her superior and deserved respect as such. If he were like anyone else in the lab, she assumed that he would either pretend he didn't see her, or simply give a curt greeting. Instead, he went out of his way to offer words of encouragement while he walked with her.

He treated her like she was important. Valued. Respected.

And for the first time in months, Sol felt like she could actually breathe on campus.

Walking into the pizza parlor, Sol grabbed the booth in the far back corner and sat hunched over the table. Her eyes were scanning the menu, but she was barely reading any of it, her stomach both unhungry and protesting the idea of anything being put in it. Instead, her thoughts swirled around Henderson and what he'd said about Clarke, what she already knew—or thought she knew about the man—and what it meant going forward. She only looked up when Amir's shadow fell over her as he sat across the booth.

"Welcome back, Sol." He brought a leather messenger bag slung over his shoulder and placed it down beside him.

Sol managed a half smile, staring at the bag until it was out of sight. "I'd say it's good to be back, but I'm not quite sure I'm there yet."

"You're here, aren't you?"

"Yes, but I'm not sure what that means. I'm not sure if I'm *back* back."

"Hey, I get it. You've been through a lot," Amir said, and despite his earnestness, Sol's smile fell. She just wished people would quit telling her that. The more times she heard it, the more it felt patronizing. Instead of showing too much displeasure, she focused on carefully retrieving the journal entry from its envelope and placed it down in front of Amir. His brow immediately furrowed and he leaned into the page.

"So I found a bunch of these entries buried in my backyard, but I just don't know what to make of it," Sol started. "I thought, maybe, you would be able to take a look at it and tell me what you think."

"You said a bunch?"

"Yes."

"There's only one here, though," Amir pointed out.

"Yeah, I, uh . . . misplaced them." Sol gritted her teeth. Even though the fault lay purely on Alice, she didn't like the idea of airing dirty laundry even to friends. Some things should just stay between a couple. "Can you just look at this one for me? Please?" she added.

Amir didn't answer. He stared so intently at the page without touching it that Sol felt uncomfortable. He knit his brow together in confusion and hummed in contemplation. Amir's eyes flitted back up to Sol and then down to the paper.

"I'm sorry, what is this?"

Sol took in a deep breath. She thought a lot about what she would say to Amir about this journal entry. He'd always been a little bit more open-minded than she ever gave him credit for, at least, more so than Alice. He could joke about ghosts and demons and not worry that someone would come out from the shadows to make him regret it. And there were times when he would paint her a new perspective, enlightening her on obscure historical events, like when he explained that twelfth-century barbers used to offer bloodletting because priests and monks (who were stand-ins for doctors) abhorred the practice.

That being said, she wasn't going to tell him how much she had in common with the author.

"And why are you showing this to me?" he continued. From the look in his eyes, he seemed more confused than judging her, like he wasn't sure where he fit into this situation.

"Because I can't show it to Alice. She doesn't like engaging with things like this."

"Things like this?" Amir pressed.

"Creepy things," she explained, crossing her arms. "Ghosts. She says it would attract more of them."

"She thinks a ghost wrote this?" He pointed to the page.

"No, just—" Sol pinched the bridge of her nose. He was focusing on the wrong thing. "I'm saying that I'm showing you because I need to talk to *someone* about this and well, you're someone."

A wry smile appeared on his lips.

"I'm someone?"

"You're someone who's getting on my last nerve." Sol glared at him. "Come on, be serious."

Amir laughed. "I'm just poking fun. But fine. This is . . . definitely an interesting piece of writing. Who's Teresa?"

"It's a resident in my neighborhood," Sol explained. "Someone from the Homeowners Association."

"Oh, it's actually a person you know?" He looked surprised, as if he wasn't expecting an answer.

Sol ignored his question. "It's a prank, right?" She wanted—no, *needed* a second opinion. She needed to know how this looked from the outside, even if it was devoid of context. Sol was too close to this thing. Her opinion was colored by her experiences.

Which was not a great thing for a scientist studying new phenomena.

"It could be." He shrugged. "I'm assuming you don't know who wrote this."

"Not a clue."

Amir wrinkled his nose. He reached across the table to the napkin dispenser and pulled a few tissues out before blowing his nose.

"Weird. I usually don't get allergies."

Sol nodded apologetically. Again, she was probably carrying pollen with her. The nasal spray she kept in her pocket did its job dutifully, but it wasn't something she could share.

"Have you spoken to Teresa about this?"

Sol scoffed. "Hard pass. The woman is *way* too touchy-feely for my comfort. I barely know her." And what was she going to say to her? That someone anonymously wrote a journal entry about her being creepy and *buried it in her backyard*? What a great way to start a new friendship.

Amir gave her a look.

"What?"

"You are not giving me much to work with here." Still, he chuckled, like Sol wasn't at the end of her rope and grasping for straws.

Sol scowled. Amir was right. There wasn't much he could go on with just this one entry. Not without at least meeting Teresa.

Amir blew his nose into a napkin again. "Kind of reminds me of the Church of the Neighbor, though a bit on the nose."

Sol blinked. The name was not familiar. "The Church of the what?"

"Of the Neighbor. It was a very niche cult in this area—so obscure, I'm not surprised you haven't heard of it." He waved the term away, as if that would soothe her anxieties. If it were the Church of Anything Else, it might have. But that word . . .

Neighbor sounds a little too close to the neighborhood motto. Invest in a *neighborly spirit.* Hearing him say it, something seemed to click, and she couldn't help but feel that motto connected with something vaguely churchlike.

She pulled out her phone, getting ready to type. "Would I be able to find more information about it online?"

Amir took a moment to scratch his chin. "You might find one or two things about it on the internet, but I think the most information I've found was from an old book I got at a thrift store—and even that section was barely a page."

She was already on a browser, though, and Sol found a very old article that looked like it had been printed from a microfiche and re-scanned online. She spun the phone around so they could both see it and she and Amir pored over it together. The article was about a man named Gregor Foer who not only escaped the cult shortly before it dispersed but was completely nonsensical when speaking about it.

"Foer Says Not To Trust The Neighbor," written in the *Middletown Press* back in 1893.

Don't trust the neighbor. That's what Corinne said. Sol's hair stood on end as she quickly skimmed the article.

Gregor Foer, the man known as the only escaped member of the Cult of Esther Rhodes or the Church of the Neighbor, was recently institutionalized after harassing various people in Cromwell. Among his rants was a startling sermon on how they attempted to induce group telepathy through cannibalism and repeated and lengthy submersion in water. Sources say that he is a prime candidate to be studied on the helpful effects of lobotomies on the unwell.

"Who is Esther Rhodes?"

He shrugged. "No one really knows. She's something like an urban legend, even among historians."

Incredulous, Sol looked at Amir. "Shouldn't someone who engages in cannibalism to encourage group therapy be a little bit more . . . infamous? The likes of Bloody Mary and Vlad the Impaler had all manner of stories told about them."

Amir snorted. "In fairness, it wouldn't be the first time a cult used hallucinogenic drugs. It happens. And I don't think there was any actual cannibalism, so maybe that's why it isn't as sexy as those other ones you mentioned."

Sol went back to her phone, frantically searching for more information. Unfortunately, there wasn't much at all.

"Why did you ask if I thought this might be a prank?" Amir suddenly asked. Sol rubbed the space between her eyes.

"My house's previous owner has a kid who said he'd found something hidden in the backyard. I thought he was just trying to spook me. But these entries didn't feel like they were written by a kid."

"Definitely not!" Amir said. "Kids these days are actually into way more gruesome things."

Sol could feel the conversation tipping back into the "Amir's kids" category and needed to cut that off at the pass. The man was a doting father who loved to bring up his children at every opportunity. Sometimes, it was genuinely entertaining. Other times, like right then, Sol just didn't have the energy for it.

Sol gave a noncommittal, "Is that so . . ."

"If it were Jazmine pulling a prank, she probably would've found a way to bring up something more recent to the area."

Sol's eyes flicked up. "Like . . . a suicide?"

Amir looked taken aback. "That's a bit grim. But . . . yes, probably. Actually, now that I think about it, I remember her having a bizarre obsession with Maneless Grove before. What did she call it? It was a little catchy, the Maneless . . . something."

Sol waited anxiously for Amir to continue, only to breathe when he shook his head.

"I can't remember, but maybe it'll come to me. I just don't understand why she's into all of these morbid things all of a sudden."

"She's at that age," Sol remarked vaguely as she returned the entry to the envelope.

"Did you have a phase like that as a kid?" Amir asked.

Oof, now there was a topic Sol didn't want to touch. Her teenage years were filled with a lot of self-doubt and self-deprecation. It was little wonder why she was so anxious most of the time. The ground she stood on had never been sturdy, so when something put her off balance, it was instant vertigo. It was the age when she realized Papi wasn't actually fun—he was just always buzzed. And Mami went from being a buzzkill to someone Sol realized she was never really safe around.

That being said, she did like to sneak rock songs from time to time.

"Not in a way to be concerned about." Sol changed the subject quickly. "Hey, would you be able to send me that book when you get the chance?"

"Of course." Amir glanced at his watch. "We should order soon, the lunch rush will be coming." Surprisingly, Sol discovered she had an appetite once again.

Later, after the two finished their meal and split off, Sol sat in the parking lot and thought carefully about the cult and Esther Rhodes and how it all tied to Maneless Grove. She didn't know nearly enough. *No—check that.* She didn't really know anything. At the moment, there were too many variables to draw her own conclusion. She needed more concrete information and that meant starting with what she had and building from that.

And what she had was this: It didn't seem possible that someone Randy's age could have heard anything about the cult. Seeing as Randy never even uttered the name Esther Rhodes, he clearly knew less than Sol did. So there was something genuine about the pages. That was at least something. And while Amir couldn't offer much more than that, hopefully the book he mentioned would help fill in the blanks.

Sol's phone vibrated right before she put the car in drive. It was a text from Amir.

> Just remembered! It was the Maneless Missing, and it was a 19-year-old who disappeared a few years ago from that neighborhood.
>
> I think his name was Sean.

TAILGATING

S ol tapped her fingers along the steering wheel of the car, stomach roiling as she fought the rising panic.

"*You're being followed,*" a voice whispered.

She jerked her head up and scanned the rearview mirror. No one was sitting in the back seat. No one was with her.

"Not this shit again." She cursed, then readjusted her mirror at a stoplight. The person driving behind her ducked down in a blur, rousing immediate suspicion. Sol narrowed her eyes. She didn't recognize the car. It wasn't the Subaru her wife drove. It was a small car, a Toyota—that meant nothing to her. And anyway, who would be going out of their way to follow her?

"I'm being paranoid," she said.

"*You're not,*" the voice said again. Sol gripped the steering wheel. Behind her, a long row of cars started up a chorus of honks. The light was green, she needed to get moving.

She hit the gas, hoping to lose the stalker. An unnecessary but quick turn here and there should do the trick. She wanted to get to her house and worried this would take her out of her way, but Sol knew she was still well on her way home—she could feel the pull of the neighborhood like a magnet. It was cloying, like a whiny pet. It needed her . . . and a part of her needed it. But she was still at least one highway away from the gates. The neighborhood whined and Sol ached to soothe it.

I'll be there soon, she promised to no one. All she knew was that she needed to get home. That, for maybe the first time ever, she *wanted* to be back in the neighborhood. And she would be.

Just not until she got rid of this creep.

"He's still following."

Sol ignored the voice. She was alone, there shouldn't be a voice at all. Looking back, there were two different cars behind her and they both had their turn signal on—no Toyota in sight. She did it—the mysterious stalker was finally gone.

And ahead of her was Maneless Grove. Sol blinked, not realizing she was so close to home already. She didn't remember getting on the highway at all—was it possible she took an unintentional shortcut? Sure, why not. Even a scientist like Sol could believe in small miracles.

As she entered the neighborhood, she felt the cloying cease, the pet glad its owner was finally home. She breathed in relief and eased her foot off the gas pedal. The neighborhood was awash in a comfortable glow of streetlamps. The trees clapped. Even the homes, empty as they were, greeted her with a smile. She was happy to be back. Happy to be with them, her community, the Grove. She finally felt like she could settle down here, like she could really put down roots.

"Enjoying it?"

Sol's eyes flickered to the rearview mirror. Her jaw dropped.

"Corinne?" Sol whispered. The old woman sat behind her, hands folded neatly over her lap. This couldn't be happening. She couldn't be seeing Corinne of all people. Corinne was—

"Dead?" The woman finished her thought. *"You should know nothing ever stays dead here. We're just . . . in the roots."*

Sol swallowed. "Veronica said the same thing."

"About her parents."

"Yes."

Sol bit the inside of her cheek. She had seen the Kennedys twice already and neither was the way she would have liked. The car jolted— Sol had driven onto the sidewalk. She course corrected quickly.

"Mind the road."

Sol nodded, but spared Corinne another glance. Her skin was grayed out, like she was powdered with a foundation that was too light for her. Sol remembered making that mistake in college once when she tried makeup for the first time.

No, this isn't like the makeup. This was different. Looking a little closer, she noted a sprout poked out from Corinne's lightly curled hair. Her nose appeared stiff and bumpy, as rough as Papi's calloused hands.

Corinne then mouthed something.

"I'm sorry?"

"*Mind the road,*" she repeated, though Sol was sure that wasn't all Corinne said. She made sure to glance back and once again corrected her steering. As she did, she heard something besides words—when Corinne spoke, there was a light buzzing in the undertone of her voice. It was the same sound she always heard with those voices.

"What is that?" Sol asked, turning down another street. She was now just circling the block, afraid that if she stopped for even a moment, Corinne would dissipate, never to be seen again.

Sol strained her ear. The woman definitely said something this time, in too low a whisper to catch.

"What?"

"*. . . told you not to trust the neighbor I told you not to trust the neighbor I TOLD YOU NOT TO TRUST THE NEIGHBOR—*"

Scraggly branches grew out of Corinne's eyes, roots crawled over her hands and Corinne jumped forward, clawing fervently at Sol.

Screaming, Sol hit the brakes. The squealing tires competed with Corinne's voice.

"*ITOLDYOUNOTTOTRUSTTHENEIGHBOR!*" The shriek turned guttural. Corinne—or whatever it was in the car with her—hacked up a cough that morphed into a choke. Sol could only peek through the impossible foliage to see that a strangling vine was coming out of Corinne's mouth.

Tearing at her seatbelt, Sol threw herself out of the car. Her ass hit pavement first but she didn't stop crawling backward until she was a few feet away from the car. She stared through the windows, heart jackhammering its way through her chest. Corinne was gone. The branches and vines were gone. It was just her car, dome light on, illuminating the darkening street.

Sol scrambled to her feet. She pushed down rising bile and blinked away tears.

"What was that?" Sol whispered at first—then shouted. "What the fuck was *that*!" She looked around, searching for answers. The glow of the homes and streetlamps did nothing to soothe her. It was just another street, another house, another light, in a row of unending streets, houses, lights, stretching on into the horizon like the first time she got lost.

"*Get back into your car*," the voice whispered, different from Corinne's, yet incorporating it. Like it was more than one person speaking.

"No," Sol choked out. She couldn't. She wouldn't. It would be lunacy to act like nothing happened. Corinne was there, in her back seat, being strangled by roots and vines, until she wasn't. Sol could still feel the prickled pain of scratches across her face.

"*Someone's coming*," it hissed.

Sol didn't hear the roar of an engine until it was already halfway down the street, slowing to a stop behind her car. The headlights were stronger now, blinding her temporarily even as she squinted to get a view of the suspicious Toyota.

And the voice that came out of the car was like a jarring slap.

"So *this* is where you live," Clarke said, slamming the door behind him. "Nice place. How'd you manage to swing it?" He smiled like he meant it, but Clarke was the last person Sol thought to see—made even more dire as this night was unfolding the way it was—and that made him unpredictable at best, and dangerous at worst.

"What are you doing here?" Sol asked, backing up. Hadn't she lost him? How did he find her?

Clarke ignored her skittish behavior, confidently striding over. He was taller than her, but was also a beanpole. She'd never been intimidated by him, especially not physically, seeing how Sol had been raised on a healthy diet of carbs and protein, but now, on this street, alone . . .

She looked around, seeing if there was anywhere she could run to. Anywhere she could get away from this man who couldn't possibly be here for anything good. She realized he had *never* been up to any good. Sure, he wore thick glasses and had a nasally voice and was so soft-spoken and well-mannered that he came across as nonthreatening to most people. But that was clearly a mask he wore.

Truth be told, Sol never knew what made a person as quietly vicious as he was. Sol agonized over it for months, pored over every interaction she had with the man. Did she not greet him enough? Should she have invited him to coffee like Amir did with her? Nothing was so internally devastating as the conclusion that the fault had to lie with her. There was something wrong with *her*. *She* should have tried more. Been more charismatic, more accommodating, more, more, *more*. Sol would have given up teeth if it meant being on good terms with the man who was destroying her career.

And that made her angrier than she'd ever been.

He chuckled. "Why do you look so upset?"

"I don't know—because you tried to ruin my life and are now invading my space."

"Your space." He shook his head. "How the hell is any of this *your* space?" he muttered.

She had no response to that, so, clenching her teeth, she asked what had been pressing on her mind all day. "I heard you confessed."

"Yes."

"I've been wondering why."

He stopped. "Funny you should say that, because I've been asking myself the same thing."

Clarke was careful in the way he dressed. Even though he was thin as a pencil, he made an effort to get tailored suits, polish his shoes, and keep a clean-shaven appearance.

Except now that he was closer, Sol noticed he was disheveled, dirt rubbed into the collar of a Nirvana T-shirt, and ragged sweatpants to match. A five o'clock shadow was coming on strong. If it wasn't for his voice, she might not have known it was Clarke at all.

"What do you mean? You confessed. That's what happened."

"Yes, that's what happened. But how'd you do it?" He came forward again. Startled, Sol stepped back once more, trying to keep the distance between them.

"How'd I do what?" She glanced over her shoulder, hoping that someone in a nearby home was watching. *It always feels like there are eyes on me here. Where are they now?*

"How'd you get me to confess?"

Sol widened her eyes. Did she hear that right?

"You think I *made you* confess? We haven't even interacted since your accusation!"

Clarke gave a noncommittal half shrug. Sol couldn't believe it. Even after all this, the fact that he *willingly came forward himself* was supposed to be her fault? If Sol was a neurologist, she'd like to study his brain to see where it went wrong.

"I didn't do anything." Sol glared at him. "At all. Not once did I ever do anything to you, to drag me through all of that. If you were feeling guilty, then that's on *you*."

Clarke snorted. Sol's eye twitched. This was *funny* to him?

"But I don't feel guilty! That's the thing. Why should I? You said I dragged you through all this? Please! You're *fine*. You would've been fine. You think Yale was really going to let go of their only . . ." He gestured to her, mild confusion and disgust taking over his face. "I mean, come on, you publish a new article in the *Journal of Molecular Biology* like every year or something. Who else can say that?"

He stepped forward again, voice suddenly low. "How does *anyone* get to do that consistently?"

They get to do that because they're just that good. Because I'm just that good. Sol chewed on the inside of her cheek. Her blood pressure was rising quickly.

"I worked hard," she said. "Like I always have."

"Sure, maybe. I'm *sure* that's it. I'm sure it has nothing to do with *anything* else." He dug his hands into his pockets, and now she was worried there might be a weapon in there. Once more, she looked around. *Should I just run? Can I outrun those long legs?* He kept moving forward, saying, "But I've worked hard too. And yet, for *some reason*, my papers are never accepted."

"So . . ."

"So I just needed you to not submit for one year, just to give me an edge. You might think it's a waste of time because *so many people* submit their work, but the way I see it, I'm just evening the odds."

She was nervous, but she was also angry. He tried to destroy her to get a stupid paper published? It seemed so small—so petty. And so goddamn wrong.

"My papers were accepted because they advance the field. I don't know why yours weren't. But if that's how you see it, then your math is bad." She still couldn't figure out an escape, so now she was just stalling. Maybe if all he wanted to do was vent, he would go away. Not that she had a lot of confidence in that—judging by the way he was dressed, he was obviously going through some kind of breakdown.

"*Probably from being blackballed.*" A voice giggled.

Clarke froze. He glanced about and then locked his eyes on Sol.

"Did you hear that?"

"Hear what?" Sol swallowed—but her poker face was not as good when she wasn't prepared. Clarke broke out into a smile.

"Oh no, you're not going to lie your way out of this one. You wanted to know why I confessed?" He flicked a knife out of his pocket.

Sol brought up her hands, defensively. "Clarke, I can see you're upset—"

"*Shut up.* I woke up one morning, and there was this loud buzzing noise. At least, I thought it was buzzing. But then I realized it was like a million voices talking all at once. And they just wouldn't stop." Clarke was just an arm's length away from Sol. If he so much as whipped that knife toward her, he could easily slash her.

She sucked in her breath, focusing on making herself as small as possible, but ready to run. Her car was starting to look so much safer.

"*Told you.*"

"What is that!" he yelled, knife shaking. "Tell me how you're doing that!"

"I'm not—I'm not doing anything!" Sol pleaded. She held in a choking sob, hoping to keep her vision clear so she would be ready for whatever came next.

"Hello?" The door to the house behind her suddenly opened. A young woman with hair in a long braid poked her head out of the door frame. She wrapped a robe around her middle and stepped out. Sol racked her brain for a name.

She sniffled—nothing came. *Please help!*

"Is there something wrong?" the woman asked, eyeing both of them suspiciously. Clarke had the good sense to hide his weapon, but terror remained on Sol's face.

"What's going on here?" the woman asked.

"I saw this suspicious woman on the street and I'm trying to figure out what she's doing here."

Sol looked at Clarke, then at the woman. And in that moment, she knew what he was doing. Here was a white man confronting a Black woman in *this* neighborhood. Who was this random lady supposed to believe? Sure, she could prove herself if the cops came, but the last thing a person of color wants to see is a cop car roll up in the dark of night, especially when they are still "working out the truth."

He's going to get me shot . . .

The woman was staring at both of them, and Sol noticed the cell phone in her hand. The woman seemed to lift it to dial, but then put it in her pocket. "You need to leave, sir."

Sol could scarcely believe it. And she really couldn't believe it when the woman said, "I know Sol. I don't know you. And I know *everyone* in this community. So please leave before I'm forced to call the cops."

She knows my name?

"*Of course she does,*" the voice said.

Clarke's playful smile melted into a thin, surly line. He nodded, a flex in his jawline that put Sol on edge.

"Hope you have a good night, Sol," he said quietly. "Hope it won't be your last." Straightening his back, he walked nonchalantly to his car like he had any sense of dignity. Sol's head spun as he calmly drove out.

That was a threat. He wasn't done.

He was going to *kill* her over this. Over *his* own crime.

This wasn't over. Not by a long shot.

"Yes, it is."

This time, the voice sounded more like the woman standing in her robe than the vague, nameless voice she sometimes heard. She twisted back to her, both grateful and terrified about whether this would reflect badly on her. Things *always* reflected badly on her.

"Listen . . ." Sol began, but she still didn't know the woman's name. More, she wasn't sure how she was going to smooth things over, but she had to try, goddammit. "I can explain. That was my coworker. He's still upset about some things between us, and I . . ." She stopped, realizing the woman wasn't listening. Instead, her eyes were narrowed, seeming to be focused on the car disappearing into the distance. The taillights were just red pins in the dark, the faint headlights trying to find their way out of the confusing neighborhood.

And then there was a crash.

Sol jumped and ran into the street. She could just barely see Clarke's car. One of the lights were out, and it might have been a bit too dark to be sure, but was that smoke rising from the engine?

"Don't worry about it, Sol." The woman smiled, patting her shoulder lightly. "We always take care of our own." The look in her eyes made hair rise on the back of Sol's neck. Then without another word, she walked back into her house and closed the door. It was silent on the street except for the dinging of Sol's car door and the hiss of the car crash.

And the faint rustling of the trees.

Following Clarke's example, Sol got back to her car and U-turned. Refusing to look into the rearview mirror for fear of seeing Corinne again, she stared ahead, careful on the gas pedal and rolling up next to Clarke's Toyota.

Or what was left of it, rather. The car was worse off than she thought. It was wrapped around a tree, hood rolled up like paper. A thin line of smoke was rising from the engine, dark and oily. Panicked, Sol jumped out of her car and was just about to knock on his window frantically when she noticed a branch pointed downward. It was the only part of the tree that appeared broken, and it somehow angled itself perfectly so that it went clean through the windshield.

And into Clarke's temple.

APRIL 10

I dreamt about it.

The place that woman spoke about. Where I can get away from the buzzing and the voices and the prying eyes. She didn't say exactly that, but I know that's what she meant by privacy.

It's a house. Specifically, one of the homes in Maneless Grove. It took me a while to find it. The streets like to turn and twist, keeping you confused and trapped. But more than that, when I saw it in my dream, it wasn't the view from the street. I wasn't standing on the sidewalk, looking down at the lawn leading to the front door.

I was standing in the backyard. And instead of one of those weird identical white trees, there was a dark brown tree practically grafted to the house. The bare branches seemed to claw at the home. The trunk had veins in it that curved down to the base, throbbing like it was feeding on the heart of the neighborhood.

I woke up in a cold sweat but couldn't get it out of my head. To be honest, I didn't think it actually existed. I thought I only dreamt about it because it was similar enough to what I'm surrounded by. The same pale-yellow houses with identical trees and suspiciously empty streets. Like no one's ever home.

But when I found this house, when I walked across the

sidewalk and looked across to the front door, I could feel the difference. Something about it was colder than the rest of the community. Quieter. More dead. From the front, you can't see that out-of-place tree and to be honest, I don't think I want to.

I just need a place where I can actually think my own thoughts.

THE VIEWING

It came as no surprise to Sol when they drove up to the funeral home to see that the entire community was there, paying their respects to the old woman.

"This is . . . a lot," Alice remarked, taking another pain pill. Sol narrowed her eyes at this—at both the comment, considering how often *she* got side-eye for saying such things, and at the pill. Hadn't Alice already taken one this morning? Alice didn't notice. "When they talked about having a neighborly spirit, I thought they were exaggerating."

In some ways, it was a little jarring. Sol had just seen Clarke gruesomely killed—death by impaling tree branch was not a way she would have thought he'd go (and she'd envisioned his death a *lot* the last few weeks). It unnerved her because he hadn't even been driving fast or, from what she could tell, dangerously. How could he have hit the tree so hard that it caused a tree branch to snap without so much as damaging the trunk? How much force would have been needed to pierce glass and skin and bone, all in one fell swoop? Sol wasn't a physicist, but she gathered it needed to be a lot.

On the other hand, Corinne died at home. In a familiar place. And here was the entire force of the community to crowd around her, speaking nothing but good over her life. Celebrating her. Corinne deserved this, Sol thought. She just couldn't look into the rearview mirror again.

But this was how it was supposed to be. Good people lived long, comfortable lives, with loving friends and family. Bad people like Clarke . . .

Well.

The funeral home was small and near enough to the community

that many carpooled. Three vans were still unloading in the parking lot of the San Gutierrez Funeral Home. Most were people Sol hadn't met but still gave her a nod of acknowledgment as though they already knew her.

"Hi, Sol. I'm glad you could make it." Teresa walked around her car to greet her. Instinctively, Sol stepped back.

"Sorry, I'm just . . . I don't like being touched." The idea of going dizzy here and now was anxiety inducing. She'd rather have a breakdown at home.

"Understandable. Well, if you need anything, just know that I'll be around."

Sol stopped her before she turned away. "Wait, I wanted to ask . . . the situation about Clarke—"

"All taken care of," Teresa reassured her, a kind smile turning smug if only for a moment. "The police already know it was an accident. You don't have to worry about anything."

Confused, Sol deflated and watched Teresa disappear in the crowd of people entering through the front door. There were so many people— were they all from Maneless Grove? She tried to commit some of those faces to memory. It would be good if she could recognize her neighbors at least in passing. And it would be even better if they recognized her. After the incident at the Kennedys', she wouldn't be shocked if there were already whispers about the crazed Black woman who unnecessarily called emergency services. Bad news traveled fast, especially in small, insular communities. Sol could imagine anyone who knew her by reputation would wonder what drama followed her today.

Sol caught herself—this wasn't about *her*. She was at a funeral, for God's sake. No one was going to be thinking about what brand of crazy she came packed with. Today was about Corinne.

She took a step forward and stopped.

The woman who saved her from Clarke was here. She stood within the crowd, still as a statue while everyone else flowed around her like a river. There was a hardened look in her eyes and she held Sol's stare like they were both co-conspirators in a larger plot. Her lips parted; she mouthed something quickly before turning away, disappearing in the crowd like Teresa just did. Like it was the easiest goddamn thing to do to just melt into this group.

Alice grabbed her hand. "Are you going to be okay?"

Pay attention. Those were the woman's words. As heavy as the feeling they inspired in Sol.

Sol didn't meet Alice's eyes at first. "Yeah," she lied. "Two bodies in one week is just a little rough on me." It was a good enough excuse that Alice did nothing but squeeze her hand. Clarke was the one secret she didn't have to keep from Alice. The man followed her home, threatened her with a knife, and then scurried off into a tree, bad luck coalescing into one final moment for him. His body was picked up within the hour, his car was towed, and the night moved on for the rest of the neighborhood, like nothing ever happened.

She scanned the crowd for Nadine, mentally preparing herself for the eventuality of them meeting. She hadn't gotten Amir's text out of her mind since she'd seen it and out of . . . respect? Unease? She couldn't find it in herself to bring it up to Alice.

It was one thing to know someone likely killed themselves in her own home, it was another thing to think it might have been Nadine's son, the "Maneless Missing." Someone who suddenly disappeared some-odd years ago and was later found dead in a house fire. Specifically, the house fire that happened in her home. The house fire there was almost no evidence of.

Maybe it wasn't even the same house! Sol wanted to believe. But what were the odds of two fires in the same gated neighborhood, both started by someone who was clearly distressed?

The few online articles about the tragedy parroted the same information—Sean was a troubled kid, a loner, someone who needed help but didn't get it, and if anyone else was suffering in the same way Sean did, they should consider reaching out to the Suicide and Crisis Lifeline which was available 24/7.

Sol wasn't sure she completely bought it. It was one thing for a nineteen-year-old—a *kid* by her standards—to run away from home, and yes sometimes troubled kids did attempt suicide, but normally it was through overdosing, or turning on the car in a closed garage.

Something low effort and somewhat painless. Death by immolation was a step too far for a child.

Unless he only lit the house on fire and not himself. That would make more sense.

Except why would he run away only to stay in the neighborhood? She thought about all the times she'd driven out of Maneless Grove— and of her walk through the woods—and wondered if he'd somehow gotten lost too.

If the only escape he could find *was* fire.

Which all made Sol want more clarity on what happened to Sean. Maybe Papi was right and she was just a chismosa like her mother. In a very odd way, she hoped it was just that and not that she was paranoid about something entirely new. But she was connected to it, even if just tangentially, and she had to know.

"Are you sure you're okay to miss work today?" Sol asked Alice instead. It was a Friday, and while they were neighbors, the fact of the matter was that they had only known Corinne for a short time. Funerals were best suited for friends and family of the dearly departed, especially when it came to explaining time off to an HR department.

"They won't miss me," her wife said, a little colder than Sol expected. She could see the sting of being passed up for a promotion was still fresh. Was it weird to find a small comfort in knowing they were in the same boat? Of knowing that employment would never be a completely even ground for women like them? Even when the two proved their competence time and time again (*competence? more like excellence*), the evidence could so easily be ripped away from them unceremoniously and without warning. The game was always rigged. It was a painful reminder that, really, they only had each other.

Sol steeled herself as she and Alice walked toward the funeral home.

The building was very cool. The air conditioning bore down on Sol, raising goosebumps all over her arms and the back of her neck. It wasn't until she fully entered the viewing that she understood why. The room was filled wall to wall with friends and acquaintances of Corinne Munro. Next to the casket was a large portrait of her, a loving smile and brightened eyes looking up toward the sky. Sol's breath caught in her throat. This was how she was meant to see Corinne last. Full of joy, and life. Not roots and wood taking over her skin. Whoever painted the portrait captured her well.

On her left and right, rows of chairs were filled with people either weeping or speaking in hushed tones. A mass of people were waiting in line just to pay respects. Hands went into the casket, as if they were making sure she was truly stiff enough to be buried. Then they walked back down the aisle.

Ahead of her, Sol saw Hope gripping the edge of the casket and shaking her head. Her husband then pulled her into a hug at the exact moment that she began to openly sob.

Sol glanced at Alice. Her own wife was very good at keeping a poker face, and Sol wished she could match that energy. Unfortunately, despair found cracks in her armor and she found herself already struggling to keep a calm composure. It was like the morning of Corinne's death all over again.

Sol looked around, hoping to find family of Corinne somewhere. A nurse asked if Sol was her daughter—so perhaps she had at least one.

"Are . . ." Sol swallowed, parched throat growing drier by the second. "Are there only white people here?" The crowd around her bristled but she didn't care. Sol squeezed Alice's hand again to get her attention. "Hey, are you seeing this? Did Corinne not have any family?"

Alice gave her a solemn look. "This community was her family."

The whole room suddenly became cast in a different light. The more Sol scanned, the more she confirmed it was truly only white people. And where did they all come from? Where were they all the other times Sol was out in the street, trying to find her way home?

Shit, is this my future? Good God, she needed more Black friends.

"Have you found any seats yet?" Alice asked. Sol blinked and shook her head.

"There are some seats right there."

When she looked, Finnian was pointing to a few seats in front of him. She stalled, not wanting to be too close to him, but after confirming she had no other choice, she led Alice the way up the aisle.

Alice was the first to greet him as she sat down.

"Hi, Finnian," she whispered.

"Hi. It's nice to see you two here," he said. Sol made a quick glance in his direction and noticed his eyes were puffy and red. He held a napkin in his hand and pressed it to his crooked nose.

Another Finnian. Sol tried not to stare too hard. *A different one.*

"Gosh, I'm never good with these things." He chuckled, embarrassed.

"It's okay, don't worry about it," Alice replied. "Were you and Corinne close?"

"Ha! Of course. I used to bring her fresh produce from the community garden all the time."

Alice nodded sympathetically. "That sounds really nice. I'm . . . sorry for your loss." She put a hand on his shoulder and from Sol's view, it looked like he was holding back a gross sob.

They really were close, Sol thought as she turned away from him.

"You're so kind," Finnian said.

Roy came into view, eyes just as red as Finnian's. "Alice, Sol, thanks for coming." He held out a hand and Alice shook it. While Sol still hadn't forgiven him for the overly friendly meeting at the welcoming party, she did the same.

"I know you two hadn't really known Corinne that long, but it's nice of you two to stop by." Roy sniffled and then coughed into a handkerchief. Whatever was ailing him seemed to still be at it.

"It's the least we could do." Alice gave a small smile. "Though it was hard to find seats. It's like the whole neighborhood's here, huh."

"It really is." Roy looked around. Sol followed his line of sight. True, she recognized quite a few people she had already met. But the funeral home was packed with so many others. People she wasn't even sure really *lived* in the community. Maybe if she looked hard enough, she'd find the other Finnians.

Eyes falling down, she noticed even the children were organized in lines with their families, tearstained cheeks and soft whimpers marking them as if they were in danger of breaking out in loud cries.

"I didn't realize she was such a loved member of the community," Sol mumbled.

Roy shook his head. "At Maneless Grove, *everyone* is important. We're not just alone in our own worlds here. We're part of a whole. That's what makes it special." Suddenly his hand was on Sol's shoulder and he squeezed it. "And don't worry. One day, you'll understand it too."

Sol's body went cold at both the touch and the words. Then she quickly stood up. "I'm going to go see Corinne," she announced, and shuffled off. The line to the casket was slow moving. The only thing that Sol was grateful for was the fact that there was no one on the line that she was familiar with. It saved her from the hell of small talk and allowed her to use most of her energy thinking about what happened to Corinne.

And her last words.

Don't trust the neighbor.

Why those words? The elderly woman had only recently gotten back from the hospital and now she was dead. And yet Sol believed she had been visited by Corinne . . . and warned by her. She just didn't know what the warning meant.

Sol envisioned her choking in bed, a hush of whispers calling her to the grave. If it wasn't for the fact that Corinne seemed afraid during their last visit and her strange dream, Sol might have written it off as it just being her time. But seeing her in the back seat of her car, talking about the roots, whatever they were, and the fervent desperation she was trying to instill in Sol . . . she was terrified. There was something off, something strange about this neighborhood that Corinne knew.

Don't trust the neighbor—but which one? Nadine was an obvious suspect, but when placed next to the handful of different Finnians in the lineup of suspicions, or the all-knowing HOA vice president, Teresa, or the pushy, no-boundaries Hope, or the yet-to-be-believed bigot Lou—it really could have been any one of them.

Unless she meant the Church of the Neighbor. Sol almost scoffed at the thought. That cult had been dead for over a century now—if it had even existed in the first place. So who should Sol talk to first?

"Are you feeling better?"

Dealer's choice it was.

"Yes, though I'll admit I was shocked. I just wasn't expecting that to happen."

Teresa was close enough to brush Sol's shoulder. "No one ever does. Death is just like that."

The line moved ahead. Sol was close enough to Corinne to see part of her boots. They shined in the light and made Sol think about the walk they had before the stairs accident.

"It's not your fault."

The statement startled Sol.

"What?"

Teresa stared ahead, as though she hadn't said anything. Then she repeated herself.

"She died in her sleep, Sol. The fall didn't do anything to hasten her death."

Sol steeled herself when she stepped close enough to see her face. Corinne looked like she was just peacefully having a nap. It was such a sharp contrast from the look of pain she had when a crack shot through her hip.

Like the crack in that trinket . . .

"I-I wasn't thinking it was my fault," Sol said, defensively.

"Just making sure." Teresa hummed. "It's very easy for a person to blame themselves over the death of a new friend."

She didn't know how to respond to that, and luckily she was saved from having to because it was finally Sol's turn. She came to the head of the casket and looked down on the stillness of her old neighbor. A lump rose in her throat and her lungs seized up for a moment. Corinne had died in her sleep. It was the most peaceful way to go and still, Sol wasn't sure if that was really how she went. Twice since she met Corinne, she had watched the woman's eyes turn fearful, pained, and desperate. It wasn't a lot, but the depth of those emotions stayed with her.

And after she was dead? More desperation, more fear. Sol reached up to the curve in her cheek where the sting of a scratch should have been.

"It wasn't my fault," she whispered to the dead woman. The words felt like a lie.

A minute later, Sol was able to let go of the casket and walk back. Teresa gave a sympathetic smile that made Sol's skin crawl, but instead of retreating faster, she slowed her pace as a question came to mind.

"Is Nadine not here?"

Teresa shook her head. "Nadine's not good with funerals."

Because of her son. Sol understood the implication even without being told outright. Still, she frowned.

"I thought the two were close." It seemed that way to Sol, especially given how Nadine talked about her.

"Ha! Well . . ." Teresa's mouth hung open, like she was deciding on the next word or an explanation. But after a few more seconds, she went back to a sympathetic smile and an empty look in her eyes. Sol shuddered and took that as her cue to leave.

She mumbled pardons all the way down the line of the people waiting to get to the casket, and hoped to quickly get back to her wife and her seat.

Only one of them was there.

"Alice?" Sol looked around the room. Familiar faces mixed in with the unfamiliar, but Alice wasn't one of them.

"Are you looking for the short Asian woman?" a stranger asked, as if there were *any* other Asian women at this funeral. "She went outside. I think she just needed some fresh air."

Sol thanked the man and hurried.

Luckily, Alice wasn't too far from the entrance. Sol spotted her right away, standing by a potted tree hugging Finnian tightly. By the look of her shaking shoulders, Sol knew that Alice was crying. Sol stopped in her tracks, fully perplexed. Alice was supposed to be the stoic one here. Hell, she hadn't had more than two conversations with Corinne before she died.

She slowly jogged over, eyeing Finnian cautiously. If he noticed her coming, he outright ignored it and whispered something in her wife's ear.

"Hey." Sol put her hand on Alice's lower back. "Everything over here okay?"

Alice pulled away from Finnian, tears streaking down her face. Almost immediately, she began wiping her tears away and forcing a smile. Sol froze again.

"I'm fine, sorry, it's just—it's so sad."

"So everyone says," Sol muttered. The words came out of her mouth before she realized it. The look of confused shock on Alice's face told her that yes, she said it out loud and should hope no one else heard her.

Alice recovered quickly and instead asked, "Did you get to pay your respects?"

"Yup. I'm ready to go now." Sol looked over to Finnian. Whichever one he was now, she'd like to be away from him.

Don't be like that. You're one of us now. Sol blinked. His lips didn't move, but that—that was definitely his voice. She glanced at Alice, but it was clear she wasn't in on whatever new level of telepathy they were on.

She looked back at Finnian. It was very slight and lasted for half a second, but Sol could have sworn she saw a smirk.

"Oh, before you go, Roy and I were wondering if you were free to join us for brunch," Finnian asked.

"Uh, today? Right now?" The invite was much too sudden for Sol's liking. Even Alice couldn't force her into this.

"No, sorry—this Sunday."

"Oh, I would love to," Alice answered first. Sol sent her a look but she didn't catch it. Finnian looked at Sol expectantly and she found it surprisingly difficult to say no.

She gritted her teeth as she answered, "Sure."

"Great! I'll text you the address and we can meet there at about eleven thirty."

"Sounds great."

Sol waited until the two were in their car before turning to Alice.

"What the hell was that?"

"What was what?" Alice blinked, putting the car in reverse.

"Could you not make plans for us at the drop of a dime?"

"I didn't make plans for *us*, Sol." Alice shot a glare at her. "*I* said that *I'd* love to go. You didn't have to say you'd go too."

Sol opened her mouth to argue but when Alice sniffled, she shut down purely out of confusion. Alice hardly batted an eye when she went months without speaking to her parents for constantly picking at her weight. What sense did it make for her to go ruining her makeup over a woman she knew for less than a week?

"Are you okay?" Sol asked.

"I'm fine." Alice still didn't look at her. Sol rolled her eyes and shifted closer to the window.

After a moment, she asked, "Did you notice Nadine didn't show up for this funeral?"

"Nadine's not good with funerals."

Which were the exact words in that exact inflection Teresa had told Sol not too long ago . . .

Sol shifted in her seat, suddenly uncomfortable with the fact that Alice was driving. "I thought they were close, though."

"Ha! Well . . ." And then silence.

The same response again?

This time she couldn't just let it slide. "What does *that* mean?" Sol looked at Alice again. Her wife's eyes remained on the road, only moving to glance at the rearview and side mirrors.

"Hm? What does what mean?"

"I asked you about Nadine and you said she wasn't good with funerals." When Alice didn't answer, Sol continued. "Then I said I thought they were close, and you just did a weird laugh and said, 'Well.'"

"She's just not good with funerals, jagi. I don't know what else to tell you."

Alice's words were so soft, Sol wanted to believe her. But that didn't answer the question of why she suddenly mimicked Teresa perfectly in the span of thirty seconds. She wasn't sure how to ask about that, though, and so decided to shift the conversation just a little.

Treading carefully, Sol asked, "Do you know . . . *how* Sean died?"

"Ah, I don't," Alice answered. "Nadine doesn't like to talk about it."

Sol sank into her seat.

Loners don't do well in Maneless Grove. That's what Nadine said the last time they spoke about Sean. Sol still didn't know what to make of it. It was easy to believe that Sean took his own life—*too* easy, in fact. But for his own mother to call him a loner—and to use that as a threat against Sol—had her convinced there was more to all this. Still, suddenly asking a woman how her son died was beyond even her usual tactlessness.

"Are we still going to the spa tomorrow?" She watched her wife's reflection in her window.

"Yeah, I think so. Nadine hasn't canceled."

Maybe that's the perfect time for my usual tactlessness.

APRIL 19

The neighborhood is trying to keep me away from the house.
It's obvious. The way it takes me nearly an hour to find my
way over even though it shouldn't take me more than fifteen
minutes. It doesn't like that I come here. It doesn't like that it
can't get to me so easily.

I guess that's why I keep coming.

The woman comes too. Or rather, sometimes she's just here.
She comes in through the back door, like she was always in
the backyard. She comes in smelling like smoke. I don't know
why but it's the only thing I can remember about her. The
smell of smoke. The sound of crinkling fire.

Is it bad that I already trust her so much? Or is it because
I don't trust anyone else? She doesn't lie to me, not like the
others do. When I ask her why I can't remember something,
she doesn't give me a fake smile and laugh like I told a joke.
She tells me the truth, even if it doesn't make sense.

Like the other day, I asked her why I can't remember
anything else about her. Not her name, not her face, sometimes
not even the sound of her voice. She said—or I think she
said—it's because of the Neighbor. It's already gotten to me.

Maybe if I had gotten to this house sooner, I'd be able to
remember her.

INNER BLISS

Inner Bliss Spa was a midsize building with stone walls and a fake waterfall pouring into a fake pond with a stone statue of two fish crossing each other. Their heads pointed up just halfway out of the surface of the fake pond, mouths squirting water in a continuous arc. Sol zoomed out of the Google image as much as she could before trying to move on to the next. It wouldn't go. These were the only images of the spa that were put on Google Maps, and they included stone fish with chipped, horrifying eyes.

She scrolled down on her phone. Only one anonymous review that gave it 5 stars and a short description about it having a "good atmosphere." Were they actually going to a spa or were they going to get murdered?

"Thanks again for inviting us along," Alice chirped as she strolled out the front door toward the van. Sol trailed behind her, eyes still glued to her phone. She might have been talked into carpooling, but she was *not* in the mood to socialize.

"Please!" Nadine waved her off graciously. "You're doing me a favor. I mean, I didn't actually think I would win the contest. It would be a waste otherwise."

Sol rolled her eyes. She already didn't trust Nadine and having looked into the Maneless Missing case, she had even less reason to do so. The missing person report was several years old, before Sol and Alice had even heard of the community. No leads, just shrugs from the police and the conclusion that he might have run away. Then suddenly, he was found dead in a vacant house fire. The word "suicide" was thrown around, but that was it. A very clean wrap-up that didn't allow anyone to ask questions. And why would they? Poking around a grieving mother's story was a crass thing to do.

Yet, that was exactly what Sol was going to do. She climbed into the van, barely looking up from her phone. The drive to the spa was supposed to be short, maybe twenty minutes, give or take. And if they were only going to be there for about an hour or so, she could count on this entire trip being no more than two hours. She had two hours to broach the topic of Nadine's dead kid. Maybe she would start by talking about the history of the house. The fire that Corinne mentioned, and what might have caused it. Nadine would have something to say about that.

I'm sure she'll love to talk about it.

But Sol didn't care. She felt Nadine slide in next to her and became tense.

"Sorry, I thought you were just going to be riding shotgun." Sol looked to the empty passenger seat.

"No, but if you'd like to take it, you're welcome to it!" Nadine said with all the charm of a preschool teacher. Harmless. Except her body was pressed against Sol, like a constant reminder that she couldn't get away easily. She'd be sandwiched between Alice and Nadine and with the way the two liked to talk . . .

"Yeah, I think I will," Sol grumbled, climbing into the front. She cast a quick glance to the driver—a pale woman who stared blankly ahead. She wordlessly put the car back into drive and started down the road.

"Thanks for the, um, ride," Sol muttered. The woman didn't respond. Instead, Nadine jumped in almost immediately.

"Oh, right. I should introduce you." Nadine patted the other woman on the shoulder. "Bethany, this is Alice and Sol. Bethany also lives in the community and is one of my closest friends."

So is Bethany not going to say hi?

"*Right, because you're so social,*" a buzzing voice responded. Sol's jaw fell. She tried to catch her wife's eyes in the rearview mirror.

"Something wrong, Sol?" Alice asked, furrowing her brow in mild concern.

Sol began to sweat. "You didn't hear that?"

"Hear what?"

"Nothing. I thought—nothing." She twisted back around and sank in her seat. In the rearview mirror, Nadine smirked.

Sol looked away quickly.

Alice and Nadine chattered on in the back. The engine roared as the group picked up speed. Sol gripped her seat and eyed the woman next to her. She hardly blinked.

But she did speak.

"*Nice to meet you, Sol,*" it returned. "*We're the neighbor.*"

It took everything to not rip open the door and dive out of the moving car. Instead, Sol bit the inside of her cheek and closed her eyes tight. The light buzz of its voice became static, drowning out everything else in the van. When Sol opened her eyes again, she was still sitting there, but had the jarring feeling that she was outside of the scene. One step removed, not quite connected.

Except she still felt the static. It hummed under her skin, caressing her cheek, and nuzzled against her pulse. Sol's breath caught in her throat. The voice chuckled.

"What's going on?" Sol whispered. She could feel the static winding itself around her skull. She reached into her scalp and found herself frustratingly stopped by flesh and muscle. Sol dug in until the pressure became a sharp pinch and—

"*Don't do that,*" the voice said, shedding layers of static. It almost sounded human. It almost sounded like—

"Corinne?" she whispered, carefully. Sol's eyes instinctively went to the rearview mirror again. Luckily, she only saw Alice and Nadine, so engrossed in their own conversation, they didn't notice how Sol was on the verge of peeling her skin off. Corinne said not to trust the neighbor—what was she doing here now . . . talking *as* the neighbor?

Nadine once said the dead keep on living in the community. Was this what she meant?

"*If you make yourself bleed, you'll only worry Alice. Do you want to worry her?*" The static built up again, sounding less like Corinne. Sol slowly put her hands down. "*Good. We're just trying to help.*"

Trying to help. The words dripped with a condescension that made

Sol hesitant to accept it as fact. Because who were they trying to help? It certainly wasn't her. She didn't need their help, whoever this was. She needed it to stay out of her business, out of her home, and most importantly—out of her mind.

The laughter started like a trickle until it became a rushing river. Long and forceful, and rising in volume. Heat spread across her face like a wildfire. She didn't have to look back at Nadine or Alice to know they weren't hearing any of this. They weren't being laughed at or made a spectacle like she was. They were enjoying themselves, looking forward to a relaxing day at the spa.

Sol was the only one that was out of place. The only one who didn't belong—and she knew it.

Sol squeezed her eyes tight until she could force the tears back in. It felt like years before the laughter died down and she let out a gasp of relief, happy to be free of buzzing until she felt a sparkling sensation in the back of her head. The static-like feeling shocked its way through her skull, from neuron to neuron and then all at once.

Sol could *feel* connections starting to form from ideas to thoughts to sensations. She wasn't sitting next to Alice, but she could feel the rub of her arm just as easily, as well as the pressure of a cold leather steering wheel under her hands. Her stomach felt like it was widening again, and Sol instinctively pushed against that sensation until it petered out to nothing, certainly not yet ready to feel any sympathy pain from Nadine again.

Her rejection was met with a growl and the image of a branch piercing Clarke's skull. Within seconds, it became more than that. It was as if she could feel herself turn into dark wood, could feel its point shove into skin then bone then brain. A cold shock rolled over Sol's body, limbs falling numb, her breath slowing while her vision darkened.

It was like a threat, being told she had to accept being part of the community or reap the consequences.

Or like she *owed* them.

"*We take care of our own,*" the memory of the woman reminded Sol.

The static pushed onto her shoulders and down her back. The icy feeling of death washed itself away with the voice and suddenly, Sol could breathe easily again. No panic about where they were going or how long they'd be there. No paranoia about trees or journal entries or dead bodies. Sol was just in a van, with her wife and two friends, on their way to a spa.

Sol's phone buzzed. She pulled it out and grimaced at the caller ID. *Harrison's Senior Living Center.*

Ignore, she thought, her thumb already going to the dismiss button.

"You should take that."

She hesitated for a moment, then picked up.

"Hello?" She turned away from the group.

"Hi, I'm Irene from Harrison's Senior Living Center. Is this . . . Marisol Reyes?" Up until Sol's name, the line that Irene spoke sounded rehearsed, like this was just one of dozens of calls she was making today. It probably was.

"Yes. Is there something wrong with him?" Whatever was happening with Papi better have been an emergency. Maybe she could use it as an excuse to get out of the spa day.

"N-no." The nurse coughed. "He was just . . . concerned because you hadn't taken the time to visit him in the last two weeks."

It definitely was not an emergency.

"I'm busy. Let him know I'll see him soon." Sol hung up before Irene could respond. As nervous as Irene sounded, Sol wouldn't be surprised if her dad had badgered her into calling Sol. It couldn't have been normal to call the next of kin for anything other than emergencies. Irene was probably new. She would learn not to give in eventually.

Or she wouldn't. Papi had that slick charm when he really wanted it. Sol had been a victim of it for long enough, that was for sure.

"Is everything okay, Sol?" Nadine suddenly asked. "You look a bit . . . upset."

"Actually, I'm fine." She was surprised to really mean it. Seeing as her father's call didn't even send her spiraling into a bad mood, which was not the norm. She frowned at her phone, not sure if she liked nonchalance being thrust onto her. Focusing on the voice again, she whispered, "Are you . . . in the roots?"

A laugh came like a chorus of shaking trees, and that seemed like both an affirmation and a complete non-answer. Still, excitement bubbled up in Sol's chest as colors seemed to brighten on their own. The voice broke apart into hundreds of chatters, each coming from a unique source.

"If you consider changing your finances here..."

"I can get your insurance rates lowered..."

"This will increase your ROI by fifteen percent..."

Sol dipped in and out of each conversation, feeling dizzier with each one. She didn't understand half of them, but she knew what she was hearing was real. Same as the emotions that infected her—all at once, she felt like grinning, giggling, sighing, baking a cake, going to the gym; intermittent fasting sounded nice. She considered cutting out carbs, switching banks, buying that cute yellow dress from Anthropologie, even though it's always been out of her price range. What if she straightened her hair? Ran a 5K? Anything and everything she wanted suddenly became more accessible. No anxiety to hold her back. If she needed someone's help, there was always a connection to be made somewhere.

It was amazing, and yet it was also a vortex, sucking her in.

I'm not ready I'm not ready I'm not ready—

Sol pinched her arm and focused on the rumble of the van to anchor herself within it. The disorganized chatter melted together into an intoxicating buzz that spoke with one voice.

"No need to hold back," it finally answered. *"We can help you be ready."*

Unsure any of this was real, Sol let her head loll over to the side to be able to see her wife, to give her one more thing to ground her. Because of that, she ended up catching Alice hunched over in the corner. She had covered her mouth and was whispering quickly into her phone. Sol had to strain her ear to catch it in time.

"We can talk later, Aunt Julie." Alice hung up.

Sol's mouth fell open. "Was that your aunt?"

"Mhm." Alice forced a smile and looked straight to Nadine. "It wasn't important. You were saying, Nadine?"

Nadine picked up the conversation, but Sol was stuck in that little moment. Alice *never* called her aunt "Aunt Julie." It was always "Imo." Moreover, she never opted to speak in English rather than Korean with her. It just wasn't her instinct.

I speak English with Papi, she thought, wondering if it were any different. *But I'd never call him Father or Dad.* Sol wondered if Alice had gotten into a fight with her aunt—but that didn't seem possible either. They were so close—closer than Alice was with her own parents, even.

But what else could it be? Why the change *now*?

"What does it matter?"

Because it *did*. Those little things mattered. It was part of what made them who they were. Made them unique.

"Things change," it said with a shrug. *"And uniqueness is for those on the outside."*

Again, she spun her eyes around the van, looking at the other three women. But were there three other women? Was she even a fourth? *"Yes and no,"* the voice said, seemingly pleased.

But Sol was anything but pleased. She glanced between Nadine and Alice. They were too engrossed in their conversation to notice anything wrong with the woman in the front passenger seat.

"Does the whole tree get upset when one leaf is blown away?"

Sol was not prepared for the metaphor, so she also took a moment to register the threat.

"Not a threat. Never a threat. Never a need."

And that, more than anything, made Sol's blood run cold to the point where she was actually shivering. She looked to turn off the AC, but worried about touching another person's car. Except she wasn't quite sure if this was a person's car or, as the voice had alluded to, just a leaf. Bethany remained quiet for someone who was supposed to be one of Nadine's closest friends.

"Hey, Bethany," Sol called out to her.

"Don't disturb her. She's driving."

Sol shut up.

Sol studied Bethany intensely. Her paleness rivaled that of the children in the neighborhood, but other than that, she seemed like every other suburban housewife. Mousy brown hair. Pink athleisure sweat-suit.

And utterly silent. Even Alice paid no attention to her, which was very much out of character. Alice was what most people considered a social butterfly—charismatic and very easy to get along with. By contrast, Bethany was a shadow.

Like a random leaf left on the driver's seat.

The van slowed on a turn. As Sol peered through the windshield, she narrowed her eyes on the fish statue, spewing water in an arc. Bethany pulled into the first parking spot she found.

"We're here," she said, in a raspy voice that didn't match her age and scared Sol as much as anything during this short drive, which was saying something.

She sounds like Veronica, Sol realized. Her hair stood on end with that connection, but once more the brief tinge of horror was already being melted away by static. The van rocked from side to side as everyone filtered out. Everyone but Sol.

"You'll feel better if you go with the flow. Like Alice."

Sol followed her wife with her eyes. Unlike her, Alice seemed to be really enjoying herself. Her smile was bright, and she stood tall, dancing from foot to foot. She was clearly excited for this. Considering the bad news about the promotion, Alice might have even needed this.

But the gravity of the situation far outweighed any superficial comfort. Despite Sol's own shaking nerves, she would pull Alice aside the first chance she got and speak quickly.

After all, she never knew who was listening.

Laughing at something Nadine said, Alice looped arms with her and led the group to the spa building. Sol's fingers dug into her palms. Now how was she going to get her away from Nadine?

The static moved down to the crook of her elbow, simulating the feeling of being held in the same way. Sol reflexively slapped it away and followed the group in. The inside was at least ten degrees cooler than the outside, with a low hum vibrating through the walls. She was already breaking out in a cold sweat, but the strong air-conditioning made her shiver even more.

Ahead of them was a blond receptionist just putting down a phone.

"Hello! Reservation for three?"

"Four, actually." Nadine pointed to Bethany. A brief moment of surprise went through the woman's face and she smiled apologetically. Even she didn't realize Bethany was there. The neighbor seemed to be very good at hiding its presence.

"*It's one of our gifts,*" it admitted.

Though there was a sinister undertone to that. An unspoken "We could make you go missing, if we wanted." Sean may have had *some* amount of attention when he disappeared, but Sol was Black and butch. She knew she would not get the same courtesy.

"*Relax,*" the voice seemed to command. "*It's a spa day.*"

Sol stepped beside Bethany. Upon closer inspection, Sol could see she had muted green eyes. She tried to engage in small talk, if only to make her stare seem less impolite while Nadine and Alice closed in on the front desk.

"So . . . Bethany . . ." Sol swung her arms beside her. "How do you know Nadine?"

Bethany slowly turned her head. "We're neighbors." She stayed like that, refusing to turn her head back. Sol couldn't tell if the blank expression on her face was purposeful or not.

"Okay. How long have you been neighbors?"

"Since I moved in."

"Right," Sol said. "When was that?"

Bethany didn't answer. The head of her shadow uncharacteristically twitched and Sol stiffened, cold fear snaking its way down her spine.

She was startled by a sudden arm around her shoulder, quickly recognizing the cloying scent of perfume and the press of a belly against her side. Nadine was way too touchy-feely for Sol's liking and she was about to say something when the sound of Alice's laughter put her off, though she couldn't place why.

"Okay, we're going to start out with head-and-shoulder massages,"

Nadine explained, leading them down a long hallway. "They can do backs if you don't mind undressing for it but as you can see—" She paused to rub her stomach, a playful pout on her lips. "I'm probably not going to be able to have that luxury. You all enjoy."

Undressing? That meant there would be a separate area for them to slip into robes. That would be Sol's moment, her chance to bring Alice's attention to the neighbor. Or at least admit to her that she was terrified to the point of vomiting and would rather go home *right now, please.*

"I think Sol and I will just stick to the head-and-shoulder massages," Alice announced, shocking Sol. Alice looked thoughtful as she explained, "She doesn't really like being touched and to be honest, I don't know how comfortable I am undressing for a stranger."

Any other time, Sol's heart would've soared to hear that. Instead, it sank hard and fast.

"Well, we all have our limits." Nadine glanced at Sol. It might have been her imagination but the pregnant woman almost looked amused.

Sol's spine stiffened, and she entered the next room first. Despite having never been to a massage therapist or a spa center, Sol looked around, nodding at every detail of the setting like she was checking them off a list. The tiles were black and sleek, polished enough for Sol to see her reflection. In the center of the room were two massage beds, each with a white towel folded on top of it. Along the walls were cabinets filled with more towels and tiny bottles. Sol assumed those were oils.

But it was what was between those cabinets that made Sol stop in confusion.

Sinks. Four sinks, evenly spaced next to each other. Chairs in front of them.

Sol's mind flashed to childhood memories of going to the Dominican salons back in New York. The long lines of chatty women waiting to be seen by hairdressers with clawlike acrylic nails. The smell of burnt hair in the air and the feeling of her scalp getting scrubbed raw.

"*This won't be the same experience,*" the voice assured, and just like that, anxiety was flushed from her system. Sol looked around again, seeing the setup with a fresh pair of eyes.

Here there was no long line, no clawlike nails, and most importantly, no lingering smell of burnt hair. Just beds, chairs, cabinets—and sinks. It was, in an odd sort of way, terribly mundane. Sol could feel the voice was waiting for a reaction of some sort. There wasn't any.

"*Exactly.*" It hummed, pleased. "*Just lean into the new experience and enjoy.*"

"What's all this?" Sol turned to Nadine and gestured toward the sinks.

"Oh!" Surprise colored the other woman's face. "Right, you've never done this before, I presume? That's all right. For the head massage, they do like to really get at the roots and wake up the scalp, so they wet the hair and massage in a peppermint oil. It's unorthodox, I know, but it really does feel invigorating. Trust me."

"*Trust us.*" The voice overlapped with Nadine's.

The cold fear snapped back. Sol let out a short gasp, the emotion as jarring to her as it was familiar. Ironically, unease came easy to her. If she wasn't suspicious of everything and everyone at all times, who was she, really?

Her stomach tightened instinctively and she turned to the door just as four women in all-white scrubs stepped in. They were all smiling brunettes who sized up Sol's group. Sol noticed a twitch in their eyes, their smiles falling a little flat when they looked at her.

Resting bitch face. She forced a smile. It didn't stick.

The voices roared in laughter again, a live audience reaction to Sol's personal comedy show. She winced and couldn't help but turn away from the massage therapists. The fewer eyes on her, the better.

"Okay, so we have a changing area just on the other side of that door," the leader said. "There are fresh robes to change into as well. Who would like to start on the bed first?"

Alice gestured to Bethany who was already halfway to the changing room. "It'll just be her, I'm afraid."

"A-actually." Sol swallowed. "Alice, wouldn't it be a waste not to get a full-body massage? I mean, we came all the way here."

Alice blinked, a mix of surprise and concern on her face. "I just don't feel comfortable." She searched Sol's eyes for a moment. "Are you okay?"

"Can I talk to you alone for a minute?" Sol whispered.

"Right now?" Alice frowned.

"*Don't do it,*" the voice warned her. "*You know she won't believe you.*"

"It won't take long." Sol pleaded with her eyes. "Please?"

Alice sighed. She took Sol's hand and she led her out of the room with an apologetic look. "Sorry, everyone, we'll be right back."

"Don't worry, we can wait." Nadine smiled, though Sol noticed it was only to Alice. The massage therapists nodded, parting to let them out, and once they were in the hallway, Sol waited until she could hear a murmur of voices from the room before taking a breath.

And then all at once, she blurted, "I know you said you don't like talking about creepy things or the supernatural or ghosts because you think it'll attract bad things, but there is something very real and very bad following us *right now* and I don't know why you can't hear it but I can and it's called the neighbor, I think—"

Alice pressed both hands against Sol's mouth, stopping her immediately. Her wife smiled. Looked up and down the hallway. And then back to Sol, whose heart was less of a beat and more a constant vibration.

"I get it," Alice finally spoke. "You're still upset about the pages I threw away."

Sol pulled her hands down by the wrists. "That is *not*—"

"And you only came along because you agreed you would and you didn't want to make us look bad."

Sol's mouth slackened. Where exactly was she getting this from?

"*From you,*" it said.

"There!" Sol's eyebrows jumped up. "It just spoke again. Tell me you heard that—"

"Sol!" Alice hissed. "For once, could you just be *normal*? Why does everything have to be a mass hysteria event with you? If you're not anxious about how white people will see you, you're nervous about being the only gay person at a party. If it's not that, it's because you're

butch. Why can't you just be yourself, *confidently*, and say fuck everyone else?"

"Because I *can't*." Sol glared. "Everything that happens *to* me or
around me *does* depend on how Black I am, or how gay I am, or how
butch I am, or how Latina I am, and most of the time, it depends on
all four!"

It wasn't just an anxiety thing. It was her *real life*. If Alice was tired of
this, how did she think Sol felt? If she wasn't constantly careful, if she
didn't stay on her toes, it could *very* easily be the difference between
life and death.

"You're hurting me." Alice winced, pulling her hands away. "Let's
continue this talk later, okay?" And without another word, her wife left
her standing there and went back into the room.

"Told you."

Sol rubbed her temples, unsure what to do now. In the end, she followed Alice in.

Immediately, the massage therapists split apart, each practically
running to any of the other women. When two arrived at Nadine's side
and gave each other an intense stare down, Sol realized what the issue
was. None of them wanted to deal with Sol's hair.

She shot a look to Alice that said, *You see this, right?* Alice rolled her
eyes and sat down next to Nadine.

"So how much longer do you think . . ."

Sol tuned out of their conversation. Instead, she looked down at
her reflection. From that angle, her head was a mess of tight coils that
would prove unforgiving to any hands that would attempt to part them.

From experience, Sol knew it was *really* not that difficult. Just some
water, leave-in conditioner, and a wide-tooth comb would've done
the trick. But a quick glance at the brunette's pin-straight hair told Sol
they probably had never seen a wide-tooth comb before, much less
had reason to use it.

Had Sol known this was what the spa experience entailed, she might
have even done the hard part for them.

"Sol!" Nadine's voice snapped her out of her thoughts. "Aren't you
going to sit down?"

Nadine was already seated, a white towel draped around her shoulders. Sol's thoughts went back to the salon in her childhood. Something about walking to the seat made her feel like she was walking to the gallows.

She slowly sat down on Nadine's other side. Just like always, the pregnant woman was getting between Sol and her wife.

Behind her, the massage therapist sounded like she was rummaging through the cabinet. "Where is it . . ." she muttered to herself. Sol glanced over and saw she was reaching all the way to the back. Her name tag read *Riley Morrison*.

"Uh . . . Riley?" Sol spoke up. "Is something wrong?"

"Yes! No!" Riley turned back to Sol, a half-empty bottle in her hand. "Sorry, I was just grabbing this."

Sol recognized the brand without even taking a long look at the label. It was Carol's Daughter peppermint oil.

"This will be fine, right?"

The fact that the bottle was half empty gave Sol some pause. It *used* to be a staple in natural hair care before the company was sold off to the highest—white—bidder and the ingredients were changed to something Sol's scalp didn't agree with. She hadn't used anything from that brand in years.

God, I can't even do my hair *without white people interfering. And Alice thinks I'm just being dramatic?*

"I'm uh . . . not a fan of that brand, actually."

Riley's face fell. "Oh, uh. Sorry, I was just told that, well, you know . . ." Her voice trailed off. "This is . . . this is what the Black community uses, right?"

"You know what?" said Sol. "How about we just skip the head portion of the head-and-shoulders massage? I already massaged my scalp plenty this morning."

There was a mix of relief and confusion on Riley's face.

"Are you sure?"

Sol tried that smile again—it still didn't feel right. "Uh-huh. I'm sure."

"Okay, then let's move over to the next room. These chairs don't pull apart from the sinks and I guess they didn't set up the new seats in this room."

Sol didn't know what she meant but she was happy to go along with her. She followed Riley to the door and looked back. Alice's eyes were closed, already lost in the calming sensation of peppermint oil being rubbed into her scalp. There was no point in asking if she was going to be okay here.

Unlike her, Alice seemed to be fine wherever she went.

Sol glanced at Bethany, who was just as motionless, and then over at Nadine. The pregnant woman rubbed her stomach while chatting quietly with the massage therapist behind her.

Sol clearly wasn't needed. Or wanted.

Harrison's was calling again.

"Do you need to get that?" Riley asked while rubbing circles into the back of Sol's neck. Sol had to admit the sensation was calming—up until she saw the caller ID.

"It's fine." She hung up. "It's just my dad."

Sol tried to lose herself in the massage but could already feel Riley trying to force small talk.

"So, he's at Harrison's Living Center?" Riley whistled, impressed. "Heard that place is pretty fancy. Like, with a pool for water aerobics and everything. Your dad must be loving it."

"Yeah, you'd think so, huh?" Sol muttered. Unfortunately, the only thing he liked to do there was hit on nurses. The last conversation she had with him about his nurse Rosa made her ball up her hands.

Just focus on the massage, Sol. She took in a deep breath. This was easier when she had the feel of static to guide her—but no, she wasn't going to rely on it. It used Corinne's voice to calm her down, it clearly couldn't be trusted.

There were so many connections . . . The more Sol thought about it, the more she wondered just how far those connections went. Could she use them so she never had to deal with another Clarke ever again?

Could she use them to more easily steer clear of homophobes and xenophobes and God knows whoever else might have a problem with her being who she was?

"Are your in-laws there too?"

"Nope!" Sol said, quickly. "They're still in Korea."

"Oh! How nice." It was a polite comment, that meant *I don't really know what to say to that.* Then Riley went, "Have you been?"

"For the wedding."

Riley's hands were moving farther down to Sol's shoulders. As nice as it felt, it was annoying to not be able to shrug as an answer.

"Wow!" Another polite comment. Riley was really scraping the bottom of the barrel. "So since I'm not doing a more thorough head-and-shoulders massage, I'm just about done here. Do you want to rejoin your group?"

"I can find my way back."

While Riley cleaned up, Sol made a speedy exit, then stopped short outside the other massage room. She heard her wife's voice.

"I just really thought I had it this time, you know?" Alice said. "After all the work I do, you'd think I'd be recognized for it."

Nadine made a sympathetic noise. "Oh, honey, I'm so sorry."

The tone in their voices made Sol hesitant to interrupt. Alice didn't even want to speak to *Sol* about the work situation. She thought that it was because Alice was still processing her disappointment—but was it just because Sol wasn't reliable enough?

Then again, Sol hadn't even told Alice about getting her job back. Why was that? Normally, it would've been the first thing out of her mouth—but it kept slipping her mind as she became preoccupied with other matters. Her hand wavered over the doorknob.

"At this point, I really just want to quit. Maybe take some time to think about switching careers."

"Have you spoken to Sol about it?" Nadine asked. Her voice peaked just loud enough for Sol to hear it clearly. She narrowed her eyes.

Alice made a sound that was something between a scoff and laugh. "Sol's just going to worry about how we'll pay for our mortgage. We can't *both* be jobless. Besides, I haven't even told her about signing the association agreement."

The world around Sol stopped. Her jaw dropped. Alice did what?

The voice returned. "*It was going to happen eventually.*"

"Shut up," Sol whispered. The static remained under her skin. She'd do anything to tear it out. Instead, she lingered at the door, anger rising by the second.

"*Why are you so upset? It's not a big deal.*" The words repeated until it became the truth. It wasn't a big deal. It wasn't even anything to be upset about. So what if Alice decided to sign a flimsy piece of paper, adding them to a growing body of a homeowners association? There were so many perks to it. It cost them nothing to join, and it would give them everything they needed. It was a hell of a deal. Sol was lucky to be part of a generous community.

If it's not a big deal, why did we have to join? Sol thought, burning through the rationalizations.

"Oh, I don't think she'll care too much about that," Nadine said. "And honestly, you did the right thing. You mentioned how she wanted a garden, but has she actually tried to make one? It's hard work. She's better off just using the community garden."

Alice laughed. "I know, but still. It's not really so much the garden as it is the idea of having to keep secrets. We don't keep secrets from each other. She'll definitely lose it."

Yeah, no shit I'd lose it. Just like Sol thought, there was something off about the association, the neighbor—and something very rotten about the roots. The buzzing became louder, vibrated harder behind her ears. It was a warning, Sol knew. Take a step back, breathe, and above all do not enter the room in a state of rage.

If she did, the buzzing suggested, it would not end well.

"You might be right," Nadine mused. "Considering how she freaked out at the Kennedys."

Gripping the doorknob, Sol burst through the door. The massage therapists and Alice jumped, but the other two were hardly startled.

"You're a fucking snake. You know that, Nadine?"

Alice looked up at Sol in horror. Then she narrowed her eyes. Sol shook her head, pleading for her not to ask.

"Nadine, do you want to tell me what happened at the Kennedys'?"

The pregnant woman playfully grimaced, as if pretending to look uncomfortable. Sol considered it a new fourth expression. "It's nothing bad!" She backtracked. "It's just . . . Sol was feeling some concern about your neighbors from across the street and took it upon herself to call emergency services."

That was a tactful summarization of the incident.

". . . But obviously, the paramedics weren't pleased when they came in and saw no dead bodies."

Nadine, you drama-hungry bitch.

"*What!*" Alice yelled. "When did this happen? Why didn't you tell me?"

Sol glared at Nadine. She remained seated, hands folded calmly over her stomach.

"You still haven't told Alice?" She blinked, innocently. "I hope I didn't get you into any trouble . . ."

Sol sneered at her over Alice's shoulder. "You are *so* full of shit, Nadine."

"Hey!" Alice pushed her back. "You have been nothing but ungrateful and rude to Nadine since the moment you met her. And you know what? I'm sick of it. She hasn't done anything to deserve it."

"She's a shady bitch, Alice. That's probably why Corinne looked afraid of her when she was in the hospital and why she didn't bother showing up to the funeral."

"Nadine isn't good with funerals!" Alice was shouting now, and like gas to an open flame, Sol doubled down with a worse response.

"No one's good with funerals! That's normal! But you know what isn't normal? Neglecting to tell us that *her son killed himself in our house.*"

The room was silent. And then it was chaos. Nadine's face crumbled into a perfect sob, bringing all the massage therapists to her like bridesmaids to the bridezilla. Alice grabbed Sol's arm and pulled her to the door.

"Go home, Sol," she said icily.

"Alice, wait—think about it—"

"Even if that is true, to bring that up here and now of all times—you are very lucky that I'm not *thinking* of *divorcing* you."

That shut Sol up. She looked behind her at all of them just one last time. Nadine blubbered. The massage therapists were trying to calm her down. The only person paying attention to Sol was Bethany and she was just as expressionless as before—but only for a moment. Right as they made eye contact, Bethany's face brightened up with a smirk on her lips.

Then she winked, and Alice slammed the door closed.

"Don't worry. We always take care of our own."

THE INVITATION

Sol didn't go home—not at first. She stood outside of the spa for several minutes, feeling the cool breeze from the fake waterfall brushing against her skin, when her cell phone buzzed again with a call from Harrison's. She declined the call and instead ordered a Lyft. Her self-destructive habits made her want to turn this bad day worse— why not see the man who was ready and willing to make that happen?

"*Don't go.*" The voice was firm, more solid. It repeated the words over and over again, until Sol went blind with the rising noise. And with the noise came distracting sensations. Her shoulders reacted to firm massages being given to her wife. Somewhere in Maneless Grove, a kid was carving into a tree again, pulling bark into pieces. Chewing, swallowing. She tasted blood and mint and—who was making lasagna this early in the morning?

Sol didn't realize the Lyft had arrived until it honked its horn in front of her. That shook her out of the roots, at least enough to slide in the passenger seat.

The neighbor collective became active in conversation, a low but steady stream of words filling in as background noise. Sol could barely make any voice out over another.

"...*pruning?*" one whispered. A rush of opposing voices drowned it out. Others murmured in agreement in the background.

Sol rubbed her eyes. She wished someone would have warned her that being connected to the neighbor meant she would always be carrying the equivalent of an internet comment section in her head.

"Thanks..." she muttered to the driver, and stumbled out of the car. The path to Harrison's Senior Living Center was pristine, lined with fresh azaleas. It made Sol think about the massage therapist's comment. What the hell could Papi ever complain about *here*? The buzz of voices trickled down as she entered. Finally, silence.

Sol was halfway past the nurses station when a familiar voice shouted over the counter.

"Are you Marisol?"

Sol looked behind her to see a stout woman with *Irene* printed on a name tag. She looked much younger than Sol had imagined and was failing to turn her grimace into a smile.

"What's going on?" Sol asked.

Irene paused for a second to sneeze. Again. And again. And a fourth time.

Sol looked down on her sleeves to see a dusting of pollen once again. Sol would need to invest in a lint cleaner and give herself a roll-over every time she left the neighborhood.

Eventually Irene said, "Your father was sent to his room for being a little . . . colorful with the other guests."

He was cursing everyone out for breathing in his general direction. Got it. The man could be insufferable.

Sol turned on her heel. "I'll go deal with him."

There were days when this felt like a badge of honor—her devil-may-care attitude toward Papi, knowing that she was the only one who could really handle her father. But today was not one of those days. Today, she was three seconds away from either a fight or getting lost in the bottom of a bottle of vodka. And God help her, she was already on thin ice with her wife. If she was going to explode, it might as well be toward the person who deserved it most.

Sol stopped at the end of the hallway, in front of a door that only had one name on it.

Jose Reyes. There was a little whiteboard where both he and nurses could write what needed to be done for the resident. Most of the time, it was empty, but today, it read, *To be left the hell alone.* The atrocious handwriting really nailed home the fact he wrote it himself for once.

Sol knocked calmly at first. When no answer came, she knocked again before entering.

"¿No puedes leer?" he snapped almost immediately. Then he squinted toward the door and scoffed. "Ah, it's you. Guess you finally remembered I haven't died yet."

Unfortunately.

"I've been busy." She crossed her arms. Sol remained by the door, a nonverbal threat that she would leave just as easily as she arrived if he so much as gave her a less-than-kind look.

"Too busy to see your own father?" Papi sucked his teeth. "Maybe it was better that your mom passed away early. She would've hated to see how ungrateful you've become."

Sol gritted her teeth. There was that word again. *Ungrateful.* Truthfully, it wasn't the worst thing she'd ever been called by him, but it still dug into her skin.

"You had them call me multiple times today."

"You didn't visit in two weeks. What was I supposed to think?" Papi put a tissue up to his nose and blew it quietly. He gestured to the trash can on the far side of the room and stared at her, expectantly.

Sol rolled her eyes and took the napkin to the trash can.

"So what, you were worried about me?"

"You say that like it's a surprise."

No, it's a lie, actually.

Outside the bedroom, small giggling children ran by. It made Sol wonder if she'd ever had that kind of energy—happy and lively. All she could remember was being tensely quiet. A nearby nurse firmly yelled, "No running!"

Sol took a moment to close the door.

"What's wrong with you?" Papi said. "You're too quiet."

It was almost on impulse, lying to him about being okay. Sol never liked to open up to him about how she was *really* doing, no matter how good or bad it was. And now things were *especially* bad, but in ways she couldn't really articulate—not to him. Then an idea came to her and she put on a cold smile.

"Well, Papi, I was actually having a really nice morning at the spa with my *wife,* but you had called so many times that I thought I'd come over to see what the emergency was. But . . ." She sighed and gestured disappointedly at the old man. "You're fine. So I rushed out of our appointment for nothing."

It was like the room dropped ten degrees. The look on Papi's face was . . . chilling but just *so* satisfying. The lie had done what it needed to.

"I see. So you're saying I'm not important. Even after everything I've ever done for you. You know what, it's good that you don't have kids. I can tell they'd only end up selfish like you."

Sol laughed derisively. She'd had years to think about what it was like growing up under the intense hand of her parents, constantly looking over her shoulder and weighing the pros and cons of what it would feel like to fight back. She never did, not really.

When she had the option and ability to leave, she was out. And yet for some reason, she still visited. She visited her mother's grave once a year on her birthday, and she was visiting her father weekly until he joined Sol's mother in the ground.

Sol thought she knew why she visited even though there was never much kindness between them. But lately, she was starting to wonder what the point was.

"If your takeaway is that children only end up as bad as their parents, what does that say about you?" She gave him a withering stare.

Papi reached for the nearest newspaper and rolled it up.

"Malcriada," he growled. "Come closer! I'll teach you to disrespect your father."

She took a step forward before the neighbor whispered, "*Don't.*" It tickled her ears, keeping the static low as if careful not to overwhelm her.

Sol stared at the bed where Papi lay. Constant back pain kept him either in a bed or a wheelchair—which was to say that he couldn't lift a finger against Sol until she decided to be in range. It was the first time she realized she had control over something in their relationship.

I can just leave.

She snorted. The idea of just leaving tickled her. Why did she have to subject herself to his rudeness? She had a great if not quirky community to get back to, a nice house, a fulfilling job, and a hot wife.

"You think this is funny?" her father yelled at her, oblivious to the voice.

"*You can have so much more than this.*" She could work on her so-cial skills, become the head of the biology department. And why stop there? If she wanted to learn to trade in stocks, earn passive income, there was someone just a root away to help her. She'd never have to work a day in her life if she didn't want to. Corinne hadn't worked in years and she was still a beloved member of the community. If she wanted kids, she could even adopt Veronica. The neighbor would let her, she was sure of it. The little girl no doubt needed a new set of living parents.

Her brain lit up with new thoughts, new possibilities, a new life ahead of her. The roots went far and deep.

"*Just leave.*" It would be so easy. A quick turn and a few steps. Sol held her breath while she considered it.

"I have to go." She exhaled. "But before I do, I need to ask you some-thing."

She reached into her pocket and pulled out her phone. Static flooded her fingers as she found the picture and turned it around to him.

"What do you know about this tree?"

Papi narrowed his eyes. "I can't see from that far. Come over here." He snatched the phone from her and squinted at the screen. "This is . . . strange. Is that your house behind it? Who built a house that close to a tree? It's practically going into your basement. This is what you spent so much money on?"

Sol took back her phone, scowling. "Do you know what it is or not?"

"It looks like a strangler fig. But those shouldn't be growing any-where but Florida." He smacked her arm with the newspaper. "And watch how you talk back to me! I didn't raise you to be like this!" He continued to bop her over and over again. The static moved into her feet, and solidified around her tendons like rope.

No—like roots. It plucked at her ligaments, jerking her backward until Sol was out of reach from the newspaper.

"Hey! Where are you going? You better come back here!"

She stumbled out of the room, the feeling of roots shooting down the length of her arm and slamming the door shut. Nearby, a nurse jumped, sending small pills scattering across the floor.

Sol took a moment to catch her breath. The feeling of roots under her skin dissipated, becoming nothing but static again.

"*You should listen to us next time,*" the neighbor warned her again. She shook, violation provoking her into anger—and fear.

"*Don't make a scene.*"

Sol forced her shoulders down and unballed her fists. The nurse was still gathering the scattered pills. She bent down to help her.

"Sorry," Sol said.

"Don't." The nurse stopped her. "I'll get them. But look, I've been working here for a long time. There are generally two types of visitors. The kind that drop off their parents, never to see them again unless there's some kind of emergency, and the kind that are actually close to their parents and do make an effort to visit regularly."

Sol stood quietly. The neighbor was still milling about in her head, watching her carefully.

The nurse pointed a long finger at Sol. "You're neither. Actually, you're worse. It's clear you don't want to be here but you still visit every week anyway. The only good thing about you is that you visit when no one else is around so at least you're not bothering other visitors with your fights."

Static rested on Sol's shoulders, making her tense up.

Don't, she pleaded.

"*Relax. Just talk to the nurse. You're not in any trouble.*" Yet it still wrapped around her spine, a light reminder of what it could do. "*Talk. Why do you keep coming back?*" It turned her head to the nurse. Her mouth opened, and out came the first excuse she could think of.

"I have to. It's . . . it's a Dominican thing, okay?" She had to be around until he died, at least. Others would complain that she would still need to visit his grave but at least then he couldn't complain if she didn't.

The nurse rolled her eyes, grabbing the last pill on the floor.

"It's always a Dominican thing. Or it's a Puerto Rican thing or a Mexican thing. Sometimes it's a Catholic thing. I don't know. All I know is you're making my job more difficult every time you get him riled up." The nurse tossed the pills away and changed her gloves. "If you can't stand him and if you know he can't stand you, what's the point in torturing yourself by visiting?"

The neighbor murmured in agreement. The truth could not be clearer—visiting Papi was bad for Sol. She got nothing out of it, no apologies for poor treatment, no acknowledgment of her achievements, and as far as her wife was concerned, Sol was essentially in the closet.

A sympathetic voice pierced through the buzz. "*Stop going to the hardware store for orange juice.*"

"What else am I supposed to do?" Sol blurted.

To not visit would weigh too heavily on her mind. Neither was healthy but at least by being there, she'd have chosen the lesser regret.

The nurse made a face before she answered. "I'm a nurse, not a therapist. Maybe you should start there."

Sol still hadn't heard back from Alice by the time she got to the house. Well, not that Sol had messaged her first. Usually when the two had a fight on this scale, Sol would let Alice cool off and the best way to know when she was finished cooling off was when she reached out to Sol. Or when Sol apologized.

And she was *not* going to apologize.

As soon as the Lyft rolled up in front of the house, Sol could feel the neighbor receding. A sense of dread welled up in her, like she wanted to avoid going inside at all costs.

But Sol could see something wedged into the front door. She tentatively walked forward, relief shocking her bones as the neighbor melted away. It prickled at her back, like it was trying to stick. Once she got to her porch, it disappeared.

Sol sighed. Home was safe—at least for now. A bright yellow envelope was stuck into her doorframe. She eyed the mailbox a few feet away. Whoever put the envelope there didn't want Sol to miss it.

Unlocking the door and pulling the envelope out, she opened it to find an invitation to a summer bonfire.

"Hey there, Sol!" Finnian's chipper voice startled her. "How are you doing? Looks like you got your invitation already!"

When had he materialized on her porch? Did the neighbor send him in advance?

Sol stared at him for a second—confirming he was half a foot shorter than before. A different Finnian who would pretend to be the same. She looked back to the invitation.

It said it was their sixth annual bonfire and potluck. Everyone was encouraged to make something for the event, as long as it was keto-approved, low-carb, gluten-free, sugar-free, nut-free . . . the list went on. At some point, it specified that white bread would be allowed as long as it was made from almond flour, but wasn't almond flour made from nuts?

"I really hope you can make it!" He smiled. "It would be a nice way to enjoy the warmer weather, don't you think?"

Sol was in no mood to pretend to be a functioning person today. The most she wanted to do was get a bottle of wine and lounge on the couch for the rest of the night since she was sure that was where she'd be sleeping anyway.

"Sure, the bonfire sounds like fun times," she said dryly, and was about to close the door behind her when Finnian's foot got in the way.

Alarmed, Sol raised her eyebrows.

"Actually, I had another reason for coming by." His voice lowered. "I wanted to make sure you and Alice were still on for brunch with Roy and me tomorrow? We'd like to get to know you two more . . . and maybe get a second chance at getting back into your good graces."

If he was connected to the neighbor, he should have known that ship had long since sailed. Still, she fumbled for a response that was less aggressive than *There's not a snowball's chance in hell that'll happen.*

She settled for, "That's not necessary."

Finnian didn't remove his foot. And the way his eyes bore into hers, she could tell he wasn't taking no for an answer.

What are the chances that if I call the cops, I'll just end up being the one arrested?

She wasn't going to gamble that either.

"Please," he whined. "Roy feels terrible about what happened at the welcoming party."

He should. He crossed a line that you're quickly approaching.

"Okay." For now she would give in—but later, she would block his number. "I'll talk to Alice about it." She would not.

"Thank you."

The moment he stepped back, Sol slammed the door shut and locked it quickly. Then she tossed the invitation into the nearest waste-basket.

I need a drink.

Sol knew she would regret it even as she descended the stairs to the basement. Nothing made her feel worse than having to go behind her wife's back. But today was rough, Nadine was shady, and Finnian was too pushy for her liking. Plus, Alice was mad at her anyway. Might as well commit to the betrayal.

She found the box in the back corner of the basement easily, shifted papers aside until she found the flask.

She couldn't believe she needed it so soon. The hardest liquor Sol had—so rough and caustic that it was meant to be mixed with soda or juice. Drinking it by itself was considered dangerous. But the flask was easier to hide than forty ounces of whiskey.

She took no more than a few swigs—she didn't want to drain it completely. Everclear was illegal in so many states that it was hard to find even in the legalized states. Hardly anyone kept it well stocked.

Sol's throat burned. Her stomach warmed. In a moment, she knew she would feel it in her extremities, so it would be best if she lay down before her stumbling became obvious.

She reached the top of the basement stairs easily and went straight to the couch. As she sank into the cushions, her thoughts slowed with the help of the Everclear. What was she doing with this? She had her job back, she really *should* be preparing for her return to Yale. It would get her out of the house, and things between her and Alice would go back to normal. She could have it all, with the help of her new friend.

Except if there was one thing she didn't like, it was a chorus of voices constantly chatting in the back of her head. She didn't like the sensations that seeped into her life, or the way they could easily hijack her arms and legs, twist her in whatever direction she didn't want to go.

Sol wanted her freedom. She wanted her *privacy*.

Sean wanted the same thing and found it in this house. *Her* house.

So why did he try to burn it down?

APRIL 26

I can't stay here forever. I know that much. Mom and Dad keep calling for me. They won't come in this house. I can tell they feel its deadness, the way it's disconnected from everyone. They don't want to be disconnected for even a moment. They're too far gone.

I don't want to leave. I can't take it, being out there. If you're not strong enough, the thoughts, the feelings, the memories, it takes you over. It's like someone else moves in, and you just have to deal with a sudden change in personality.

And I'm not strong enough to stop that. I don't know if anyone could ever be. Is Mom even Mom anymore? Is Dad? Is anyone still who they say they are? I can't tell. Every time they speak, I hear someone else.

Except the woman. She's not like the others. I know how that sounds, but she really isn't. It's like she's constantly under the radar. No one takes her over. But she still hears and sees everything. She can choose how she lives, what perspectives to discard, what kind of memory she wants to keep. She floats above all of that.

She says if I had come here first before everything, she could've protected me. But now, there's only one way to be free of all of this.

I just hope I'm strong enough to do it.

THE PHONE CALL

S ol's phone rang. She wanted to ignore it in favor of a deep nap but when she saw who it was, all the warmth in her face quickly turned cold.

"H-hello?" she stammered, tongue still heavy with the effects of Everclear. Her other hand gripped the flask—she didn't even realize she had brought it up from the basement.

"Marisol, hello." Alice's aunt spoke softly, almost apologetic. There was the sound of running water from the sink in the background. "Have you spoken to Alice lately? Is she okay?"

Sol wondered if this had something to do with how weirdly Alice answered Julie's phone call earlier. She decided not to tell her aunt about the fight.

"Yes, she's fine. Why?"

Sol realized she was sitting very stiffly, as though Julie could even see her. Even so, she couldn't force herself to relax. Aunt Julie commanded respect and Sol cared what she thought of her. Alice's aunt was a psychiatrist in Toronto and taught Alice everything she needed to know about how to best support Sol not just during this difficult time with her job, but several years ago when she was first disowned by her parents. In an odd way, Sol felt both incredibly grateful to Julie but also terrified of the woman. Having the power to save a relationship came with the caveat that they could also have the power to destroy it. Sol did her best to stay on Julie's good side.

"I called her earlier today," Aunt Julie told Sol, "but it seemed like she didn't understand what I was saying. She just said she would call me later—but she never did." The rushing water suddenly stopped. Sol imagined Julie shut off a nearby sink. "I tried calling back several times but she never picked up. I thought maybe something had happened to her phone."

"I don't think so?"

Sol pulled the phone away from her ear long enough to check the time. She didn't know how long the spa session was supposed to last but it was barely half past noon. Maybe she went to grab food with Nadine and Bethany. She hoped not. "I think she's still with her friends."

"Was Nadine with her?"

"Uh, yes." Sol wondered if she could grab a glass of water from the kitchen and sober up fast. Her words weren't slurring but the slightest indication that she was drinking again in front of the one other person Alice trusted was catastrophic.

"Ah, I see. I guess that's why she called me 'Aunt Julie' instead of 'Imo.'"

"She's never called you that before." Sol didn't need to ask. She knew how strange that was, what a difficult place it was to feel concerned about it. Maybe to others, it wasn't a big deal. It conveyed the exact same thing. *But it was bigger than that.*

Alice didn't respond in Korean and was changing her manner of speaking. She went shopping at Trader Joe's! Was that not an indication that something was deeply wrong?

Julie tutted. "Honestly, the way she acted, it was like she suddenly forgot Korean. I blame that Nadine."

Suddenly forgot Korean.

Sol thought about what she read in the journal entries. Sean mentioned forgetting things. But Sean was a white kid, living among white people. Maybe he forgot arguments he had, promises people made. Things not linked to identity.

For Alice and Sol? There was the danger of losing their entire culture. The realization made her freeze. How had she not thought about that?

"I don't understand what she is doing. She's not usually like this."

"She's been very stressed lately," Sol offered and quickly felt childish for it. Trying to defend her wife from her aunt-in-law was something she wasn't used to doing. She didn't even have much experience in defending herself from her own parents.

"That's no excuse for her to be ignoring me." Julie let a few more words slip in Korean and it made Sol's head spin. "Please let her know to call me as soon as she can."

"I will try."

The call ended just as abruptly as it started. Sol's hand fell to her side and she stood there, dazed and wondering what the hell just happened. She regretted not keeping up with her Korean for situations like these.

It was rare for anyone in Alice's family to call Sol directly. Eun-hee and Kwang-ho were the kinds of parents that didn't intrude into their daughter's life, but after what Alice told Sol about them sending her away when she was a teen, she could see why Julie picked up the mantle of raising Alice. And if she were now acting strange to Julie, that'd be a cause for concern.

The front door swung open. Sol buried the flask between two couch cushions and twisted herself around. It was unfair how much more refreshed Alice looked compared to Sol. Her skin glowed, and her hair looked silky, if a little damp.

Sol felt like she had a layer of dirt covering her from head to toe. And the way Alice looked at her only doubled the feeling.

"I'm not apologizing," Sol blurted. Alice rolled her eyes and crossed the living room to the stairs.

"Did we get our invitation to the bonfire?" Alice asked.

Sol opened her mouth and thought to lie. She decided against it.

"Yeah, it's in the trash. They should really start sending emails instead, this is just wasting paper." This was another reason Sol didn't drink Everclear too often. It made her bold, unmoving. The two of them argued more when she had something like this in her system, and she didn't like it. But it also helped her find her own boundaries and hold on to them.

Alice turned to hold Sol's stare. She said nothing the entire time, only looking at Sol like she was looking straight through her. Then she turned around her and went straight to the wastebasket.

"Are you just going to ignore me like this?" Sol asked. Alice didn't answer. She just leaned down and picked the crumpled invitation out of the trash. Her face softened and gave Sol a disappointed look.

"Seriously?" Alice sighed. "What is going on with you? You've been acting crazy lately."

Sol's face fell. "I have been as reasonable as I can be. I at least try to talk about what's bothering me—you just want to ignore all of it."

Alice pursed her lips together.

"What happened at the Kennedys'?"

Sol threw her hands up. What was the point of rehashing this? "Didn't Nadine already tell you?"

"I want to hear from you." She looked at Sol with steady eyes. Studying her. Sol was almost sure Alice could tell she'd been drinking again. That she could tell Sol wasn't quite right—that there was something wrong with her.

Sol forced down a lump in her throat. "Remember that little girl I was telling you about? Veronica? She keeps running into the middle of the street, following me around, just acting completely bizarre for a girl her age. I got concerned and went across the street to talk to her parents about it."

"And?"

Sol saw them hanging from the ceiling. Decaying. Dead. The rot was so strong, Sol could practically taste it through the door.

"They . . . weren't there." Sol cast her eyes down. Embarrassment was one thing. Shame made her feel smaller. "Nadine says they're fine, but I haven't seen them once. Their car is always parked in their driveway, collecting dust. Doesn't that seem strange to you?"

"No. I've seen them," Alice said.

Sol stared at her, incredulous. "When?"

Alice shrugged and ran a hand through her hair. "Usually when I get up to go to work. They're always waving at me through their window."

"The window that always has its curtains closed?" Sol narrowed her eyes.

"Well, they're not *always* closed," Alice retorted. "And if they are, maybe it's because they don't like their neighbor watching them from across the street."

"Oh, do *not* turn this around on me," Sol shouted. It felt a little silly to have this argument while sitting on the couch, but she knew if she stood up, she would stumble. And if she stumbled even once, Alice would know she'd been drinking. "I have been doing my best to mind my own damn business in this community."

Alice blinked. "Really? And is dialing 911 your version of minding your own business? Is throwing Nadine's son's suicide in her face minding your own business?"

Sol froze, recognizing the immediate tension in the room. Her eyes fluttered and she struggled to find a good comeback. But then she looked at her wife, and a new thought hit her. Alice's expression wasn't so much one of disbelief at Sol's accusation—but rather rage that she would have the audacity to bring it up. The new realization made Sol's stomach turn to lead.

"Alice . . . did you already know that? About this house?" Sol asked. "Did you already know that Nadine's son . . . did that here?"

When Alice didn't respond right away, Sol jumped up. "You fucking *knew*? This whole time?"

"Oh my God, like you weren't keeping secrets from me!" Alice yelled back.

Sol's head spun. The empty air became thick with betrayal. The walls of the house felt less like solid wood and more like treacherous bars. She sucked in as much air as she could—there wasn't enough. There was never enough.

Sol needed to get out of there—out of the house, out of the neighborhood. She could hear Corinne yelling at her again, not to trust the neighbor, not to get entangled in the roots. It choked her to death and now it was wrapping around Sol.

Sol tripped over herself to get to the door, but Alice beat her to it.

"Get out of the way," she said.

"Not until you talk to me." Alice's eyes were suddenly brimming with tears. Sol searched them, looking for proof that Alice knew more than she was letting on. Did she already know about the neighbor? Did she hear the voices? How much did she already know about this place?

"Why are you looking at me like that?" Alice asked. "Listen to me. I know it's a little fucked up—"

"A *little* fucked up?" Sol shook her head. "That's supposed to be your friend's *kid*."

Alice rolled her eyes. "Like you ever cared about Nadine."

Sol took a moment to breathe. She stared at her wife again, catching the way her jaw flexed. Alice's cheeks were flushed red. Even as calm as she tried to be, the anger showed its hand easily. Sol took this hint and tried to make sense of it.

"That's your friend."

"I know," Alice admitted. "But don't you think she would rather have someone she knows live in a place like this, rather than some stranger?"

You sound like we're living on her son's grave. Because they kind of were. And that made the whole situation even more insane to Sol.

"Is she the reason you went behind my back to sign the association agreement?" Sol asked. It wouldn't have mattered if she was—but Sol needed to know.

"She didn't have to. Everyone else is . . ."

"Pushy." Sol finished her sentence. It was understandable. When Sol thought about Hope trying to sneak into the house through the back door, it still sent her into a fit of rage.

Alice looked down and stepped out of the way. The door was now fully accessible to Sol. She could take the car and drive as far as the neighborhood would let her—or just run if Clarke was any example.

Sol was tempted to just go without a word. Alice lied to her about something so monumental that was fully in her right to know. Would she have opted to move into this place after knowing the whole truth? Probably not. She would have preferred to stay looking on the housing market, watching homes get snatched up by more and more investors, skyrocketing property rates while rent increased year by year with no end in sight . . .

Alice would have gotten desperate at one point or another. Again, it was understandable. As mad as she was, Sol couldn't blame Alice too much for her secrets.

But how much did she *really* know?

"Before you go," Alice began. "You should know—I have spent my *whole life* just trying to make do with what I can get. I couldn't get my parents to talk to me, so I had to live with Aunt Julie. I couldn't get a decent house with no sordid history, so yeah, I took up Nadine on her offer and applied for us to move in here. And I can't live here *peacefully* without being hounded at every step to join the goddamn association, so I fucking *signed it.* I'm not proud of what I had to do if it meant we had a chance of a happy life here."

Sol whispered, "You said 'Aunt Julie' again."

Confused, Alice looked up. "What of it?"

"She's been calling." Sol wasn't sure how to broach this topic without sounding insensitive.

Alice's reaction was subtle, a twitch in her right hand before forcing it to relax.

"Yeah, I said I'd call her later." Alice strutted toward the staircase, stopping as soon as Sol got in her way.

"And she said you didn't," she said. "She said you even refused to speak Korean to her."

Alice's expression hardened. "What does that matter when we can both speak English?"

"You started shopping at Trader Joe's," Sol pointed out.

"That was *one* time. Christ." Alice pinched the bridge of her nose. "I'm starting to notice a trend with this line of questioning. Am I suddenly not Korean enough for you?" She let out a biting laugh, clearly offended.

Sol's nails dug into her skin. Maybe from another standpoint, all of this seemed like minuscule changes, unimportant and hardly worth causing an argument over. But to Sol, this was monumental.

"I'm just saying, you've been acting weird. It's noticeable even to your aunt."

"You know what's weird? Hiding the fact you called emergency services on our neighbors," Alice said. "And if you want to talk about *noticeable* changes, let me ask you—when was the last time you called me 'querida'?"

The question was like a gut punch. Had it been a while? So long that even Alice noticed? Her wife stared at her, unblinking.

"You didn't even realize, did you." It wasn't a question. Alice was fully aware of all the ways Sol's behavior changed down to every facial expression. Strangely enough, Sol's heart felt a little lighter with this realization. It meant she hadn't completely lost her wife to the roots.

It might even mean she could still save her. Save the both of them.

"I might have been . . . preoccupied," Sol muttered.

Alice frowned. "So preoccupied, you haven't kissed me in a long time." She leaned in. The smell of fresh mint cleared Sol's Everclear buzz momentarily. She imagined hands traveling on Alice's body, pulling her clothes off, and getting into the longest fuck session ever known to humankind.

Alice's lips brushed Sol's and all thoughts stalled for a moment.

Trying to regain her footing, Sol whispered, "I'm still mad you didn't tell me about Nadine's kid and this house."

"And I'm still mad you didn't tell me about the Kennedys." Alice deepened the kiss. "So we both agree we're still mad at each other?" Sol was sure Alice could taste the liquor on her tongue—but if it mattered at all, Alice gave no indication. She moaned into the kiss and Sol took it as permission to start shedding layers.

Fuck, she tasted so sweet. Sol could chase the Everclear aftertaste with just the woody tang she savored on Alice's tongue. The flavor was reminiscent of a very specific wine she couldn't place at the moment.

The two traveled up the stairs hazardously, unable to pull away for more than a few steps at a time. Alice nearly tripped backward in the hall when shimmying off her pants and Sol followed her into the room, all instinct, no thoughts. Just hands, tongue, and mouth on neck, ass, and thighs. Eventually, Sol remembered to say a few words she promised to pass on.

"You need to call your aunt."

"Shut up," Alice responded, diving between Sol's legs.

It was odd how her brain worked under Everclear. When drinking it, Sol was bold and confident in herself. She recognized it the moment Alice said Sol was acting crazy lately—it was the first time she took that opinion, raised it into the sunlight of her mind, and outright rejected it.

Because as it turned out, when Sol compiled the evidence of everything she had experienced, she recognized how logical each and every one of her steps were.

A stair disappeared? Study the phenomenon and attempt to replicate it for verifiable data.

An old woman seems to be afraid of the pregnant neighbor? Investigate why that might be, don't just turn away.

Continue to experience odd occurrences? Track down the last owners and obtain first-account witness stories.

Sol was being perfectly logical. And as she rode on between waves of pleasure, she held on to that confidence, so tight that it burned in her chest.

Because Alice was definitely hiding something.

APRIL 29

I'm scared.

THE CONNECTION

Sol was hungover—something she should've anticipated. After all, even with only taking small sips of the liquor here and there, the potency flooded her system, and she found herself passed out on the bed with drool on the side of her chin. Light felt piercing to her eyes and as she shifted to a seated position, she heard pacing in the hall. Sol rubbed her face as heels clicked into the room.

"Awake yet?"

Sol slowly looked over to Alice. Her brain felt like mush.

"Barely," she finally said. "Are you going somewhere?"

Sol noticed that Alice was dressed to go out, a silk peach top with white jeans. Her hair was let down instead of pulled back into a ponytail.

Alice raised an eyebrow at Sol. "Finnian texted me and wanted to make sure we were still on for brunch. Not that you were going to remind me."

Sol groaned.

Of course. When it rained, it fucking poured.

"I'm not feeling so great, actually." Sol rubbed her temples.

"How about this? You take some painkillers and come with me anyway and I will *pretend* like you didn't taste like rubbing alcohol last night."

That seemed like a fair enough compromise. Sol nodded as she massaged her face. There were lines on her from sleeping uncomfortably in bed. Looking down at herself, Sol found that she somehow managed to put on a shirt and boxers before passing out. Alcohol and rough sex tended to put her on autopilot.

"Are we going to talk about it?" The elephant in the room. At the moment, it could have referred to any number of things. The fact Alice hid from her the knowledge that someone died in this house, how she signed the housing agreement without Sol's approval, Alice's *insistence* on avoiding anything that made her uncomfortable.

But really, Sol meant all of it. She wanted to talk about how Alice could, time and time again, feel so comfortable throwing Sol under the bus. She pretended—no, *believed* it was for Sol's own good. Like she couldn't trust her wife to be levelheaded and make a single decision for herself, not without some prodding. Even seeing a therapist was Alice's idea.

Sol waited for an answer. In the silence, Alice seemed to consider giving one.

"Have a glass of water, take some medicine, and get ready. Brunch is in an hour." Then Alice stomped off. Whichever room she went into, Alice slammed the door behind her, purposefully aggravating Sol's headache. Sol rolled her eyes at the pettiness and massaged her face deep enough to fully wake up.

I need to be less hungover for this, she wished. Somewhere, in the back of her head, Sol could hear whispering.

Cliff's Diner was quite a ways from Maneless Grove. It was surrounded by small thrift shops on one side and a row of neatly trimmed lawns with baby deer statues on the other.

The sight of it made Sol think back to the requirements of the Homeowners Association and she mentally ticked off everything about the houses that would drown them in so many fines, they'd have to rent a room to pay it all—which would, in turn, be another fine. Dandelions peppered the end of the driveway and Sol counted that as one. One of the houses was a bland pink, a color that was not approved at all so that would cost them as well. The house on the end had a Black Lives Matter sign in the window—something that Sol wholeheartedly agreed with, but she could imagine the neighborhood getting into an uproar about whether or not that counted as "political."

When Alice slowed the car down, Sol looked up to see cursive neon lights spelling out *Cliff's* over the spotless window of a brick building. Through the glass, Sol could spot a number of people quietly eating amongst themselves. Clearly it was a popular spot.

I don't want to be here. But she knew she didn't have a choice. After all, Finnian had something to tell her, didn't he? That was why he was so pushy about brunch in the first place.

Once parked, Sol trailed after Alice to the building. Finnian and Roy stood just on the other side of the door. Sol's eyes lingered on Roy, noting just how much more sickly the man seemed today. He was even paler than should be possible for a white person. It was concerning and made her wonder if it was a good idea for him to be out at all. And more, whether what he had was catching. The blue of his veins sprawled more visibly under his skin, reminding her of roots.

"We're here!" Alice announced. "And we're ready to *eat*."

"Oh, I hear that!" Finnian said, leading the way. Sol eyed him as she entered. Was he actually Finnian? Or just another guy with red hair who claimed to be Finnian? Sol tried not to think of them as off-brand Finnians, but the differences between each one always forced her to do a double take. How could she be sure that they were always the same person?

"Table for four?" Roy said to the nearest waitress. The young woman seated them immediately and handed them a stack of menus.

"I'll be back in a moment to take your drink orders." She smiled.

Once she stepped away, Roy turned to Alice. "You know, I have to say, it really is nice not being the only gay couple in the neighborhood anymore."

Sol's eye twitched. This talk seemed familiar. Was Roy just rehashing the same conversation? She tuned him out, already not wanting to be here. Between the fact that Alice was treating her less like her wife and more like a petulant child and the fact that the couple in front of them was unable to take no for an answer, she was ready to crawl under the table for the rest of the meal.

"You were the only ones? Our condolences," Alice joked, eyes still on the menu.

"Ha-ha," Roy said. "But seriously, it was a nightmare. I think some-one once jokingly asked which one of us was the top or bottom. You'd think straight people would've learned to mind their own business by now."

Sol stole a glance at her phone. Brunch was never her thing. Conversations went on for too long. People talking between bites of food annoyed her. The fact that there was no sense of urgency, that everyone lingered, like they couldn't part with the table, confused her. A meal was meant to be eaten and done with.

"A meal is meant to be shared."

Not this again. Sol shut her eyes tight and focused on her breathing. The buzzing was rising again, a mix of chatter and laughter that left her too nauseated for someone with very little in her stomach. When she opened her eyes, it seemed someone had laid a drink menu in front of her. An assortment of fruit-flavored cocktails stole her attention and her mouth watered. She found herself thirstier than ever.

"Why not have a drink?" the voices echoed.

Why not? She deserved it, didn't she? If Alice was going to keep secrets from her, lie to her, and make her feel insignificant for it, didn't she deserve to get some kind of compensation for her trouble?

But I'm no better. Under the surface of Sol's self-righteousness, her shame simmered. Temptation was hard enough without the prodding. She wiped her sweaty palms on her jeans and pushed the menu away.

Roy snorted, like he heard a funny joke. He raised the drink menu, a shine in his eyes that said he was going to surprise them with a good proposal.

"Why don't you and I get mimosas? Here, they *really* don't skimp on the champagne," Roy said to Alice. Sol's attention flitted back and forth between them, then settled.

"Oh, that sounds really good," Alice said. "I think I'll have a mimosa then."

Which immediately made Sol the designated driver. The voices giggled like they had pulled a bait and switch. Of course, Charlie Brown, Lucy will definitely hold the football in place. It was stupid of Sol to think otherwise.

Roy called a waitress over and ordered for the two of them.

"So how've you been doing, Sol?" Finnian asked. Roy and Alice looked at her expectantly and Sol froze. It might have just been her imagination, but even the noise in the background seemed to drop in volume.

"Uh, fine? I guess?"

The noise picked up. Alice and Roy looked away from her, content with her answer. It was like a flip had switched—time stopped and moved forward depending on her participation.

"I'm really glad you could join us," Finnian said a little quietly. Sol's eyes darted from Alice to Finnian—she was engrossed in another conversation with Roy altogether.

"Well, that makes one of us," she said truthfully. Finnian's smile tightened.

"Don't be like that. We just want to get to know you. Just like how you want to get to know us."

Sol looked down at Finnian's hands. They were folded over, nails neatly trimmed and cleaned. His skin looked well moisturized and soft for someone who spent so much time tending to a garden.

"Inner Bliss Spa?" she asked.

He shrugged, nonchalantly. "Why not take advantage of a discount?"

So the idea behind Nadine winning a free treatment was also a lie. Noted.

The man leaned halfway onto the table toward Sol. Anyone who looked over would think they were co-conspirators in something. Sol waited for Alice to catch on to this, but she and Roy didn't notice anything amiss on the other side of the table.

"If you have something to ask," Finnian whispered, "just ask. But we should get to ask something of you too. It's only fair."

"Why are you whispering?"

"I thought it would make you more comfortable." He pulled back and shrugged again.

"Since you don't like talking to us."

Sol jumped out of her seat, pushing it so far back it clattered against the ground. All the noise in the diner died and Alice stared up at her in horror.

"Sol. What are you doing?"

"I . . . he—"

"Sit. Down." Alice gritted her teeth. "For the love of God, if you were going to make a scene, you could've just stayed home."

She wanted to argue that there was no way Alice would have let her stay home—she had *wanted to* stay home, but she realized it *was* becoming a scene. For while the other patrons in the diner pretended to go back to their own conversations—she could *feel* them staring. She could hear the laughter, the taunting being pointed at her like sharpened knives. It was enough to make Sol shake with rage. Her chest rose and fell and soon enough—there came the fishbowl effect. Her vision stretched and Sol's hyperventilation was the only sound for miles.

Everything else became muffled, like it was being held under a pillow or pushed behind layers and layers of walls. Sol might as well have been in another room entirely.

Bewildered, she took a moment to look around. The other people weren't eating. They were scraping empty plates with utensils, simulating having a meal, but no one had so much as a glass of water.

And for some reason, she couldn't make out their faces. Eventually, the waitress returned with a pitcher of mimosa and two glasses for Roy and Alice. The sound of liquid pouring into the glasses was closer to a trickle.

Finnian's sharp laughter came back into focus as he twisted himself toward her.

"Sol?" His voice cut through the muffled noises clearly and he gave her a vicious but knowing smile. "Why don't you sit?"

Unsure what else to do, Sol slowly picked up her chair and sat. The fishbowl slowly lifted, and sound returned. Looking down at the table setting, Sol's hand shot out with a panic and grabbed the napkin-rolled utensils. She undid the roll with a frenzy to get to the butter knife. If she were quick, she could probably stab Finnian a few times before someone called the cops.

"You don't want to get the cops involved," Finnian said. "It wouldn't save you."

She knew that, of course. Her experience with the paramedics told her any authoritative body would likely be influenced by them. Who was she kidding? Even without the influence, she was always going to lose to a white man. Clarke was just an outlier. The status quo was here to stay. Sol slowly put the butter knife down.

"Why are there so many of you?" Sol asked before she clarified: "So many Finnians."

His face twitched with annoyance.

"You said I could ask any question," Sol reminded him, then looked aside. Alice was hardly paying attention to her—to their conversation. Too wrapped up in whatever she was talking about with Roy. Or maybe Sol's side of the table was being hidden—the same way that Bethany's presence appeared minute at the spa.

Not that Finnian needed any help. Alice never liked acknowledging anything out of the ordinary. Sol's drinking problem? Sure, she could handle that. Some white guy's grasp on their immediate reality? That was a step too far for her. She'd rather pretend it didn't exist.

Sol could feel Finnian's attention on her, studying her like she would eventually break. From the corner of her eye, she could see his finger tapping the table repeatedly. A nervous tic, maybe.

"We have a lot in common," he finally said. "Sometimes a group of people might . . . overlap too well. Personalities can converge onto one."

"So where's the real Finnian?"

He smirked with a turn of his head. "You've already asked your question. It's my turn. And I'll make it easy for you, because it's just one question. You're about to start working, correct?"

Sol bit the inside of her cheek. Where was this going?

"I'm getting there," Finnian said, intruding on her thoughts again. "I'm sure that while your . . . Dr. Henderson, was it? While he's completely on your side about the whole affair, do you think any of the other scientists feel the same way?"

Sol clenched her hands.

"Think about it. You were never particularly nice to anyone. You're abrasive. You keep to yourself. Clarke was the complete opposite of that and now that he's dead, some of them might not be thinking so highly of you. They might even be thinking it's a little . . . convenient that he admits his fault, resigns, and suddenly dies in the same neighborhood you live in."

"I didn't *do* anything!" Sol shouted. Her pulse pounded loudly, as blood rushed to her head. The anger was dizzying.

And as she looked over the entire diner, she realized none of the other patrons reacted. Alice hadn't even so much as blinked.

Finnian raised a hand. "I know. We know that, don't we?"

The whispering neighbor collective agreed.

"I'm saying, we can make sure that the thought doesn't cross anyone's mind. You just have to . . . drop a few seeds. Spread some more pollen."

"What are you talking about?" She seethed. Confusing her with nonsensical words would not stop her from knocking him upside the head. It was not like anyone would notice.

Finnian chuckled, pressing a hand to his mouth. "You're right, no one would notice, but I would prefer if you didn't resort to violence. You could end up hurting other members."

"Like I give a shit—"

"Including Alice."

Sol straightened up, nostrils flaring. Right. Of course, it would affect her wife. Mad as she was, even Sol wouldn't stoop so low as to hurt Alice, even as collateral damage.

"But to answer your earlier question," he continued. "Our ability to connect with each other mentally? It's all because of the trees. The aspen. Grind up some bark, sprinkle it into food or ingest some pollen, and you start to get . . . absorbed into something bigger. Call it the will of God, call it evolution, but that's how we've been able to get ourselves connected like this."

Reaching for her glass of water, Sol took a few sips. Rage was urging her to launch clear across the table and beat Finnian senseless. But she heard the low churn of whispers in the background. Not from the other patrons, but from the neighbor. All eyes were on her. If she so much as raised a hand to hurt Finnian, they would not hesitate to make her regret it.

"So, you're a tree?"

Finnian snorted. "Is that what you took away from it?"

"How does it work?" She ignored his amusement. It just didn't make any sense. The world was filled with trees, and yet the hive mind was limited to just this one neighborhood? There had to be something else. And if she knew how it worked, inside and out, maybe she could find a way to shut them down.

"Ha!" Finnian laughed, then covered his mouth. "Sorry, that was just so cute. You know what? I'll humor you. What do you know about aspen trees?"

They were thin. They were tall. They were made of wood.

He rolled his eyes. "Come on, you have to at least *try*. Aren't you a biologist?"

"I'm a *molecular* biologist." Sol scowled. "I don't work with trees. That's botanists." Her expertise was with parasites, and that was about it.

"Arguably, the largest organism in the world," he began, spelling it out for her, "is the Pando Tree—an aspen grove. While not so large, Maneless is such a grove. And we have found a way to help it grow. To form a . . . *symbiotic* relationship with aspens, so to speak."

Sol's jaw fell. So that's what he meant by evolution. Not people turning into trees, but rather people *linking* with trees.

Does that mean their one weakness is fire?

Finnian tutted. "Let's be honest, most organisms are weak to fire. But for us—no, not really. Ever heard of controlled burnings? Aspen trees are adapted to fire in such a way that they regenerate prolifically after a burning. I mean, do you know how much better Roy's health got after Sean's little . . . accident?"

Sol winced. "He was a kid."

"A kid who we now honor with our yearly bonfires." He raised his glass of water like it was a toast, then drank it. "Listen, we're not evil people, all right? We just know what we want and we work together to take it. And haven't we been good to you, Sol? Got you your job back. Kept you from getting stabbed by that crazy coworker."

All things she didn't really ask for. If anything, *Alice* deserved that promotion for doing everything to appease them.

Did you deserve to get stabbed?

That brought her up short.

"Well . . . we've already got Nadine at that firm," Finnian continued with a shrug. "Alice is more of a backup for when Nadine goes on maternity leave. You, on the other hand—we could really use a connection at Yale."

It infuriated Sol the way he responded to her thoughts as if it counted as an actual conversation and not just invasive and controlling.

"*Fine.*" Finnian let out a fake sigh of exasperation. "I'll wait until you *actually* speak before I respond. You are so demanding, you know that?"

And the neighbor laughed.

Sol clenched her teeth and chose her next words carefully.

"If I said no?" She wasn't sure what they were asking of her—if they were even asking for anything. They just wanted her to go back to work? How did that help *them*? Whatever they wanted, Sol refused to be their puppet. "What, are you going to make me go like you made me leave my dad in the nursing home?" She still remembered how she felt her body moving on its own, muscles and tendons stiffening and jerking to get her to leave the room. Pain didn't begin to cover it.

"What are you talking about?" Finnian pouted. "You've *already* been doing plenty! Going to all those therapists, walking on campus, seeing your friend Amir."

Sol's eyes widened. How did they know his name?

"As powerful as our community has gotten just inside our gates, we can't plant aspens all over the world, you know. They're not even native here—I bet your dad would have told you that if you asked," Finnian said, and she shuddered that he knew so much about her. He went on. "The pollen you spread, although temporary compared to the actual trees, is key."

Oh, fuck. The memories came back to her. All the times she sat with Amir or Dr. Moore or the nurse at the senior center as they sneezed and complained about allergies—she was *infecting* them?

"Any more questions?" Finnian asked, so smug he seemed to radiate condescension.

Sol struggled to find her voice. "Where is everyone? I never meet more than the same few people. No one's ever home." It wasn't as important to know this, but it was still a curiosity she had to satisfy.

"On the contrary, everyone's *always* home. Normally in bed or just working in their home office. Not many people can handle being far from the community. Just those who are the strongest," Finnian admitted.

Sol slackened her jaw. Never leaving home, never interacting with other people—the way these people lived seemed unsustainable at best.

"That . . . doesn't seem healthy."

"Oh?" He blinked. "Isn't it how you live?"

She cut her eyes at him. That wasn't the same thing. She had a *choice* in where she went and who she spoke to. It couldn't be helped if she just chose to stay home and speak to no one.

"So how am I supposed to do whatever it is you want if I can't leave the neighborhood?"

"Oh, you can absolutely leave. So can Alice. Haven't you noticed, you're in and out every day. It's what makes you our best candidates."

Sol rubbed her temples, trying hard to think.

Finnian cooed. "Aw, headache again? Why not try the painkillers that Alice's been taking? They work *wonders* for her." Reaching out, he placed two small blue pills on the table in front of Sol. She swatted them away, letting them fall to the floor and roll under a nearby table.

"Yeah, I didn't think so." He tutted.

She looked to her wife. Even now, Alice was drinking mimosas faster than Sol could count.

"Don't feel so left out." Finnian called her attention. "You're still part of us—even if you're a little reluctant. We try to put a little bit of aspen into everything—the marble stones, for one. Even the wine." He winked.

Sol's stomach sank at the memory of their first night at home. The wine the association put in their gift basket.

"We did our best to find out what you liked." Finnian looked proud. No, *smug*. They had been planning this from the very beginning, from the first day they moved in.

"Why?"

"Because we want to be a *community*—of one mind, Sol. To share each other's knowledge, strengths—each other's *pain* is the way we stay strong. Whatever one of us lacks, another makes up for."

"You *drugged* us."

"Ah, ah, ah! There are no side effects that suggested being under the influence. It was really just an . . . extended hand. An open door to the connection," Finnian explained. "Besides, think of all the ways we can help. Imagine if your dad moved into this neighborhood. Imagine what it would be like if we could just . . . *prune* his personality just a little bit. Make him softer around the edges, more *understanding* toward people like us. Toward you."

As Finnian spoke, his words felt like cool water, running over her mind, flowing through all the ridges of her brain and soothing her. Papi could be less of a gross misogynist, less of a homophobe. The image slipping in her mind was even of someone who could *apologize* for all those years of pain she suffered. She imagined the lumbering man, standing tall, posture straightened. He would no longer smell like he showered in beer. He would hug her and meet Alice and maybe she could move on from the trauma of being stabbed.

They could change him like they changed Lou.

Sol's hands shook. It wasn't the thought of the change that she hated—but rather that she preferred Papi actually be himself, even if that meant he stayed the same incorrigible asshole he was all his life. Because at least then, he would still be her father. Not some watered-down facsimile of himself.

"You can't . . . you can't just *fix* that. It isn't yours. It's *my* pain and you don't get to pretend like you share it."

Finnian's response was a deep sigh. "Fine, we can leave him out of it. It really doesn't matter to us. Our main priority is *you two*." He gestured to her and Alice. "See, you moved into our community—our roots, so to speak. And Alice is taking to it just fine—but you? There's something . . . off about you. Something holding you back from fully being integrated."

"I thought you said I was already one of you?"

"See, you are but you aren't. You're just . . . not quite there yet and we're not sure why. It's like screwing nails into the trunk of a tree. Sure, we can grow around it but it's . . . uncomfortable for us."

Sol put both elbows on the table and leaned down. The pressure was intensifying and every metal scrape against the porcelain plates felt like a slice into her frontal lobe.

"Are you why Alice is forgetting Korean?"

"I don't know. Do you feel like you're forgetting Spanish?"

It was a rhetorical question. It felt more like the words were outside of her grasp, being moved further and further away. Eventually, she could grab on to it, remember certain words and phrases. But it took longer than she felt comfortable with.

"What if we moved?"

"Hm." Finnian leaned back into his seat. "You could try. Though I think you'd find that *very* difficult. For someone as integrated as, well, *Alice*, we would have to prune her."

The threat was subtle but there. Corinne was pruned. Did Sol want to leave so bad that she'd risk killing her wife?

"But let's be rational about this," he said, pushing the issue aside. "If you're *so* worried about the language situation, you should know it always comes back. She'll adjust soon enough and so will you . . . as long as you help us expand. We already have other communities. Andor's Grove, for one. But we really want to grow into the workplace as well. If we do, people just might be able to leave their homes more often. Become active in other parts of life."

"So that they can keep spreading the roots." Sol filled in the blanks.

Finnian nodded with a gleam in his eye. "It's only fair since we helped you get your job back."

"Fuck the job. I don't want this."

"Do you think I want to feel the effects of pregnancy? Right now,

Nadine's in bed, trying to keep her feet elevated so they don't get too swollen. Teresa's husband, Noah, has IBS and is lactose intolerant so now Roy can't even have his favorite Ben & Jerry's ice cream."

"They have dairy-free ice cream," she breathed. The pain was subsiding.

What she saw on Finnian's face was worse.

His smile was practically ear-to-ear. "*Now* you're getting it. To be part of a community, we all have to make sacrifices."

"Like you did with Corinne?"

Finnian's smile faltered. Even considering her current predicament, Sol took pride in getting under his skin.

"Corinne was . . . old. And the painkillers she was taking after that incident at your house were affecting Nadine's pregnancy." He swallowed, looking away from Sol. "It's unfortunate, but her pruning was necessary."

"She was your friend." Sol remembered how he cried during Corinne's funeral.

"We all have to make sacrifices." His smile was tight. "And besides, even in death, we don't lose our connections. Corinne is still with us. She's just . . . part of the neighbor now."

Sol wasn't so sure. "Fine, whatever. Justify this shit all you want, I don't care. But what about the shadows?" The moving shadows on a still Veronica, or a vacant Bethany—both seemed like a tell for something even more sinister.

"Shadows?"

"You know what I'm talking about." She waited for him to understand her, but the look on his face betrayed him. He really didn't know what she was talking about. Maybe she was wrong.

The conversation died between all of them as the waitress returned with a pen and notepad. "Okay, are you all ready to order?"

Sol felt her appetite run from her but mumbled a half-hearted order for French toast. Alice barely made eye contact with her the entire time.

"Speaking of food," Finnian began. "You should really think long and hard about what you'll make for our bonfire potluck. I know the food restrictions can be discouraging, but I'm sure you'll figure it out."

Sol rolled her eyes. If any of them were smart, they would leave her out of the festivities completely. And if they had any sense, they wouldn't touch whatever food she made.

"Because of the poison?"

"Because of the spice," Sol retorted, irritated by his lack of boundaries.

Finnian chuckled. "There are no boundaries with us. You'll learn soon enough." He turned away from her, jumping back into conversation with Alice and Roy. Sol quietly seethed, blood boiling at how they cornered her like this. Whatever she did to them, they would just take it out on Alice. And if she didn't help their plan progress, who's to say they wouldn't just prune her immediately? The implication was there.

Sol pushed back her seat and made a beeline for the bathroom. She could splash her face with cold water for years and it wouldn't cool her head.

"Aren't you glad we had this conversation?" the neighbor asked.

All this time, Sol knew there was something distinctly wrong with this neighborhood. Their hidden agenda felt obvious, and there always seemed to be a target on her back. Alice thought she was being paranoid, her therapist thought she was just depressingly lonely. But now, she got definitive answers for all the strangeness.

Most days, Sol loved to be right.

This wasn't one of those days.

MAY 2

I'm almost ready. It took a while to find the gas line, and even longer to get enough wood to fill up the room I'll be in. I needed the woman's help for that one. I've been too afraid to leave the house because what if the neighborhood confuses me again, pulls me away from here? What if by the time I walk to the tree on the sidewalk one house over, I'll blink and already find myself clear across the community?

To be honest, I'm still scared. She says it won't hurt and I believe her but I don't know what to expect afterward. What if it's worse than being here with the Neighbor?

She says it's the only way. And that if I don't do it soon, she can't help me.

So I have to go through with this.

P.S. I finally remember her name. It's Esther.

THE MEAL

"How have you been, Sol?" Dr. Nieman asked.

"Not great." Sol chewed on the nail of her thumb. It should have even easier to lie, to pretend to be fine—but Sol knew what she looked like. Sleep was elusive and the bags under her eyes deepened. There were stains on the sweatshirt Sol never got around to changing out of. Since brunch, Alice would coldly say she was fine, that nothing was wrong.

It should have made Sol feel guilty to decide that she would go see Dr. Nieman almost immediately after finding out she was unintentionally spreading pollen and hive mind influence to anyone she was in contact with. At this point, she couldn't pretend to be completely innocent in the neighbor's schemes. Like it or not, she was helping them by being here.

But she needed to talk to *someone* and she could not stomach doing one more boring intake session with someone new. Maybe it was a strange, twisted form of Black solidarity that made her choose the white therapist over the Black one. Like choosing to protect Dr. Moore by keeping the infection away from him.

Great, now I really am a parasite.

On the other hand, Sol came to speak specifically about one thing and as Dr. Moore indicated in just one session, he could not be trusted to stay neutral about her being gay.

Sol didn't feel comfortable even sleeping next to Alice, so she went to the couch once again. And even then, she couldn't sleep. Instead, Sol went out and bought three large bottles of vodka. Alice was just about ignoring her anyway, there was no point in keeping up appearances.

Still, Sol didn't touch the alcohol. She left them in the trunk of her car, untouched. She found herself unmotivated to even engage in her worst behavior. What was the point now?

Dr. Nieman frowned. "Would you like to explain what's happening?"

Sol curled into herself with a hug.

"Something's wrong with my wife. She's not herself lately and I don't know what to do."

Confusion permeated Dr. Nieman's face. "Okay . . . what do you mean she's not herself lately?"

A lump rose in Sol's throat. "She's not calling her family, she's not— she's not making the food she likes to make. She suddenly wants to quit her job!" Her eyes brimmed with tears. "She doesn't look at me the same way. It's like she's a completely different person." She painted the unhinged truth with a normalcy that could be easy to digest. After all, the best- and worst-case scenario over telling the truth would be the same: Sol would be institutionalized.

And she couldn't leave Alice all alone in Maneless Grove.

"Can you think of any reason why that would be?"

Sol struggled to find an ordinary reason. "She didn't get the . . . the promotion she wanted."

"I see. Is it possible she is a little depressed? Maybe she doesn't want to disappoint her family and so she hasn't reached out."

Sol couldn't help but scoff. It was much deeper than that.

"You don't agree?"

"It's just . . . she's gone through rough patches before. But she's *never* not talked to at least her aunt, let alone her parents. Even stranger"— and Dr. Nieman's eyebrow quirked at this—"she's stopped speaking Korean to them. It's . . . it's like she's forgotten her own language."

"That does sound pretty serious," Dr. Nieman mused. "But again, a lot of that can be explained by depression."

"Losing language?"

"Lethargy. The lack of effort. If she's been speaking English for so long, maybe that's now her default?"

"I—" But Sol couldn't say. It didn't add up for her, but what Dr. Nieman was saying did have a logic to it, and unless she added, "I forgot to mention she's taking aspen-pollen pills that are altering her brain and making her part of a cult," there wasn't much more she could say. Instead, Sol asked about something Dr. Nieman *might* actually be able to help with.

"Fine—okay, not fine, but let's say that's the case. Why is she then taking it out on *me*? I thought depressives shifted inward."

Like me.

Dr. Nieman put down her pen. "Sol, when you were much deeper in your despair the last few months, were you taking it out on her?"

"No." She pursed her lips together. "I mean, I was still trying not to drag her down but . . . no, I wasn't taking any of it out on her."

"Then I think it's safe to assume that whatever she's going through may not have anything to do with *you*."

Once more she was right . . . in a way. Alice was changing because of the full force of the community influencing her thoughts, feelings, maybe even what she was seeing. Sol may not have been as quickly influenced due to her susceptibility to migraines and her distinct lack of trust of others, but Alice tended to lean toward seeing the good in people.

She nodded then, as if again acquiescing. "How do I . . . get her to open up to me, then?"

She realized what she was asking was much different than what Dr. Nieman may interpret, but it was still worth a shot. So far, she was more helpful than she knew.

"Why not find a way to reconnect with her? Find that one spark that brought you together in the first place."

Sol looked down. The wooden floors had swirls in them that looked like faces. She knew exactly what it was that initially brought them together—and it wasn't a good memory.

"My parents kicked me out when I was in college," Sol finally admitted. "Alice took me in."

"That's . . . a start." Dr. Nieman nodded meaningfully. "So you connect her with home—with *being* with her. Yet that's still something superficial. What about what really brought you *together*? That made it not just about a shared living space, but a shared life? What kickstarted those feelings in the first place?"

Sol opened her mouth and then closed it. She thought about it intensely, *really* tried to pin it down. But the more she shifted through her memories, the more she realized the feelings grew gradually. There was never just one thing or one moment that sealed it. Hell, they never really *talked* about it. Aside from the wedding, they never even celebrated dating anniversaries. It was all so casual until it wasn't.

"We cook for each other," Sol started. "And *with* each other. And she used to watch a lot of variety shows and K-dramas with her family. I wasn't into them at the time, but the way she would passionately talk about them made me want to learn Korean just so I could watch them with her without subtitles."

Something dawned on Sol then. It wasn't one thing—it could never be one thing. It was the totality of it. Again, Dr. Nieman had hit the nail on the head, even if she wasn't aware. *I want to share my life with her—share* everything *with her.*

Everything but this.

Maybe the realization was the start she needed, though. Because it was clear Sol only ever wanted to spend time with Alice. What still wasn't clear—what was always a mystery—was why Alice wanted to spend time with *her*. For as long as they'd been together it was a miracle she never took for granted.

Again . . . until now.

"I don't even know why she likes me." Sol didn't know she said this out loud until she looked up to see Dr. Nieman.

"You don't know *why* your wife likes you?" Her eyes were wide with shock and amusement, and a smile that she was trying and failing to hold back. Sol's cheeks became hot.

"She's literally married to you, I'm pretty sure she more than *just* likes you." Dr. Nieman chuckled.

Sol sank into her seat. "Okay, *fine*, she clearly likes . . . *loves* me," she corrected herself. "I'm just saying, I don't know what it was for her like it was for me."

"So then why don't you find out?" She leaned forward. "Try to re-connect over a meal. Maybe go out for dinner or stay in and make it romantic."

Sol grimaced. "That's kind of cheesy."

"It's just an example, but I'll note it's only cheesy because it's a tried-and-true trope. Ultimately, though, it's about making sure there's time for just you two, nothing else. If you're concerned about your wife and feeling a little insecure in your marriage, there's always the option to re-create those early feelings you had for each other."

"And what if they're not there anymore?" Sol's stomach tied itself into knots. She didn't even want to *think* about that possibility—that Alice didn't love her anymore. Because if she didn't, there wasn't much Sol could do to save her marriage or Alice.

"Well . . . let's cross that bridge when we get to it."

Dr. Nieman gave her a polite smile. Sol gritted her teeth and looked away. For the rest of the session, Sol kept her questions and answers purely mundane—nothing supernatural going on with her at all. Not that Dr. Nieman would believe it.

As soon as the session was over, she practically sped out of the office. Though she didn't want to go home, there were few places Sol could find it in herself to loiter. She was a homebody for a reason. Her previous worries about her home turning on her were also for good reason. It was her one haven, where everything could be reliably *hers* and unchanging just like her.

Except it wasn't. For once, Sol was nauseated at the thought of going home.

But at the same time, she couldn't stay away. The farther away she was, the more her stomach felt like a rubber band stretched too far. She would snap if she didn't get back quick enough even if she knew it wasn't safe.

And she didn't want to admit it but the buzzing of whispering voices in the background became soothing to her. Intoxicating. The closer she got, the more she wanted to drink it in, fall into the thoughts and sensations like it was her favorite brand of vodka. She could see why very few people left their homes. If they could be in this calming bliss all the time, why wouldn't they?

Sol gripped the steering wheel so tight, her knuckles were taut. She hated it but couldn't fight it. Home was always somewhere she wanted to be. Home was where Alice was. No matter how much Alice changed, Sol would always want to be there with her.

So maybe . . . maybe it was okay to just let it go. Lean in. Someone else could handle the wheel.

Sol slowly drove the car through the streets and into Maneless Grove. Her stomach knot loosened until she came home—then she was startled by the view of Alice's car in the driveway.

She went inside and quickly found Alice in the kitchen, already working on dinner. There was an array of odd ingredients spread out all around the counter. Panko breadcrumbs, cannellini beans, olive oil, green onions, and just a small jar of cumin. Nothing that had a spice rating above a jalapeño.

"You're home early, Alice." Sol proceeded carefully. "Did something happen at work?"

"No, actually. Just decided to scale back the number of projects I'm on. There's really no point in working myself to the grave when I'm not going to be recognized for it."

Sol couldn't argue with that. She noticed an opened container of quinoa on the counter.

"What are you making?"

"I'm trying this new thing called quinoa patties," Alice said as she stirred something into a small boiling pot. "How was therapy?" She tossed the question over her shoulder.

Sol's eyes darted all over the kitchen. There was something distinctly wrong with the image—worse than the food Alice was making. Sol just couldn't pinpoint what it was.

"Uh, it was fine," she stammered. What was she missing? It felt so obvious, like it was staring her in the face. Alice stopped stirring but she didn't turn around and that made Sol's view all the more unnerving.

"Sol? You're gawking." And then she went back to stirring.

Sol kept trying to find the source of her discomfort. It was subtle, like her clothes suddenly fit wrong but the fabric was so soft, she wouldn't notice. She thought back to Dr. Nieman and her suggestion—trying to connect with her wife. Sol took hesitant steps forward, brought her hand to Alice's lower back.

Deciding to ignore the deep, cloying feeling of wrongness, she asked, "Need help cooking?"

That was when Alice looked up at her and Sol saw what was wrong. Alice was cooking with her right hand. She had been left-handed her whole life—when did that change?

And her hair was several shades lighter and curled. How did Sol miss something as obvious as that? She was right in front of her, practically looking like a different woman altogether, and still Sol's mind was directed elsewhere.

Alice smiled. "Of course."

That was different too—cooking. Sol and Alice liked to dance around each other in the kitchen, flawlessly stepping around and up to each other to pass ingredients, exchange laughter, and sneak small bites when the other wasn't looking. The result was often a lopsided meal—too much rice and not enough banchan. This time, there was no banchan. There wasn't even rice.

Sol tried to move around Alice, but she found herself in the way more often than not. Her feet tripped over her wife's, and she spent more time apologizing for the action than laughing.

And Sol didn't like quinoa enough to sneak bites.

The two were out of sync. As time went by, reconnecting seemed less and less possible.

It was when the two sat down to eat that Sol couldn't take the wrongness anymore.

"You changed your hair," Sol commented.

"Do you like it?"

Sol liked anything that made Alice happy. But Alice didn't seem happy—she didn't even seem like Alice.

"It's cute."

And that was true, at least objectively. Alice was attractive to Sol no matter how she changed her hair—Sol just wanted to know *why*.

"Why the sudden change?" Sol took a small bite of the patty. The grains felt unpleasant in her mouth and tasteless to boot.

Pick a struggle, patty.

"I don't know, just thought it would be fun!" Alice said. Even her voice was half an octave higher. It lilted upward in a way that felt unnatural.

"When did you come back home?" Sol asked. She tried not to sound like it was an interrogation even though that was exactly what it was.

"Not too long ago."

Sol did the mental math. Dyeing and curling hair took some time—when did Alice leave work?

"So did you leave work in the middle of the day or . . . ?" Sol's voice trailed off.

Alice never answered. Sol watched her cut up her patty into small squares before eating each one. Not knowing what else to do, she copied Alice's movements. At first it was done with the intention of getting Alice's attention again, a sort of playful mocking, *Ha-ha, look at how weird this is*—then Sol found it oddly calming.

Everything became background noise, from the squeal of knife against plate to soundless sensations. It was dissociating without quite being dissociating. Everything faded and she was focused intensely on the patty, making each slice as identical as possible.

And then, something changed.

In a blink, her hands became a different color. Lighter. In another blink, they were older. In another, the plate itself was different. Every time she shut her eyes and opened them, she saw something different about her hands, the plate, the cutlery she was using. But two things remained the same throughout all of it—the food and the cutting movement.

Again, she blinked, and suddenly she was watching herself. Making the same hand motions, lifting each square piece to her lips, chewing three times and then swallowing. Sol noticed that from across the counter, she looked less tired—the bags under her eyes receded and her posture was better. She wondered who was sitting in her body, the same way she was sitting in Alice's. Maybe it was Nadine. Or it could have been Terry, Bethany, a child, anyone could have been there, swapping viewpoints with each blink.

Then it occurred to her—Alice *wasn't* eating. At least not now. She cut up the same patty, chewed three times, and swallowed, but now was just watching Sol make her way through a dull meal.

You look better, Alice thought with a kind of vague sadness that Sol couldn't understand.

"What?" Sol spoke through her own lips. And just like that, she was shoved back into her body and having much more vivid sensations. Bits of quinoa stuck uncomfortably between her teeth. Her stomach was nearing capacity and aside from the aftertaste, she had little memory of chewing or swallowing. It took Sol a moment to remember her vocal cords and repeat herself.

"What did you say?"

Alice's eyes were wide and indecipherable, but the smile remained intact.

"I didn't say anything."

Not out loud, of course. Sol knew that.

She asked, "Remember that time I asked you to do that yoga class in college?" It was their second semester of junior year. Though the yoga class wasn't a requirement to graduate, they needed a course credit in the humanities and arts, and for some reason, yoga seemed like an easy A.

Or at least, a way to blow off steam between the hard-science courses.

"Oh yeah." Alice laughed, in spite of herself. "You didn't even own yoga pants. I had to buy you a pair."

The pair was stuffed in a box somewhere in the basement. Sol was sure it didn't even fit her anymore, but it meant a lot to her that Alice would gift her something since she was strapped for cash, so she kept it as a memento.

"It was one of the few classes I had where we weren't the only non-white students there." Sol would never be able to hold the crow pose for longer than five seconds, but she looked forward to that class the most because it was the one time she didn't feel completely out of place.

The best part about the class was the silly games Alice, Sol, and their Nigerian friend Ife came up with. Every time they were told to go into cobra pose, the three would count how many cracks they heard in their backs and call each other by the number for the rest of the class as if it were their name.

Sol briefly wondered where Ife was now. Hopefully not in a community like this.

"Why are you bringing that up now?" Alice asked.

Sol wasn't sure. Uneasy, she looked back down at her plate. It was empty. Alice reached across and gathered her plate.

"I'll load up the dishwasher. Why don't you get ready for bed?"

Similar to the fishbowl effect Sol got with her migraines, the table stretched out in front of her, lengthening the distance between Alice and her. She panicked and blurted the first thing she could think of.

"I thought we could watch some of your favorite variety shows together."

Her vision stopped stretching, but the distance didn't decrease. Alice's lips became a thin line, and she gave Sol a once-over. Hesitant but still hopeful, Sol stepped around the kitchen counter and came right up to Alice. It felt like ages, traversing the distance between them, but once she was there, Sol didn't want to walk away.

"Sol?" Alice's voice was small.

Was this how it was going to be? Pretending like nothing was happening, that these changes were *fine*, that being stripped of their identities in increments was just a drop of a sacrifice in return for some cultish idea of a greater good? Language was not like ice cream. Having to abstain from one was not the same as abstaining from the other. Alice had to realize that . . . right?

"Are you really happy like this?" Sol asked. It was the one thing she actually *wanted* to ask.

Alice's eyes fluttered and she took a step back. Sol grabbed her hand to keep the distance from returning.

"It's fine." Alice shook her head. "It'll work out. And when it does, we use it to our advantage, right?"

"I don't think we can keep ignoring how this is hurting us just for some perceived future leverage," Sol pleaded, eyes brimming with tears. "Is not being ourselves the way to be happy?"

They had their fights like any other couple, of course. There were times when Sol loved to annoy Alice, argue until she was blue in the face just to prove she was right about something minuscule.

But the moments when they were happy? Truly and honestly happy? It was because Sol was Sol and Alice was *Alice*.

Or did Alice not love Sol for being herself?

Tell me this isn't it. She wanted to know desperately. *Tell me you've always loved me just as I am.*

"Nothing stays the same forever," Alice whispered, hand slipping out of Sol's. A frantic determination lodged itself in Sol's chest. She grabbed Alice's hand again, lacing her fingers between her wife's.

"No, but what if I could do something about this?" She was practically begging. "I could be better on my own. I don't need *their* help."

"You needed their help for your job."

Sol swallowed. Liquid emotion was threatening to pour out of her eyes. "That's not fair." *And not necessarily true. I didn't even have a chance to defend myself. Sure, I'm glad it hadn't come to that, but I also did have a reputation as an excellent researcher* before *Clarke's accusation to support me* . . .

But even she was pretty sure that was all a load of crap. If the neighbor hadn't intervened, what was she actually going to do against misogyny, bigotry, and the will of a mediocre white man?

Alice gave a small shrug, avoiding Sol's stare. She stepped away, focusing on rinsing a greasy plate before placing it in the dishwasher. Sol refused to move.

Alice sighed. "Go to bed."

"No." The desperation turned sharp. Sol was indignant. "You kept Nadine's sick secret, lied about the homeowners agreement *and more* for what? You didn't even get the promotion you wanted so bad!" It was a slap in the face and Sol knew it, but she wasn't going to let this go. It was actually insane how far Alice went for these people. Aligned herself with them just for them to call her a *backup*.

"I know you did not aspire to be second place to anyone—much less a white woman who needs the support of an entire cookie-cutter neighborhood just to do her job half as well as you," Sol continued.

Though her back was to Sol, she could sense irritation piling up across Alice's shoulders. Her fingers curled tightly around the edge of the counter.

"I'm sorry, okay!" Alice shouted, visibly shocking herself. She quickly cleared her voice, keeping her emotions under control. But it slipped, showed just how easily Sol managed to get under her skin.

Alice lowered her voice. "Yeah, I fucked up. I get it. I know. I shouldn't have kept throwing you under the bus like that. I just . . ." Her shoulders shook.

Suddenly, Sol was right there, taking her head in her hands and wiping her tears away.

"What do I do now? What are we supposed to do now that we're stuck here?" Alice sniffled. The full force of regret came out in quiet sobs.

Sol pulled her into a hug and whispered, "Do you remember what you said our first night here?"

Alice shook her head.

"You said we take care of each other. So, let's just do that, okay?"

MAY 4

I noticed something odd about the woman.

Her shadow moves even when she doesn't. I wanted to ask her about that but there's no time left. Today is the day.

I will bury these pages under the dead tree in the backyard. If anyone finds them, well . . . I hope you find a better escape than I did.

But before you do, please tell my mom and my dad I'm sorry.

Their names are Nadine and Terry Adams.

I'll write their address below.

THE GUEST ROOM

Sol looked down at the array of inoffensive (and frankly bland) food items she emptied out of the fridge and pantry. There wasn't much. Potatoes, but those were too carb heavy. She had rice and pasta but neither were on the approved list of gluten-free staples the association allowed at any event. She baked cookies once for Corinne, but the sugar she used was also not approved by the association. She looked back at the list that came with the invitation—no gluten, no dairy, all processed food was banned, keep everything keto-friendly, paleo-friendly, skip the butter, if anything *must* be fried, it had to be fried in very specific oil not to exceed a certain amount—how did anyone live like this? How could anyone *eat* like this?

They couldn't. Sol had seen Roy devour a tower of pancakes during brunch. The welcoming party had all sorts of table goodies (though Sol opted for a more liquid diet that day). Absolutely no one restricted themselves this heavily when it came to food. Was this a punishment? Or a test? If she used the wrong flour or added a dash of normal iodized salt instead of sea salt, was that grounds for pruning?

The countertop became bare. The most Sol had that skirted just underneath the regulations was a clove of garlic, a wilting bag of spinach leaves, and a pitcher of water. Not even the oranges could be squeezed into a recipe—they were technically out of season, and the association frowned upon making use of anything that might have been GMO.

And the *seasoning*. Sol worried that if she so much as tried to add Goya Sazón into ground beef for a tame baked pastelito (which really should just be fried), someone would accuse her of trying to raise everyone's blood pressure. The gochujang also sat in the fridge, unused, and she had to avoid the red pepper and chili powder, and couldn't even use a soy sauce base for anything because *someone* in the community was afraid of a little preservative.

What else did that leave? Ginger, of course, along with rice vinegar and sesame oil (although she'd recently read that even sesame was becoming a big allergen—she just had to hope the community here wasn't as up on FDA regulations as she was). Maybe if she sauteed it together with the garlic cloves and the spinach leaves, she could claim it was a new kind of salad.

"Fuck me, these people are impossible," she mumbled, rubbing her temples to keep the headache from returning. Sol would have asked Alice to help, but for once she didn't want Alice home for this. The longer her wife was home, the less she felt like Alice. She noticed it in her small tics.

Sometimes Alice chewed on her nails when she was annoyed—other times, she picked strands of hair from the nape of her neck. But lately, Alice leaned more on her right side with a hand on her hip like she was carrying extra weight. She hardly cursed when she was irritated, she just sighed and said things like, "Well, at least we have our health."

Sol never thought she'd miss her wife so much even while sleeping next to her. No, Alice had to spend as much time away from the neighborhood as possible. The changes had to plateau eventually. And until they did, Sol would be on kitchen duty to get ready for the bonfire tonight.

She threw a pan on the stove and felt her phone vibrate. An email from Dr. Henderson confirming her first day back at work—she'd answer it later. The idea of spreading seeds and pollen to infect others at Yale made her guts twist. But returning without having any backup after the shit Clarke put her through? Inconceivable.

Flicking on the stove, Sol moved to crush the garlic under a knife before stopping.

It was low and probably nothing, but she thought she heard a rhythmic tapping in another room.

Did I imagine it?

No, there it was again. *Tap, tap, taptaptap, tap, tap . . .*

She turned off the stove and stepped into the living room. The tapping sounded like it was coming from upstairs.

"Alice?" Sol yelled, knowing she couldn't be home from work yet. The tapping stopped. Then it started up again. She moved toward the source until it stopped. She stood and waited until it continued, and she followed.

It was an odd game of Marco Polo. Like something was beckoning her closer but didn't want her to get too close. If Alice were here, she would have said there was an intruder in the home. Sol would not have agreed. Whatever was making the tapping noise could see Sol enough to know where she was.

Finally, Sol stepped into the guest room, which was more or less acting as the storage room until they could figure out a more appropriate use for it. Boxes of unpacked items were lined against the wall and old lamps were huddled in the far corner. They hadn't even been in this house for long and yet there was a thin line of dust covering every surface.

Sol waited for the tapping to start again. She strained her ear to listen for it, absolutely sure that it was coming from this room. After a few minutes of dead silence, she sighed and turned back to the door.

It wasn't there.

Stunned, Sol twisted herself around. Every wall was just that—a wall. There was no door or lining to suggest a door had ever been there. She pressed her hand flat against the wall where the door had been. Just a smooth surface.

Okay, this cannot be real. This cannot be real.

She was frantic now, punching into the wall until her knuckles were sore. The pain was enough to convince Sol that she wasn't asleep.

"Doors just don't disappear!" she yelled.

Neither do stairs.

Fuck.

Going toward the noise was supposed to help her uncover what was making it, not trap her in a makeshift tomb.

The thought made Sol's breath catch in her throat. If the room was airtight, she only had so much air left.

No, she refused to believe it. Grabbing the nearest lamp, she struck it against the wall again and again. It made a dent, filling Sol with some hope until a few blinks later, it was gone. All the dents and depressions made in it were healed over as if it was never struck.

It's healing itself.

Sol became frantic. Smashing the lamp in again and again, the only thing she accomplished was breaking the lamp in two. She grabbed another lamp and continued the destruction; it broke moments later. Tears ran down her face and screams racked her body. She needed to get out.

Somewhere on the other side of the wall, her phone rang. She heard its faint chime, like a mocking giggle far out of reach. Sol dug her nails into her palms. The pain was sharp; she wasn't having a nightmare. She tore into the wall, only succeeding in removing a layer of dried paint and half a fingernail. Her bloodied hand shook.

Sol sank to her knees. There were not enough words in the world to describe the emotion that dug into her. It wasn't a hopelessness or even a madness that spread from her chest to her fingertips. It was the feeling that she had somehow stepped completely out of the world— out of reality. She was detached from everything and everyone in this room that had no doors. Isolation that had become existential.

She shut her eyes, finding an odd comfort in darkness. In the dark, she could at least pretend she was not in the guest room at all. She imagined herself to be in the living room, lying on the floor, but at least a little closer to the earth.

In the dark, she could imagine being anywhere but here.

In the dark, she heard something. It was deep and groaning, like a strong wind pressing against an old wooden shack. It didn't push very hard, but Sol got the distant feeling that something was trying to force its way in. Unlike when the community tried to, this didn't produce a headache in her.

Alice? Is that you? she called out in thought. Then something else— the distinct sound of a crinkling fire.

THE CULT OF ESTHER RHODES

Sol reached out to the neighbor, listening for that hum of voices in the background—and heard nothing. Just an echoing silence through and through.

Oh great, the one time she actually *needed* their help, and they weren't accessible. What kind of game were they playing at?

Sol sniffled and looked up, stilling at the sight of a shadow across the room. It was tall with gangly limbs, and appeared to stare down at her.

"Who are you?" Sol pressed her back against the wall.

The shadow figure answered by shedding another shadow. It stepped aside, becoming a different form. A smaller figure with thicker limbs. Then another shadow stepped out. A figure missing a limb. Repeatedly, the shadows duplicated, until they filled the room so much that there was hardly any light. The room quickly dropped in temperature and Sol shivered.

Sol noticed a pair of shadows had a thin line between their heads and the ceiling.

The Kennedys.

"I thought you were all part of the neighbor," Sol whispered.

Slowly and in unison, the shadows shook their heads. They turned and walked into each other, reforming into the gangly-limbed form. The room brightened considerably with a soft haze of rippling light.

Then the figure stretched its long hand down, crossing the threshold where the wall met the floor, and slinked farther along toward Sol. Unnerved, Sol jumped up and tried to escape through the wall.

"No, no, no, no, no!"

When the hand touched her, a shock ran through her body. Her body convulsed, crashing to the floor, as images shot rapidly across her mind. Swinging axes. Knives carving into bark. Roots reaching deep within the earth, twisting and curling in pain, leaves shaking in terror. A deal made between a shadow and a mistaken cult leader.

A nameplate in the garden.

Once the hand pulled away, Sol sat up, gasping for air.

"The nameless." She choked. As the community used the trees for its interconnecting abilities, the trees reached back through that same channel and developed a quiet consciousness.

And the consciousness was hungry. It was always hungry, watching, absorbing knowledge, minds, names. It hid in the background, allowing the neighborhood to think it was a passive source of strength while using the strangler fig tree in Sol's backyard to hide many of the dead it took.

And those who were still living? Slowly being fed on, becoming vacant bodies to puppet over time.

It was never a symbiotic relationship, like Finnian thought. It was a parasitic relationship.

Sol rubbed her palm, absentmindedly. The first time she touched the fig, it stung her, claiming her first. It allowed her to see everything and everyone within those gnarled roots. And all within the neighbor's blindside. She was just as much part of the nameless as she was part of the neighbor.

And it knew what she wanted most.

"Fine," she spat. "Let's make a deal."

Sol strolled up to the large redbrick building with a Tupperware of spinach in one hand and a bag filled with her own personal surprise in the other. It should have felt odd to Sol, that though there was a promise to give her a tour of the neighborhood, this would actually be the first time she'd walk into the town hall itself. During the welcoming party, everyone milled about outside, not once looking to the building or acting as though it were open for use. The building just sat there, a perfect cylindrical tower in the center of the community.

It should have felt odd—but Sol was beyond that now. The buzzing of voices was smooth, nearly a hum. She'd get to know every inch of the neighborhood and its inhabitants in due time.

Glasses clinked together loudly as she walked to the entrance. A set of glass double doors was adorned with balloons strung together and floating side by side. Between them, Sol's reflection in the large window greeted her in yoga pants with a loose shirt tied at her hip. Her thick curls were pulled back into a ponytail, sleeked with gel and revealing her heart-shaped face. The trees clapped in the distance, tugging a coy smile from her lips.

"Hello?" She carefully let the bag on her wrist gently slide down to her elbow before knocking. "It's Sol!"

The door swung open. One of the Finnians smiled at Sol, though a mix of curiosity and shock flicked through his eyes.

"Sol, you're early," he answered, taking in her new look. "We haven't even got the gas tank over here yet."

"I figured I'd come and help set up." She shrugged, stepping into the door frame. Finnian seemed to take the hint well enough; he smoothly stepped out of the way.

"That's . . . very nice of you."

Inside, the town hall looked very well used. Rows of wooden benches arranged in a semi-circle around a stage. In the very center was a pulpit. Sol's eye twitched, imagining that this must've been where the church originally congregated. She set her Tupperware aside on one of the benches and took a moment to walk the length of the room.

Folded up chairs and tables lined the wall, along with boxes and decorations. Sol's eyes darted to a corkboard with a large calendar on it. Today's date was circled for obvious reasons and next to it looked to be a directory complete with pictures of every board member of the Homeowners Association.

"I just finished bringing up the rest of the supplies we need from the basement," Finnian said, trailing behind Sol. The door to her right creaked open. Another Finnian froze just as he poked his head out. Sol nodded and watched him slide another set of folded chairs through.

"This is the last of them," he said, his voice cracking with an accent she couldn't place. Then he slipped back inside, shutting the door behind him.

"Looks like you got a handle on everything here." Sol raised an eyebrow.

"Everything but the gas tank." He forced a chuckle.

Sol placed a hand on his shoulder. "Why don't you let me handle that?"

Finnian stared intently at her, darkened eyes clashing with a friendly smile. She could feel him sizing her up, curious to know what game she was playing at. Her expression remained placid, cool. Even when she felt something palming through her mind, worming its way into her thoughts, she let it grasp at nothing. If Finnian was hoping to get a rise out of her, he'd simply have to try harder.

"You're sure?" he asked, suspicious.

"No." Sol giggled. "Oh my gosh, I'm joking. You're so serious! You should lighten up. Here, take this." She removed the hanging bag from her elbow and pressed it into his chest.

"What's this?" He furrowed his brow, feeling the weight of glass and liquid. Sol was already halfway to the door when Finnian looked inside. His eyes immediately widened. "Wait a minute. This is a lot of Grey Goose. I'm not sure if we can allow this."

She twirled around.

"What's wrong with it? You can pour a little bit in some juice. Ooh!" Her eyes lit up. "Have you ever made a bay breeze cocktail? It's to *die* for. Just throw in some pineapple and cranberry—a perfect blend for end-of-the-summer festivities, don't you think?"

"It's just we don't normally take something like this—"

"Finnian." Sol stopped him with a look. "It's gluten free."

His mouth flapped open, struggling to find a response. Sol took the advantage to head out.

"Oh, could you make sure to put that spinach in a fridge somewhere? Thanks!" She tossed her head back in a laugh. The two of them would not get along, would not be friends whatsoever, but if all she had to do was play nice? Sure, she could do that.

Anything to get ahead.

THE BONFIRE ANNOUNCEMENT

The glow of the fire reached far, illuminating much of the event field and all the people gathering for drinks and food. Sol watched the children run sporadically with a quiet deliberation. Their shadows cut across the lawn and occasionally, Sol would catch a new shadow peeking out toward the older crowd.

"Hey, Sol," someone said, stealing her attention. Teresa strolled over with Hope in tow. The way the bonfire light caught their faces, their smiles twisted into something mocking and patronizing. "Thank you so much for your . . . interesting addition to our bonfire potluck."

Each of them held a clear cup in hand, still full, with a swirl of red and yellow. If Sol peeked behind them, she might see her spinach concoction sitting on the table, gathering a rogue fly or two. She wasn't bothered and would not give them the satisfaction of mistaking she was.

"Well, given the restrictions on such short notice, I could only work with what I had," she admitted, taking a long, cool drink herself. Sol could barely taste the alcohol in it, if at all. Finnian still seemed to be apprehensive toward her. That was okay, she could work on that.

"Oh, but I thought you weren't working. Couldn't you have run out to get other ingredients?" Teresa prodded. Sol gave a bashful, calculated smile.

"I'll actually be returning to work soon, so I've been busy preparing for that. I'm surprised you didn't know. Nadine didn't tell you?"

Hope looked askance at Teresa and her face fell. The doubt wasn't fully there, but Sol could rouse it just a little more.

"It's fine, I'm sure she's been busy with the pregnancy." Her eyes darted around the lawn, pretending to scan the crowd. "Where is she, anyway? I noticed she wasn't at the welcoming party last time. Is she also not good with social events?"

"Not lately. It isn't . . . good for her to be at these events." Teresa glanced down at her cup.

Right, the alcohol. Nadine couldn't be present while she was pregnant. Everything affected everyone else. Even those who hadn't been born yet. Sol tried to mask her delight with another sip. Her mind was definitely buzzing and this time it wasn't with voices.

"That's a shame." She wrapped both hands around her cup. "I'm sure she hates having to miss out like this."

"She's due to give birth any day now, though, right?" Hope perked up. The more Sol thought about her, the more she realized what this woman was like—sort of a personal gofer. Kind of like one of those helicopter seed pods on maples, fluttering around and able to move about in a way the tree couldn't. They sent her to practically break into Sol's house that one time, didn't they? Except . . . was that role diminishing? It'd been a while since Sol had seen her. Hope looked a little older, pudgier. There was a tinge of fear in the way she carried herself, like she knew she was past her prime. She only ever seemed to play the support role in this community.

Are you next to be pruned?

Hope's eyes widened, and Sol acknowledged her with a gentle smile.

"True, but then she'll have to start breastfeeding and even then, I've heard you have to steer clear from alcohol and all sorts of things. Could affect the milk." She shrugged. "But you know, good on her for prioritizing her health. And as neighbors, we should step up and take a few things off her plate. It takes a village, right?"

Teresa nodded, a slight twitch in her face giving her away. It wouldn't do for a president to keep prioritizing their own. And if that had to continue on for another year or two, well . . .

Sol downed the rest of her cup and stepped away. "I'm getting another drink." She locked eyes with Hope as she finally took a guilty sip.

Don't worry, I won't tell.

Alice leaned over the drinks table. Another stressful day at work had her knocking back another cup and putting it aside. Sol placed a hand on her lower back.

"Having fun?"

"How is there barely any alcohol in any of these but I'm still feeling drunk?" Alice hiccupped.

"Because you've had a lot." Sol eyed several empty cups, strewn over the table. Normally, she was the one who would be drinking herself into a stupor. But not today, not right now. Sol could get buzzed if it suited her, she just couldn't go too far. She had a point to make, after all.

She took her wife's hand and spun her so they were facing each other. "Do you want to head home? I can have one of the Finnians drive you back."

Alice hardly reacted to the odd phrase with anything more than rubbing her face with the back of her hand. But that was par for the course when Alice had this much to drink. Her cheeks were reddening, and even her hand felt clammy in Sol's.

"Yeah, that might be a good idea." Alice stumbled. Sol held her steady as she searched for the nearest redhead. Her gaze latched on to one, moving to the outskirts of the party. His eyes were glazed over, but that wasn't from the drink. His cup was still full, just like most others at this party.

She smiled at the shadow attached to this Finnian, a bit too bulky for his actual shape. It swayed as if waving high and she beckoned the actual man over.

"Finnian, you haven't had much to drink, right?" she asked. "Would you mind dropping my wife off at home?"

He blinked, not realizing he had walked over. "Sure, yeah." He dropped his drink on the table and gently looped his arm in Alice's. It was a relief to know even something—some*one* mentally vacant could still be courteous. The two walked off toward the parked cars.

"This is a new look for you, Sol."

Sol braced herself as she turned. The voice was familiar—the person was not. A woman wearing slacks and a satin blouse. All sleek, no name brand but probably expensive all the same. She was followed by two other women, dressed similarly, with hair parted down the middle and curled at the ends.

"Hey, you." Sol clocked the woman as Peach from the welcome party. Sol was never given a proper name but at this point, she didn't care. Peach plucked a drink off the table and made eye contact as she took a sip. Sol resisted the urge to roll her eyes. The most aggressive this woman could be was still passive.

"Yeah, I had to dig these old yoga pants out of storage. Haven't worn them since college, can you believe they still fit?" She gave a playful little twirl and glanced at the entourage. "You're one less today?"

"Evelyn's not feeling well," one of the other women responded. Might have been Chartreuse or Magenta, Sol couldn't tell. They weren't wearing their respective colors. Evelyn must've been the one wearing blue.

"I'm sure she'll be missed." Sol pouted, knowing she would likely never see that woman again. *And then there were three.*

"We heard from Finnian that you helped set up. And brought the drinks," Peach noted, finger tapping her cup. Her snakelike eyes seemed to be sizing her up. "What are you up to?"

Sol gasped, feigning offense. "Am I not allowed to just indulge in neighborly acts?"

Peach cocked an eyebrow with a smirk.

"Okay, fine, you caught me." Sol laughed, then dropped her voice low as if harboring a secret. "I was just thinking . . . the elections are coming up, right?" Sol scanned the faces of each of the three women, leaning in. Their eyes shined with curiosity. They could smell drama like sharks smelled blood.

She looked at the fire and wondered why a grove of aspens would want such a thing so close to them. But then she also thought about what Finnian—whichever one she'd been talking to then—had said about forest fires being cleansing.

That's why Sol was here. Why she was getting them all drunk. Why she made sure there was alcohol to keep Nadine away. Because she *was* going to be with Alice. She *was* going to be herself and have her home and not be just another branch waiting to be pruned.

No . . .

She was going to burn it all down to the fucking ground.

She smiled at the women, and they recoiled just a touch, which made Sol smile even more.

Now you get it, you stupid Karens.

"I'm thinking of running for president."

THE NEW BEGINNING

Three Months Later

Sol sat at the local Havenstar Cafe, pulling apart the wrapping of the sandwich she had just bought.

"Couldn't wait until I got here?" Amir huffed playfully as he walked up.

"When have I ever waited to eat with you?" She licked off a rogue line of mayonnaise from the side of her thumb. "This isn't a fancy restaurant, I've literally only got a ham sandwich and an apple."

"Fine. Just a moment then while I buy something."

Sol picked up the sandwich and bit into it. Ham and cheese with mayo was basic, and really the bread was a little stale, but oddly enough, she didn't mind it. Maybe her tastes were changing?

When Amir returned, it was with a similar sandwich and a bottle of water.

"You look like you're doing much better." He eyed her new look. She actually wore women's slacks, and a pink blouse cuffed at her elbows. It gave her a new shape, one she wasn't opposed to but still didn't like the attention it brought.

Sol furrowed her brow. "You've said that the last five times we've met." And it was all in the last week.

"I know, but this time it's true." He laughed.

"Wow. Ass." Though she knew he wasn't exactly lying. After winning the association election, Sol was tripping over herself trying to balance all of her new responsibilities. So many eyes to see through, so many ears to hear from. It resulted in a sort of sensory overload that lasted longer than she would have liked.

It got easier when she attached more shadows to bodies. Less thoughts, less feelings to deal with. Less buzzing in her head unless someone was *really* trying to get her attention. It did wonders for her mental health. And the nameless was grateful for her generosity. Parasites, by definition, could not live without their host. And if the host was thriving in abundance, who would miss the excess resources?

Even if those resources were minds.

"Sorry about forgetting to send you that book," Amir said with a frown. "I meant to, I promise I just . . . forgot, I think?" His brow furrowed. The confusion on his face told her all she needed to know. The pollen made Amir's mind a little fuzzy. Things could slip here and there if he wasn't in constant connection with it.

And at the time, it wasn't like Sol was eager to keep visiting Yale.

"Don't worry about it." Sol waved it off. "Turns out, the journal entries *were* just a weird prank." Sol took a second bite. Her own grumbling stomach was starting to settle down.

"Huh. Can't say I'm not a little disappointed." Amir undid his sandwich's wrapping. "Anyway, what've you been up to, Sol?"

"Well, other than work, the association has been keeping me busy," she responded.

"Ah, right. What's the phrase . . . an idle mind is the devil's playground? You're the kind of person where that rings true."

Sol shrugged. "Can't deny what makes me tick." She reached for the apple on the table.

"Being president for an entire association sounds like a lot of work, though. How are you balancing it with all your other responsibilities?"

"You know what they say—many hands make light work. It's such a good community, I'm able to delegate a lot." She smiled to herself. "How are the kids?"

"Fighting." He bit into his sandwich. After quickly chewing and swallowing, he continued with, "Every day is a new grievance between them. If it's not about who's hogging the bathroom, it's about someone *not* touching someone else."

"Must be tough."

Amir laughed. "Don't ever have kids."

"I'll take kids over my dad any day," she said, finishing her sandwich. "Did I tell you, a few weeks ago, he stole a medicine cart to roll out of the nursing home?" A side effect of sensory overload was that she sort of just . . . forgot about him. Long enough for him to believe something terrible must have befallen her, so of course he concocted a half-baked plan to rescue her. Or yell at her. Knowing him, it was probably both.

Sol snorted at the funny thought of him rolling through the neighborhood, screaming her name. At best, he would've been a nuisance and at worst, he would've gotten arrested. No one would've known what to do with him.

"You know, the more I hear about him, the more he sounds like a handful."

"That's an understatement. He calmed down after I paid him a visit. And brought a little gift." The little marble gift sat on his windowsill, basking in the sunlight. Almost immediately, he softened by miles. The number of times he raised his voice in any conversation was reduced to zero. Nurses found him much more pleasant.

And Alice got to formally meet him—even if he was a little confused about where he was at the time. Sol and Alice's relationship had never been stronger.

Those deteriorating minds won't last long, though, she reminded herself. As easy as it was to make the nursing home another feeding ground for the nameless, she had to put more work on establishing it for Yale.

That would likely take some significant effort, since she was a scientist, often working alone in a lab and away from the much younger students.

But she could do it. And it would be worth it.

"By the way, Sol, did I tell you, my wife got in touch with a real estate agent?" Amir said, finishing his sandwich. "With all their bickering, I think she wants to finally have more space for our kids. The agent said there was actually a really nice home in a gated community near Maneless Grove."

He met Sol's gaze. "Have you heard of Andor's Grove?"

"Of course." She smiled. The new opportunity made her mouth water. "I think I have a few connections there. Want me to put in a good word?"

ACKNOWLEDGMENTS

I'm not going to lie, a lot of this book could not have been written without so many people's help. First, I'd like to thank Dani Moran, the sensitivity reader I hired to get much of Alice's Korean backstory correct. She was instrumental in understanding what Alice's personal beliefs would be, and thorough when it came to cultural differences in the household. I'd also like to thank Ra In-Sang, who was there at the start of writing this book and helped me with the romanization of Korean phrases.

Thank you to Stanley C. for help in fleshing out Amir's character. Though much of the information didn't make its way into this book, I learned a lot about the Partition and how it would have affected families to this day. (Extra thanks to Stanley's mother who chimed in with more nuance from an older generation.)

Though my therapist will likely never read this book, a lot of our sessions helped me work through the internal issues I was having. It's not easy being a queer Dominican with unaccepting family. My gender is often overlooked and underappreciated and any complaints I have are consistently demonized. In that way, I sympathized with Sol more than I wanted. If it wasn't for my therapist helping me work through these issues, I'm not sure this book would have been written at all.

Thank you to my agent, Kristina Perez, for believing in this book from the very beginning. I couldn't ask for a better agent!

Finally, I want to thank my editor, David Pomerico, for not only supporting such a challenging novel but encouraging me to dig deeper and not pull my punches for anyone. Having him and the team at William Morrow in my corner really made me feel like this story was important. I can't tell you how much that means to me. Thank you.

ABOUT THE AUTHOR

Vincent Tirado is a nonbinary Afro-Latine Bronx native. They ventured out to Pennsylvania and Ohio to get their bachelor's degree in biology and master's degree in bioethics. Their debut YA novel, *Burn Down, Rise Up*, was the 2022 winner of the Pura Belpré Award and was a finalist for the 2022 Stoker Awards and 2023 Lammy Awards. Their sophomore YA novel, *We Don't Swim Here*, was called "a chilling ghost story" by *Publishers Weekly*.